SO-ALL-684

WHITE
MOUNTAIN BRIDES

SUSAN PAGE DAVIS

WITHDRAWN

BARBOUR
PUBLISHING

Return to Love © 2008 by Susan Page Davis
A New Joy © 2008 by Susan Page Davis
Abiding Peace © 2008 by Susan Page Davis

ISBN 978-1-60260-583-1

All rights reserved. No part of this publication may be reproduced or transmitted in any form or by any means without written permission of the publisher.

Scripture quotations are taken from the King James Version of the Bible.

This book is a work of fiction. Names, characters, places, and incidents are either products of the author's imagination or used fictitiously. Any similarity to actual people, organizations, and/or events is purely coincidental.

Cover Model Photography: Jim Celuch, Celuch Creative Imaging

Published by Barbour Publishing, Inc., P.O. Box 719, Uhrichsville, Ohio 44683, www.barbourbooks.com

Our mission is to publish and distribute inspirational products offering exceptional value and biblical encouragement to the masses.

 Member of the
Evangelical Christian
Publishers Association

Printed in the United States of America.

Dear Readers,

Writing these stories was a foray into my roots. About twenty years ago, I learned that in 1689 one of my father's ancestors was killed and another captured during the massacre near Dover, New Hampshire. Richard Otis, a blacksmith, owned one of several garrison houses in the settlement of Cochecho. On the night of June 28, his home and most of the other fortified houses were attacked by Pennacook Indians. Richard was shot as he rose from his bed. His son Stephen and daughter Hannah were also killed. His wife and new baby, Margaret, were captured, along with a son, several more daughters, and at least three of his grandchildren. In all, twenty-three people of the town were killed and twenty-nine captured. Four of the five garrisons in Cochecho were burned.

The Indians split into small bands and divided up the captives. Richard's daughters Judith, Rose, and another—probably Ann—were taken, but were rescued near what is now Conway, New Hampshire, by a party of men who pursued that band. It is through Judith's line that my father was descended.

As to the children who made the long trip to Canada, they were parceled out in different locations. One boy, called Jean Baptiste in Canada, was captured at age 9 and severely wounded. He was given to an old Indian woman to raise, later married a Canadian woman, and never returned. Francoise Rose, 11, was sold to the French and married a Frenchman at age 18. The baby, Margaret, was sold to the French with her mother. She was raised by nuns in a convent and re-christened Christine. She returned to Dover, New Hampshire, at the age of 45 and married a colonist there. Her mother, Richard's widow, married a French Canadian man and never returned to New Hampshire.

It was the story of these children that gripped my heart and inspired me to write about three young women—all fictional—who became captives at Cochecho and journeyed to Canada. This book tells of their return, five years later, and the community's difficulty in accepting them. I hope you enjoy these tales, and that knowing a bit about the real events suffered by so many at that time will make them real to you. Come visit me at my Web site and tell me what you think: www.susanpagedavis.com. I also recommend a visit to the Woodman Institute museum in Dover, New Hampshire, where the last standing garrison home of the 1600s is preserved in a pavilion, and artifacts found at the site of the Otis garrison may be seen.

Blessings!
Susan

RETURN TO LOVE

Dedication

To our dear little granddaughter, Reagan.
I wish we lived closer so I could spend more time with you.
I love you forever. Marmee

Glossary:

Banns—a public announcement, especially in church, of an upcoming marriage

Byre—a barn

Goodman—a social title for a yeoman farmer or householder who did not attain the rank of gentleman

Goody—a shortened form of *goodwife,* a term of civility applied to a married woman in humble life

Ordinary—a tavern or eating house

Relict—a widow

Chapter 1

Cochecho, New Hampshire, 1689

Richard Dudley bolted upright, his heart pounding in the dark. The sound that had wakened him came once more—a distant but terrible shriek, splitting the night. Only an Indian out for blood could make that gruesome noise.

"Richard!" His father's forceful voice came from below.

"I hear it."

"Quick! Wake your sister. We must run to Otis's."

"I'm awake," came Catherine's voice from behind the half partition that separated their sleeping areas in the loft.

Richard scrambled to pull on his breeches and shoes. A moment's hesitation could mean death in an Indian raid. He leaped down the ladder, pausing only to be sure Catherine made it safely down in her billowing skirts. His parents hadn't built up the fire, and only a faint glow from the coals lit the room. Richard sensed movement and knew his mother was gathering emergency supplies. No doubt his father had dashed to grab his loaded musket that hung above the door. Richard groped his way to the corner where his own weapon leaned against the wall.

"Stephen," his mother gasped, and Richard's heart sank at the thought of his younger brother.

"He'll be safe at Otis's garrison," her husband said. "It's ourselves we must worry about. Catherine?"

"Here, Father."

"Come, then."

"Take this." Their mother's voice was low and urgent. She pressed a sack into Richard's hand, and he knew it held food. He suspected his mother and Catherine also carried food or blankets. They had discussed sudden flight many times across the supper table and practiced it once before when an outlying farm was raided and the warning came to fort up at the nearest garrison.

That would be Otis's, the closest fortified house. The blacksmith and his large family offered protection for other settlers whenever needed, as did Waldron, Heard, and other prominent men in the struggling community. Their houses were fenced all around and built of sturdy oak, with rifle loops instead of windows above and the second story protruding over the first, so that attackers could be fired down upon. Richard prayed the people within would be safe, as well as the other families who were certainly running toward them.

The four of them crept outside and headed silently across their newly planted cornfield, avoiding the path. Richard cringed with each step, knowing he crushed tender plants he and his father and brother had worked hard to nourish. But worrying about that was senseless now. If they did not make it to the safe haven, the corn would not matter. His thoughts flew to the Minton family—Sarah and her parents. They were closer to Waldron's garrison. Had they made it there in safety? He couldn't think of her now. Distraction could mean death.

His mother stumbled, and his father reached to steady her. Richard hurried on, taking the lead and hearing Catherine panting behind him. Ahead, the savage screams increased, and a flash of foreboding told him they were running the wrong way, even as his feet took him onward.

They topped a rise, and Richard stopped abruptly. Catherine slammed into him, and the air burst from his lungs.

"Sorry," she gasped, clinging to his jerkin.

"Look." Richard held her arms and turned her toward what he had seen. A fiery glow lit the sky ahead.

His parents came up beside them and stood silent for a moment except for their labored breathing.

"Otis's is burning." His father's voice quivered with hurt disbelief. The stronghold they had counted on, near the center of the settlement, had been attacked.

"Stephen," Mrs. Dudley breathed.

The two men said nothing but watched a moment longer. Richard's heart ached, and a bitter taste filled his mouth. His brother had gone to the Otis house yesterday to give a day's work in exchange for the blacksmith's sharpening of the Dudleys' tools.

"Major Waldron's?" Richard asked.

"Aye. But we must take to the woods," his father said.

Richard felt Catherine shudder, but it was the only wise course. They dare not stay in the little house or travel in the open. Another glow burst on the sky, beyond Otis's garrison.

"Come," his father hissed, and Richard hurried after him, watching the forms of his mother and younger sister in the near blackness. They crossed the stone wall at the far edge of the cornfield and scurried into the woods, slower now. His father halted every few yards, and they all stood stock-still, trying to quiet their breath, listening. Far away they heard fiendish yells.

Ten minutes later, they emerged from the forest. The smell of smoke broke over them in a wave. A woman's piercing scream sounded, much closer than the other cries, and Father backed up, pushing them against the trees. An unearthly shriek reached them, and then flames burst against the sky scarcely two hundred yards away. A cottage's thatch crackled and then whooshed into roaring, orange fire.

"That be the Mintons'." His mother cringed back against him.

Richard swallowed hard, but his nausea only increased. Three days ago, he had walked to the Mintons' and asked the goodman's permission to call upon his fifteen-year-old daughter, Sarah. Instinctively he moved forward, but he felt his father's strong hand on his arm, holding him back.

"Nay, son. Be not hasty to throw your life away," his father said. "Let us pray they went to Waldron's."

They crouched together, out of reach of the fire's light, until the only sounds were occasional snappings from the dying conflagration and the gentle roll of the river beyond. A breeze sighed through the trees, and the branches above them swayed gently, rustling their young leaves.

Richard's heart was like a stone in his chest. He sent desperate snippets of prayers heavenward. *Almighty Father, help them to escape. Help us all to live!*

"Richard, come."

At his father's word, Richard stood. Catherine seized the hem of his jerkin, but he pried her fingers loose and whispered, "Stay here with Mother."

He and his father ducked from tree to fencerow, silently approaching the ruined house. A few yards from the smoldering heap, his father grunted and stumbled. Richard hurried to his side and knelt by the body he had tripped over.

" 'Tis Goodman Minton," Richard whispered, recognizing his neighbor more from the familiar clothing revealed in the fading firelight than from the man's mangled features. The embers of the house shifted, and a sudden burst of light showed more than he wanted to see—the bloody head, relieved of its scalp and bashed in mercilessly. Richard turned away and retched.

Father touched his arm gently and pointed. "His wife is yon."

Richard inhaled deeply and scooted toward the prone form, keeping low. Her outer skirt had been torn away—textiles were one of the first things savages looted. Or perhaps she had fled the house without it in her terror. Her petticoats were tangled about her ankles, and she, too, had been scalped. Fighting horror, Richard reached for her wrist to check for a pulse. People were known to have survived scalping before, but Goody Minton's life had seeped away.

His father crouched beside him, and Richard whispered, "She's gone."

"Pity. The savages are between us and Waldron's now. We must hide until morn."

"Sarah—"

His father clapped his shoulder. "No, son. She's with her parents in glory, or she's been taken."

"But she and her sister could be lying nearby, needing help."

His father hesitated and looked around. "See you any others?"

Richard peered all about, wishing one moment to find her and hoping desperately the next that he would not discover her mutilated like her parents.

"Nay."

"If it's quiet, we'll return at first light," his father said. "Come. We've others to think about."

His father faded into the darkness, back toward the trees where they'd left Mother and Catherine. Richard hated to leave the spot. He rose and flitted to the fence. Goodman Minton's byre had burned, too, and the animals were likely stolen or running loose. Quickly he circled the ruins of the buildings. The house was still so hot he couldn't get close. He would return at first light and sift the ashes if need be. He searched the yard and found a pewter plate and several articles of clothing strewed willy-nilly on the ground. The savages had plundered before they put the torch to the house. He jumped at a sudden movement. A piglet sprang from beneath a bush and squealed, streaking toward the river. Then the night was eerily still.

Cries broke out again at a little distance, and he knew at once they came from the direction of Major Waldron's garrison and gristmill. Richard crept back to the place where his family waited. His mother wept softly against his father's shoulder. Catherine squeezed his arm so hard he winced.

"Any sign of Sarah or Molly?" she hissed.

"Nay."

"Hurry," said their father. "They likely won't come back here, but we must find a thicket in the forest and wait for dawn."

They hurried into the trees, away from the destruction.

Chapter 2

1694

Five years, Sarah Minton thought. Five years since she had seen the town. Its contours were the same, but structures had changed. She shivered. There was Waldron's mill—but she knew the mill had burned the night she was captured.

She and her family had fled their home in hopes of safety. As Indians battered the front door in, they had escaped out the back lean-to, running toward Major Waldron's garrison. Half a dozen painted savages had leaped on them just outside their door. A warrior dragged Sarah away, and she heard her mother scream behind them. He had pushed her before him toward the river. A short time later, restrained by the burly Indian, she saw the Pennacook empty the gristmill of corn and then watched flames leap skyward from it. Yet here it was, rebuilt on exactly the same spot, looking more prosperous than before.

The men who escorted her and the other redeemed captives back to New Hampshire from Canada had answered their questions about that awful night. As she had feared, her parents were killed in those first moments of surprise. She had hoped that her younger sister, Molly, had survived and escaped. Failing that, perhaps Molly had been carried away by another band of Indians. But the captain had told her gently that Molly's body was found the next day in the charred ruins of their house.

Many dwellings were put to the torch and nearly thirty settlers hauled to Canada. Major Waldron was tortured and slain by the angry Pennacooks. Yet his place of business looked just the same now, as though the horror had never happened.

Sarah wiped beads of sweat from her forehead and shuddered. Merely walking into the village where she had spent her childhood brought on a dread that compressed her lungs and made breathing a chore.

"Be ye well, miss?" the leader of the expedition asked her.

Sarah nodded. She hoped they would stop for water soon. The hot sun had made their last few days of travel uncomfortable, and the vivid memories parched her throat even more.

Captain Baldwin nodded and moved on toward the center of the village of

Cochecho. The governor had appointed him and three others to ransom and retrieve as many captives as they could. The French had turned over a dozen prisoners in the city of Quebec. They had then rounded up and handed over several more like Sarah from the surrounding Indian villages. Some were from Cochecho, the rest from other villages in the colony.

Their company had spent the last month on the trail—twenty redeemed captives and four negotiators from New Hampshire. One of the men, Charles Gardner, she remembered. He'd been a lad living not far from her family in Cochecho, beside the river. He and Richard Dudley were friends.

Her heart skipped at the memory of Richard. She hadn't asked about him on the long, arduous journey, for fear of receiving another blow. Captain Baldwin's news of how her own family perished in the massacre was grief enough for her to carry. But now she couldn't help but think of the Dudleys and wonder if they, too, were slain. As long as she didn't know, she had the memory of him; she didn't think her heart could bear it if she'd lost Richard, too, and so she stared at the village.

So many houses, built near the green for safety. Outlying farms were always in danger. Several new families must have arrived in town during her absence, in spite of the threat from the natives. If not for the mill, the curve of the river, and the rise of land toward the meetinghouse, she wouldn't have recognized the place.

She plodded along with the others, behind Christine Hardin and ahead of Mrs. Bayeux and her children. *Home.* She'd dreamed of it for so long, and yet her exhaustion robbed her of joy. What, after all, was home when one's parents and sister were dead and the town was full of strangers who'd come to fill the ranks? Would she and the others be welcomed with kindness, or would they be shunned because they had lived among the savages and the hated French? She closed her mind to those thoughts and focused on the remaining short walk to the meetinghouse.

A woman and a boy came out of a thatched cottage and stared at them. More people flocked toward the path as it widened out and became the village street.

Sarah eyed the first few but soon realized she was searching for the features of her mother. . .her sister. . .her father. . .and all were gone! She stopped looking and put one aching foot before the other, dogging Christine's steps.

"Welcome back!"

She looked up and saw the minister, Samuel Jewett, and his wife, Elizabeth, coming to meet them. He'd come to Cochecho the year before the attack; the new, young parson and his family had been unprepared for the rigors of frontier living but eager to serve the people of the village. They seemed glad to see the captives. That countered some of Sarah's apprehension about how the villagers would receive them. She wanted to smile at Goody Jewett, but her exhaustion shortened her breath so that she could do nothing but keep walking.

Captain Baldwin broke away from the column's head and grasped the Reverend Jewett's hand. The line of travelers faltered for a moment, but the pastor turned with a sad smile and gestured toward the meetinghouse.

"Come, my dear people. We shall gather with the townsfolk and see how many of you can be reunited with loved ones."

Christine began to walk again, slowly, and Sarah followed her. Perhaps when she'd had time to rest and to accustom herself to the little village once more, she would be able to respond to the people.

Those lining the street seemed as much at a loss for words as those returning. Their faces were pulled taut in anxiety, their expressions curious but not loving. Some appeared to be fearful, others disapproving, but they all looked exceedingly clean and civilized.

Sarah focused on the back of Christine's tattered dress. She knew her own clothing hung in as bad repair. Five years ago, if a woman had entered the village in such a state, would Sarah have welcomed her? Or would she have hung back? If her mother had stood beside her, she hoped she would have had the courage to reach out and embrace those who had endured the unimaginable. But she wasn't sure her mother would have done so. She recalled vague rumors and hints of the unacceptable character of people who had been among the savages. Did the villagers think of her that way now? She looked into the face of a woman she didn't know and saw her shrink back, drawing her little girl close to her.

The meetinghouse was ahead. At last they reached its shadowy doorway and stepped inside, out of the cruel sun.

◆

"Richard! They be home!" Young Ben Jewett, the minister's oldest son at twelve years, panted as he ran along the path from the village.

"Baldwin's back?"

"Aye." Ben leaned on the snake fence, sucking in air. "Father sent me to tell everyone. They're going to the meetinghouse."

"My brother?" Richard asked.

"Don't know. I ain't seen 'em."

Richard shouldered his hoe and ran toward his father's dwelling. They had reinforced the sturdy wood frame house since the attacks and built a palisade all around it. Spaces between the upright staves allowed them to see out over the cornfield and fire muskets through the barrier if need be. He paused to open the gate. "Baldwin and the others have returned from Canada."

His father turned from where he chopped wood near the doorstep. "Did they bring back any of our captives?"

"I don't know. Folk are gathering at the meetinghouse."

His father slammed the ax down into the chopping block and headed for the door. Richard hesitated. Of course his mother and sister would want to come, too. The tug in his heart was too powerful to wait, and he turned and ran for the village. He passed the Youngs' place and the Mayburys'. Villagers hurried ahead of him on the path. He came to the green and cut across it, dodging the grazing sheep, and saw trickles of people approaching from all directions.

At the edge of the street that passed the meetinghouse, he stopped. Men and women lined the track, and children wriggled between them for a better look. Richard caught a glimpse of Charles Gardner, his friend who had gone with the negotiators. His great height made him conspicuous, and Richard's heart gladdened at the sight of his boyhood chum, though Charlie looked weary and thinner than usual. Surely he and the others had been successful.

He edged around Goodman Maybury and stopped short. A line of weary, dirty travelers moved slowly along the street and into the meetinghouse: women, mostly, some with babies or young children clinging to them; two middle-aged men; and a couple of half-grown boys, but none the right age and size for his brother.

Richard's heart seemed to fall to the bottom of his stomach. He watched with pity as several girls limped along at the rear, gently encouraged by Captain Baldwin and William Gunn, another of the party who had gone to redeem the captives from the French. The young women were rail thin, their clothing ragged and their feet bare.

What agony they endured to come home. Richard swallowed hard. There must be others he hadn't seen yet, who had already entered the building. Perhaps his brother was among them. And perhaps—dare he even think it—Sarah Minton?

"Any sign of our Stephen?"

He turned at his father's voice and at the same time felt his mother's fingers clutch his sleeve. Their desperate faces brought his heart back up to his chest, where it sat heavily, like one of the stones he was everlastingly digging from their cornfield.

"Nay, but mayhap I missed him."

His sister, Catherine, sidled in next to him, her face drawn as she gazed at the new arrivals.

A woman cried out, and Richard flinched. Goody Bates ran forward and seized the hand of an emaciated young woman at the end of the line.

"Be ye my sister? Anna Hapworth?"

The young woman stared at her for an instant. Recognition lit her eyes. With a sob, she fell into Goody Bates's arms.

Richard swallowed the lump in his throat. That couldn't be young Anna Hapworth—but it must. He would never have recognized her. Five years ago, she'd been a plump young damsel of ten who sang at meeting with an angel-sweet voice and chased about the churchyard with the boys after service until her mother reprimanded her. Flaxen hair and rounded cheeks, Richard recalled. This thin, careworn female looked older than Goody Bates—who was three years her sister's senior and had married just last spring. It couldn't be little Anna. But the two entered the building weeping, with their arms about each other and Goodman Bates, the new husband, on their heels.

"Let us go inside," his father said. They followed the other villagers into the meetinghouse and, out of habit, sat in the pew where the Dudley family always sat of a Sunday. The congregation waited in hushed anticipation. Slowly a murmur swelled as people craned to see the faces of the new arrivals, hoping to trace familiar lines in their forms and recognize those they had grieved so long.

The Reverend Samuel Jewett stood behind the pulpit, and the room went silent.

"Good day, my brethren. It is with joy that we receive souls who were lost to us. Since this warfare broke out and the peace with the natives hereabouts ended, we've seen many of our kind stolen and hauled away captive. Those who are sold to the French north of us, we've several times been able to bring back, and occasionally we also gain release of some who have been among the villages of the Indians. Captain Baldwin will now read us a list of the captives redeemed from the French in Quebec. Families may take their loved ones home. A few from other towns will be escorted thence on the morrow."

Captain Baldwin, still in his traveling clothes, a leather jerkin over his linsey shirt, woolen breeches, and boots that appeared to be coming unstitched at the toes, rose and faced the people.

"As ye all know, many souls were taken from here after the massacre in '89, and several more likewise in raids since then. A few young people were recovered at Conway soon after the massacre." Baldwin nodded toward the Tuttles' family pew, halfway back on his right, and Richard knew he spoke in deference of Judith Otis Tuttle, who sat there with her husband. A band of men led by her brother had brought back Goody Tuttle and her two sisters just days after their capture.

Captain Baldwin went on: "Others were taken many miles to the west, we are told. Indeed, some of our congregants may still be living in the city of Montreal or thereabouts. However, having heard that several people of this township were sold and enslaved to the French in Quebec, the governor sent us there, and there we did go and redeem as many souls hailing from this colony as we could with the funds allotted. Indeed, we bought back all the French admitted to having in that area. Welcome them back, my friends."

He looked out over the silent crowd then glanced toward the row of captives squeezed together in the front pew. "Though it be long since these have gone from us, and travel between us and New France is fraught with peril, we've been able to locate some of our own village. Some were taken in the massacre and have been gone from us five full years. Others were taken after, here and in other settlements. Firstly, I give you Joanna Bayeux, formerly Joanna Furbish of Cochecho."

A woman stood and turned. In her arms was a babe of no more than a twelvemonth, and a wee boy clutched her skirt. Richard tried neither to stare nor to do the calculations.

"Her husband, Goodman Furbish, were killed in the massacre five years ago," Captain Baldwin said. "Be there any of her kin to claim this poor woman and her children?"

A man near the back called, "Aye. She be my niece."

He didn't move from his seat, and Madame Bayeux searched the crowd. Her eyes focused on someone, and she waited.

"Be ye able to give these poor ones shelter?" Baldwin asked.

Behind the Dudleys, a shuffle and stir proclaimed the man's movements.

"My wife wishes to take her in, but we've not much room. Mayhap someone else can take the children."

A collective gasp went up from the congregation. Richard glanced uneasily at his parents. His father scowled, and his mother sat with her lips pressed in a tight line, staring at Madame Bayeux, whom they had all known as Goody Furbish.

How could they not claim their own kindred? The babes must be the children of a Frenchman, Richard decided from the look of them. But that shouldn't matter. Her husband here had died the night of the attacks. Everyone knew that. She had probably married again in Canada. And the tykes were small enough that any strange ways they'd begun to learn could be trained out of them.

Joanna Furbish Bayeux clutched her baby closer and reached for the toddler's hand. Mrs. Jewett, the pastor's wife, stood and walked over to her. "Come, my dear. I'll help you get settled at your uncle's house."

Joanna said nothing but followed her slowly down the aisle. The man who had spoken turned and walked out of the meetinghouse. His wife rose and met her niece and Mrs. Jewett in the aisle.

"Yes, come with us, Joanna. We'll come to an arrangement, I'm sure."

When the group had left the building, Captain Baldwin cleared his throat.

"James Fitch of Summersworth. He shall be taken home by boat in the morn." He consulted his list. "Elizabeth Perkins of this town."

As the girl stood and turned, a woman cried out. "My Betsey! I did not know ye, child!" A tearful reunion followed, and the girl left with her mother and stepfather.

Next was Mary Otis, a granddaughter of Richard Otis, the town's blacksmith who was murdered and his garrison home burned the night of the massacre. Her aunt and uncle, John and Judith Tuttle, tearfully received her and left the building.

The litany continued, and Richard's hopes sank lower and lower. Several of the redeemed young people had no surviving family members to claim them, as their entire families had been murdered or captured in raids. Farmers offered to take in children and young adults to help with chores in exchange for their keep, and Baldwin and the minister allowed it. Richard supposed they were thankful to find places for the orphans.

Baldwin neared the end of his list, and the parishioners who had not yet found a lost relative remained in their pews.

"We have these four young women left," Baldwin said. "All are destitute, their families having been annihilated or otherwise succumbed since the attacks. Little Hannah Lesley is now but six years old, and she does not remember the attack, nor her parents, God rest their souls. Her father's farm was sacked and burned in '91, and she has lived in a convent these three years. The older three I have spoken with during our journey, and I have confirmed so far as I am able that they have no living kin. If any one of you can give them a place in your home, speak now. Jane Miller."

No one spoke.

"Christine Hardin."

Again silence.

"Sarah Minton."

Richard caught his breath. Sarah? Which one of them was Sarah?

He stared as the last of the three stood and faced them. Her gaze never left the floor. All of them trembled, but Sarah, if it were truly she, looked terrified. Her once-lustrous hair lay matted and dirty against her skull. Her tattered dress hung about a wasted frame. *If she would only look up*, Richard thought. If he could see into her eyes, he would know if this was Sarah, the girl he had loved— or dreamed of loving. But she continued to stare downward with dull eyes. He inhaled carefully and swallowed the bile that surged into his throat. This was not Sarah. It couldn't be.

People shifted uneasily. Catherine stiffened beside him and whispered, "Richard!"

"We'll take the wee one," Goody Sampson called. She heaved herself to her feet and shuffled forward, muttering something about "popish ways."

17

No one else came forward. Richard shot a glance to his right. His father was eyeing his mother, but Goody Dudley sat rigid, avoiding his gaze. Richard's lungs squeezed his chest until he could barely breathe. He felt sweat drops bead on his brow and trickle down his back beneath his shirt. He wanted to speak, but his throat hurt so badly he couldn't even swallow.

After a long, quiet minute, the Reverend Jewett spoke.

"My wife and I shall give these three shelter in our home until other folk feel led to take them in. I know the Lord has a place for each of them."

Chapter 3

Sarah felt a stirring in her heart. She was not capable of gladness, but she felt easier—less hopeless—when she heard that Christine Hardin and Jane Miller would be with her at the minister's house, if only for a short time. They were all close to twenty years of age and would have some companionship.

Sarah had developed an almost silent friendship with Christine on the long journey. They hadn't known each other before their captivity. Christine's family lived down the coast, and their farm was attacked a year after the massacre in which Sarah was captured. Even their experiences in Canada varied vastly. Christine's years in the convent were a far cry from Sarah's with the Pennacook Indians. But something passed between them that first day in Quebec, when they were brought before the governor and handed into the care of Captain Baldwin. It was perhaps a recognition of intelligence and commonality.

Jane, the girl who had married a French voyageur, also kept her own counsel for the most part, but she had let fall bits and pieces that told Sarah she was frightened of returning to the English settlement in New Hampshire and the reception she would find there. Sarah had heard her pleading with Captain Baldwin in their camp one night to scratch her married name off his list and present her using her maiden name, instead of as a Frenchman's widow. It seemed the captain shared her misgivings and did as she had asked, for he had announced her today as Jane Miller. Even so, none of the villagers had offered her refuge.

The villagers rose and filed out of the meetinghouse, and the unclaimed three waited for instruction. It flashed through Sarah's mind that the Reverend Jewett had offered his home to three young, single women while his wife was out of earshot. What if Goody Jewett disapproved?

One of the last groups to leave the room caught her eye. An older man and woman, a girl with hair that glowed auburn as she passed through a ray of sunlight from a window, and a young man waiting for them at the door.

Richard!

Sarah caught her breath. A spark of hope kindled in her heart. He reached to steady his mother as she approached the doorway and the steps. He looked taller to Sarah, or perhaps his mother had shrunk and was shorter than she used to be.

Goodman Dudley and his wife weren't old, exactly—in their forties, she supposed. But the hard life they led at the wilderness outpost had taken its toll, and both had aged considerably in five years. Goodman Dudley's hair and beard were graying now. Sarah doubted she would have recognized him if she hadn't noticed Richard and identified the family.

Richard didn't look her way. Surely he had heard Captain Baldwin speak her name. But he and his parents had not moved to claim her or even to welcome her. She studied Richard's face before he slipped out through the doorway. He was older, of course, more mature, more sober. She recalled how his face had looked five years ago. Many times in the Indian village she had called his likeness to mind: his laughing face that never failed to ignite joy in her; his gentle, golden brown eyes; his reddish, downy beard, young and soft looking. She'd never had the chance to touch it, to see whether it was as silky as it looked or wiry like her father's dark beard. Richard had come by to see her once—only a few days before the attack—and had mentioned, blushing and anxious, that he wished to speak to her father for permission to call on her. But today he showed no recognition, let alone any attraction. Sarah's heart felt heavy, like the lump of lead from which her father shaped his musket balls.

The Reverend Jewett turned from his low conversation with the captain. "Well, ladies, we shall proceed to the parsonage, and I'm sure Mrs. Jewett will join us soon and inform you of where you shall sleep, but I suspect it shall be in the loft with our girls. The boys can bed down by the hearth for now."

He waited, as if expecting them to gather belongings. When none of the three young women moved, he cleared his throat and tried again. "Yes. Follow me, ladies."

Sarah glanced at the other two, and Jane gave a slight lift of her shoulders and stepped after the minister. Sarah and Christine followed. The parsonage lay only a few yards down the street and downhill from the meetinghouse.

Just as they were about to enter the little house, the Reverend Jewett stopped and looked toward the green. "Ah, Goody Jewett is coming now."

His smile dawned so bright that Sarah believed he was considerably relieved. His shoulders straightened. "Wait here just a moment, ladies."

He joined his wife a few yards away and spoke earnestly with her. His back was to them; Sarah couldn't hear his quiet words, but his wife glanced toward them and nodded. Then she said distinctly, "Of course, Samuel. What other can we do?"

Her husband said something, and she looked up at him for a moment. Sarah thought she said, "We must trust the Almighty."

She approached the three girls smiling. "I'm so pleased that you are coming to board with us. You'll find us a bustling household with the five young ones.

I expect we shall be cozy." She searched their faces. "Miss Hardin?"

"Aye," Christine said.

The goodwife's gaze settled on her. "My husband says the captain will put out further inquiries for you, lest we overlook some family members of yours. So far as we know, there are none, but apparently you remembered someone in Hingham."

"Yes, I. . .had an uncle there, before my father removed to the Piscataqua River."

Mrs. Jewett smiled. "Well, perhaps we shall hear good news after a bit. Come, now. I'll show you the house, and my husband will fetch the children. I left them with old Goody Deane when we heard that your party had returned."

They entered the plain little house, and Sarah paused just inside the door to let her eyes adjust to the dim interior. A family of seven lived in this one-room cottage, and now they were adding three adults to the clan? She doubtfully surveyed the sparsely furnished room. A straw tick covered with linen and quilts lay neatly made up in the corner farthest from the hearth. No bedstead, but that was not unusual for a family on the frontier. The entire north wall was comprised of a fireplace large enough for her to stand in, with the massive stone chimney spreading into a wall that included a bake oven. That at least was a luxury Mrs. Jewett could enjoy. Many of the pioneer women did their baking outside or in covered kettles on the hearth. Rough-hewn boards made the table and benches. Clothing and utensils hung neatly from pegs on the walls, and a spinning wheel and loom claimed most of the floor space in the east side of the room.

Sarah recalled two little towheaded Jewett boys five years ago and a baby girl, but from what their hostess had said, two more children had joined the family since Sarah's departure.

They all climbed to the loft, and she quickly counted pallets, surmising that four of the children habitually slept there.

"I believe we'll put you up here with Abigail and Constance." Mrs. Jewett stooped beneath the slanting roof and picked up a stack of folded clothing. "Perhaps my husband can borrow an extra straw tick for the boys, or we can make a new one."

"I can sleep on the floor," Christine offered.

"Oh, there's no need of that. And boys can take such conditions easier than young ladies."

"We can help you make the extra," Sarah said.

"Thank you, my dear. I've a couple lengths of linen, and more on the loom."

"I should love to weave again," Christine said. "I did so in Quebec, and the sisters said I had a touch for it."

Mrs. Jewett clasped Christine's arm. "Thank you. I don't like to ask any of you to work."

" 'Tis only fit that we do," Christine replied.

Sarah nodded. "You are most gracious to give us our keep, ma'am. We'll do all we can to help you with the housework."

"Yes," Jane said. "And we can help with the children, too."

"If we are a burden on your family, we might be able to hire out and help others," Sarah suggested.

Mrs. Jewett smiled. "We shall see what the Lord brings us."

They followed her down the ladder, and just as Sarah's feet touched the puncheon floor, the door flew open and a fair-haired boy of twelve dashed in.

He pulled up short at the sight of the four women grouped near the ladder to the loft. "Uh. . .where's Father?"

Mrs. Jewett's lips puckered, as though caught between a smile and a frown. "Really, Ben, where are your manners?"

The boy ducked his head. "Pardon, miss." He glanced warily at the three strangers, and Sarah suppressed a smile.

"How do you do?" she asked.

Ben gulped. "I be fine, miss."

"That is Miss Minton," his mother said. "No doubt you met her when you were a little boy, but mayhap you don't recall. And these be Miss Miller and Miss Hardin."

Ben nodded and muttered, "Good day."

The door swung open once more, and the Reverend Jewett herded his younger charges inside.

"Well, here we are, and quite a large family we make." The pastor smiled on them all, and the little ones hung back. He handed the baby to his wife and touched each child's head as he introduced them. "You've met Benjamin, I see. Here we have Abigail, Constance, and John. The wee one is Ruth."

Sarah smiled at the children and wondered how it felt to have three scarecrows suddenly plunked into your family. The pastor took the boys to the loft to rearrange the pallets and retrieve their clothing while his wife supervised preparation of the evening meal. Sarah realized she was famished, but that was nothing new. They'd been on short rations for the monthlong trek from Canada.

Mrs. Jewett put Jane to work mixing corn bread batter while she took Christine with her to milk the cow and Sarah went with Abby and Constance for water. By the time they returned to the house with their buckets, the two little girls were chattering eagerly with Sarah about the rag dolls their mother had made them.

As they reached the doorstone, an elderly woman approached carrying a linen sack.

"I be Goody Deane, next door." She dropped the sack on the step.

Sarah studied her face. "I remember you. Your husband is a cobbler."

"Was," the lady said. "He passed away three years gone." She nudged the sack with her toe. "The parson told me they have extra mouths to feed, so I brung some dry beans."

"How kind of you," Sarah said. "Would you like to come in?"

"Nay. There's no need."

"I'll tell him and Goody Jewett."

Goody Deane's wrinkled face crimped into even more folds. "Be ye one of the Minton girls?"

"Yes, I'm Sarah."

The old lady nodded. "I mind your parents. They were good people. Pity they was scalped that day."

Sarah swallowed hard. "Aye."

"Well, ye had a hard time, I'll warrant, but 'twas not so hard as their'n, eh?"

The thought had never occurred to Sarah. In fact, she had wished many times during her first year of captivity that she had been slain with her parents. "I. . .suppose."

"Aye. This life is not easy, be it here or among the French."

Sarah did not correct her assumption or tell her that her five years had been spent in Indian camps.

"Good night, now." Mrs. Deane turned and hobbled toward her tiny cottage, the roof of which sagged even more than that of the parsonage.

Sarah called good night and hurried the little girls inside. Mrs. Jewett had brought in the milk, and she scurried about the hearth with Jane and Christine.

"Mama, Goody Deane brung us some beans," seven-year-old Abigail called.

"Brought, child."

"No, she brung 'em. She told us so."

Mrs. Jewett straightened and pressed a hand to the back of her waist. "Ah. Then so she did, but in this house we say *brought*."

The boys and their father came in bearing armloads of firewood, and they sat down at the table. The hostess insisted that the three newcomers sit with them to eat.

Sarah started to protest but realized that the dishes and benches would not allow all of them to partake at once, so she took a spot on the bench by John. The nine-year-old stared up at her with big, solemn eyes until his father chided him to bow his head for prayer.

The pot of beans had simmered all day in the oven. Goody Jewett served them with fresh corn bread and dried pumpkin made into sauce. The good, hot food quickly filled Sarah's stomach. She missed the taste of meat, which was a staple in the Indian village, but realized it might be a scarce commodity in the settlement at early summer, especially in the humble parsonage. But a pewter cup of frothy milk was set for each of the young ladies.

◆

"Drink up, now," the pastor urged. "Our cow freshened last month, and milk we have aplenty. When you've finished your portions, my wife will fill the cups again for the boys."

Sarah, Jane, and Christine had not spoken of their intent, but when they had eaten rather meager helpings of food, as if by prior agreement, they stood.

"Ma'am, you and your daughters must sit now and let us serve you," Sarah said softly.

Mrs. Jewett opened her mouth as though to protest, but when her husband nodded, she sat at Sarah's place without comment. Quickly Sarah and Jane rinsed their plates and filled them, while Christine took little Ruth, who was barely a year old, and began to feed her pumpkin and milk.

By the time all had eaten and the table was cleared, Sarah thought she might fall asleep on her feet.

" 'Tis time for the children to be abed, and you girls must needs retire, as well," Mrs. Jewett said.

"I thought to speak with the young ladies a moment," her husband countered. "You tend the children, Elizabeth, and give me just a few minutes with our guests."

His wife nodded. After instructing the boys to lie down on the large straw tick in the corner, she laid little Ruth between them. Then she shooed Abby and Constance up the ladder and followed them to the loft.

The minister smiled at the young women. "Please do not fear me, ladies. I shall not bite."

Sarah gave a slight laugh and Jane's lips flickered in a smile, but Christine eyed him dubiously.

"Come, sit for a moment and tell me a bit of your experience," the reverend urged, and they all obeyed. Sarah sat on the edge of the bench she'd occupied for supper and waited for him to interrogate them.

"Miss Minton."

"Yes, sir?" Sarah asked.

"The captain said you spent most of your captivity in the wilderness with the Pennacook."

"All of it, sir."

"Ah. I must ask you—please do not take offense—if you have retained your faith."

"Aye, sir." Sarah could see that he wanted more. She licked her cracked lips. "I had no fellowship all this time, sir, but I prayed every day."

He nodded. "Your parents were good Christians, members of this church."

" 'Tis true."

He leaned toward her across the plank table. "Did the savages try to impose their heathen ways upon you?"

She stared at him, not certain of what he meant. "I. . .was made to dress like them and learn their talk. But I am yet a Christian, sir."

"Good, good." He turned his scrutiny on Jane. "Miss Miller."

Jane stared at him as though she were no longer capable of blinking. "Aye?"

"You were given in marriage to a voyageur, I am told."

Jane looked away, her cheeks coloring, and Sarah felt embarrassed for her. " 'Twas not my choice, sir," Jane whispered.

"I trust not. Tell me"—the pastor cleared his throat—"would you say that your husband treated you with respect?"

Jane opened her mouth and closed it. She shifted on her bench and looked down at her hands, which she held clasped tightly in her lap.

Sarah couldn't bear seeing the girl's discomfiture any longer. Not only was a man she'd just met questioning her about the intimate details of her married life, but two half-grown boys lay within earshot. She reached over and pressed Jane's hand.

"Begging your pardon, sir," Sarah said, "but we be greatly fatigued. We know you desire only our good. Mayhap we could share our stories with your wife on the morrow, and she could relay to you such bits as you need to know."

She thought a slight flush stained the parson's face beneath his beard, and she looked away. It was not her intention to be rude to the minister, but she felt he exhibited great insensitivity. Jane's grateful glance confirmed this suspicion, and she knew that even if the reverend refused her suggestion, the broaching of it had succeeded in some measure.

"Perhaps you are wise, Miss Minton." He glanced up toward the loft. "I'm sure my wife can help you ladies with any need you might have at this time. I wish only to ascertain that you have kept your Christian faith throughout your ordeal."

"I assure you I have, sir," Jane murmured.

He eyed her for a moment, but Jane would not meet his gaze. At last he nodded and turned to Christine. "Miss Hardin."

"Yes, sir?" It came out as a little squawk, and Sarah wished she could pat the girl's hand, but Jane sat between them. Christine had been cloistered three years and had studiously avoided the men who accompanied them home.

The parson gazed at her and frowned. "Well, I expect Miss Minton is right, and we should postpone a discussion of your spiritual state."

"Thank you," Christine whispered.

He pushed away from the table. "Go on then, ladies. I wish you all a good night's sleep now that you are back in a Christian home."

They bade him good night and scrambled up the ladder to the dim loft. Sarah was glad to escape, but she knew Jane and Christine felt even more relief once they were out of sight of their host.

"There, now," Mrs. Jewett said, rising from the edge of the straw tick where the two little girls were curled up together. "Be ye settled for the night? If ye need aught. . ."

"I believe we shall be very comfortable," said Sarah.

"Ma'am," said Christine, "we don't wish to put the children or yourselves from your beds." Her face went scarlet, and she gathered bunches of her skirt material and worked it through her fingers.

Mrs. Jewett touched her sleeve. "Don't fret, now. The girls will be comfortable. I wanted you each to have your own pallet. My husband will move the boys over to the hearth, and I've thick blankets for them to lie on. We shall all sleep well, I trust, and tomorrow we'll see if anyone can lend us more bedding."

Sarah lay awake long after the little girls had drifted into gentle slumber. A while later, she heard Christine's breathing change to a steady rhythm. Jane lay silent, over beneath the slant of the roof, and Sarah wondered if she was also beset by horrible memories.

But thoughts of the future loomed nearly as gruesome as her recollections of the past. Richard had abandoned her today. She couldn't deny it, and it reopened her long-standing grief. A month ago, a spark of hope had kindled in her breast. At last she would leave the Pennacook village. She would go to Quebec. She'd been bought back with money hard earned by the colonists, as Christ had redeemed sinners to form His church. She was free!

But now. . .what could she look forward to? A life of serving others in exchange for her bread and shelter, it seemed. The man she had dared to hope was still alive and cherishing her in his heart had refused to acknowledge her. The tears flowed down Sarah's cheeks toward her ears.

God above, she prayed silently, *I am not ungrateful. I do thank Thee for bringing me here. I thank Thee for Thy mercy and love. Show me what Thou hast for me, Lord, and I shall perform any duty Thou settest me with thanksgiving.*

Her tears gushed afresh, and she swallowed against the huge lump in her throat. *And I thank Thee for answering my many prayers for Richard and his family, Father. I thank Thee for keeping them safe. And I ask Thee, please. . .*

She blinked hard, not sure what to ask for. Richard no longer loved her. He'd forgotten her, or if not forgotten, he had at least put her memory aside. Perhaps he loved another. A terrible thought clutched her. He could have married some other maiden. Five years was a long time to ask a young man to wait. He was two and twenty now. Had he spent these years alone, or had he found another companion?

A deep sob came from under the eaves, and Sarah flinched. Jane was awake, too. Did she cry for her lost parents and siblings? Or for her husband? The voyageur had died on his last river trip, she knew. Had Jane loved him? Did she miss him now? And did she feel as alien and misplaced as Sarah did, with only loneliness ahead?

Dear Lord, please. . .help me learn to stop loving Richard.

Chapter 4

Richard toiled all morning in the cornfield. The fine weather had allowed him and his father to plant early this year, and if all went well, they would have an early crop. He worked his hoe methodically, prodding loose the weeds and clumps of grass that grew up between the foot-high stalks.

All the while, he kept his musket slung over his shoulder. It made hoeing harder, carrying the extra weight, but the colonists knew better than to work their fields without ready access to weapons. This cornfield lay more remote from the village than some. He and his father had pushed back the forest as they cleared the field. They'd begun the spring of the massacre year, and Stephen had helped, though he was only a boy of ten. He'd gathered the brush they cut and thrown it on the bonfire and helped pick up stones and load them on the sledge the ox pulled.

After the raid that June, the Dudleys and other farmers had given up clearing new land for a while. Some families had left Cochecho and gone to Portsmouth or even Massachusetts, wanting the relative security of the larger settlements. Some had stayed, even after their families experienced devastating tragedy. Young Richard Otis, whose father's garrison house was burned that day, stayed on. His father, brother, and sister were killed, and a dozen or more members of his family captured. Richard Jr. escaped the savages. He and his brother, Nicholas, and three sisters, who were captured and later rescued, remained part of the community. Young Richard Otis had recently obtained a grant of land in Dover, where he had set up his smithy and carried on the work his father, Richard Sr., had taught him.

The perseverance of people like the Otis family had inspired the others, and soon the men were back at work in their fields. They teamed up to guard each other while they worked through the rest of that summer and harvest.

But one can't go on living in terror. Gradually Richard Dudley had seen a change in his father and felt it in himself, a calm determination. Owning land was worth the risk, and they continued to clear and tame it, always watchful, ever diligent.

A noise startled him, and he dropped the hoe. In less than a second, he had the musket ready in his hands and stood still, waiting and listening.

It came again, a step too loud for an Indian. Whoever it was didn't try to hide his presence. A figure appeared at the tree line, and Richard exhaled and lowered his musket. Charles Gardner had come through the patch of woods that still separated their two farms and picked his way now through the rows of bright green corn.

Richard couldn't help smiling at the sight of his friend, returned unharmed from his journey. Charles's butternut yellow linsey shirt splashed a bright spot amid the green and brown of leaf and soil. Richard lowered the butt of the gun to the earth and waited.

"How's your corn coming?" he called as Charles came closer.

"It's doing well. Thank you for hoeing it while I was gone. I didn't know but what the frost would take my early planting."

"Nay, if I'm any judge, I'd say every kernel sprang up twice. Your field is thick sown."

Charles nodded. "I thought you'd want to know about Stephen."

Richard walked toward him and stopped when they were close enough to talk quietly. "I hoped to speak to you yesterday, but you left so quick. . . . I thought you must want to get home and see to things."

"Yes," Charles agreed. "But your family must wonder about him."

"We do." Richard eyed him without much hope. "You. . .found no news of him?"

Charles sighed and looked off toward the village path. "I heard of where he'd been, but. . . They didn't bring him forth, though we asked for Stephen by name."

"But they turned other people over to you—ones who were taken the same night."

"I know."

Richard looked down at the ground. Of course Charles knew. "You think. . . he's still with the natives, then?"

"I do." Charles shifted and looked over his shoulder; then he surveyed the field and the path before he spoke again. "Look, Richard, boys that age. . . I mean, he was ten, right?"

"Yes."

Charles sucked in air between his teeth and blew it out again. "Ten years old. Boys that age, they think it's wonderful. I mean, look at you! Breaking your back every day, and for what? A little corn, a few pumpkins, and fodder for the sheep. Boys get off in the wilderness and find they don't have to work every minute. Instead they can hunt and play and run wild."

"Is that the way you felt?" Richard asked, for Charles, too, had been captured but was redeemed after two years in the wilderness. For that reason, he was chosen to go with the negotiators. He knew the ways and the language of the Indians. The governor counted on him to get back captives who had been adopted into the tribes. Richard eyed him with new speculation. He'd known the experience had changed his friend, but Charles had never spoken so frankly about his feelings. To suggest that a Christian would prefer an uncivilized, heathen existence might be construed as heresy. "When they took you," Richard asked, looking deep into his friend's eyes, "were you glad to be free?"

Charles winced. "Not at first. I was scared out of my wits, and of course I hated them for what they did to my folks. But. . .after a while. . .after I'd got over being scared. . ." He shook his head. "You learn they aren't so bad, the natives. It's just that their ways are so different from ours. It's a completely different way of looking at things. And they wanted me to be their son. They gave me the best of what they had, and they let me do pretty much as I pleased, once I'd got used to their ways and they were sure I wouldn't run off."

"So. . .why did you come back?"

"Well, I didn't have much choice." Charles kicked at a clump of grass that Richard had hoed up, roots and all. "The governor's man came to the village and gave them money and told them they had to turn me over. My new family didn't like it, but they had to."

"You were sorry to come back?" Richard stared at him, unable to think it.

"At first, I suppose I was. I mean. . .for what? What was there here for me? My parents were dead."

"You got their farm back."

"Yes." Charles frowned. "After I came back, I realized all I'd lost. Not just my parents and Walter."

Richard swallowed hard, remembering Charles's younger brother. He hadn't survived that long ago raid, either.

"At first, I didn't want to think I had anything to regret," Charles said. "It wasn't my fault I'd been taken. But then. . .then I started back to meeting, and every Sunday I'd hear the reverend talk, all quiet and soft about God and His grace and what He'd done for me. And I started to think about how I'd turned my back, not just on England and Cochecho but on God. I'd given up my faith, and willingly so. And that scared me worse than the Pennacooks had the night of the raid. It's for eternity." He eyed Richard anxiously, as though his friend's comprehension was crucial.

Richard nodded. "That's what I worry about most with Stephen. It hurts that he would forget us and take on the savages as his own people. That he would perhaps have the chance to escape and not take it. But even worse is the idea that he may not think at all about God now. It's been five years, Charles."

"Yes. I can't hold out any hope to you."

"You think he wants to remain in Canada, then."

"Either that or the natives are determined to keep him. They've taken him away from the settlements and hidden him well. They'll probably keep him away until we stop asking about him."

"But. . .we got those others back."

"I know. Some from '89. Some from scattered raids since then. Five years is a long time, though. Too long for a child, perhaps."

Richard felt salty tears in his throat. "I can't give up hoping."

Charles reached to clasp his shoulder. "I know. And I will say I'm glad now that I was brought back. That God brought me back. I thank Him for that. 'Tis a hard life here, on the frontier. But it's eternity that counts."

Richard managed a smile. "I'm glad you're back, too. I had no idea how difficult it was for you."

"Well, sometimes, even now, I think about the family I had up there, and. . .awful as it must seem to you, I miss them. When I went to look for Stephen, I thought perhaps I would see my Indian family again. But when I came among the tribes, I realized I'd come too far back into civilization, and I couldn't go back to their world. And yet. . ." Charles tilted his head to one side and gave him a tired smile. "You'll tell your father?"

"Yes. He may want to speak to you, though. Get particulars on what you did to effect Stephen's release."

"I'll talk to him anytime. This first disappointment will go down hard. Tell him all I've said to you about your brother. If he needs to know more, he can come see me or Baldwin. We did all we could."

Richard watched him walk to the trees carrying his musket and fade into the forest with only a quiet rustle. He stood for a long moment in silence; then he slung his own gun over his back and stooped for the hoe.

Two more hours of good daylight. No sense going to his father now. They would discuss it over supper. It was too cruel. Yesterday he'd seen his mother's face when they left the meetinghouse bitterly disappointed. Mother's heart was so torn over losing Stephen that she could not even think about giving aid and solace to those who had returned.

Sarah.

Richard felt a deep tug below his heart, but he clenched his teeth and kept hoeing. He would not think about the ragged, gaunt young woman whom Captain Baldwin had named as Sarah Minton. She wasn't Sarah. At least, she wasn't the Sarah he'd known. She was horribly changed. And if the outer transformation was so great, how different was she inside? Would she flush scarlet when she left the church on Sunday, as she had five years ago, just because he'd lingered near the steps to get a look at her? Would she laugh at the feeblest jest he offered for her amusement? Would she let her bonnet fall back the way she used to on a fair June day, so the breeze could ripple her spun gold hair?

Sarah has no one. Richard hoed faster, ignoring the voice that said, *"You ought to have claimed her."*

She must be twenty now. They could be married. Immediately he thrust that thought away. The idea repelled him now. She had lived among savages for five years. How could he even think of sharing his life with a woman who'd lived that way? His hands shook.

"How do you know what she's been through?" the inner voice taunted him. He didn't want the details. Didn't want to know if she'd been mistreated. Just to look at her, he would guess that she had. She'd lost every shred of confidence. She was not the same girl who left here so long ago. He would bury the dreams he'd had of her returning one day. The reality was nothing like he had imagined. Too much time had passed, and the stamp of her ordeal was too deep upon her. As Charles had said, you couldn't go back.

He jabbed the hoe savagely into the roots of a grass clump. He would *not* think about Sarah.

A sudden sound startled him, and he looked quickly around, his heart racing. The shadows had stretched long without his noticing. He ought to have headed home ere now.

A flicker of movement at the edge of the field caught his eye, and he stood still, letting the surge of fear and the urge to fly dissipate. A medium-sized boar was rooting at the farthest row of tender corn plants.

Probably offspring of Father's sow that had escaped last fall. The feral pigs made havoc of the gardens, and the settlers shot them at will, only worrying about ownership if the animals they killed had earmarks. If so, the hunter would take the carcass to the owner and split it with him.

Richard's family was nearly out of bacon, and the hams they'd smoked last fall were long gone. The only meat they'd had lately consisted of fish from the river, an occasional squirrel, and a tough old rooster. A bit of fresh pork would go down well. He inched his musket around from his back, slowly lowered the hoe, and worked the gunstock up to his shoulder.

The shot rang loud in the stillness. Probably he'd frightened the nearest farmers. Ah well, it was worth it. The boar leaped and plummeted to the earth. Richard stopped long enough to reload before going to retrieve it. Approaching the edge of the woods unarmed at twilight would be foolhardy.

Even with his musket primed, he approached his kill with caution, watching the trees, not the boar. He grabbed the pig's hind feet with one hand and pulled it along the edge of the cornfield, walking backward and still holding the musket pointed toward the woods. When he reached the path, he hefted the carcass and walked quickly toward home. In broad daylight, he'd have gutted the animal in the field, but he wouldn't take a chance on staying outside the palisade so late.

His father met him at a bend in the path, also carrying a musket.

"Ah, son! I heard a shot, and I was sure it came from our field."

"Aye, Father. We've plenty of meat here."

His father pulled the boar's ears and examined them in the fading light. "No markings. 'Tis probably ours, but it's so warm we'd best share with the neighbors anyway. 'Twould spoil before we could eat it all."

Richard nodded. "I'll take some to Charles Gardner tomorrow."

"Mayhap the parson needs meat," his father mused, taking the hoe from Richard's hand. "The Jewetts took in three extra yesterday."

Richard didn't want to talk about the captives. At least not about Sarah. He could divert his father's thoughts from the poor young women at the parsonage with the news he'd learned. "Charles came to the field two hours past."

"Did he?"

"Aye." Richard paused as his father opened the gate in the tall fence then lowered the boar to the grass inside. "He says he'll come round if you like, but. . ."

"But no word of Stephen."

Richard nodded. "I'm sorry."

His father clenched his teeth and inhaled slowly. " 'Tis what I heard from Captain Baldwin. I had a word with him today in the village. He told me Charles went to several Indian encampments and spoke to some of the very savages who wrought the terror here. But they denied having our boy. Baldwin says they lied, but he couldn't do any more than that. He'd spent all the ransom he had for the ones they brought back, and the French were not happy with the insinuation that they were not giving over all they should. Baldwin asked them to punish the savages who killed so many here, but they would do nothing. They told Baldwin he was lucky they released the captives on hand."

"Well." Richard leaned his musket against the wall of the house and pulled out his knife. "Have you told Mother?"

"Aye. She's taking it hard."

"Of course. We all hoped."

His father nodded. "You can't ask a mother to quit hoping her child will return." He laid a hand on Richard's shoulder. "We'll hang that pig and tend to it after supper, son."

Five minutes later, Richard entered the house, his hands and face scrubbed clean at the washbasin on the back stoop and his hair raked into place with his fingers.

"Sit down, Richard." His mother placed a trencher of samp on the table, the parched corn dish that stood them well when fresh foods had been exhausted. Applesauce from dried apples, nuts gathered last fall, and a small amount of cheese filled out the meal.

Richard and his father sat down, and Catherine removed her apron and joined them. His mother poured milk for all of them and then joined them at the table. After Father's blessing, they attended to their food. Richard took plenty of samp. At least their corn had held out through the long cold season, and they would soon have a few fresh vegetables. His mother and Catherine had already gathered a few wild greens, and they'd had one feed of asparagus.

"Richard killed a fine young boar," his father said.

"Praise be! We shall have fresh meat again." His mother smiled on her son. "I was going to ask you to take time from cultivating the corn and go fishing tomorrow."

His father proceeded to tell them all that he and Richard had learned about the captives that day and the futile search for Stephen.

" 'Tisn't fair!" Catherine thumped her spoon on the table, and her mother scowled at her.

"Hush, now," said her father. "God above is just, but He never promised us He would be fair."

Richard stayed out of it. He'd heard his father's pessimistic logic often enough. The gist of it was that if God treated them fairly, they'd all be doomed.

"But those savages get away with kidnap and murder," Catherine protested. "We have to grovel to the French and bribe them to return our loved ones. I misdoubt I shall ever see my brother again. Captain Baldwin as good as told you the French know where he is."

"Nay," said her father. "That was not his meaning."

Catherine inhaled as though she would retort, but her mother's sharp gaze silenced her. "We don't know for certain that Stephen is even alive this day," Goody Dudley said.

"You think. . .he's dead?" Catherine asked.

She must have thought of it many times, Richard told himself. Five years was a very long time. So many things could happen to a boy gone feral. He'd often considered the possibility that Stephen had met his death, but the family had never openly discussed it.

"It might be better than thinking he's living as an infidel." Mother got up and took the steaming kettle from the fire. "Who'll have tea?"

Richard declined. What they called tea was steeped leaves of wintergreen, and he'd just as soon do without.

"Well, I don't think it's right," Catherine persisted. "We've got all these other people back—Mary Otis and Sarah Minton, and a slew of folk we don't even know—but not Stephen."

Richard clenched his fist below the table. If only Catherine wouldn't mention Sarah in her prattling.

"We could have taken one of those children with no families. I could at least have had a little sister or brother."

"Hush," her father said softly, as Mother set a cup of tea before him.

"We'll not be bringing any captives into this house," Mother said sternly. "No telling what those young folk have learned in Quebec. I won't be letting them spread strange notions here."

"But. . .if Stephen were found, you'd take him back."

"Of course we would," Father said. He raised his cup and blew on the surface of his tea.

"Then why shouldn't we help one of the others? We could have Sarah Minton here." Richard caught his breath, but Catherine plunged on. "I'd like to have a sister, and Sarah was always a good girl. I don't understand why we didn't speak for her. She was a neighbor and a friend."

"You don't understand the way things be, child." Her mother sank wearily into her chair.

Catherine's brow furrowed. "Richard, you always liked Sarah. Don't you think we should have taken her?"

He shoved his stool back and stood. "Hush, Cat. You heard what Mother said." He turned and went outside. He knew he'd been rude, but he couldn't stand another moment of her chatter. Why had they let her go on so? Mother usually made Catherine sit quietly at the table, but tonight she'd gobbled away like a turkey.

He walked around to the back of the house, where he and his father had hung the boar. There was enough moonlight for him to butcher it now. He might as well. Anything, even hacking up a pig, was better than thinking about Sarah's plight.

But as he set to work, images of the two Sarahs beset him. Sarah, the lovely, healthy girl he'd fallen for as only a seventeen-year-old lad can fall. And the bedraggled, emaciated, and, yes, unrecognizable figure he'd seen yesterday in the meetinghouse.

Heavy footsteps approached, and he kept working. Father would rebuke him, and justly, for leaving the table in so discourteous a manner.

The footfalls ceased, and he sensed his father standing behind him, watching as he skinned the boar. Neither spoke for several minutes.

Father cleared his throat. "You'll take a quarter round to the Jewetts' in the morn? After you see Charles?"

Richard kept on for another minute, trimming the skin loose from the pig's legs. "If you wish," he said at last.

"We should do at least a small part in caring for those poor creatures."

"Aye."

Father stepped around where Richard could see his troubled eyes in the moonlight. "Catherine spoke of sending some clothing or material for the redeemed ladies."

"What did Mother say?"

"She will allow it."

Richard didn't comment on the fact that he had avoided the question. He'd never heard his parents quarrel, but since Stephen's abduction, his mother had changed. She rarely smiled anymore, and her whole manner seemed harder. Poor Cat! She'd been just twelve when it happened, an age when a girl needed her mother's care. And now his sister had turned argumentative. What was happening to their family?

"Perhaps Catherine would like to go along with me tomorrow."

"I suppose that might be well, with you to watch out for her." His father stood there for a few more moments, watching him work. "Stephen's going has been hard. We haven't spoke much, you and I. Is there. . .anything you'd like to say?"

Richard stopped working and stepped back, looking directly at him. His father looked old and tired. "I wouldn't know what to say," he admitted. "Except that I'm sorry. About Stephen, and for my rudeness this evening."

His father didn't protest. They understood each other for perhaps the first time in five years. "I'm sorry, too. You've suffered with the rest of us." He nodded at the carcass. "You needn't cut that up tonight. Leave it for tomorrow."

"Nay, the wolves will smell it," Richard replied. "I'm surprised they're not sniffing round the fence already."

"I'll fetch my knife and help you." His father turned back toward the house.

Chapter 5

The sun bore down on Sarah's shoulders as she hung clean clothes on the line behind the Jewetts' home. Mrs. Jewett had kept her boys busy all morning hauling water so that the guests could bathe and scrub their threadbare clothing. While their meager wardrobes dried, the three young women had taken turns wearing their hostess's extra dress and a skirt Christine had hastily fashioned from a length of linen. Christine was now confined to the house in the linen drape and worked at the loom while Mrs. Jewett prepared the noon meal. Jane scrubbed some of the family's clothes in a cauldron behind the house while Sarah hung the wet garments.

Jane's thin cotton gown had dried first, and she had put it back on. Sarah's was still damp, and she wore Mrs. Jewett's Sunday frock, taking care not to muss it. The woolen fabric felt a bit itchy and was more suited to cool weather, but Sarah was happy to wear it, even for a short time. The one dress they'd given her in Quebec, to replace her tattered doeskin dress, was now little better than a rag. After a month's hard journey, it was almost beyond repair, but Sarah had mended torn elbows and a drooping hem before washing it, realizing she might have nothing else to wear for some time.

Jane wrung out some white squares of cloth and carried them to her, dripping. "These are the last of Ruth's clouts." She handed one of the baby's cloths to Sarah and snapped the other out; then she hung it over the length of woven vines that served as a clothesline.

Sarah did the same. "A job well done."

"Yes. I'm glad to be clean and glad we could help Goody Jewett by doing up the baby's things. I'm afraid we've made a good deal of extra work for her."

Sarah shot a glance at Jane as they walked toward the cauldron. "Have you thought about what shall become of us?"

Jane pressed her lips together. "Somewhat. Perchance I could hire out as a dairymaid or a laundress. Although yesterday none seemed eager to take me into their household."

Sarah nodded. "I've had the same thoughts. The Jewetts have been most kind, but we can't all stay here. We're squeezing them out of their own home, and they can't afford to keep us. Still, no one wants a girl who's lived among savages tending their babies or baking their bread."

"Aye, the same can be said of a girl who married a Frenchman and lived as his wife more than two years."

Sarah lowered her eyelashes, feeling heat fill her cheeks. "I'd think your state of widowhood would make you more respectable in their eyes."

"Wouldn't you just?" Jane shrugged. "Seems a dead Frenchman counts far less than a dead Englishman. Help me dump this."

Together they carried the big kettle of dirty water to Goody Jewett's kitchen garden and poured it out on her neat rows of herbs and beans. Although Sarah tried to save Goody Jewett's dress a soaking, her effort was only partly successful, and she ended the chore with an edging of mud around the front of her skirt.

"Now I'll have to wash this out when my dress is dried."

Jane squinted at her soiled hem. "Let it dry. That may all brush out."

Sarah nodded. There was more she wanted to ask Jane, but she didn't care to embarrass her. She saw that Jane was watching her, too, and wondered suddenly if her companion was as curious as she.

"Did Goody Jewett speak to you this morning?"

Jane gave her a wry smile. "Oh yes. She seemed a bit nervous. I expect the parson gave her a catechism to drill me on."

"Oh?" Sarah blinked and shook her head. "He means well, I think."

"Of course he does. And his wife is a dear." Jane's lips curved just a little as she shrugged. "I answered all her questions. If they deem me not fit to be around their kiddies, then I shall have to go."

"They wouldn't put you out." Sarah stared at her. Where could they go if the Jewetts wouldn't have them?

"I hope not. I daresay Goody Jewett wouldn't think of it, even if I'd denied my Protestant faith." Jane looked up at Sarah. "My husband was of the Romish faith, you see. It's not allowed here."

Sarah picked up the kettle by the bail and headed back toward the house, deep in thought. "So, it's only that one thing they wish to know? Our spiritual state?"

"That and whether we retained our virtue."

The words rather shocked Sarah, and she stopped in her tracks. "You mean—"

"Nothing. Just be forewarned. Our hostess will probably ask you some very close questions."

"But you were married."

"Yes, thank God. But to a man not of our faith."

"But still. . ." Sarah dreaded going into the house now. What things would Mrs. Jewett ask her about her life with the Pennacook? She swallowed hard. At least it wouldn't be as difficult as if the minister performed the inquisition.

They set the kettle bottom up near the back wall and rounded the corner of the house. Entering the dooryard was a young couple. Sarah gasped and halted, recognizing Catherine and Richard Dudley.

"Sarah?" Catherine came forward eagerly and extended a hand to her. Across the other arm, she held a bundle of cloth. "Do you remember me?"

"Of course." Sarah felt a flush stain her cheeks once more. "Catherine, let me present Jane Miller."

Jane nodded and dropped a slight curtsy.

"And my brother Richard." At Catherine's bright words, Richard shuffled forward a few steps and nodded without looking directly at either Sarah or Jane. He carried a bulging sack.

Catherine scowled at him when he didn't speak and then turned back to the two young women. "Richard shot a boar last night, and we brought you one of the hindquarters."

"I'll tell Goody Jewett." Jane whirled and dashed into the house before anyone could protest. Sarah wished she were the one to escape.

"I brought you an extra shift of mine and some material for a bodice," Catherine said, holding out her bundle.

"That's very kind of your family." Sarah took the cloth. "Won't you come in?"

"Oh. . ." Catherine darted a glance over her shoulder at Richard, but he was staring at the ground, his face grim.

At that moment, Goody Jewett and the two little girls burst through the doorway.

"Catherine!" Abigail's shriek could no doubt be heard all the way to the gristmill.

Catherine laughed and clasped hands with the little girl. "Good day!"

Constance reached her then, and Catherine knelt to embrace her.

Sarah looked over their heads at Richard, who listened as Mrs. Jewett instructed him on where to leave the sack. He nodded and strode off around the corner of the house without so much as a glance at Sarah.

"Won't you come in and visit, Catherine?" Goody Jewett asked.

"Oh, thank you, but no, we mustn't. Richard has a full day's field work awaiting him at home." Catherine rose and smiled down at Constance and Abby. "I'll see you at meeting on Sunday."

"Promise?" asked Abby.

"Promise." Catherine smiled once more at Sarah. "I'm glad you're back. And I'm sorry about your family."

Sarah felt tears burn her eyes, but she managed a nod and a murmured "Thank you."

Richard came from behind the house, and just for an instant, his gaze rested on Sarah. She caught her breath, and her pulse quickened.

He broke the look and nodded at Mrs. Jewett. "I hung the sack where you said, ma'am."

"Thank you both, and please thank your mother for her kindness. We're most grateful."

Richard nodded and turned away without another word.

Catherine stammered quick good-byes and hastened after him.

Sarah helped Mrs. Jewett herd the children toward the doorway, where Jane was peeking out with the baby in her arms. Sarah took one last glance at the departing guests. Catherine appeared to be scolding her brother, probably for his lack of courtesy, if Sarah were any judge.

She may as well face it. Richard did not want her. Perhaps now no man in the colony would want her. Prosperous families hired young women to help with the housework and food preservation. But none had offered to house her, so she doubted they would hire her. Perhaps if she went to Portsmouth or Exeter, she could find a billet with strangers.

The hurt Richard's intentional indifference had inflicted festered and brought a bitterness to her heart. For five long years she'd avoided the pain of hopelessness, thinking always that rescue would come, and when it did, her family and friends would rejoice with her.

Not so. Richard had no intention of resuming their friendship. He'd escorted his sister on her errand, probably under duress, but Sarah needn't expect more from him, ever. He probably congratulated himself this moment that no one else had come along and seen him and Catherine standing in the Jewetts' dooryard with her.

Mrs. Jewett approached her after the noon meal. The reverend went to the meetinghouse to prepare his sermon, and his wife asked Sarah to help her in the garden, while Jane watched the children and Christine returned to her weaving.

"Sarah, think ye what ye'd like to do with yourself?" Mrs. Jewett asked as she bent over her parsley bed to pull weeds.

"Why, yes, I thought I'd try to get work," Sarah said. "I'm strong, and I know how to sew and keep house."

"A possibility," Mrs. Jewett said, "though most of the families hereabouts have the help they need or cannot afford to pay. Have ye thought of marriage?"

"I. . ." Sarah ducked her head, letting the brim of her bonnet hide her face. "I'm not sure I'm ready to be a wife."

"Nonsense, my dear. You must be all of twenty."

"Aye."

"Then unless there be some reason, some past mistreatment that has prejudiced you. . ."

An odd way to put it, Sarah thought, but she sensed the lady's struggle to get information from her without appearing cross.

She continued pulling weeds. "Nay, I. . .was not mistreated. That is, I was made to work hard, and betimes we went hungry, but. . ."

Mrs. Jewett eyed her anxiously. "Then the savages—the men, that is—they made no. . .advances toward you?" She stood and rubbed the small of her back. "I regret having to ask you girls such questions. My husband feels it necessary, if we are to help you, to know exactly your situations, so that we can represent you honestly to the community. If a man was interested in marrying a strong young female, he would have a right to know if she'd. . .been sullied."

Sarah froze with a clump of grass in her hand. This was what the villagers thought of her and the other girls. Tales of abuse doubtless ran through the colony. She'd heard whispers herself as a girl. One wife would visit another and drop hints of such happenings over their quilting. Captives were tortured and degraded. The women were so horribly used they would not wish to return and face their families if given the chance.

She tossed the grass to the earth and looked up at Mrs. Jewett. "I know you mean well, ma'am, and I tell you in truth, though I feared such things, I never was harmed in that way. Once we reached our final destination, a Pennacook woman whose daughter had died took me as her own. I worked for her and her family. They clothed me after their fashion and treated me as well as they treated their own daughters. I was less fearful then, though at times I did think a man looked on me with designs. . .not honorable." She shuddered and closed off the memory. "My adopted mother did not force me to take a husband, though this last twelve-month she seemed to wish to see me settled, for she was growing old."

Mrs. Jewett's face expressed sympathy and a tenderness that made Sarah look away. She hadn't thought about it before, but Elizabeth Jewett was quite pretty, despite the calluses on her hands and the fatigue lines at the corners of her mouth. Sarah felt her kindness to be genuine, and her heart went out to Goody Jewett as it never had to the Pennacook woman.

"Well, then, in time we shall surely bring that wish to fruition, though not as she foresaw it. There be several bachelors and widowers hereabout. Once your captivity is not so fresh in folks' minds, I expect one of them will tell himself, 'Now there is a very handsome young woman.' My husband shall have to turn away suitors, I'm bound." She nodded and stooped once more to her task.

An uneasiness filled Sarah's heart. She didn't want to be handed off to some farmer or woodsman who needed a cook and housemaid. Was she ready to be married, even if it were to someone she liked as much as she used to like Richard? And what of Richard? He had shunned her. He was not the potential husband Goody Jewett imagined. It would be another man, perhaps one much older than she, left with several motherless children. What would marriage be like with a stranger? Bits of Jane's conversation flitted through her mind. She'd lived with Monsieur Robataille, the Canadian voyageur, for two years, and for a good part of that time, he'd been away on the trading expeditions that earned him his living. But Sarah had the distinct impression that Jane was happier during the months Robataille was away than during his stints at home.

That night, she again lay awake. They had borrowed a tick from neighbors and filled it with fresh, sweet hay for the boys, so she no longer felt guilty at forcing Ben and John to sleep on the floor. She had the new shift of sturdy linen from Catherine. Her body, hair, and clothing were clean, and her stomach satisfied with the plain food at the parsonage.

But the problem of her future kept her mind racing hither and yon, seeking a resolution. And if she slept, dreams would come. Dreams of that night so long ago, when she'd been pulled from her mother's grasp and hauled away in the darkness. . .

Below, she heard the soft murmur of the pastor's voice and his wife's quiet reply.

She rolled over. Jane seemed to be sleeping tonight, and Christine's snores rivaled young Abigail's.

In a lull between the homely sounds, she heard the Reverend Jewett say distinctly, "We must ask the Lord to provide husbands for all three."

"That would be best," his wife agreed.

Sarah covered her ear with her bent arm and heard no more, but she started a barrage of her own prayers. *Dear Father in heaven, You know what is best. But please, if You have any pity on us, I don't believe a one of us wishes to be married just now. I know I don't. At least, not if it's to someone besides Richard.*

She sighed. Marrying Richard was not an option. Long into the night, she wrestled with that bleak thought. At last she breathed one last prayer.

Lord, help me to be willing to do whatever You want. Even though I can't have Richard.

Chapter 6

Richard trudged along behind the sledge the ox pulled.

"Ho!" he called when they had gone a few paces.

The beast halted, and Richard and his father bent their backs to one of their hardest chores—pulling rocks from the soil and piling them on the sledge. Many were so large it took all the strength of both men to move them. When the load filled the sledge, one of them drove the ox to the edge of the field, and they hauled the rocks off and piled them onto the half-finished stone wall.

The drudgery afforded Richard plenty of time to think. Against his will, or so he told himself, his thoughts ran to Sarah with eager feet. He imagined going to Pastor Jewett's house to call on her, and Sarah running to welcome him with a joyful smile and open arms.

He flushed and glanced toward his father. Enough of that! If he let himself muse on such daydreams, his parent would surely guess his unseemly thoughts. It wasn't an impure notion precisely, yet he couldn't shake the feeling that it was an improper one.

Young men were allowed to think about eligible young ladies. But Sarah, though he'd rejoiced to learn she lived, was no longer eligible, at least not in the eyes of his parents. And he must respect his parents, even though he had reached his majority and could think for himself. They were right.

Weren't they?

Sarah lived five years among the heathen.

"*So?*" his spirit argued as he hefted a stone to the sledge.

So, she has taken on heathen ways.

"*Are you sure?*"

Decent folk won't receive her.

"*The parson and his wife receive her.*"

But they must.

"*How so?*" The little voice persisted, and he chose a very large rock that needed all his energy and concentration. Yet when he had strained and groaned and moved it to the sledge, the question remained unanswered, and he could not help arguing with himself again.

They must, because God commands them to love and serve the flock.

"And does not God command you to love the brethren, as well?"

Aye, that He does. But even if I were to overcome the repulsion I feel when I contemplate her experience, I mustn't go against my parents, who are good people.

"And how do you define goodness? Think on the tale of the Good Samaritan. Were not those who passed by the injured man good people, respected in their communities?"

By the end of the day, he was mentally and physically exhausted.

"Come, son," his father called. "It's a good day's work we've done. Let us head for home ere darkness catches us."

Richard plodded to the sledge and dropped one last stone on the load. His father had already unhitched the ox.

"Shan't we unload this tonight?"

"Nay," said his father. " 'Tis only half a load, but twilight falls. We'll come back at first light."

Richard walked wearily beside his father. His shoulder ached where his musket rested on it. Side by side, they shuffled toward home, where a beam of light shone out from the little oiled paper window and through a gap in the palisade.

"Father."

"Yes, son?"

Richard said nothing as they walked toward the gate, knowing that once he broached the subject, he couldn't unsay it.

They paused at the gate, and his father looked at him in the dimness. "What say ye, Richard?"

"I. . .was thinking of Sarah."

His father grunted and opened the gate.

"Is there a reason I should not marry her?"

His father turned slowly and stared at him. Richard felt the unaccountable urge to apologize, but something deep within held him back.

After a long moment of silence, his father said, " 'Twould be a mistake, I fear."

"Why, Father? Her parents are dead. Don't you feel we have sort of an obligation to her?"

"No more than the rest of the town has." His father shook his head. "Best leave it be, son."

"But—"

"Your mother's grief is fresh. She's struggling with the idea that she has to give up on Stephen. He may as well be dead, and she needs to grieve him properly. To bring someone else into the family, someone who has been among the heathen and perhaps learned to sympathize with them. . . Nay, son. Not now. If you've a mind to marry, better to look toward one of the girls who has remained in the community and been faithful at church."

"It wasn't Sarah's fault that she was captured."

"That's so. But think, Richard. She was enslaved by Indians. She may have been compromised. And if not, she has surely embraced some of their savage ways. I know you had notions about her in the old days, and I was not displeased. But things have changed. She is no longer the ideal wife for a God-fearing man."

His father stepped inside the fence and waited for him to enter. Richard stood still. A dark, bleak ache swept over him.

"Son?"

He walked through the gate, and his father closed it firmly.

◆

For two more days, Richard let his father's verdict simmer. On Sunday, his family walked to meeting and sat in their regular pew. Sarah sat in the front with the parson's wife and children and their other two boarders, Miss Hardin and Miss Miller.

From where Richard sat, he could see Sarah, sitting straight and still between the taller Christine Hardin and little Abby Jewett. A streak of sunlight found its way in through the open window, and he thought he caught a faint glint of gold from her hair where it fell below her cap. Not the glorious luster that had gleamed from it of old, but a hint, or better, a promise. Her hair was clean now, though still limp, but the mats and tangles had been combed out. Still, he wouldn't have known her from behind if he hadn't known of her presence in the Jewett household and recognized the fabric Catherine had carried to her a few days past.

All through the reverend's two-hour sermon, his heart warred with his brain. He knew it was sinful, but he couldn't keep his thoughts on what the pastor said. Instead he thought of how thin Sarah's shoulders looked and how she had toughened during her absence. That soft, rounded cast to her face was gone. Her cheeks were gaunt and her eyes sunken.

But that will change, he told himself. A summer in the village with good eating and loving friends, where her labor would be less strenuous than it had been in Canada, would restore her. All she needed was fresh, creamy milk and a good pudding every day, and a kind word or two from one who loved her. If only he could be the one to provide that for her!

When the service ended and they rose, he realized he couldn't tell what the parson had expounded. He sincerely hoped his father didn't quiz him on the sermon. Though he was no longer a child to be chastised, it would still embarrass him.

He lingered, hoping to get a closer view of Sarah, but she stayed at the front with Goody Jewett and the others. She never turned toward them while he watched.

"Come, Richard," his father urged, and he followed his family outside.

A few neighbors spoke to him. He nodded and answered with as few words as possible. He swung around to look back at the doorway, but still Sarah did not appear.

"There be Goodman Fowler and his two daughters," said his mother. She and Catherine went to speak to the young ladies, and his mother threw him a meaningful glance. All too clearly, he saw that she wished him to go and speak to Dorcas and Alice Fowler. In a flash, he knew his father had said something to her about Sarah.

Richard felt betrayed. Although his father had counseled him not to mention Sarah for fear of upsetting his mother, he had gone and done it himself, warned her that Richard had once more turned his attention to the girl he'd admired so long ago. He went to join a cluster of men who discussed cutting an early hay crop and pretended not to notice his mother's glances.

By the time the four headed home at last, he had come to a decision. He would visit the Jewett home on Monday and ask to speak to Sarah. He would ask her what had happened to her since she was removed so cruelly from the village. No more of this speculation. Mother and Father feared she was no longer fit to live among them. Well, he preferred not to pass judgment until he learned the truth. He would ask her straight out what her captivity was like, how she was treated, and if she kept her faith.

◆

A moment's doubt overtook Richard when he raised his hand to knock at the Jewetts' door. For an instant, he considered turning and striding quickly along the path toward home. But as he hesitated, the door flew open. Richard topped the pastor's height by three or four inches, but Jewett stood above him on the floor of the cottage, so he found himself eye to eye with the minister.

Richard caught his breath, stepped backward off the doorstone, and nodded. "Morning, Reverend."

"Ah, Richard. May I help you?"

Could he, indeed? Richard cleared his throat and adjusted the musket on his shoulder.

"I. . ." Why on earth hadn't he brought something as an excuse for this visit? He felt the blood rush to his face and hoped his beard covered his discomfiture. "I thought perhaps to have a word with one of your guests."

"Aye?" The pastor relaxed just a hair and smiled. "Which one? All are about the place, I believe. Myself, I'm about to go over to the meetinghouse for some quiet while I study. The children's exuberance makes it difficult here, you understand. But perhaps I should stay?"

"Oh no, sir. Don't discommode yourself. No need at all."

Did a shade of disappointment cross the parson's face? "Well, Miss Hardin and Miss Miller be inside helping my wife—"

"It's Miss Minton I've come to see."

"Ah. The garden, then. She seems to find peace in working the soil. I've warned her to stay within hailing distance of the house and not go to the far corners of our little cornfield without company."

"Aye, sir, I understand you perfectly. Though your house be in the center of the village, we cannot count on safety."

Jewett stepped outside and closed the door. "I'm not wishing to be nosy, Richard, but I stand as a father would to these young ladies now. Might I inquire the purpose of your call?"

"Well, I. . ." The awkward uncertainty assailed Richard once more, coupled with the knowledge that his actions went against his parents' wishes. "I wanted to fully express my condolences to her. We were longtime neighbors and. . .her family and mine. . ."

"Of course. I only ask that you speak to her within full view of the house and any passersby. We mustn't give occasion for gossip when the returned captives hold so fragile a position in the parish. It is my hope to see them reconciled fully into the village in time."

Richard found it difficult to swallow around the painful lump that had risen in his throat. So the parson knew just how deep the mistrust and fear went. He wondered if Jewett knew his parents' intolerance. And his own, when it came to that. Only Catherine had shown a truly magnanimous and forgiving spirit. "Yes, sir."

The pastor eyed him thoughtfully and nodded. "Pray for these ladies, Richard, and the other returned captives, as well. I've visited several of the families who have been reunited with loved ones or taken in orphans. It will take them time to feel comfortable in our society again. Not only those who lived among the savages. Some who lived in the city are finding it hardest. I could tell you about one girl who was a kitchen maid to a wealthy family in Quebec. She had finer clothing and better fare than she has here with her own people."

"Does she wish to go back?" The idea startled Richard.

"Nay, I think not, but she must reconcile her memories and her expectations. Well, then, I'll be on my way. Good day." The pastor nodded and walked up the slope toward the meetinghouse.

Richard rounded the house and spotted Sarah almost immediately, hoeing steadily among the knee-high corn plants. He supposed she didn't mind working in the little cornfield Pastor Jewett had planted that spring. Among the Pennacook, cultivating corn and later grinding the dried kernels into meal must have been among her major duties. But now she hoed good, English soil, with the promise of good company, a filling meal, and a snug berth when the day's toil was done. Was she happy to be here among her own kind? Of course she missed her family. Had she known they were all dead when she left here? Or had she hoped to come home and find them waiting?

And what had she hoped of him?

He walked slowly toward the edge of the corn. No turning back, now that he'd spoken to the parson.

Her slender form bent to the task. She was too intent on her work, he thought. A warrior could sneak up on her easily. But at that moment, she straightened and whirled toward him, and he saw that he was wrong about that. She was not only alert, but instinctive fear had seized her when she sensed his presence.

When she saw him, she ceased her motion for a second and then raised a hand to wipe her brow. Their gazes locked, and she stood immobile.

"Sarah." He spoke her name so softly she couldn't possibly hear it from where she stood, but he saw her lips quiver. She raised the hoe and carefully hiked her skirt just enough to let her pass between the corn plants without disturbing them.

When she reached the edge of the plowed ground, she stopped and rested the hoe blade on the ground. Richard approached one step, then another. About six feet from her, he stopped.

"Good morning." She squinted a little and rocked on her feet, as though she might dash for the house.

He nodded. "I. . ."

The sun glinted off her hair, and for an instant, he saw the old Sarah. The core of her beauty was still there, and it grabbed him so strongly that his stomach lurched.

She took one more step toward him, and he could see the depths of her blue eyes.

"Are you well, Sarah?"

"Aye."

"Be you going to stay here with the Jewetts?"

"For now."

He considered that. Did she have plans? "And then? Will you leave us again?"

"Should I?"

"Nay, but. . ."

"But?" She cocked her head toward her left shoulder and studied him. "The people here treat us differently now than before we were taken away."

"Do we?"

"You know you do."

His mouth went dry. "We don't—that is, I don't mean to."

She said nothing but stared, unmoving, until his guilt spurred him to close the distance between them.

When only two feet of salty New England air separated them, he gathered his courage. "Sarah, I regret how I acted last week."

"Oh?"

"Yes. I. . .couldn't. . ."

"You couldn't bear to look at me and claim me as your friend? You couldn't stand to think that I might have joined the Pennacook in their heathenish ceremonies, is that it? Or perhaps you speculated I'd become worse than a slave to them, I'd thrown away all decency and virtue, I'd—"

"Stop it."

They glared at each other.

Richard couldn't help noticing how alive she looked in that moment. Her cheeks, though still thin, were flushed a becoming pink, and her eyes sparked with passion. He gave a small cough and tried again. "My father—"

"Your father has nothing to do with it, or he shouldn't have! You are a man grown. If you can't own me as your friend—as someone you once cared about—before the whole village, then I won't have you skulking around now apologizing, when none else can see you. I've heard the things people are saying, Richard. If you believe them, you're not the man I thought you were. I thank God I spent the last five years depending on His mercy, not yours."

She turned and walked back into the cornfield, where she wielded the hoe with jerky strokes.

So that's the way you accept an apology. If you think you can cultivate a man's heart the way you do a corn patch, you're mistaken, Sarah Minton.

He hefted his musket and made for the path.

Chapter 7

Sarah rued her dismissal of Richard before she reached the end of the row she was hoeing. Of course he was confused and curious. She should not condemn him for taking things slowly in renewing their acquaintance, and he *did* come in private to talk to her, when there were no busybodies listening. Why had she berated him for it? He was trying to sort things out without generating gossip.

She paused and wiped the beads of sweat from her brow. The day had turned quite hot, and her vigorous hoeing, along with her anger, had warmed her. She would stop when she got to the end of the next row, near the house, and go in for a drink of water.

Looking back along the file of young corn plants, she realized what she had just done. Richard had come and said he was sorry, the very thing she had longed to hear since that first painful day when he had ignored her. And she'd sent him away with a blistering rebuke. She wished she had heard him out and explored the depth of his feelings.

He'd said he regretted his actions, and he'd mentioned his father. Had Goodman Dudley led the family in shunning the returned captives? Had he forbidden his children to befriend them?

If such were the case, then she should be grateful that Richard had taken matters into his own hands and come to her, despite his father's feelings. Catherine, too, had shown kindness in bringing her the material for the new clothes she so badly needed. Were the children perhaps more fair-minded than their parents? The Dudleys' younger son, Stephen, was taken captive when Sarah was. Surely the family would not treat him this way should he return to them one day.

Sarah leaned on the hoe, weary to the core. She was tired of always trying to figure out what people thought and how they felt. Why couldn't one be straightforward in dealing with folks? But when she considered that, she wasn't sure she could abide complete honesty among the villagers. If some did not hide their true feelings, their contempt and distrust would show plainly, and chaos would erupt.

A breeze lifted the brim of her bonnet, and she welcomed its relief. It also stirred the leaves of the nearby forest, and she realized how far she was from the pastor's house. She began to chop quickly at the weeds in the next row, working her way steadily back toward the humble parsonage.

The next day it rained, and Sarah spent all morning with Jane, stitching a new dress while Christine continued to weave. Sarah gave Abigail a scrap of the linsey material and a needle so that she could practice her stitches. The three young women had been left with the little girls and their sewing while Elizabeth Jewett joined her husband in calling on several ill parishioners. The two youngest children napped in the loft.

"Mrs. Jewett despairs of finding me a husband," Christine confided to the other two girls when Abby ran outside to the necessary.

"Must they try?" Sarah asked.

Christine shot the shuttle through her web. "It seems the reverend thinks they must. But he fears I'll be harder to unload than you or Jane."

Sarah knew it was true, for she had heard the pastor and his wife discuss Christine's situation during her captivity. The Puritan minister practiced great toleration and charity by harboring one who had lived in a convent. But even with the Reverend Jewett's support, others in the strict community would continue to wonder if Christine had apostatized.

"You gave him your word you've remained faithful," Sarah said.

"Of course. But people have long memories hereabouts."

Jane bit off the end of her thread. "At least you've no foreign marriage to live down. Goody Jewett told me the village gossips' tongues are wagging. I suppose I shouldn't have gone back to my English name. They wonder if I was really married and if Monsieur Robataille is truly dead, or if I just up and walked away from him when Captain Baldwin came on the scene. I thank the Lord I had no babies to bring back with me, as crass as that may sound. These staunch Englishmen wouldn't want to take on a Frenchman's offspring. Look at Madame Bayeux. Her own family didn't want her children. Though I hear they've kept them after all."

Sarah felt heat redden her cheeks. "The truth is, I don't believe I wish to marry."

"Me, either." Christine nodded and ran the shuttle back and forth. "I'd be happy to live as a servant in someone's house, so long as I'm not mistreated."

"Well, I don't know as I'd want to work for someone else all my life," Jane countered.

"That's because you've had your own home," Sarah said. "It must have been good in some ways to be a housewife and run things your own way."

Jane's lips pressed tight together as she bent over her sewing. "I suppose some days were not so bad. But I'll tell you this: A wife without hired help works harder than a servant girl."

A wail came from the corner bed, and Sarah jumped up. "There's Ruth, awake from her nap. I'll get her."

"And I'd best start putting dinner on the table," Jane said. All knew their hosts would return home soon for the meal.

By the time Sarah changed Ruth's clouts, Constance had wakened. Sarah carried Ruth to the bottom of the ladder and watched while the four-year-old descended. Abby came in from outside.

"There, now, girls, you can play with Ruth while we prepare dinner." Sarah set the baby on the quilt that covered the parents' low bed in the corner. Constance obliged by fetching her rag doll and holding it out to Ruth.

As she worked about the hearth with Jane and Christine, Sarah decided she would have another talk with Goody Jewett that evening. She knew the pastor and his wife meant well, and perhaps it would be best for the community if all the young women found husbands. But the idea of being parceled off to a man she hardly knew repelled Sarah. Yes, much better to serve as a hired girl for one of the wealthier families, perhaps at one of the garrison houses.

Richard's image flitted through her mind. Not the Richard from her past, young and optimistic, but the new one—sober, suspicious Richard, who was not ready to trust her even as a friend, let alone as a woman he could love. She doubted he would ever regain the carefree heart he'd had as a lad. He'd seen too much. All of the villagers had. And of course, he'd lost his own brother.

Sarah empathized with Richard and his family. Not knowing your loved ones' fates was perhaps a step worse than seeing them killed. She knew that when the negotiators went to Quebec, Charles Gardner had done his best to get wind of Stephen Dudley's whereabouts, but the Pennacook had closed ranks and kept any whisper of information from him. The Dudleys must be heartbroken.

During her captivity, Sarah had wondered about her own family. Her mother's scream had haunted her, but still, for five years, she had hoped some of her kin might have survived. Captain Baldwin had dispelled those hopes soon after she met him in Quebec City. Both her parents had been cut down by the savages, and her sister, Molly, had apparently died in the fire that leveled their house that night. The captain speculated that Molly was dead before the fire began, but even so, Sarah fought nightmares of her younger sister engulfed in flames.

She shivered and plunked the pewter plates down on the table harder than she'd meant to.

"Are you cold?" Christine asked. "Goody Jewett has a shawl hanging on the peg by the door."

"Nay," Sarah whispered. "Thank you, I'm fine."

But she knew she wasn't ready to go off to live with strangers yet. In just a few days, she had begun to feel secure here with the Jewetts. Until she came back to Cochecho, she'd had hopes of being reunited with her family, though she'd been torn from them in the dark of that awful night and looked back to see flames rising. Still, she had told herself they might have gotten away. As long as she didn't know, it was possible. But since she'd learned their fates, the awful dreams had assailed her.

She would like to stay here awhile, she believed. If the Jewetts would keep her on, she would like to help them with the chores and tending the children until the nightmares stopped.

That evening she found a moment to speak to Goody Jewett, after they'd washed the dishes together, while Christine and Jane put the little girls to bed.

"Of course we want you to stay with us until you're ready, Sarah," the pastor's wife assured her.

"I don't like to be a burden on you." Sarah lowered her gaze, afraid to see rejection in her hostess's eyes.

"Nay, you are a help to me. You've worked in the garden and done the washing. You young ladies are a blessing to me just now." Goody Jewett sneaked a look toward where her husband and the two boys sat at the table, going over the lessons the minister had set for his sons that morning. "You see, we expect another wee one by Christmas. I should be glad if at least one of you stayed with me that long."

Sarah caught her breath. Was this good news? A sixth child coming, and Ruth just beginning to toddle. The parson's family already stretched its resources as far as they could. But Elizabeth smiled at her and squeezed her hand. "My husband hopes for another boy."

Sarah smiled back. "I'm sure that would please him. But. . ."

"But what?" Elizabeth waited for her to speak.

"What if we all three stayed? That would be hard for you. The people won't keep bringing food, will they?"

"We shall see. And I'm sure you girls will find places within a few months' time, whether through marriage or employment."

Sarah wasn't so sure.

◆

Richard set out early for the village to buy provisions for his mother, an empty sack in his hand. Better to get it done and be home before nooning. Then he could put in a full afternoon of work around the farm.

He came within sight of the long, low trading post, built many years earlier by Major Waldron. After the major was killed in the massacre, the post was taken over by Joseph Paine. He traded with the Indians but also stocked supplies from the outside world for the settlers.

As Richard drew close, he spotted two figures going into the store: Sarah and one of the other girls boarding at the Jewetts' house. He pulled up short. He

53

almost turned around and went home; however, that would mean another trip to the village, and his mother would scold him for not bringing her the sugar cone and vanilla he had promised to fetch. He ran a hand through his hair and made up his mind. He would only nod to them, unless Sarah initiated a conversation.

As he entered, he noticed a middle-aged couple talking to the trader, apparently haggling over a length of woolen cloth. *Trust Goodman Ackley to squeeze every ha'penny before he let it go.* His wife's sharp tongue would only add to the sport of the trade. Richard thought he would stay away from the trader until the Ackleys were done dealing with him.

Several men stood near the cold hearth, deep in conversation. Richard supposed they chose that spot out of habit—their warm gathering place in the colder months of the year. The two young women had wandered to the far side of the long, low-ceiled room, to where the herbs were stored.

Richard's quest for vanilla beans would take him near them. He paused along the wall where tools hung, eyeing the fox and beaver traps. The two young ladies seemed to have found the item they wanted and stepped away. He drew in a deep breath and walked toward the bench, though he would have to pass close by them.

"Good day." Sarah's soft voice sent a shiver down his spine.

He stopped abruptly between the cinnamon and the lard tubs. "Good day, ladies."

Sarah smiled in the dimness, but the other girl—Jane, was it?—averted her gaze and gave a perfunctory nod.

"How is your mother?" Sarah asked.

"Very well, thank you." He didn't know what else to say and stood there mute for a long moment. Her eyes were gray in this light, but her hair somehow caught a glint from the rays streaming through the window across the room.

Sarah twitched, and he was almost sure her companion had nudged her with a not-too-subtle elbow.

"Pardon us," Sarah said. "We must fill Goody Jewett's list."

"Of course." Richard quickly chose a handful of vanilla beans and carried them to the counter. Trader Paine was still talking to the Ackleys, but he broke away from them and came to tend to Richard's purchase.

"Will that be all?"

"Nay, my mother requests a cone of white sugar if you've any on hand." Richard slid a coin toward the trader.

"Indeed I do." Paine bent beneath his rough worktable and lifted a heavy object wrapped in paper and set it on the surface.

Richard opened his sack, and Paine lifted the sugar cone. As they worked together to fit the unwieldy object into the bag, Richard heard Goody Ackley, who stood three feet from him, mutter something about "those shameless girls the parson took in."

Richard turned and stared at the woman. How dare she say such things about Sarah and her companion? But sure enough, she was eyeing the two young women across the store with a contemptuous sneer on her lips.

"I beg your pardon, ma'am?" Richard said in a voice loud enough that the men at the hearth broke off their words and looked toward him.

"Nothing," said Goody Ackley, glancing toward her husband.

"Strange," Richard replied, his anger taking hold and spurring him to speak when ordinarily he would have kept silent. "I thought I heard you comment on the parson's houseguests."

"Oh, it's strange, all right." The goodwife wrinkled her nose, and her eyes nearly closed as she flicked a glance toward the two distant figures. "Strange that our minister would harbor fallen women in his household."

Richard felt heat surge through his body. "That is vile language. You ought to be in the stocks for speaking such base things about women who were carried off against their wills and have shown only meekness since their return."

"Here!" Goodman Ackley stepped between Richard and his wife and glared up at the tall young man. "Don't you speak to my wife like that. The idea of a churchgoing man defending a jade who's lived years with a French trapper!"

Before he gave any thought to his actions, Richard pulled back his fist and smacked the man's jaw.

Chapter 8

Ackley fell backward and tumbled to the floor. His wife gasped and knelt over her husband. Richard winced and rubbed his knuckles.

"You—you—you wild young jackanapes," Goody Ackley sputtered at him. "I'll have the constable on you!"

"Nay," the trader said calmly, throwing Richard a weary smile. "'Tis you and your husband who should fear the law, ma'am. Dudley is right about that. Folk are put in the stocks for far milder slander than the two of you have uttered here this day."

Richard nodded gravely at Paine, picked up his sack, and turned to go. To his dismay, he saw that every eye in the trading post was on him, including those of Sarah. Jane Miller's face was scarlet, and Sarah's a stark white. For a moment, no one moved. Then Sarah slipped the item that she'd held onto the nearest shelf, and the two young women headed silently for the door.

Richard looked at the trader, and Paine returned his gaze with a resigned look. All Richard could gather from it was Paine's support, but regret that the incident had occurred in his place of business. Even though he disliked the Ackleys, Paine would have to trade with them in the future, just as he traded with the nearby Indians nobody trusted.

Richard nodded and walked out. Outside the door, he stopped in surprise.

Sarah and her companion huddled together under the eaves, and Sarah stepped forward as he emerged. "Richard, thank you. I hope you are not hurt."

"Nay, it was nothing." He looked past her and saw that Jane stood apart with hunched shoulders. Tears trickled down her cheeks.

"Allow me to see you ladies home," Richard said.

"We'll be fine," Sarah assured him. "But I needed to thank you for taking our part. You didn't have to."

"I know." He shrugged. "They spoke nasty lies. I probably overstepped the bounds of propriety, but I didn't feel I should let it go."

Jane looked him in the face for the first time. "Sir, you don't know how often people speak such things. You can't be about to silence them every time."

"Nay, but if one man speaks up one time and others hear, perhaps the next time the others will take your part."

Sarah reached out to squeeze his arm. "You speak truth."

"Come." He hefted his sack, wincing at the stab of pain in his knuckles, and started along the path toward the parsonage. They walked without speaking, with Sarah between him and Jane. When they reached the parson's dooryard, he smiled ruefully at them. "Perhaps Goody Jewett will go with you next time, though young ladies ought to be able to do a bit of trading without fear."

"Yes." The troubled frown between Sarah's eyebrows accentuated her thin face. She wasn't fully recovered yet from her ordeal, he realized, but she was beginning to regain the weight she had lost. No longer did her features bear that emaciated look.

Richard's pulse quickened as he surveyed her. In another month, she would have regained her beauty, he was sure. He cleared his throat. "Would you like me to go back and fetch Goody Jewett's needs for you?"

Sarah shook her head. "Thank you, but nay. I shall tell the reverend what happened today, and I expect he shall want to settle this matter himself."

◆

She watched Richard leave, striding down the path with long, confident steps. He had done what she'd longed for the day she returned, and now she was in turmoil.

True, he had defended Jane and Christine, as well as her—mostly Jane—and he probably would have done so had she not been present. Instead of disheartening her, that raised her appreciation of his action even more.

This was the Richard she'd kept alive in her heart for five years. This was a man who stood for truth and protected the poor and downtrodden. She had not been mistaken all this time. Richard had grown into the man she had dreamed of loving.

As she pondered this, she had no hope, in spite of her fierce attraction to him. Richard didn't want to marry her. The townspeople looked down on her now. Even if he had wanted to marry her, she couldn't saddle him with that burden.

She turned toward the door, certain that the right course for her would be to remain single and serve God however she could.

Jane stood waiting for her on the doorstone, watching her keenly. She raised her chin. "He's a good man. He put himself in danger of censure for us."

"Aye." Sarah went in with her, and when Goody Jewett heard her tale, she left the children in care of Christine and Jane.

"You and I will go straight to Samuel," Elizabeth Jewett declared, taking off her apron.

Sarah walked behind her to the meetinghouse and waited meekly outside while Elizabeth went inside to tell her husband what had happened at the trading post.

The Reverend Jewett came to the door and looked out at her, his blue eyes filled with concern. "Are you and Miss Miller all right, Miss Minton?"

"Yes, sir," Sarah replied. "Jane was mortified, but Richard Dudley's actions will be put about the community ere nightfall, I'm sure."

"Oh, I've no doubt," the pastor agreed wryly. He looked toward the river, where the trading post lay. "I expect I should go have a word with Goodman Ackley, and also with the trader." He leaned against the doorjamb, and Elizabeth peeked out beside him.

"Think ye the constable should be notified?" his wife asked.

"Not by us. Richard and Paine heard what was said. They can lodge a complaint of gossip if they wish."

"What if. . ." Sarah gulped and looked up at them. "What if Goodman Ackley sues Richard?"

Pastor Jewett shook his head. "If he's determined to do that, he can, but it seems to me he'd have no case. Most people will sympathize with Richard."

"Are you sure?" Sarah asked. The majority of the community still seemed to look on the former captives with distaste.

The parson slid his arm around his wife and pulled her against his side.

Sarah pretended not to notice. Such a display of affection was seldom made in public, and she doubted Reverend Jewett was conscious of his act as he spoke to her.

"I'm sorry you young ladies have seen the cruel side of the sinful nature. I'll speak to Goodman Ackley and his wife. It may not do any good, but it's part of my job to keep peace in the parish. If they won't listen. . ."

"I wouldn't expect a quick apology," Elizabeth said, and her husband frowned.

"Well, I'd best get over to their house." He dropped his arm to his side and walked down the steps of the meetinghouse.

"When you speak to Mr. Paine, would you bring me the candlewicking and pepper Sarah and Jane went for, if it's not too much trouble?" Elizabeth asked.

"Surely. And afterward, I shall come back here to finish planning my Sunday sermon." He looked up at the blue sky. "Odd. It's on forgiveness."

◆

As the long summer days passed, Richard threw himself into the work of the farm, often toiling at his father's side from first light to sunset. During his hours of steady labor, Sarah's face often flitted through his mind.

But more and more, another haunted him—Stephen.

His brother's capture angered him. The negotiators who redeemed the captives had done all they could and spent every penny they had but found no word of Stephen.

As time passed, Richard saw his parents, especially his mother, grow old before his eyes. Her hair whitened, and her step slowed. Catherine seemed to be taking on more of the housework, and their mother spent more time in her chair, knitting or simply sitting with her hands folded in her lap. She spoke little and smiled less. Richard knew she grieved for Stephen, perhaps more heavily than when he first left them.

When the corn stood nearly to his waist, Richard and his father turned to haying. In order to keep livestock through the long, harsh winter of New Hampshire, they needed to stockpile hay, corn, and cornstalks to feed the cattle, sheep, and chickens. In winter, when they cut trees to dry for the next year's firewood, they always cut in a pattern that would open up new fields for them to grow hay. The number of livestock they could keep depended on the winter feed they could produce.

Richard eyed the gardens and the hayfields often, counting off the days until he might leave his father for a while. Goodman Dudley still had his strength, though he also showed his age in swatches of gray hair at his temples. But to provide for four adults and gradually improve their life, he needed the help of his grown son.

In mid-July, after the first cutting of hay was safely stacked, Richard dared broach the subject. As they were milking one evening, he took his wooden bucket of milk and went to where his father was finishing with the second cow. "I want to go to Canada, Father."

His father's hands paused in the rhythmic motion of milking then went on. "It is too dangerous."

"Charles said he and Baldwin's crew were received well enough when they went."

"They had the governor's backing. What could you do that those men did not do, son?"

"I don't know, but if I don't try, I will always wonder."

His father sighed and stood up, lifting his milking stool and bucket. "I can't let you go, Richard. Imagine how your mother would take it if anything happened to you."

Richard turned away disappointed. *I will wait until after the harvest*, he told himself.

A fortnight later, he gathered his courage, and on a quiet evening, he left his parents' home and walked once more to the parsonage.

◆

After supper, Pastor Jewett took all the children but Ruth for a walk to the river so they could enjoy the evening breeze that came up from the sea, tempering the heat of the July day.

Goody Jewett sat in her chair by the open doorway, lulling Ruth to sleep, while Sarah, Jane, and Christine made short work of cleaning up the kitchen.

As Sarah hung her damp linen towel on a peg to dry and Christine set the last pewter mug on the shelf, Mrs. Jewett called out to an approaching visitor, "Good evening, sir, and welcome."

A deep voice replied, "Good even to you, ma'am."

Sarah felt a shiver of anticipation as she recognized Richard's voice. For the past month, she had seen him only at Sunday meeting. He sometimes spoke to her briefly, no more than a "Good day." His sister was more vocal, often stopping to chat with her and the other young women. But sometimes as Sarah left the meetinghouse with Goody Jewett and the children, she would see Richard gazing at her from across the yard, and she often wondered where his thoughts led.

"Be Sarah Minton about?"

Her heart leaped at his quiet inquiry, and she fumbled with the strings of her apron.

"Let me help you," Jane hissed, pushing her around and seizing the ties.

"Why yes," Goody Jewett said, shifting in her chair so she could call into the room. "Sarah? A visitor has come a-calling."

Sarah pulled in a deep breath and stared at Jane. She'd told the other girls she didn't wish to marry, and yet a glorious hope dawned in her heart when she realized Richard had come all the way into town to see her.

Jane smiled and squeezed her arm. "Best see what he wants."

Sarah's knees trembled as she walked slowly toward the door. The setting sun streaked the clouds behind Richard with pink, mauve, and scarlet, but the display could not rival the burst of joy inside her.

"Welcome, Richard." She ducked her head, conscious of the eyes watching her.

His smile was contained and nervous. "I. . .wondered if we might walk. With Goody Jewett's consent, of course."

Mrs. Jewett smiled. "You may, provided you stay within sight of this house, sir." She struggled to stand without disturbing the sleeping little girl in her arms.

Sarah reached to take Ruth from her. "Let me take her to the loft."

Goody Jewett drew back. "Nay, I think Christine is waiting just behind you to do that task for me. Your guest awaits." She smiled gently, and Sarah let her arms fall to her sides.

"Aye." She glanced again at Richard. He had retreated a few steps and stood waiting for her.

"Come in before full dark," Mrs. Jewett murmured as she passed her, and Sarah nodded.

Delicious coolness bathed her as she stepped outside. Richard met her gaze then looked down at the toes of his boots. "Perhaps we could stroll along the near edge of the fields?"

"Certainly." She walked beside him around the house and to the border of the corn that now reached her waist.

Richard looked out over the rows and pulled in a deep breath. "Parson looks to make a good crop this year."

"Yes, we've had fine weather. Enough rain, but hot days for growing." She felt a bit silly, discussing weather and crops with a grown man. But that might be better than addressing the real reason Richard had come. Her pulse throbbed faster, and she stared straight ahead as she walked.

"I've been thinking about Stephen a lot these days," he confessed as they reached the end of Pastor Jewett's field and moved on to the edge of Goodman Bryce's. "Charles Gardner tells me he's likely been adopted by an Indian family and is happy there. What think ye?"

Sarah's giddy feelings fled as the memories of her own Indian family and the lean years in the Pennacook village returned. She had imagined that Richard came with thoughts of courting, but instead he only sought her out for her knowledge of the Indians. Still, it was better than being shunned, and perhaps they could restore their old friendship over time.

"Charles is probably correct. When he came to my village to redeem me, my people—that is, the family who adopted me—hid me at first. But after they had talked a long time, they brought me out and handed me over to the white men. I was overcome with joy and fear and disbelief. Charles asked me right away about Stephen, and I told him all I knew, which was little."

"You'd seen Stephen in Canada?"

"We were in the same group when we were taken, but they split into smaller bands before we came to the village where I lived most of the time. The warriors who took Stephen went off westward—toward Montreal, I supposed—but I had no real idea where they'd taken him. I did see Stephen one more time, about two years later. His people came through where we lived and stopped with us a few days."

Richard stopped walking and stared at her. "I didn't know this. Were you able to speak to him?"

"I tried." She looked back toward the houses of the village. "I saw a chance the second day, when he was out with some of our boys, practicing throwing knives. I pretended to be working, but I moved closer until he looked up and saw me. I said his name. *Stephen.* He looked at me as if I'd spoken in Greek. And he turned and walked away. I was going to follow him, hoping he would acknowledge me when he was away from the others, but my. . .mother—the woman who. . ." She glanced up at Richard in confusion. Would he understand, or would he think her disloyal to her own family?

He arched his eyebrows. "Your Indian mother?"

"Yes. She came up behind me and seized my arm. She dragged me into her lodge and wouldn't let me go out again until the visitors were gone. I ground corn and worked hides, all the while praying for another chance." The memory of the painful bruise on her forearm made Sarah wince, and she rubbed the spot, although it had long ago healed. "I never saw him again. I'm sorry, Richard."

"It's not your fault."

"Perhaps. But if I'd bided my time and been discreet. . . Oh, I'm so sorry I can't give you better news." Tears flooded her eyes, and she wished she'd kept her apron to wipe them with. She raised her arm and swiped at them with her sleeve.

"Shh."

Richard touched her shoulder, and that made her sob. She wasn't sure whether the tears were for Stephen, or for Richard and his family, or for herself.

"He's probably not unhappy," she ventured.

"Aye. I fear you are right." Richard frowned, and she wished she could unsay the words.

"It's better than. . ." She stopped. Was it really better than what had happened to Molly? Would she rather know Molly lived contentedly among the savages than that she had died in the slaughter that bloody night? Seeing the crosses in the churchyard with her parents' and sister's names carved on them had brought it home to her a few weeks ago. Molly was at rest. But Stephen roamed with the warriors. Perhaps he would even take part in raids against English settlers.

In Richard's face, she saw the same turmoil she was feeling.

"I want to try to find him," he said.

"No, Richard. Don't go. It will only bring you deeper grief."

"Don't you see? While I do nothing, I feel as though I've betrayed my family and my faith. I can't let my brother go wild and heathen without trying my best to stop it. I can't, Sarah."

She drew a shaky breath and reached out to him.

Richard took her hand for a moment and held it in his strong, warm one. "I'm glad you at least had people who didn't mistreat you too badly."

She nodded. "It was difficult. They live in extreme poverty most of the time, but they know no other way. When they have a good harvest or a successful hunt, they do put food away for the lean times. But it always runs out during the winter." She shivered. "As you say, I had it better than some. I worked hard. I learned new skills. And I tried to be the daughter my new mother craved."

"They had no children of their own?"

"Oh, yes. She had three grown sons. Her husband died before I came there.

And she'd had a little daughter years ago who grew to about the age I was when I went there. I think that is why they chose to keep me. She wanted a girl to replace her daughter who had died. I was the right size, and I suppose I seemed docile but strong and healthy. I later learned that the man who had captured me and took me to her was one of her sons. When I could speak their language well enough, she told me she had asked him to bring her a daughter to comfort and serve her in her old age, as his sister would have done."

Richard looked down at her with troubled brown eyes. "They give no thought to the mothers grieving here for the children they've lost."

"It is true." She looked around and noticed that the sun had dropped below the dark evergreens. "We must return," she said.

"Aye. Thank you, Sarah."

They walked back toward the parsonage, and although one more bit of information surfaced in Sarah's mind, she wasn't sure whether or not to tell him.

As they approached the house, he paused for a moment. "I plan to go," he said earnestly. "Sarah, if you go to meeting one Sunday and I'm not there, you'll know I've gone to seek Stephen."

"I wish you wouldn't. You will not find him."

He only clamped his lips together and gazed off into the distance.

Sarah sighed. "If you do go. . ."

"Yes?"

"I can tell you the names of the family that adopted Stephen. I learned them after they took him away again. I asked other young women in our village, and they told me the names. And your brother's new name."

"Charles told me nothing of this."

"He probably did not want to cause you more sorrow."

"But you told him when you first saw him in Canada this spring?"

"Yes. It made him hopeful that he could succeed in his mission, but not so." She eyed him with sadness, fearing she had only made things worse for him. "Charles knew the land, the people, the language, and he still could not find your brother."

"I know." Richard took a deep breath. "You will write down the names for me?"

"If you wish it."

"Thank you. I will find Stephen."

Sarah's heart ached. Richard had no idea how rigorous the journey would be or the discouragement that awaited him. He refused to consider the danger he would encounter. Had she just destroyed her only chance of a happy future?

Chapter 9

A fortnight later, as soon as the morning dew evaporated, Sarah and Christine went out to gather petals from the blossoms lading the rosebush at the corner of the parsonage. Christine had learned at the convent how to distill rosewater in a Dutch oven, and she had promised to make some for the pastor's wife to use in her baking.

"It's a pity to ruin all the flowers," Sarah said as she held a stem carefully between its thorns and stripped off the pink petals.

Christine held the basket beneath Sarah's hands to catch the colorful bits as they fluttered down. "We won't need all of the roses. Let's save a few of the best blooms and take them to Goody Jewett." She glanced up and nodded toward the village street. "Yon comes your beau and his friend."

Sarah looked over her shoulder and saw Richard Dudley and Charles Gardner approaching them. Her mouth went dry, but when she glanced at Christine, she realized her friend was even more uncomfortable.

"I'll take this inside," Christine murmured.

"Nay, stay here," Sarah said. Richard and Charles had left the street, and by now it was obvious they intended to converse with the two young women.

"Good day, ladies," Richard said, doffing his hat.

Christine lowered her gaze and nodded.

"Good day, Richard," Sarah said. "Mr. Gardner."

Charles pulled his hat off and stood, holding it and looking at the ground. Sarah took in their appearance. Both held muskets and carried full packs on their backs.

"Charles and I are heading to Quebec," Richard said. "He will take me to the village where he redeemed you, and we will begin our inquiries there."

At a loss for words, Sarah looked into the depths of his eyes, rich brown shot through with gold. She sensed a challenge in them, and the set to his chin told her that nothing she could say would deter him. She looked to Charles instead. "Mr. Gardner, can't you dissuade him from this quest?"

"I'm afraid not, ma'am. And if he must go, then he must."

She turned back to Richard. "You've asked your friend to tread again the fruitless paths he trod a few months ago?"

"Nay, Charles is the one who suggested I might like a companion."

Charles nodded decisively, though his frown showed his disapproval. "I should hate to see my dearest friend undertake this unhappy mission alone, and so I've determined to go with him. At least I can translate for him among some of the tribes, and as you say, I've walked these paths before and can guide Richard. We will travel speedily, the two of us. We hope to be back before snowfall."

"But, Richard, I thought you were going to wait until your father had his harvest in."

"I cannot do that and hope to make this journey before winter. Father has agreed to trade work with some of the other men in my absence."

With early August upon them, Sarah realized they had only three or four months of good traveling weather ahead, and it would take all of that for them to go on foot into the northern wilderness, make their inquiries, and return.

"So. . .you are going now? Today?"

"Aye." Richard gazed at her and took an uncertain step forward, standing just inches from her. "We spoke to Parson Jewett ere we came here. He promises to uphold us in prayer. Will you do the same, Sarah?"

"Of course." A great sadness swept over her. She wanted to reach out to him, to embrace him and plead with him not to go, but that would be useless and most indecorous. "If you get to where I lived, you might have better success if you take a gift."

"We've a few trade goods, but we cannot carry much." He glanced toward Charles.

"I picked up a few knives and some tobacco at the trading post," Charles said.

She nodded. "You might learn something from the women, too. When I was captured, the warriors stole many trinkets and household goods, but the old woman who adopted me was most pleased by. . ." She paused as a lump rose in her throat and tears pricked her eyes at the memory. "Her son brought her some English clothes. They like to get them. Her favorite thing was a bright apron pieced from scraps of red and green cloth. I thought. . ." The tears filled her eyes, and she took a deep breath then went on. "I thought it was one made by Goody Waldron, and old Naticook used to wear it hung about her shoulders like a shawl. It made me laugh to see her wear it that way, but. . .it made me cry, as well."

Charles said, "If we had more men, or a pack animal. . ."

Sarah nodded and reached into the pocket tied about her waist. "Here. This is small." She pulled out a square of soft, fine linen on the corners of which she had stitched bunches of roses. "Take it. If you come to my village, ask for Naticook. Give her this and tell her I am happy with my people. Perhaps she will tell you where Stephen's band lives."

Charles accepted the handkerchief and tucked it into his vest. "Thank you."

Christine stirred. "If you can carry more—"

"I think not, but thank you, ma'am," Charles said.

Christine ducked her head and reverted to silence once more, staring down at the ground.

"Your parents. . . ," Sarah ventured.

Richard frowned. "They are not happy about my decision, but Father understands that I must do this."

She looked long into his eyes and again saw his resolve and a plea for approval. Regardless of those watching, she reached out and touched his sleeve. "God speed you, Richard."

"Farewell, then." He nodded briskly and gave a quick glance that included Christine. Then he and Charles turned and walked back to the village street and turned west, the way Sarah and the others had come into the town nearly three months ago.

"His family wished him not to go," Christine said.

"So it seems. And I can't blame them. They've lost one son, and the journey Richard is undertaking is a dangerous one." Sarah watched until the two young men disappeared from sight.

"And yet they long as much as he does for any scrap of news."

"Yes, I'm sure that's why his father let him go."

"He's a grown man," Christine said. "Surely they couldn't stop him."

"Nay, but Richard would not defy his father." Sarah sighed and looked at the fragrant basket of rose petals Christine still held in her hands. "Have we enough now? Let us go and make our concoction. Perhaps I can go over to the Dudleys' one day and help his mother and sister put up food for the winter. I can even work in the hayfields if they'll let me."

"Goodman Dudley would never allow you to work out in the fields all day."

"I did it in the Indian village on many occasions, hoeing corn from dawn to dusk."

"Still. . .Parson and Goody Jewett let you tend their garden, but they won't have you stay out there all day in the hot sun."

"True," Sarah said as they walked toward the house. "Elizabeth is very kind. She always insists I wear a bonnet and come inside frequently to rest and refresh myself. Life at the parsonage is far different from the Pennacook village."

She thought of her life there, where Naticook saw her fed and clothed but never expressed concern or affection, requiring instead constant work. Here the arduous work seemed pleasant, and the expectation that she would spend the next winter with the boisterous Jewett family in a snug little house with plenty of firewood stacked outside made the future pleasant to contemplate, rather than frightening as she'd found it during her captivity.

"His family will miss Richard sorely, though," Christine said.

"Aye. In a few days, I will ask permission to visit Goody Dudley and Catherine."

"I'll go with you. Perhaps I can do some mending or spinning for the goodwife."

Sarah smiled at her friend, knowing Christine would not have made the offer if she wasn't sure they would find only women in the house when they paid their call. After her years in the convent, Christine was not used to men and still cringed when they were around, though she seemed to be getting used to the parson's booming voice and energetic presence in the Jewett household. She seldom walked in the village and always hung back with the children on Sunday, as though she hoped no one would speak to her. Sarah thought Christine quite lovely with her tall, willowy form and grace of movement, but Christine seemed unconscious of that and wanted only peace and solitude. Sometimes Sarah wondered if Christine would ever be happy, or if she would live out a fearful, lonely life at the loom.

"Mayhap we'll get enough rosewater today that we can take Richard's mother some," Sarah suggested.

Christine smiled a tiny, timid smile. "I think the gentleman has plans for when he returns."

"If they find Stephen, you mean?" Sarah asked.

"Regardless of whether they find him or nay. He looks like a man of a mind to court."

Sarah felt the blood rush to her cheeks. "Come, we have much to do."

◆

Sarah's opportunity to visit the Dudleys came sooner than she had expected. Only three days after Richard's departure, Catherine Dudley arrived panting on the Jewetts' doorstone at noon, while the family sat at dinner.

"Pastor, come," Catherine gasped. "We need you."

The Reverend Jewett jumped up from his stool at the table. "What is it?"

"My father. He dropped a tree on himself this morn. My mother found him when he did not answer the call for dinner."

"Shall I come?" Elizabeth Jewett asked.

"I'll go," Sarah said quickly. Goody Jewett's pregnancy had begun to show, and Sarah knew she often felt nauseous in the morning and fatigued easily.

"How bad is it?" the pastor asked. The minister was indeed called on often when accidents occurred, though for nursing of the sick, Goody Baldwin was often summoned. The captain's wife was known for her skill at midwifery, and between her and the Reverend Jewett, the people of the parish got by without a trained physician.

Catherine leaned against the doorjamb. "He surely has broken a leg and perhaps done other damage to his innards."

Elizabeth got up and hurried to her. "Sit down, child. Rest a moment while my husband and Sarah gather some rags for bandages."

"Mother has his worst wounds bound up." Catherine took a seat and accepted the dipper of water Jane silently offered.

"Has your mother any willow bark?" Elizabeth asked.

"I don't know. We got him to the house with the ox cart, and she told me to hurry to bring Pastor. I didn't stop to see all that she would do for Father."

While they spoke, Sarah dashed about and grabbed a basket and her shawl. Christine, Jane, and Elizabeth tossed several items into the basket, including the fever-reducing willow bark, a few rags, and a bowl holding half the blueberries the children had picked that morning.

The parson didn't own a musket, but he carried a sturdy walking stick whenever he went about the village. He fetched it and reached to take the basket from Sarah. "Are you ready, ladies? Ben, you come with us, and you can run back to give your mother the news after I've looked at Goodman Dudley. Let us not delay any further."

He stepped outside, and Sarah and Catherine followed. Ben trotted ahead, and the other three walked along together until the path narrowed at the edge of the village proper. Then the pastor took the lead, and the two girls walked behind him. He kept up a moderate pace so that they wouldn't tire, and soon they were within sight of the Dudleys' palisade. Ben had outdistanced them by a few yards, but he waited for them outside the tall fence.

Catherine had left the gate open in her haste, and they entered the compound and stepped up to the house. Catherine hastened in ahead of Sarah and the reverend to announce their arrival.

"Oh, Pastor, I'm so glad you've come," Goody Dudley cried. "There's no one better than you to pray over folks and set bones."

"How is he?" Catherine asked, searching her mother's face.

"Much the same as when you left," Goody Dudley replied.

"Let me see the patient," the pastor said as he leaned his staff in the corner.

Sarah waited with Catherine in the kitchen, and Ben sat down on the doorstep. The Dudleys' home was divided into two rooms on the lower level, with a bedchamber boarded off beneath the loft. From within the chamber, Sarah heard Catherine's father murmur a greeting to the Reverend Jewett. Moments later, his moans reached her ears.

Catherine jumped up and grabbed the iron kettle that sat on the hearth. "We must fetch some water. There will be much washing to do."

Sarah picked up an empty bucket and followed her outside.

"Ben, you may help us," Catherine told the boy. "Have you a well at the parsonage?"

"Nay. We draw our water from the river."

"Well, we have a nice dug well, and you may lower the bucket and haul it up again and fill our vessels for us. Sarah and I shall carry the water into the house."

This kept them bustling for several minutes, and they had just finished filling every pot and pail available, and even a washtub, when Goody Dudley came from the inner chamber.

"How is Father?" Catherine asked.

"The parson needs help in setting the leg, and it is still bleeding some."

"Can we help him do it?"

"Nay," said her mother. "He advised me to send young Ben to the nearest neighbor." She went to the door and instructed Ben on the errand. "After you tell him to come, your father says you are to go on home and tell your mother the parson will be home ere nightfall."

"Aye, ma'am, I'll have Goodman Ackley here in a trice," Ben promised. He tore out through the gate and down the path toward the village.

Goody Dudley turned back into the house. "What good girls you are. Just look at all the water you've hauled." Her eyes focused on Sarah for the first time. "Thank you for coming."

Sarah nodded. "I thought perhaps you'd need help after the pastor leaves. I could do chores while you sit with your husband, ma'am."

Catherine squeezed her arm. "How kind of you! Shall you sleep here tonight? I've been lonesome since Richard left, and there's no one on the other side of the wall at night."

Sarah glanced up at the loft, where a rough partition separated the two sleeping areas. "If your mother has no objection, I should be happy to." She threw a guarded glance at Goody Dudley.

Her hostess hesitated only a moment. "I'm sure Catherine would find your presence a comfort."

"It would comfort me exceedingly," Catherine agreed. "But, Mother, does the parson think Father will mend all right?"

"He says it will take time. It's a bad break, and Father's midsection is bruised severely. Some ribs may be broken. After the leg is set, the parson will wrap his middle. He will need to rest for several weeks, I'm sure."

"Oh, Mother!" Catherine flung herself into Goody Dudley's arms and sobbed. "Why did this have to happen with Richard gone?"

"There, now." Her mother rubbed Catherine's back. "I'm sure the Almighty has His purpose in this, though I've not had time to consider what that might be."

"Perhaps the parson can tell us." Catherine pulled back and sniffed. "What shall Sarah and I do now, Mother? I was going to pick beans today, but. . ."

"Why should you not?" her mother asked. "Reverend Jewett will probably be some time attending to your father. I expect he will want you girls out of the house while he and Goodman Ackley set Father's leg. Now, I must gather some linen for him to use to wrap his ribs with."

Sarah gave her the rags Goody Jewett had sent. She was glad for a reason to be outside when Goodman Ackley arrived. She had not forgotten his cruel remark about Jane, though weeks had passed since the incident at the trading post.

"Come, Catherine," she said. "Let's get the beans and cook some for supper."

"But the washing. . ."

"We shall do that later," Sarah assured her.

Goody Dudley nodded. "Yes, after the doctoring is done, I shall gather up all the soiled bedding and clothing to be washed."

As she and Catherine headed out to the kitchen garden, Sarah saw Goodman Ackley puffing up the path toward the house.

"Let's see who can fill her basket first," Sarah said.

Catherine entered into the game and dashed to the rows of beans, swinging her gathering basket.

A few minutes later, both containers were filled to the brim. Sarah wished they hadn't picked so fast, for now they had no excuse to stay outside. "If we had a pot, we could snap the beans out here in the shade," she suggested.

Catherine frowned. "We filled all the pots with water, remember? But mayhap we can dump out my basket and use it for the snapped beans."

They sat down on the grass and set to work, breaking off the ends and snapping the pods with their fingers, filling Catherine's basket with short lengths of green beans.

"I know Charlie Gardner would come help with our field work if he hadn't gone with Richard." Catherine sighed and reached for a handful of beans from Sarah's basket.

"Your other neighbors will help," Sarah assured her.

"Oh, I know it, but everyone is busy this time of year. Mother will hate to ask them."

"Don't fret about it. The parson will likely set up a time for different ones to come. That's what they did when Isaiah Pottle was injured. And perhaps he'll let Ben come stay during harvest. He could be a big help."

"Well, they won't be harvesting the corn or the oats for a while yet," Catherine said. "I can feed the livestock and milk and gather the eggs. I do a lot of that anyway."

"And I will stay as long as you wish and help you with those things and with the cooking and the washing. . .whatever you and your mother need done."

Catherine reached to squeeze Sarah's hand. "Your coming is a blessing. I was very frightened when I saw how badly hurt Father was. I'd been moping around for days anyway, since Richard went. But now—oh, I know it will be hard for Father to rest, and I wish he wouldn't have such pain, but I'm glad you're here. I haven't had a girl stay at the house for ages."

Sarah smiled at her. "I'll enjoy my visit."

When they entered cautiously, bearing their baskets of snapped beans, the Reverend Jewett and Goodman Ackley were seated near the hearth sipping mugs of tea.

"Ah, young ladies! I see that your hands have not been idle." The pastor stood and bowed to them.

Goodman Ackley climbed awkwardly to his feet and ducked his head without meeting their eyes.

"How is Father?" Catherine asked.

The pastor winced. "He's resting now. Your mother is sitting with him. I'm sure he'll recover from this, but I've suggested your mother get Goody Baldwin to help her with the nursing. Of course, if Sarah wishes to stay a few days. . ."

"I should like to, sir," Sarah said, "though I'm not a skilled nurse."

"And I should like it, as well." Catherine smiled at her, and Sarah felt warmth spread through her, although Goodman Ackley still avoided looking at her.

"I must be going," Ackley said.

"Thank you for helping," said the parson.

Ackley gave a brief nod. "I'll come back to help cut Dudley's next hay crop, after I get mine done."

"That's most kind of you," Catherine said.

Ackley clapped on his hat and went out.

"Well, then," said Catherine, "I suppose we should start thinking about supper, Sarah. I wonder if Father will want to eat?"

"I recommend a light broth tonight." The pastor picked up his hat from the table and reached for his walking stick. "I shall head for home. Sarah, will you need anything brought to you for your stay?"

Sarah shot a glance at Catherine, who stepped forward with confidence.

"Oh, don't you worry about Sarah, Pastor. We shall take good care of her, and if she has need of clothing and such, she can borrow from me. I think we're nearly of a size."

Pastor Jewett nodded. "So be it. Tell your mother I shall stop in after dinner tomorrow and that if she needs anything before then, she should send you. But you girls must stay together if you come into the village."

71

"We will," Sarah promised. No one mentioned Catherine's solitary dash to the village to fetch the parson earlier. Everyone knew that utmost caution was needed since the Indians had begun their raids several years earlier, but in dire circumstances, one did what one had to do.

The girls worked quietly about the kitchen, and an hour later, Catherine's mother emerged from the bedchamber with an armload of crumpled linens.

"Father is sleeping," she told them.

Catherine's face paled at the sight of the bloodstained clothing and sheets, but she said only, "Sarah and I can wash those things up before supper, can't we, Sarah?"

"Yes, indeed. We've a tub of cold water waiting outside." Sarah took the bundle from her hostess and headed for the door, knowing the blood would wash out easier in cold water than in hot.

She and Catherine spent the better part of an hour doing laundry; then they went in to find that Goody Dudley had started baking a batch of corn pone on the hearth and put the beans and a bit of salt pork over the coals to simmer. The girls had picked a head of cabbage, and Sarah set about chopping it while Catherine set the table.

"The pork broth is for Father, I suppose," Catherine said. "Our meat supply is getting low again, and I see Mother only put a small piece on to cook."

"It will flavor our beans nicely," Sarah said.

She liked working with Catherine. The Dudleys' large kitchen seemed spacious and airy compared to the Jewetts' crowded house. It reminded her of the old days, when she and Molly helped their mother in the little house by the river.

At dusk, Sarah peeked into the bedchamber to tell Goody Dudley that the broth was ready. Catherine's father lay stretched out on the rope bed, his injured leg propped up with pillows. He seemed to be dozing.

Goody Dudley rose and took the bowl from Sarah. "He's restless," she said. "Sometimes he tries to toss about. I think that leg pains him a great deal."

"Shall we start some more willow bark tea?" Sarah asked.

"Aye. And I believe I'll have you girls help me fix a pallet on the floor here. It would hurt him if I tried to lie on the other side of the bed, I'm sure."

Sarah relayed the news to Catherine as they put their meal on the table. Catherine went to the doorway and said, "Mother, supper is ready."

Goody Dudley came out and sat with them in the kitchen. She eyed the table with approval. "You girls have fixed a lovely meal." In addition to the corn pone, pork, cabbage, and green beans, Sarah had set out the blueberries she had brought.

"We've gathered some bedding for you, Mother," Catherine said. "Do you want us to bring Richard's mattress down?"

"Nay, let Sarah sleep on it. I'll be fine with a couple of quilts."

"Oh, I don't mind sleeping on the floor, ma'am," Sarah said quickly. "I'm used to a hard bed."

A pained expression crossed Goody Dudley's face, and she looked away. "No, my dear. I expect I'll spend a good part of the night in my chair anyway."

Sarah ate in silence, wondering if she had blundered in alluding to the harsh conditions in which she had recently lived. Goody Dudley said no more until she rose from the table, and Catherine assured her that she and Sarah would do the dishes.

"Then I shall bid you good night," Goody Dudley said.

"If you need us in the night, call me," Catherine said.

"I shall." Her mother turned and looked at Sarah for a moment. "Thank you for coming. You're a help, that you are, and I'm sure your being here is a blessing to Catherine."

"Oh, it is!" Catherine flashed a smile at Sarah.

"Thank you," Sarah murmured.

She and Catherine hastened to clean up the kitchen then went up to the loft to arrange things by candlelight. Sarah felt a sudden shyness come over her as she entered the sleeping area Richard usually occupied. His Sunday clothes hung from pegs, and a candlestick and a small book rested on a crate beside the bed. She supposed he had taken most of his belongings with him to Canada.

"I know!" Catherine turned, her face alight with excitement. "Let's pull Richard's bed into my room, and we can talk all we want tonight."

Sarah eyed the heavy frame of the rope bed dubiously. "That might be too much of a chore."

"Well, then, I'll bring my feather bed in here and sleep on the floor beside you."

"Let me be the one to sleep on the floor," Sarah protested.

In the end, they decided Catherine's bed was wide enough for two slender young women, and they piled Richard's mattress on top of Catherine's and made the bed up laughing and chattering as they worked. They took off their caps, aprons, bodices, and pockets.

When Sarah sank onto the thick double feather bed in her shift, she thought she'd never felt anything so soft and welcoming.

Catherine blew the candle out. "I'm so glad you came."

"So am I," Sarah whispered. "Are you sure your mother doesn't mind?"

"She's thankful you're here. Why would she mind?" Catherine asked.

"I just don't want to upset her. If she'd rather I didn't. . ."

"Mother has had some dark times, but she knows good help when she sees it. Oh!" Catherine pushed herself up on one elbow. "That was rather crass of me. I meant that even though she may have seemed—"

"It's all right," Sarah said. "I know a lot of people don't like those who've been captive. They don't know how to treat us or if they can trust us."

"Mother doesn't mean to be rude," Catherine whispered.

"She hasn't been. She's been kind to me today, even though she's so worried about your father."

"Sarah, we all missed you. We missed your whole family, if the truth be told. Mother and Father liked your parents, and Molly was a dear. I'm so sorry you lost them."

"And I'm sorry you've lost Stephen."

Catherine sighed in the darkness. "It's Richard I'm fearful for now. What if he and Charles Gardner meet with some accident? Father didn't want them to go, you know."

"We must keep them in prayer," Sarah said.

"Yes. I'm glad Charlie is with him, but. . .even though Richard and Charlie are best friends, and Father respects Charlie, I'm sure, Mother still thinks he's. . .wild."

"Is he?"

"I don't know. They don't let me be around him enough to find out. But Mother has made it plain to me that I'm not to look his way when I begin thinking of finding a husband."

The idea startled Sarah, but why should it? Catherine must be eighteen, past old enough for marriage.

"Do you like Mr. Gardner?"

"Of course. But I'll probably end up with Peter Sawyer or Obadiah Perkins."

"They are more your age, I suppose."

"Boys." Catherine's distaste showed in her tone. "But I expect they'll grow up. Still, Charlie Gardner seems more alluring because so many people won't receive him. It makes him rather mysterious and appealing. I don't really think I'd want to marry him, though."

"Why not?"

"His farm is even farther from the village than ours. The elders nearly forbade him to live out there when he returned. They said he was asking to be raided again. And there's some sort of rule against solitary living. Did you know that?"

"Nay," Sarah said. "He must be brave to live way out here alone."

"I think so, but when I marry, I'd like to live in town, near the trader and other womenfolk. Or perhaps even in Boston."

"Boston?" Sarah refused to think about the bustling city. She felt herself drifting off into pleasant oblivion. "This is like having my sister back," she murmured.

"Thank you! I always wished for a sister. I hoped someday you and Richard. . ."

Sarah's sleepiness suddenly fled. "What about me and Richard?"

"I hoped you'd make a match. We all did."

"Before the massacre, you mean."

"Well. . ." Catherine rolled over; Sarah wondered if she was trying to see her face, but it was too dark in the loft. "I still hope it. He does care for you."

"I'm not so sure about that." Sarah didn't mention the fact that Richard and Charles had stopped by the parsonage and spoken to her before they left the village. That was only for advice on dealing with the Indians. After thinking of little else for several days, Sarah was sure that Richard had visited her only for that reason. He and Charles wanted every advantage, no matter how slight, that they could gain in their search for Stephen Dudley.

Catherine began to breathe with a heavy rhythm, and Sarah turned onto her side, snuggling deeper into the soft bed. Once more she felt herself slipping into sleep. She ought to say her usual lengthy prayers for the Jewett family and Jane and Christine, but she feared she was too tired to make it through the list. "God speed Richard," she whispered.

Chapter 10

Sarah and Catherine rose at dawn and put cornmeal on to cook for breakfast. Just as Catherine took up her bucket to head out to the barn and milk the cow, a "Halloo" sounded outside the palisade gate.

Sarah opened the door and called, "Good morning!"

"Morning, miss. 'Tis Silas Bates, come to do your morning chores."

Catherine pushed past Sarah, carrying her milk pail, and dashed to open the gate. Sarah knew Bates was a farmer who lived in the village and worked his own outlying fields.

He entered the palisade with his hat in his hand and his musket over his shoulder. "I be here to help you, ma'am." He nodded at Catherine; then he looked past her at Sarah and blinked, as though trying to place her and knowing she didn't belong at the Dudleys'. "Parson told us last night about James Dudley being hurt."

Catherine closed the gate behind him. "That's most kind of you."

"How is he?"

"I don't believe he's awakened yet this morning, but when he's conscious, he has a lot of pain."

Bates clucked his tongue in empathy.

"I was just going to milk our cow and feed the ox and the pigs," Catherine said. "If you'd like to do those things, Sarah and I can feed the chickens and collect eggs."

"With pleasure, miss. Shall I put the cattle out to graze?"

"If you please, sir. Thank you."

Catherine offered her milk pail, and Bates took it and strode toward the small barn at the far end of the fenced yard. He stopped just before entering it and looked back. "Oh, and we'll have a crew of men here Friday morn to cut the hay for your father."

"We're much obliged," Catherine replied.

"It seems the reverend has lined up heavy labor for you," Sarah observed. "Perhaps we can do some baking today, in preparation for the haying crew. They will expect a dinner on the days they work here."

"That's a good—" Catherine broke off and stared out through a gap in the palisade.

76

"What is it?" Almost as soon as the words left Sarah's mouth, she saw the form of a tall Indian, clad only in breechclout and leggings, on the path outside the gate. Fear gripped her. She would not allow herself to be captured again, no matter what.

Catherine backed away from the fence, her eyes large with terror. "Go away!"

◆

Sarah gulped in a breath and realized that was perhaps not the best manner in which to handle the situation. She stepped closer to the gate and said, "What do you want?"

The man grunted and replied, "Trade."

"You must go to the trading post in the village," Sarah replied. Her heart raced, and she peered through the slit between two of the poles in the fence, wondering if other warriors waited nearby. If a war party was scouting to see how many people were inside the compound. . . She recalled the raids that had ripped her and so many others from their families.

Suddenly she realized that Catherine had left her standing alone by the palisade. Her heart lurched. In the language she had learned in the Pennacook village, she shouted, "We do not trade. You must go to Paine, the trader."

The man's chin jerked up, and his dark eyes glittered as he stared at her. She felt certain that he'd understood her, although his dialect was perhaps not precisely the one she used. Without another word, he turned and flitted down the path toward Cochecho.

Sarah wondered about Richard and Charles and how far they had gone. Seeing the Indian move so freely about the settlement raised questions in her mind. Were the two young men allowed to enter the Canadian villages with as little ceremony? As the warrior disappeared from her view, she prayed for their safety.

Catherine came running from the barn with Goodman Bates behind her.

"Where is he?" Bates panted, raising his musket and pointing it toward the gate.

"Gone toward the village." Sarah leaned against the high fence and pulled in a deep breath. "He said he wanted to trade, and I told him he must go to Paine's."

"Do you think he planned to attack us?" Catherine's dismay still showed in her face.

"I don't know. I didn't see but one man." Sarah's lips trembled as she attempted a smile. "I spoke to him in his own language. I think that surprised him."

"You may have saved us all some grief," Bates said. He scratched his chin through his thick beard. "They go often to the trader, but they don't usually stop at houses along the way. He might have thought you were too far from town for help to come."

"Mayhap you'd best hurry home and check on your own family," Catherine said.

"Aye." Bates peeked out through the gate. "Think ye it's safe to open up?"

Both girls looked out and could see no strangers lurking about. At last, Catherine cautiously opened the gate. Bates went out to stand in the path, staring all about, then looked hard toward his own fields, which were out of sight beyond a dip in the road.

"Both my boys be about the place. I'll finish your milking," he decided and came back inside the fence.

"If you're worried, sir. . ." Catherine began.

He bit his lip then nodded. "I think it's all right. No alarms have sounded. My Joseph would surely have fired the pistol if aught was amiss. And I'd like a chance to speak with your father about the haying when I've finished, if he's awake then."

The girls went about their work, looking often toward the gate and the path beyond, but no more disturbances came to them. Sarah couldn't help thinking of Richard and Charles, wondering if they had met Indians on their journey. Even though she'd lived among them so long, the warrior's sudden appearance had sent a terror through her that still made her tremble as she went with Catherine toward the barnyard where the hens awaited them.

Goody Dudley bustled about the kitchen when they went in with a basket of eggs.

"Ah, there you are, girls. Milking done, is it?"

"Goodman Bates be in the barn," Catherine said. "He wants to see Father."

"James is awake." Her mother stooped to toss another stick onto the fire. "I've got his tea brewing. The leg is powerful sore this morning."

"Mother, an Indian came to the gate a few minutes past," Catherine said.

Goody Dudley straightened and stared at her. "You didn't open to him?"

"Of course not."

"Was he alone?"

"I think so," Catherine said. "Sarah told him to go to the trader."

"Sarah. . ." Mrs. Dudley eyed Sarah thoughtfully.

"Goodman Bates thought it was all right," Sarah said. "And we'd have heard the village alarms by now if there were trouble."

"Yes." Goody Dudley went to the door and stared out toward the path. "Good morning, sir," she called after a moment.

Soon Goodman Bates appeared and handed her the milk pail. "Did your daughter tell you about our visitor this morn?" he asked.

RETURN TO LOVE

"Aye, she did. What do you make of it?"

Bates shrugged. "They don't often stop and ask for food or a trade at houses anymore. But in the old days, that was common."

Goody Dudley nodded. "Well, times have changed, haven't they? You speak truth, for I remember having savages come into this very room when first we built here. James said let them have what they want for food and perhaps they'll leave us alone. And they did. But that was twelve or fifteen years past, before things got so bad."

"Aye," Goodman Bates agreed. "We thought they would keep peace then. Now we know they're never to be trusted. Is your husband awake?"

Catherine's mother went to speak to James, and then she ushered his visitor into the bedchamber.

Sarah set the table for breakfast while Catherine fixed willow bark tea and cornmeal mush for her father.

When Mr. Bates came back out to the kitchen, he put on his hat and picked up his musket. "If you ladies need anything, you let me know. I think you oughtn't to go outside the fence here without an escort, though. Just my opinion, if anyone cares."

Catherine winced and glanced at Sarah. "We've no one to protect us if we need to go out, sir, not with Father laid up and my brother away."

"Well, I or another man will come by later to do evening chores before dark. If you need aught, you tell one of us, and someone will bring your trifles to you."

"That's good of you, sir," Sarah said.

"Aye," Catherine agreed. "We'll keep close, sir."

He nodded. "Well, I didn't put your cattle out. I didn't like to think there might be savages waiting to butcher them or that you lasses might go out to get them later. Safer to leave them penned up today, I think."

He left, and Catherine carefully barred the gate behind him. The little compound with the house, barn, and kitchen garden seemed smaller to Sarah. She didn't remember this feeling before the massacre, this constant fear. She was as much a prisoner here as she had been in the Pennacook village.

◆

Sarah spent the rest of the week with Catherine and her parents within the palisade. Pastor Jewett came twice and brought a small vial of laudanum he'd obtained from the trader. Goody Dudley received it with gratitude and entrusted the parson with a coin and a piece of fine lace she'd tatted to pay for it. She doled it out to her husband when his pain was most severe, especially in the night. Sarah was glad she had it, for Goodman Dudley's moans sometimes awakened her and sent shivers down her spine. She would hear his wife move about quietly in the room below

79

and administer the dose with gentle words. Then he would grow quiet once more, and Sarah was left to her yearning thoughts of Richard and her prayers for his and Charles's safety.

Sarah and Catherine ventured out only once, when the haying crew was in the field, to pick berries in a patch bordering the path within sight of the workers. When the Dudleys' late crop of hay was dried and cocked in the meadow, the men went away with a promise to return when the corn harvest came.

On Sunday morning, Ben Jewett arrived while they were at breakfast. His mother had requested that he escort the young ladies to meeting and back, and to bring Sarah home to the parsonage if she wished to come.

Sarah realized she had enjoyed her stay with Catherine, but she also missed the Jewett family, Jane, and Christine. When she heard that Jane had burned her hand severely while pouring hot water into the washtub, she decided she should go and help out at the parsonage for at least a few days.

Christine and the young Jewetts greeted her with great enthusiasm outside the meetinghouse. Jane had stayed at home with Goody Jewett and little Ruth, but John, Constance, and Abby lined up in the family pew with Christine and Ben. Sarah promised them that she would accompany them home after the service; she explained that she wanted to sit with Catherine, so that she would not be alone in the Dudley pew and feel melancholy.

"Why don't you be a Jewett for the Sabbath day, Miss Catherine?" asked Constance, the four-year-old, looking up at Catherine with adoring blue eyes.

A wide smile burst over Catherine's face. "I never thought of such a thing, but since you have room, I believe I would enjoy it."

She settled in the next-to-front row with the youngsters. Since her return to the village, Sarah had not seen Catherine look so happy. It took only a glance along the row at the scrubbed, eager little faces to remind her what a precious commodity children were on the frontier.

When the services ended, she shed a few tears in saying good-bye to Catherine but promised to visit her again soon. Catherine went off with Ben, her stalwart protector, whose only weapons were a stout stick and a knife, newly acquired as a birthday gift, of which he seemed inordinately proud.

———◆———

Richard trod quickly along the woodland path behind Charles. Even beneath the spreading trees, the heat of the day penetrated, making his pack feel heavier by the mile. They had been away from home more than a week and had run into no serious problems, although three times they had met Indians. Richard's heart nearly stopped the first time a band of warriors appeared on the path before them. He was sure that only Charles's knowledge of the savages' ways and language had saved them from being robbed or worse.

Now Charles turned around on the path and walked a few steps backward. "Hear that?"

"Aye. Water. Must be a stream ahead." Richard was glad of it. They carried only a small supply of water to save weight, which meant they must replenish it often. So far this had not been a problem, as they came upon fresh, clear streams often, especially in the mountainous territory they had traversed in the last few days. They seemed to be coming down to more level land now, and he hoped their progress would be faster.

Charles stopped on the bank of a small brook and looked all around before getting down to the water. He stooped on a rock and bent to fill his flask.

Richard stayed above, as had become their habit, and kept watch. After a moment, he took off the goatskin water bag he carried slung over a shoulder and tossed it down to his friend. Charles filled it while Richard resumed his sentry duty. When their water supply was replenished, they crossed the stream and settled in the shadows to eat a bit of jerky and a handful of parched corn.

"I expect my corn back home has mostly been eaten by the deer," Charles said, leaning back against the trunk of a large beech tree.

"No doubt they've done some damage," Richard agreed, "but Father said he would see it cut and stored for you." He looked up between the leaves to where the blue sky hung, cloudless. "Do you ever still think about giving up farming and taking to trading?"

"Truly. The venture you and I spoke of so often as boys."

"Do you still want to go to sea?"

"Maybe. Sometimes I feel restless. I'll never have the money for a boat, though." Charles sighed.

"You always used to talk about it, when we were boys," Richard said.

"I know. But now I've gained a new respect for those who till the soil. I'd like to make the farm into what my father envisioned it. He'd only started to clear it when they killed him."

They were silent for a minute, and then Richard said, "My father says I'll have his land one day. I'm not sure I want it."

Charles eyed him in surprise. "Why ever not?"

Richard flexed his shoulders. "What good is it, rooting yourself to a place, unless you've someone there with you. . .someone who cares about it as much as you do?"

Charles smiled. "Perchance we should go to sea together. They always want deckhands on the trading ships."

Richard studied him to see if he was serious. He decided that Charles had said it in jest, but half to see whether he was serious himself. And if he seized on the idea, Charles would probably agree to sign on with him for a trading voyage.

"Nay, I think we're both meant to be farmers."

Charles leaned back against the beech. "Who's to say ye'll never have someone to work beside ye, Richard? Not many days past, we stopped to bid farewell to a handsome young lady."

"If only I could hope again." Richard shook his head and brushed off his hands.

Charles reached over with one foot and kicked Richard's boot.

"Ow! What was that for?"

"You ninny. She's home again, alive and fairly well, I'd say from the look of her. Why should you not hope?"

"I acted badly when they first came." Richard stared down at the dried leaves on the ground. "In fact, I acted so discourteously that I doubt she would ever consider me now."

"Give it time." Charles eased the straps of his pack onto his shoulders and stood. "Come, we've another ten miles in us today, have we not?"

Chapter 11

After Sarah had been a week back at the parsonage, word came that several village men would meet at the Dudleys' the next day to harvest the corn. Reverend Jewett and Ben volunteered to go.

"May I go, Father?" pleaded John, the nine-year-old.

The pastor thought for only an instant before replying, "I don't see any reason against it. A boy your size can pick corn."

"I'd like to go with you, too," Sarah said. "Jane's hand is mostly healed, and she's doing chores again here. I should like to help Catherine and Goody Dudley during the harvesting bee. It will be a big chore to feed all those men a good dinner."

"Oh, let me go, too," Jane begged. "I haven't been past the dooryard except for Sunday meeting these six weeks!"

Sarah was glad to see Jane's enthusiasm and a desire on her part to socialize outside the limited circle of the Jewett house.

The parson looked her over thoughtfully; then he raised his chin and called to the corner where Christine sat in her accustomed place at the loom, "What think ye, Miss Christine? Do ye wish to join Miss Sarah and Miss Jane and venture into the world to feed the workers tomorrow?"

"Nay, sir," came Christine's gentle voice. She didn't look up from her weaving. "I'm content to stay here and help your wife with the children. Perhaps she can rest the morrow, if we've no hot dinner to prepare."

"That's good of you, Christine," said Elizabeth, "but you should go if you want. It will give you a chance to visit with other women for a change."

Christine gave her hostess a placid smile. "I have all the company I could wish for, ma'am."

Sarah knew that Christine's choice stemmed from more than her devotion to Goody Jewett and her concern that the lady would overdo if they left her alone with the three little girls. Christine simply preferred a quiet existence and avoided company whenever she could.

◆

Ben, John, and their father joined a dozen other men in the Dudleys' fields the next morning, while Sarah and Jane entered the house and found the Dudley women already baking their bread and pastries for dinner. A cauldron of lamb stew simmered over the coals, and the little house was already heated to a swel-tering temperature. Sarah and Jane donned their aprons and plunged into the work.

At midmorning, Goodman Dudley called out from the bedchamber, and his wife hurried to do his bidding.

"Father wants to get up," Catherine confided to Sarah and Jane.

"Can he?" Sarah asked, wiping beads of perspiration from her brow with the hem of her apron. "It's only been two weeks since his injury."

"Mother helps him dress, and we bring him out here so he can sit with his leg on a pile of cushions. He wants to be up and ready to greet the men when they come in for dinner."

"That will be good for him," said Jane.

"Aye. He'll want to thank them all and talk over the latest news." Catherine smiled. "Father's tried to be patient while he heals, but he does get restless."

"It will be hard to keep him from going back to his work too early," Jane said.

Catherine went to help support her father, and he limped to the kitchen with her mother on his other side. Once settled in his chair near the door, where an occasional breeze entered to bring small relief from the heat, he closed his eyes for several minutes, his face gray and strained. He roused when Goody Dudley put a cup of willow bark tea in his hands.

"He refused to take the laudanum today," Catherine whispered to Sarah. "He wants to be alert."

A while later, Goodman Dudley seemed to have regained his spirits, and Sarah suspected the tea had taken the edge off his pain.

"Miss Minton, it's good to see you back about the place," he said with a shadow of his former heartiness in his voice. "My daughter amused me with tales of your hard work and collaboration in her adventures last week."

Sarah smiled at him as she sliced carrots into a large kettle. "I enjoyed my visit here with Catherine very much, sir."

"Shall you stay with us now?"

"I am able, if your family wishes it."

"Oh, do!" Catherine bounced to her father's side, grinning. "Sarah is so much fun, Father. She makes work a game, and she showed me how to do lovely beadwork."

Sarah glanced uneasily toward Goody Dudley's ample back, wondering how she had received the news that Catherine was learning to do beadwork in the style the Indians had taught Sarah.

The lady of the house turned from the cupboard with a stack of pewter plates in her arms. "You may stay with us as long as you wish, Sarah. I've not seen Catherine so lively in a long time as when you were with us."

"We had a letter from Richard yesterday," Goodman Dudley said. "Don't know if anyone told you."

Sarah felt a strange sensation in her heart. If it wasn't so warm in the kitchen, she would blush, but her face was probably already scarlet. "Nay, what news?"

"No news, really. He and Charles Gardner met a small group of soldiers on the trail three days out and entrusted a note to them saying they'd got on well and were making good progress."

"We must pray them along on their journey and swiftly home again," Catherine said, and Sarah gave a silent *amen* to her sentiment.

At noon, the harvesters crowded around the table set up in the fenced yard, and the four women ferried the food and tea outside from the kitchen. The pastor and one of the farmers carried Goodman Dudley out so that he could sit in the shade and converse with the men while they enjoyed their dinner.

"I believe we'll get all your corn in today," Goodman Bates said. "A few of us will go tomorrow and take in Charles Gardner's crop, but I misdoubt we can make much of it, he's neglected it so."

"He makes a shiftless farmer," Goodman Ackley noted.

" 'Tis not his fault," Goodman Fowler said. Sarah was glad to hear someone speak up for Richard's friend.

"Aye," said the Reverend Jewett. "Charles was gone three months in the spring bringing our loved ones back from Canada, and now he's undertaken another such errand. We should do all we can to help him."

"May I help again tomorrow, Father?" Ben asked.

"Aye, that you may, and if I didn't have to prepare my sermon for Sunday meeting, I would join you."

From the corner of her eye, Sarah saw Jane slip around the corner of the house. No doubt she feared Ackley or one of the others would begin to make disparaging remarks about the captives.

But Pastor Jewett looked down the table and called in a loud voice, "Ackley, how be your oxen doing? You had much grief training the young one this spring. Is he pulling well with your old Star now?"

◆

Though Jane returned home with the minister and his sons that evening, Sarah stayed another two weeks with the Dudleys. During that time, she did much to help the Dudley women dry and preserve their garden harvest to put it by for winter.

It seemed Goody Dudley would never tire of talking about her younger son, Stephen, and her hopes for his return. But when Richard had been gone a month, she became quieter and more grave.

Sarah also heard, largely from his father, how hard Richard had worked to improve the family farm.

"I planned to help Richard obtain land of his own," Goodman Dudley said with a sigh, at dinner one day.

"Do you not think it's best if he stays here with us and you clear more land together?" asked his wife. "With all the Indian scares, we've been a long time putting our acreage into tillage."

"Aye. This place wears down a man," he agreed.

"Richard has always loved boats, Father," Catherine said.

"What's that compared to the soil? If our land had fronted on the river, perhaps he would think of fishing for his living, but that's a dirty, smelly trade compared to farming. A man grows his own sustenance from the earth."

"Or hauls it from the sea." Catherine squeezed her father's arm. "You know your father was a fisherman. You've told me many times how he came from England and lived many years at Marblehead as a fisherman."

"Aye, and lost his life in a storm," said Goody Dudley.

"Well, what is worse, death at sea or death in your field when the savages come through?" Catherine asked, effectively silencing the conversation for a few minutes.

When she rose to take their plates, her mother said, "Well, it is my hope that soon we shall have both our boys back again."

Sarah eyed her carefully and decided she was now accepted enough to speak the truth to her hostess. "I don't wish to dash your hopes, ma'am, but Stephen was so young when he went away. I know captives his age often embrace the Indian ways and consider themselves Indian after a while."

"That didn't happen to you," Goody Dudley said. She turned away to take the plates to the wash pan and fetch the teakettle.

"Nay," Sarah agreed, "I never thought myself Pennacook, though I expect I looked much like them for a time."

"Never," Catherine cried. "With your golden hair and blue eyes? No one could ever think you were a savage!"

Sarah smiled at that. "Nay, my heritage was obvious to all. For that reason, they hid me when strangers came to the village."

Goodman Dudley fixed her with a sympathetic look. "You poor thing. We did wonder about you, whether you lived or died, and if surviving, how you fared."

"It was a difficult season of my life," Sarah admitted, "but the Almighty preserved me and comforted me. I never doubted His care, even if I never had the opportunity to come home."

A sob came from her hostess, and all of them turned to look at Goody Dudley. When she faced them, Sarah saw tears flowing down her cheeks.

"Forgive me, ma'am." Sarah jumped up and went to the lady's side. "I should not have talked of my life with the Pennacook. It was not my intention to distress you."

Goody Dudley took her hand and squeezed it. "Nay, child. It is not for that reason that I weep. You see. . ." She flung a quick glance at her husband then pulled her shoulders back and continued. "When you returned in May, we counseled Richard to avoid you and give up his hopes of marrying you."

Sarah felt the blood leave her face, and she held tighter to the woman's hand as her knees began to tremble. The idea that Richard still harbored such a thought nearly forced her to resume her seat.

" 'Twas my doing," Goodman Dudley said in a deep, sorrowful tone. "I knew that first day that Richard would wish to claim you, but I feared it would upset our household too much."

"Father, how could you?" Catherine looked from him to Sarah with her mouth twisted in pain.

Sarah's heart went out to the family. Their feelings and grief had been much as she suspected, and in her frequent pleading with God since then, she had fully forgiven their neglect of her.

" 'Twould have upset me, you mean," said his wife. She sniffed then managed a smile at Sarah. "And truly I would have been overset had you come to us that day. It was too much to ask, and I told my husband I could not bear the thought. Although Richard had not spoken of it aloud, I could see by his manner how deeply your return affected him. I tried to put it down to Stephen's not coming home when you did, but I knew it went beyond that."

"Sit down here, ladies, both of you," said Goodman Dudley.

Catherine had kept her place and watched them, wide-eyed and silent. Sarah sat down on her stool and patted Goody Dudley's hand as she took her place in the chair beside her.

"Richard spoke to me openly not a week after your return, Sarah," said Goodman Dudley. "I admit that I discouraged him from acting."

"Aye, to save me the sorrow of being constantly reminded of Stephen's fate," his wife said. "I see now how wrong I was. I can see that you are a staunch, godly, and hardworking young woman. You've brought nothing but good to this house since my husband was injured, and I've seen your sincerity and willingness to give of your strength to help others. It is my wish. . ."

Sarah felt as though her heart had expanded in her chest. As she looked into Goody Dudley's careworn face, she knew she could develop a love for this woman as she had felt for none other but her own mother.

Elizabeth Dudley continued. "It is my wish that you and Richard will make up your differences one day and wed." The lady nodded and looked around at her husband and daughter. "There. 'Tis said. If I've caused offense by speaking so, I beg pardon, but since I so wronged this girl, my heart has pricked me to be forthright about it. Whether you and Richard make a match or not, you are always welcome here, my dear."

Sarah's eyes filled with tears. She slid from her stool toward Richard's mother and was immediately engulfed in a warm embrace. "Thank you," she whispered. "And I shall always love your family, whether Richard comes round to court or not."

Catherine walked around the table and hugged her, as well.

Goodman Dudley smiled benevolently on his womenfolk from the chair where he sat with his healing leg stuck out before him on a cushioned stool. "Well, then," he said, "we shall all pray with one mind for Richard and Charles to return before Christmas with good news."

——————◆——————

Goodman Dudley began to do small tasks from his chair, smoothing a new bow for the ox yoke and carving a plug to fit a new powder horn. By the end of Sarah's stay, he was hobbling about on his own inside the house. When he made it to the barn one morning and milked the cow, leaving only the carrying of the pail of milk to Catherine, Sarah surmised she had remained long enough.

"Must you leave?" Catherine cried when she heard the news.

"I mustn't overstay my welcome," Sarah said. She and Catherine poked about the tall grass behind the hen coop, looking for a nest they were sure one of the hens had hidden.

"You could never do that!"

Sarah smiled at the young woman who had now become her dearest friend. "If I go now, you shall be glad when next I come. That is the gift of being not always in one another's company."

Catherine smiled, a bit teary-eyed. "I shall always be glad to see you coming. Always."

"That warms my heart. But Goody Jewett is in such a delicate condition that I'm sure my help is needed there far more than here."

"She has Jane and Christine," Catherine reminded her.

"Aye, and her husband. Let us not forget the many things he does for her comfort. But he has begun writing a pamphlet, and—"

"What about?" Catherine asked. "Is it one of his sermons?"

"Nay, 'tis an account of the massacre and how it affected the people here."

Catherine's eyes widened. " 'Twill sell briskly in this village, I'm sure."

"He doesn't do it for the money," Sarah said, "though I'm sure any extra income would be welcome. He says he does it to help people understand the captives. For that reason, Jane and I and even Christine agreed to let him tell our stories. With him so preoccupied with that and his sermonizing, he has less time for the household. With five children already to look after, and the cooking and washing for a large family. . . Christine already does much, but her preferred employment is weaving or spinning, which is much needed. But you see, there is plenty for all of us to do in that house."

"When I think of all you say, I wonder how Goody Jewett got on before you all came," Catherine admitted.

"She has much on her shoulders," Sarah agreed.

"Are you certain you don't go only to be sure you aren't here when Richard returns? He was dreadful rude to you last spring."

Sarah schooled her face to neutrality as she recalled the day Catherine and her brother came to the Jewetts' house and Richard spoke nary a word to her. She decided not to comment on Richard's behavior. "Don't worry, dear friend. I shall visit you again soon."

The next day, she and Catherine walked to the village bearing Sarah's few belongings, a sack of onions, and several pounds of apples for the Jewetts. Ben escorted Catherine safely home again.

Sarah plunged into the labor of the Jewett home once more with a light heart. All seemed happy to have her back, especially the little girls, and she made it her special duty to occupy them each afternoon so that their mother could have a quiet rest during Ruth's naps, for Constance and Abby had outgrown that ritual.

As she and Jane scrubbed the children's clothes in the yard one September morning, Jane observed, "You are happier of late, Sarah. What has come over you?"

"I'm glad to be back."

"Nay, it's more than that." Jane shrugged. "I thought you would be sorrowful, since young Mr. Dudley has gone off."

Sarah paused in her work. "I try not to fret about Richard. He may meet with some accident, it is true, or he may come home despondent if he cannot find his brother. But the time I spent with his family has gladdened my heart. I'm beginning to see for the first time how gracious God was in bringing me back here and in letting me help the Jewetts and the Dudleys. If I have no more life than this, it is enough. I am content."

Jane eyed her thoughtfully as she scrubbed one of John's shirts. "Are you certain of that?"

Sarah did not answer hastily but considered what her friend asked. Could she truly be thankful if Richard never returned? Or if he returned and failed to pursue their friendship? What if he came home and married another?

" 'Tis easy to say and harder to live out," she said at last, "but I feel in this moment such gratitude that I will say, yes, whatever God brings into my life henceforth, I shall thank Him for."

Chapter 12

The trees that sheltered the trail flamed in red, orange, and yellow splendor. Though the nights were cold, warm days made the journey pleasant, and Richard found it hard to regret his endeavor. He had seen more country than he had ever dreamed of seeing, and he loved it.

Yet this trip made him long to get home to the farm. The harvest must be in now, and fodder stockpiled for the animals. He wondered if his father had done any butchering yet. He should be there to help, but he knew that what he was doing took precedence over any chores he could perform back at the farm in Cochecho.

He and Charles had made good time to the city of Quebec. Charles's previous time in the French colony and his standing as a former negotiator for the English colonies procured them an audience with the governor. Charles had asked for a native guide, but the governor denied this request, saying that surely Charles could find his way to villages he had visited before. Charles took this as an ill omen, but they went on anyway, with their supplies replenished. Their goal was the village where Sarah had lived, which Charles believed to be their most likely starting point.

The faint path led them to a shallow but rapid stream, and they could see where people crossed, relying on rocks that stuck above the surface of the water. The rushing of the stream shut out all other sounds.

As Richard led the way to the far bank, he glanced ahead and froze, one foot on the last rock in the stream, the other on the dead grass that grew alongside. Two ruddy-skinned warriors stood above him on the bank.

Richard glanced over his shoulder at Charles and gasped. Behind them, on the bank they had left, were three more Indians. He sent up a quick, silent prayer.

Charles grimaced and touched Richard's shoulder. "Easy. Let me pass you."

His pulse racing, Richard hopped back to the larger rock where his friend stood and let Charles ease by and gain the bank. At once he began a conversation with the two warriors that Richard could not comprehend. While they talked, Richard looked back and saw that the others were approaching the same way he and Charles had come. A shiver ran down his spine, and he looked back toward his friend.

"We're going to the village," Charles said.

Richard's anxiety eased only a hair, as the three fierce-looking warriors approached him on the other side.

"Sarah's village?"

"Aye. We're not far. It's as I thought."

"Well, you didn't think we'd have an escort," Richard muttered. He mounted the bank and eyed the party of Indians cautiously. "So, they're Pennacook?"

"Aye. When I told them where we're bound, the leader here said they'll see us to the village."

Richard nodded slowly. The man Charles had indicated as leader was the vilest looking of them all, clad in deerskin breeches, shirt, and moccasins, with a hawk's feather stuck in his scalp lock, a bow and quiver slung over his shoulder, and a knife hanging at his waist that Richard could easily believe had performed many wicked tasks.

The tall warrior's companion went before them, then the leader, then Charles and Richard, followed by the other three. They walked swiftly for two or three miles through the forest. The path skirted a marsh, and at last they came to a river. On its far bank was a village of twenty or thirty bark lodges.

Richard and Charles were herded into separate canoes, and the warriors paddled them quickly across the river. A score of children and nearly as many adults gathered to watch them disembark at the village. The children thronged about them as the men led them to the largest wigwam.

Inside, the smells of smoke and sweat hung in the semidarkness. Richard paused to let his eyes adjust and was shoved from behind, farther inside the hut.

He made out Charles's figure as his friend took a seat between two warriors near the fire. Several other men already had taken their places, and Richard wasn't able to settle beside Charles as three Pennacook held the spots between them.

A long discourse followed, of which Richard understood not a word. The leader of the party that had brought them in spoke first, relating what seemed an interminable tale to an older man and the others of the village.

Then the old man spoke. And spoke. And spoke.

Richard's throat was dry and raspy from breathing smoke, and his head began to ache. He wondered if he could sleep sitting here, or if it would be advantageous to stay upright and seem alert.

After an hour of this, Charles was allowed to speak. His speech seemed to Richard, in his ignorance of the language, to be quite eloquent. After he'd talked for a few minutes, he brought out a knife and a pouch of tobacco and presented them to the elder. When the man had accepted them with a tiresome speech, Charles took out the letter from the governor of Quebec and talked some more while pointing at the paper.

The old man took the letter, glanced at it, and handed it back. He then started in talking again. Next the warrior who had met them on the trail spoke at length.

Richard's fatigue nearly overtook him, and he caught himself nodding. He adjusted his position and hoped none of the Indians had noticed or thought him rude.

At last Charles squinted at Richard across the smoky fire and said in low but distinct English, "Well, friend, they claim they know nothing of your brother."

Richard's heart sank. "Did you tell them the name Sarah spoke as his Pennacook name?"

"Aye. They say they know not anyone of that name. They say we should leave."

The cruel denial settled heavily on Richard's soul. They could not leave now and go home empty-handed after their long and arduous journey.

"The handkerchief," he whispered.

Charles's eyes narrowed as though he hadn't heard clearly, and then he brightened. Giving a quick nod, he turned back toward the elder and launched a new litany. Several of the Indians spoke in turn; then Charles spoke again, and Richard thought he caught the word *Naticook*, the name of Sarah's onetime guardian. Charles looked expectantly at Richard and held out his hand.

With eagerness, though he was reluctant to give up the pretty thing Sarah had labored over, Richard withdrew the handkerchief from his leather wallet and passed it around the circle to Charles.

His friend took it with respectful mien and held it out to the elder of the tribe.

The old man reached for the bit of snowy muslin and unfolded it slowly. He peered at it then stroked the colorful stitches that made up the flower blossoms in the corners.

Charles began speaking again, and Richard heard the name *Naticook* again.

The elder barked an order, and a younger man left the wigwam.

Nearly a half hour passed before he returned, and in his wake came a wrinkled old woman.

The elder spoke, and the woman drew near the group assembled by the fire. An oration of fifteen minutes ensued before the muslin handkerchief was finally handed round and put in her grasp.

The old woman held it reverently and turned to stare at Charles. He spoke to her gently in her own tongue, and then she rounded and fixed her gaze on Richard. He almost thought tears sprang into her eyes, but the smoke might account for that.

Charles stood and came to where Richard sat. "Stand up," he hissed.

Richard stood, and Charles spoke to the old woman, evidently introducing them. When the woman nodded, Charles said to Richard, "And I present to you Naticook, erstwhile adoptive mother of Sarah Minton."

Richard bowed at the waist, feeling a bit foolish. He should have asked Charles in advance how one acknowledged an introduction to an elderly Indian woman.

Naticook spoke to Charles, and he answered her at length. The woman shook her head, clutching the bit of muslin to her breast.

"What did she say?" Richard asked.

"She thanks you for bringing Sarah's gift and asks us why her daughter left her."

"What about Stephen?"

Charles shook his head. "Nothing."

Richard winced. "Tell her the white chief said Sarah should be with her own people, and she is happy there with those who love her."

Before Charles could relay the words, the tall warrior edged between them and spoke sharply to Charles.

"Come, we must go now," Charles said.

"But—"

"Nay, we must."

"But, Charlie, what about the governor's letter?"

"I showed it to them."

"It's not a request," Richard insisted. "It's an order to tell us anything they know about Stephen and to reveal his whereabouts to us."

Charles hesitated and eyed the warrior as he once more produced the letter and began to speak.

In what Richard assumed to be the utmost incivility, the Pennacook interrupted Charles's plea with a guttural comment, snatched the paper from his hand, and tossed it into the fire.

Richard stared at the burning letter, not quite able to believe what was happening.

"Richard." Charles's voice rose in apprehension.

Richard whirled toward him and saw that the big warrior had drawn his knife.

◆

Two Indians paddled them across the river and left them on the bank. Richard set out, dejected and weary, a few paces behind Charles.

When they had put two miles between them and the river, Charles slowed and waited for him to catch up. " 'Twill be dark soon, but I think we'd best go a few more miles before we camp."

"Charlie, I can't go home like this."

Charles frowned at him. "What more can we do?"

Richard stared at him, unable to believe this was the end. "We could. . . We could find some of their other villages, ask different people. I don't know, Charlie. I don't know." He sank to his knees on the path. "I'm so tired I don't know what to think."

He felt Charles's hand clasp his shoulder. "Come on. A few more miles at least. Then we'll talk and get some rest."

Two hours later, they lay in a thicket shivering and murmuring to each other. They didn't dare light a fire after their hostile leave-taking from the village. Richard's head was no clearer, and neither of them had generated an idea that seemed safe or meritorious.

At last Charles told him, "The elder said they will kill us if we return."

"And you think they mean it?"

"I most assuredly do. Sleep, friend. We can do no more."

Richard tossed for only a few minutes on the hard ground before his body gave in and sleep took him. How much time passed, he did not know, but suddenly he felt a hand on his shin, and he jerked upright with a gasp.

"Charlie?"

"Nay," said a strange voice. "It is Stephen."

Chapter 13

Richard's steps dragged as they approached Cochecho in a chilly rain. They entered the village, and he caught a glimpse of the parsonage roof. But even thoughts of Sarah could not draw him. He must complete his mission before thinking of visiting her.

Only a few people passed close enough for them to nod in greeting, and he and Charles took the muddy path to the farms together. When they reached the palisade outside the Dudleys' home, they stopped.

"Shall I come in with you?" Charles asked.

Richard shook his head. "I must tell them alone, I think. My mother will grieve anew. Unless—" It suddenly struck him how forlorn a homecoming Charles would have in his cold, empty cottage compared to the welcome he would receive. "Would you stop with us tonight?"

"Nay. You spoke right. Give them your news." Charles nodded. "Come to me in the morn, if you wish to talk."

Richard pressed his lips together and held out his hand. "Thank you, Charlie. You've done more than you ought. You are the truest of friends."

Charles grasped his hand warmly. "You know the path to my door, friend."

Richard watched him over the rise and faced the gate. He drew in a deep breath and blew it out again. *Lord, give me grace one more time.* Raising his voice, he called, "Father! Be ye within, Father?"

Through a crack between the posts of the fence, he saw Catherine leap down off the doorstep and run toward him. She threw off the bars, swung the gate open, and flung herself into his arms.

"Where's Father?" he asked as she nearly strangled him with her embrace. "It's nearly dark. Is he yet at the field?"

"Nay, he's within. Oh, Richard, come inside and tell us all!"

He slid his pack off his back at the door and shuffled in after her. His family had been at the table, and the remains of supper lay still in evidence. The smells of fresh bread and stewed chicken made his stomach rumble.

Richard hurried to kiss his mother. To his surprise, his father did not stand to greet him.

"You will pardon me, son, but I do not get out of this chair until I have to nowadays."

Richard stared at him, surprised that in three months his father had taken on the attitude of an old man.

"Father broke his leg," Catherine said, "but it's better now."

"Much better," his father agreed. "Sit down, boy."

Richard removed his coat and sat down heavily on a stool next to his father. "How did this happen?"

"Later," his father said gently. "We've time to talk of that. Tell us of your adventures."

Richard took the chair his mother set for him by the hearth and shook his head as he stared into the glowing fire. "I never should have gone."

He saw that they all watched him with sorrow ready to spill over in tears, for his returning alone had said the news for him. He swallowed hard and steeled himself for the added pain he was about to inflict on those he loved.

"We found Stephen."

"What?" His mother jumped from her chair and seized his arm. "Where is he? Richard, what—" She stopped and studied his face; then she slowly dropped her hand as her face lost its animation. "Tell us."

"We got to the village where Sarah had been, and they kept us a long time talking. Charlie showed them the letter we got from the governor of Quebec, but that didn't seem to sway them. We met the woman in whose home Sarah lived while she was there, but she had nothing to tell us, either."

"How horrible was it?" Catherine asked with a shiver.

Richard smiled. "Let us just say it is good to be home. Very good."

"But. . .how did you find him, if they kept quiet and would not aid you?" his father asked.

Richard nearly laughed, for he would not have described the long-winded Pennacook as quiet. But he sobered as he remembered the night that followed. "We didn't find him," he said softly. "He found us."

His mother gasped.

Richard reached for her hand and eased her onto a bench beside the fireplace. He unfolded the tale of how Stephen had learned of his presence before Richard and Charles had entered the village. "The warriors who escorted us in had, unbeknownst to us, sent a runner to another village not far away, where Stephen now resides. But he came not near while we were in the camp. Or if he came, he didn't show himself. After we'd left, however. . ." He sighed. "They drove us off. Told us to go or they would kill us. And the chief threw the governor's letter in the fire."

"Oh, wicked," Catherine cried.

Richard nodded. "At first I tried to talk Charles into looking further, but he assured me the savages would keep their word and slay us if we persisted.

I gave up hope then. And so we went. But Stephen. . ." His chest felt as though a giant hand squeezed it, and he closed his eyes for a moment. "He followed us several miles without our having a suspicion anyone was there and watched us crawl into a thicket in the dark and settle down for slumber. And then he came and woke me."

Every eye was fixed on him, but no one spoke.

"He told me he could not come home with me. He said he was. . .better off to stay there." Tears flooded Richard's eyes, and he wiped them with the back of his hand. "He truly believed that if he came back here, everyone would hate him."

His mother's tears flowed freely as she whispered, "Did you not tell him how we love him?"

"Aye. But he is a man now, among the Pennacook. He hunts with their men and—" Richard caught himself before *fights with them* slipped out. He looked around at his family and gave them a bleak smile. "He said he cannot come back to this world, and he doesn't want to try."

"But what have they there for him?" his father asked. "A hut made of branches, a life of hunting and starving and freezing?"

"I know." Richard bowed his head. "He refused to come and threatened Charles and me if we tried to follow him or if we ever came back to his people."

Catherine began to sob.

"I told him that you were all well and thinking constantly of him and wishing him home."

"What did he say?" his father asked without hope.

"That we must stop thinking so. He will not come."

Goody Dudley burst into tears, and though Catherine hurried to console her, her own sobbing nearly drowned out her mother's.

"Come, son," his father said after an interval of tears and deep thought. "Take your boots off. Have some supper. You, at least, are home now."

◆

The next day, Richard plunged into the work of preparing the farm for winter. Many tasks lay undone because his father had not liked to ask his neighbors to neglect their own work to do his. Catherine and her mother had toiled, and James Dudley had done all within his meager power.

But the supply of fodder for the livestock was less than it would have been if he'd retained his full strength and had his son to assist him. Richard would have helped him harvest more hay from the salt marsh and perhaps even glean a meager third cutting from the meadow. A few of the palisade posts needed reinforcing, and a leak had developed in the barn roof. Besides all this, James decided to butcher four pigs, leaving only two that would need winter feed.

For several days, Richard worked from dawn to sunset, racing winter. One light snow had already fallen before his return but had not stayed long on the ground. But on the fourth day after his return, snow fell heavily as he walked to the barn in the early gray light of morning. He fed the animals and had just sat down to milk the cow when the barn door swung open. He turned toward it and saw his friend in the doorway. "Charlie! What brings you out in this?"

"I thought you might need an extra hand today. Tomorrow is the Sabbath, and you've much to do this day, I've no doubt, before your enforced rest."

Richard grimaced and kept milking. "You must forgive me, friend. I meant to come to you, but I've been so caught up in my work here that I broke my word."

"Nay," Charles replied, leaning against the post where a low wall separated the cow's stall from the rest of the small barn floor. "I've no livestock, and my little corn was put up for me, so I hadn't much to do. How goes all with your family?"

"Father was injured soon after we left. Did you hear?"

Charles shook his head. "I've seen no one these four days."

"He had an accident involving a middle-sized ash tree. He's been all this time recovering and still moves slowly."

"I do hope he's not done permanent damage?"

"He says not, but at his age. . ." Richard stripped the cow's udder and set the pail aside.

"What is your intention for today?" Charles asked.

"If this snow lets up, I thought to begin cutting firewood for next year. The ground is frozen hard now, and the snow will allow for dragging the logs out." Richard stood, picked up his milking stool, and hung it on the wall outside the stall.

"I shall help you."

"We'll work together, then. But if the storm be too harsh, we'd best wait it out." Richard looked out the door of the barn. The snow fell thick and fast. "Catherine and Mother plan on shelling beans today. If it's too foul for me to work outside, I expect I shall help them."

"Then I shall help, too."

"Had you any beans?" Richard asked.

"I fear the groundhogs and deer got them all."

"Mother tells me we have plenty. I'm sure she can spare a share for your help."

"That is not—"

"Oh, hush," said Richard.

Charles came to stand beside him in the doorway. "How is your mother taking the news about Stephen?"

"She is distraught and yet more controlled than I expected. She and Father—aye, and Catherine, too—are relying on their faith to sustain them."

Charles nodded. "That is the best course, for we have done all in our earthly power."

"Aye." Richard drew in a deep breath as he stared across the dooryard toward the snug little house. "Charlie, Cat told me Sarah Minton spent much time here in my absence."

"Oh?"

"She came with the parson as soon as they heard Father was injured. And she stayed and helped Mother and Cat for some time."

"That can't be bad."

Richard shook his head, but he couldn't quite bring himself to look into his friend's eyes. What if he saw there the teasing laughter Charlie used to shower on him when they were lads?

"I. . .feel a change in their thinking. About the captives, I mean. Especially about Sarah."

"As I said, that cannot be bad. I rejoice with you."

Richard puffed out a breath. That achy longing had returned. "Hold off on celebrating awhile. But you're right. It is something. It is. . .a great thing. Mother in particular has come far in this attitude."

Charles squeezed his shoulder. "Have you seen her yet?"

"Nay. I've anticipated the Sabbath and tomorrow's meeting. But. . ." Richard looked out at the snow, now more than two inches deep on the ground. "If this keeps up all day, we'll not make it to meeting."

"Do not give up hope this early, my melancholy friend. More likely this storm shall end ere noon, and we'll break the path with little trouble."

Richard sagged against the door frame. The falling snow had, if anything, increased its density and speed of falling.

"I think I understand her better now, Charlie. How she feels, and how difficult it has been for her to return to this community."

"There is hope," Charles said softly. "Much hope. Come, let us clean up your byre and go and help the ladies shell beans."

Chapter 14

On Monday morning, Sarah set out after breakfast with Ben Jewett. Few people had come out for meeting on Sunday, but of course she, Jane, Christine, and all the Jewetts had attended. Only hardy people who lived in the village proper had made their way to the meetinghouse in the midst of the storm.

The snow had continued until midday on Sunday, leaving about eighteen inches of frozen fluff on the ground. At dawn Monday, men could be heard urging their oxen to drag heavy boards through the town to scrape the street.

"I hope the path is broken," Sarah said to Ben as she hurried along behind him carrying a basket. She had stout leather boots now—the Reverend Jewett had insisted that all the young ladies have sturdy footwear for winter, and the trader had donated one pair and given the others at cost. A thick woolen cloak of Goody Jewett's wrapped her snugly. The wind had died, and the sun sparkled on the snow, giving the illusion of warmth. Indeed, Sarah fancied the snow had already begun to melt from the rooftops.

"If it's not, then we shall break it," Ben assured her. " 'Tis only a mile."

Sarah smiled at his optimism. She was glad for his company. Ben had walked with her and Jane many times now, escorting them on their errands about the village. At thirteen, he had surpassed her in height and begun to show downy whiskers on his chin.

The trail was scraped only as far as the first two houses beyond the village, and after that there were only boot tracks where several persons had taken the path. Ben preceded her and stomped down the snow between the footprints. It was slow going and strenuous work, but Sarah reflected that the exertion was no doubt good for them both.

She wondered if she would learn any news about Richard today. She doubted he was home, though. When he returned, he would almost certainly pass through the village, and she expected he would report to the reverend on the outcome of his mission. Still, the snow had blocked many people from their purpose these last two days. At any rate, she would spend the day doing what she could to cheer the Dudleys. She'd brought a loaf of Jane's rye bread and was prepared to recite the main points of Parson Jewett's Sunday sermon for the family.

They were nearly halfway to the Dudleys' farm when they saw three young men sitting on a stone wall that edged one of the farmers' cornfields. No doubt these were the ones who had started to break the path, and Sarah was disappointed that their way would now be harder. She recognized two of the three—Felix Maybury and David Tucker. The third boy she had perhaps seen at meeting but didn't know his name.

Ben stopped suddenly, directly in front of her, and she came up short.

"What—" She broke off as the scent of acrid smoke hit her nostrils.

Ben turned and stared at her with huge blue eyes. "They're *smoking!*"

From beneath the edge of the shawl that covered her head, Sarah peered at the three young men then pulled her eyes hastily back to Ben's face. That Felix had a pipe in his hand there was no doubt. When she glanced back his way, he'd hidden it behind him, but the warmness of the air belied the thick cloud of his breath when he exhaled.

Sarah gulped down her surprise and realized that the boys' misbehavior was more shocking to Ben than it appeared to her. After all, the Pennacook, both men and women, had often smoked Indian tobacco in her presence.

"Just ignore them," she whispered.

Ben eyed her for a long moment then turned back to his task. They stomped along, and when they reached the spot where the young men had veered aside to the stone wall, he renewed his vigorous trampling of the snow.

Sarah noted that his face was red, and she feared hers had gone scarlet, as well, knowing the three watched them from where they lounged on the wall. She wondered if they realized she and Ben knew what they were doing or if they cared. Even as the thought flitted through her mind, she saw Felix slip the pipe to David, and David put it to his lips.

"Sarah," Ben hissed.

"Don't pay any mind to them. Come, I'll take the lead for a while. You must be tired."

They were barely a dozen yards past the end of the boys' trail when Felix called out behind them, "Say, young Jewett! Be you squiring ladies about town now?"

Ben opened his mouth, and Sarah whispered, "Answer him not, Ben! Come!" She turned her back to the young men once more and plodded through the deep snow, not bothering to stomp a path. The cold at once struck her as her feet plunged deep, and the snow closed in over her boot tops.

"Ladies?" The young man she didn't know guffawed.

"Oh, pardon," said Felix. "Methinks I should have said 'females.' "

David Tucker stood up and yelled, "Hey, Ben! Is that your squaw woman now?"

Sarah gasped and turned toward them. Ben had a stricken look on his face.

"What do you say, Ben?" Felix called. "Aren't you afraid she'll scalp you?" Ben lowered his gaze, and his lip trembled.

Movement beyond the boy drew Sarah's eye, and she pulled in a breath. Felix Maybury was plowing through the snow toward them. Before she could speak, he had reached them and grabbed her arm.

"Well, now, Ben, that's a pretty sweetheart you've got, though she has been tarnished."

"I'll wager she's a wild one," David laughed. He, too, had left the wall and had passed half the distance toward them.

"Let go of me!" Sarah jerked her arm from Felix's grasp, stepped backward, and overbalanced. She slipped backward and fell into the snow, her cheek slamming against the edge of her basket. She floundered to sit up.

Ben leaned to offer his hand, but Felix shoved him away. "Get back, puppy. I'll help the *lady*." Felix spoke the last word with such contempt that Sarah's blood ran cold.

Sarah rolled over in the snow and pushed herself up, facing away from Felix, but she felt his hand on her shoulder before she'd regained her feet. "Don't touch me," she snapped.

When she turned, she saw that David was holding Ben back and the third young man was coming to their assistance.

"We'll hold this mewling pup," David said, nodding at Ben. "Steal all the kisses you like from the wild woman."

Ben struggled, and David punched him. Sarah tried to pull away from Felix, but his grip on her shoulder clamped tighter.

A sudden shout from farther up the way startled them all, and Sarah swiveled toward the smooth, unbroken trail ahead. At the top of a rise fifty yards away stood a tall man in a thick woolen coat with a knit hat pulled low over his brow. Behind the long barrel of the musket he held pointed at them, she saw the hard, dark eyes of Richard Dudley.

◆

Richard advanced toward them quickly, in spite of the deep snow. His tall leather boots kept the snow out, and his long legs made little of its hindrance. He kept the musket leveled at the young men, choosing to aim at Felix, the one who seemed to be the chief offender.

"Hey, Dudley," David Tucker said, releasing Ben and falling back a step. "We were just helping these two. They got out in the deep snow and was floundering, like."

"Quiet, Tucker." Richard advanced nearer, focusing on Felix's face.

Felix seemed to realize suddenly his posture and let go of Sarah. She stepped away from him, closer to Ben.

"Well, Dudley," Felix said. "Didn't know you was back from Canada. How's your father? Is his leg mended now?"

Richard stopped three paces from Felix and stared at him down the barrel of the musket. Disgust filled his heart as the young man attempted to appear innocent before him. "If you ever touch this woman again—"

"You'll what?" Felix's question was more of a challenge.

David and the other young man backed stealthily away, but Felix stood his ground. "Next you'll be defending savages," he sneered.

Sarah and Ben were now several paces from any of the others, and Richard moved quickly. He flipped the musket end for end and swung it at Felix, catching him solidly on the chest with the maple stock and knocking him backward, where he sprawled in the snow, gasping for breath.

Richard lowered the musket and took a few steps toward him. Panting, he looked down at Felix. "As I said, don't ever lay a finger on her again. Nor any other young lady in this town."

David and the other boy turned and pelted for town, leaving their friend to haul himself erect and stumble after them.

Richard stood watching with narrowed eyes until they were out of sight. Only then did he turn and look Sarah and Ben up and down. Sarah looked fine, though her face was pale. "Be you still in one piece?" he asked.

Sarah nodded.

"Aye," said Ben with a grin. "You laid him flat, Richard!"

Richard eyed him critically. "Your eye is going all purple. Won't your mother be pleased!" He looked back toward the path once more. "I'll have the constable on them within the hour. Tucker, Furbish, and Maybury."

"Furbish?" Sarah asked. "So that's who he is."

"Aye. Goodman Furbish's eldest." *His father will not be pleased*, Richard thought.

Ben sobered. "I'm sorry, Sarah. I was supposed to protect you."

"Three on one is not a good match, Ben," she said.

He was not consoled but frowned up at Richard. "Think if there *had* been Indians."

"No, don't think it," Richard replied. The idea of losing Sarah again was beyond the realm of bearable thought. "Where are you headed?"

"Your father's house," said Sarah. "I thought to visit your family. We'd not heard you were home yet."

"Aye, but work and weather have kept me from the village."

She held his gaze with blue eyes full of concern and hesitation. When she turned to include Ben in the conversation, he remembered they had an audience in the boy, and many things he wished to say could not yet be discussed.

"Ben, you needn't go all the way to the Dudleys' with me now if you don't wish to," she said.

Ben looked apprehensively toward town, and Richard wondered if he thought the rowdy young men might lie in wait for their return.

"Or perhaps. . ." Sarah faced Richard in confusion. "Perhaps there is no need for me to go, since you are back. You could take my gift to your mother." She held out the basket.

"I'm sure they would wish for your company more than whatever delights you've prepared for them," Richard said, "if indeed you still wish to go."

"Oh, I do." Sarah averted her gaze.

Relief warmed him, routing the momentary disappointment he'd felt at the thought of leaving her now and not spending time with her as he'd planned. "In truth," he said, "my object this morning was to visit you at the parsonage. If you are not too fatigued, we could walk with Ben and rest a bit at the Jewetts' fireside and then go on out to the farm."

She looked at the boy. "Would that suit you, Ben?"

He nodded, looking from her to Richard and back.

"And I could bring you home safely this afternoon before nightfall," Richard said hastily.

"Thank you. That sounds like an agreeable plan." Sarah wrapped her cloak closely about her and surrendered the basket to him.

On their short trip back toward town, Sarah and Ben updated him on the recent events in the village. When they arrived at the parsonage, Goody Jewett and the children swarmed around to greet them. Ben's black eye brought nearly as many comments as Richard's return, and after a few minutes, Goody Jewett sent John to the meetinghouse to fetch his father.

"I can't countenance this," the pastor said as he eyed Ben's face.

"You don't think they would have seriously harmed them, do you?" his wife asked anxiously.

"From where I stood, it looked sinister," Richard told them, "and I acted as such."

"Shame, shame!" Goody Jewett wrung her hands. "Boys of our village. 'Tis unconscionable."

"Sarah, I must ask you and Richard to delay long enough to give the constable your story," the minister said.

They removed their cloaks and mittens and sat down to wait while the Reverend Jewett went to the ordinary to summon the landlord, who was also the constable.

Mr. Oliver clucked his tongue and shook his head repeatedly as Ben and Sarah then Richard recounted what had happened on the trail. The parson demanded that he arrest the young men and put them in the stocks. Oliver assured the Jewetts that the three miscreants would be brought before the magistrate and punished.

At last they were allowed to go, after Sarah received many admonitions from Jane and Goody Jewett and a silent hug of support from Christine. Richard gave her his hand as she negotiated the doorstep, but she released it as soon as she stood on the path.

They set out again on the snowy trail. Richard marveled at the silence and beauty of their surroundings compared to the noisy, crowded room at the parsonage. Sarah inhaled deeply and looked all around at the snow-laden evergreens and sparkling fields.

They walked in silence for some time, Richard with his musket and Sarah carrying the basket once more. Richard began to tell her of his journey with Charles, his elation when he met his brother at last, and the sorrow that followed.

Sarah shed no tears when he told of his meeting with Naticook. "I'm glad you saw her, and I am not surprised that she offered you no aid in finding Stephen. But neither would I be surprised if I learned she was one of those who told him of your presence."

Richard thought about what she said for a short distance then shared his thoughts with her. "Sarah, I learned some of what it meant to you to be there in that place so long. You must have been terrified."

"One cannot remain in a state of terror forever." Her smile was tinged with sadness. "Of course I was frightened at first, especially on the journey north, not knowing what would befall me. But after I'd been in the village a few months and began to feel that I wouldn't be torn out of there again, but would remain in comparative peace, I felt less anxious."

"And Naticook was kind to you?"

Sarah's eyes crinkled a bit. "I wouldn't say *kind*. She was not cruel, though occasionally she swatted me with a stick if she thought I did not move quick enough. But my lot was no worse than anyone else in the village—and better than some."

When they had passed beyond the place where the young men had accosted her and Ben, she looked up at Richard. "I haven't thanked you properly."

"No need," said Richard. "I'm only glad I came along at the right moment."

" 'Twas not the way I imagined our next meeting."

"I am flattered that you imagined it."

She smiled and trudged along with him. They had reached a stretch where only his boots had broken the snow, and the going was much more difficult. She soon fell behind and stepped in his tracks, while he quickly trod down a better path for her.

They arrived at the Dudleys' home without further mishap and told his family of the morning's events.

"Those wicked boys must be punished," Catherine cried.

"Fear not," Richard told her. "The parson will not rest until it is done. They'll be in court for assault next time the magistrate comes."

Sarah dove into the work the women had started that morning—shelling corn. His father was helping, too, and Richard despaired of having more time alone with Sarah.

"You might as well go and cut more wood on this fine day," his father said.

"Nay," said Catherine. "Not while Sarah is here to visit us."

"Guests mustn't stop the work of the household," Sarah told her.

Richard stared at her. True, he didn't often give up a fine day when he could be out working, but after all, he had planned to do so today, at least for the morning, with the express object of speaking to her. Of course, they'd had half an hour on the way here alone, but still he felt he'd been cheated.

His father rescued him by pointing to the corner, where Richard had left his ax on Saturday evening.

"Mayhap your tools need sharpening before you can spend another day in the woods."

This suited Richard's mood, and with a little thought, he was able to find several tasks that kept him inside and near Sarah.

The five of them passed several pleasant hours in conversation, and Goody Dudley was even able to speak of Stephen without breaking into sobs. "I shall never forget all you and Charles did for us, Richard," she said after Richard had given another retelling of his story. "I know you needed to settle in your own heart whether Stephen lived or no—"

"And whether he lived with the savages of his own accord," Catherine added.

"Well, yes. But as I was saying, I know you did it for yourself, but you also did it for all of us, and for that we thank you. I would never ask you to undertake such an ordeal, but since you did, you have given me peace."

"Peace, Mother?" Richard asked. "Indeed, I've seen great change in your manner since I returned, but I did not expect you would be in peace now."

" 'Tis God's peace," she told him, and a single tear slid down her cheek. " 'Tis not my peace, but He tells me all is well, and I must trust Him."

◆

With an hour of daylight left, Sarah and Richard donned their wraps. Sarah kissed her hostess and Catherine good-bye and thanked them for their hospitality. Her heart filled with affection, for she knew she had been accepted into the family circle without reservation.

As they set out for the village, Richard shouldered his musket. The air had warmed even more throughout the day, and he left his mittens hanging out of the pockets of his woolen coat. Sarah fancied the snow had shrunk several inches in depth since that morning, and the path seemed far easier to tread.

"We'll soon have you home," Richard said. "Let me take your basket for you."

"Nay, 'tis not heavy—only a skein of yarn Catherine pressed upon me so that I can knit a cap for the new babe."

Richard's cheeks colored above his beard, and Sarah realized she'd become accustomed to speaking freely about Goody Jewett's pregnancy to the women she most often associated with.

"Pardon," she murmured.

"Nay, no need."

They walked on for a few more steps in silence, and Sarah ventured, "Catherine spins the finest yarn I've ever seen. I plan to dye it yellow before I make the—" She broke off in confusion as Richard swung round in the path and stopped, facing her. Had she said something amiss?

"Sarah." He looked down at her, his dark eyes roving over her face, seeking. . .what? His gaze settled in again on her eyes, and she wished he would tell her what went through his mind in that moment.

"Richard?" she whispered.

His look softened, and he reached for her with his free hand, still holding the musket pointing skyward with the other. He touched her face, and his big hand felt warm against her cheek.

"I love you, Sarah."

She caught her breath and gazed up at him. This was a moment she had waited for these five years and more. She couldn't help smiling.

He stooped and brushed his lips against hers, and Sarah longed to throw her arms about him. Still, they were out in the open, where anyone might see, and such actions might be considered lewd behavior.

Richard apparently had other thoughts, as he drew away from her and stared carefully all around at the trees.

"Come," he said, putting his free hand to the butt of the musket. "We mustn't linger here."

They soon reached the place where the path met the village street, and Sarah walked beside him up the hill to the parsonage. With every step, her heart soared and her thoughts cast about for the right response to his declaration. Just before they entered the dooryard, she took a deep breath and slowed her steps.

"Richard?"

"Aye?"

They stopped and looked at each other. Sarah inhaled sharply, knowing he mustn't protract his stay in town if he wanted to reach home before dark.

"I. . ."

The door of the house opened, and John and Ben bounded outside.

"I feel the same way," she murmured.

The boys charged toward them, shouting a greeting. Richard laughed and let them chatter away, commenting on how Ben's bruises had spread into a fine proof of his mettle. John had a tale to tell of snaring a rabbit that day for the first time.

When they reached the door, Sarah glanced at Richard with an apologetic smile. "Shall you come in for a moment?"

"I do wish to see the parson." His significant look stopped her in her tracks, and a warm prickling spread over her.

"Father be visiting the relict Woolsey," Ben said.

"Ah. Then I shall walk that way and perhaps meet him." Richard glanced up at Sarah, who now stood on the doorstone. She thought the color in his face was higher than their walk in the cool air warranted. "I'll. . .see you again soon, Miss Minton."

She smiled. So formal in front of the boys! It was so unexpected that even Ben stared at him, though John took no notice. "Aye. Thank you for bringing me."

He nodded, shook the boys off, and headed toward the widow Woolsey's cabin with a pronounced spring in his step.

Chapter 15

The next morning, Sarah thought the pastor and his wife seemed especially cheerful—if not jubilant. At breakfast, the minister reported that the three young men who had assaulted Ben and Sarah would face the magistrate within a fortnight and were under close watch by the constable in the meanwhile.

This good news did not seem enough for the knowing smiles the couple exchanged or the beaming looks bestowed upon Sarah. She could not deny the joy and expectation that simmered within her, and she had little doubt the Jewetts' mood had something to do with that, as well.

Confirmation came soon after, when she settled near the hearth with Christine to mend clothes for the entire family. Sarah chose a shirt of John's and prepared a patch for the torn elbow, while Christine sewed a button on the parson's Sunday waistcoat.

"I wish you joy," Christine murmured, her head bent over her task.

"Oh?" Sarah asked. "And what is the occasion?"

"Goody Jewett mentioned this morn that you will be leaving us soon."

Sarah lowered the material and needle to her lap and eyed Christine with mock severity. "If it's true, then I know none of it. Shame on you for gossiping so."

Christine let out a soft chuckle. "We remarked when you left yesterday, Jane and Goody Jewett and I, how Richard looks at you now. And something must have passed between him and the reverend last night. Pastor said before us all at supper that Richard had gone to Goody Woolsey's to speak to him."

"But he did not divulge his errand," Sarah pointed out.

"Oh, surely it is known to you."

"I am surprised at you, Miss Hardin," Sarah said in the most stilted tones she could muster without laughing.

Christine's face colored. "I mean no offense. I'm truly happy for you, if this is what you wish."

Sarah picked up her sewing and took a few stitches around the edge of the patch. "I was teasing, Christine. If Richard's intent is what you think, then, yes, I believe it is what I wish, and I think I'm ready now."

Christine reached over and squeezed her hand. "I shall never marry, but I'm truly pleased for you. He is a fine young man."

Sarah wondered if Christine would change her mind one day. Perhaps, if the right man came along. . . She also wondered how she would contain her disappointment if their assumption proved false and Richard's conversation with Pastor Jewett had nothing to do with her future.

The daylight hours dragged as she watched the children and baked bread. After the noon meal, she helped the boys stack a load of firewood that one of the parishioners brought in his wagon for the parson. In midafternoon, the Reverend Jewett came home from studying and broke in upon the household with a burst of energy.

"Children, come! Get your sleds. The snow is perfect, and we shall join the Tuttles and the Otises for a sledding party."

Sarah and Jane scrambled to help the little girls get their wraps on.

"Ruthie, too," the pastor said, tossing the toddler into the air.

Ruth squealed in delight, and Christine left the loom to bundle her up in cap, mittens, and coat.

Ben and John by this time had the sleds ready outside the door, and the pastor eyed the young ladies with a challenging smile. "Come, Jane, Christine. Stretch your legs."

"I shall stay with your wife, sir," Christine said.

Sarah thought he would bow to her excuse, as Goody Jewett was within two months of her lying-in and seemed to grow more fatigued each day.

But Pastor Jewett gave her a sly look. "Nay, I've picked Sarah for that duty. She shall keep Elizabeth company, and all shall be quiet here. Perhaps my wife will have a nap."

Sarah felt a moment of disappointment, for she had not been sledding in more than five years, and the thought of rushing down the hill with one of the children appealed to her. But as soon as the thought came, she noticed the pastor's meaningful look at Christine, and she almost thought he winked at the shy maiden.

At just that moment, a deep voice hailed the boys outside, and all became clear in Sarah's mind. Richard had come calling, and her guardian was clearing the house of all the children and the other young women, leaving her alone with his wife to entertain Richard in a measure of privacy.

She felt a flush suffuse her face, and she hadn't yet laid eyes on him. The pastor hustled his daughters and Jane outside, and Christine, the last one out, pulled the door to behind her, shutting out the greetings and chatter from the yard. Sarah looked to the hearth, where Elizabeth sat in the armchair her husband had made her.

"Do you mind, Sarah?" the lady asked.

"How could I mind, with your company, dear Goody Jewett?"

"Oh, I doubt my company shall be of much consequence." Elizabeth smiled gently. "If you feel the same way as you did a few months back and don't wish to accept any man's addresses. . ."

Sarah bowed her head for a moment. Elizabeth was right. She had felt and said those things just a short time ago—that she didn't wish to marry and perhaps never would.

"Perhaps God has healed your heart," Elizabeth suggested.

"Aye." Peace washed over Sarah as she let that knowledge settle over her, and she returned Elizabeth's smile.

A solid rap came at the door—not too bold, yet not timid or tentative.

Elizabeth arched her brows at Sarah and nodded toward the sound "I believe you have a caller, my dear."

Sarah tossed her apron aside and smoothed her hair as she took the few strides to the door. No time to consider the disorder of the room. The caller would have to understand the chaos that attended a large family, especially when all had bustled to prepare for an unexpected outing.

She opened the door and stood eye to eye with Richard. A giddy anticipation shot through her as their eyes met. His lips curved upward, transforming into a blinding smile.

"Sarah."

"Aye. Welcome, Richard." She stepped back to allow him room to enter and closed the door behind him. In her mind, she cast about for the next logical phrase. *What brings you?* Nay, too bold, when she knew. *How is your family?* perhaps.

Elizabeth saved her the trouble. "Good day, Richard. You will forgive me for not rising to greet you. I tire so easily these days."

"Please do not bestir yourself." He stepped forward and offered Goody Jewett his hand.

"I shall stay right here with my knitting, if you do not mind, and you and Sarah must make yourselves comfortable. Let Sarah take your coat, and bring a bench nearer the fire."

Richard obliged and loaded another log onto the coals before he sat down next to Sarah. "Too near the flames?" he asked as she rearranged the folds of her skirt.

"Perhaps a bit." She stood and let him move the bench back, wondering if he felt as nervous as she did.

They sat in silence for a long minute, both of them watching the fire.

"How is your family?" Elizabeth asked, and Sarah almost laughed with relief.

"They be fine." Richard inclined his head toward Goody Jewett. "Father's leg grows stronger, and he's helping with morning and evening chores now. Mother seems more at peace. She and Catherine be making cheese today."

Elizabeth nodded. "Sarah told me that you saw your brother in the north."

"Aye. 'Twas not what we wished, but 'tis better than not knowing whether he lives or nay."

" 'Tis God's blessing to allow you to know," Sarah said softly.

Richard threw her a grateful smile. "I believe so," he said.

The two of them continued to talk quietly after that, and Sarah found it not difficult after all. After about ten minutes, she glanced over and saw that Goody Jewett's eyelids drooped and she had let her knitting fall into her lap. She wondered if she ought to offer to help her lie down on the bed, but perhaps that wouldn't be proper with Richard here.

He touched her hand, and Sarah jumped. When she looked up at him, the tenderness in his expression chased all thoughts of propriety from her mind. She did no more than flex her fingers and suddenly her hand was cradled in his; then he leaned close to her.

"Sarah, my dearest, I pray you have forgiven my lapse when first you returned. I deserve every rebuke you gave or thought to give me."

"Nay," she answered, breathless. " 'Twas unjust of me to scold you. I think time was needed for all of us to put events in their proper place."

He nodded, and his dark eyes seemed to blaze, though perhaps it was only the reflection of the fire. "I love you, Sarah, and I can't go a waking hour without thinking of you. Please would you—can you—consider being my wife? I would do all within my power to protect you and provide for you."

She caught her breath. "Aye," she whispered.

"We would have to stay with my family the winter," he rushed on, "but Father and Charlie Gardner will help me build us a cabin in the spring. It won't be fancy, but I'd make sure it would be solid and keep out the rain and snow, and Father says I might be able to acquire some land, though we haven't much money. But—" He stopped and stared down at her for a moment as though just taking in her response. "You. . .will?"

"Aye. 'Twould fulfill my greatest desire on this earth," she managed.

He exhaled, closing his eyes for a moment. Then his eyelids flew up, and he darted a glance toward Goody Jewett, who seemed to have dropped into a doze, slumped in her chair.

"Sarah. . ." He slipped his arms around her and drew her toward him. "If you don't think it improper. . ."

"I don't."

He kissed her then, and Sarah was bold enough to slide one hand up into his soft beard. Richard held her firmly against him, and all her anxiety fled, except one fleeting fear that Goody Jewett would suddenly rouse and see Richard passionately kissing her ward.

Indeed, as soon as he drew back, he glanced once more at their hostess, but she had not stirred. He then lingered with his arms about Sarah, which encouraged her to dare rest her head on his shoulder as they resumed their study of the fire.

◆

At the Sunday meeting, the Reverend Jewett preached a fine sermon. Sarah sat up front with Jane and the children. Christine again had remained at home with Goody Jewett, who now found it beyond her strength to walk up the hill to the meetinghouse and sit for several hours on a hard, backless bench.

Richard sat several rows behind her, she knew, but she kept from looking back. If she met his gaze, her face would surely betray her feelings. No use giving the villagers more to gossip about.

As the sermon drew to a close, the pastor entreated the people to forgive and be compassionate to one another. He read a short section that Sarah was certain came from his pamphlet, urging the people to accept as brothers and sisters those who returned from enforced servitude in a foreign land.

"And now, brethren," he cried, "I bid you join me in seeking to show greater compassion and charity. If you commit to treat thus those within the church, stand before God and man, pledging on your honor to do your part in making this a better community."

Sarah stood and heard many move behind her as the bulk of the congregation rose. For several seconds, a stirring was heard as others got to their feet. She supposed a few did not, or perhaps stood only out of shame, seeking not to be one of the few who refused to comply with so reasonable a request.

The pastor raised his eyes at last and offered a prayer of thanks for the unity of spirit among the people. When the prayer was done, instead of dismissing them, he said, "Please be seated. It now gives me great pleasure to read to you the marriage intentions of Richard Dudley, goodman, of this parish, and Miss Sarah Minton, also residing here."

As he read on through the banns announcing a marriage to take place in a fortnight, a murmur reached her ears, which she knew were scarlet now as the blood rushed to her face. It seemed a favorable, hopeful wave that swept the congregation.

When they were dismissed, she helped bundle up the little ones again, and they wended toward the meetinghouse door, where the pastor greeted each member as the people left. As they descended the steps outside, she noticed with a rush of joy that Richard waited at the bottom.

"Might I walk you home?" he asked.

Sarah looked over her shoulder at the parson, who was just descending the steps with Ruth in his arms. He bestowed a cheerful nod on them, and Sarah allowed Richard to draw her mittened hand through his arm as they proceeded toward the parsonage.

◆

A week later, Richard whistled as he set about his evening chores. The weather had turned cold, but that could not dampen his spirits. In a week, Sarah would be his wife. Catherine walked past the door of the byre with a basket on her arm, and he knew she went to feed the poultry. He tossed fodder into the ox's feedbox and sat down to milk the cow.

"Richard!" His sister ran into the warm, dim byre, panting for breath.

"What is it?"

"An Indian. At the gate."

"That's odd. You'd think if they meant us harm they wouldn't come up to the gate openly. Did he speak?"

"Nay. I saw him approaching as I went to the hen coop, and I ran to fetch you."

Richard rose and set his milking pail and stool where the cow could not reach them. "The gate is properly barred?"

"Aye. This happened before, while you were gone."

"Oh?"

"Sarah was here," Catherine said. "She spoke to the man in his own tongue, and he left."

Richard nodded and took a hayfork from where it hung on the wall. "I shall see what he wants. Go to the house and tell Father. He'll get his musket."

Cautiously he crossed the dooryard. He could barely make out a dark figure through a slit in between the logs of the palisade. The man was just outside the gate. Richard glanced toward the house and saw that Catherine had gained the doorway. He wished he had a better weapon than the two-tined hay fork.

A foot from the solid gate, he stopped. He couldn't see the warrior now, though he knew he was there. His heart beat fast, and he tightened his grip on the handle of the fork. "Good day," he called. "What do you want?"

"To see my mother."

Richard felt as though his chest were being squeezed by a giant. He rested the fork on the snow and reached for the bars; then he drew back his hand. "Stephen?"

"Aye, Richard. Your brother."

Richard closed his eyes and leaned against the gate. "God be praised," he whispered. He opened his eyes and threw the hayfork aside then hurried to remove the bars. When the gate swung open, he beheld the young man he had only seen in darkness on the trail.

Stephen, at nearly sixteen, was almost as tall as Richard, but thin and wiry beneath the deerskin clothing he wore. On his feet were moose-hide boots and short snowshoes. His dark hair was pulled back and liberally greased, and he carried a leather pouch, a bow, and a quiver, slung over his shoulders.

Richard realized Stephen was staring at him, as well, no doubt taking in his bushy beard and his knitted mittens and warm woolen clothing. He was glad he had set aside the hayfork.

"Richard!" his father yelled from behind him. "Everything all right?"

Richard didn't take his eyes off Stephen but called, "Yes, Father."

His brother's eyes darted past him and flared as they focused, no doubt, on his father.

"Welcome home, Stephen." Richard opened his arms wide.

Stephen looked at him in momentary confusion; then he slowly stepped forward into his embrace.

◆

Richard paid a visit to Sarah two days later and begged her to walk out with him. Goody Jewett was happy to give her an errand at the trading post, and they set out together.

As they left the house, he looked down at her, noting with sweet anticipation how a lock of his future bride's golden hair glimmered in the sun where it peeked from beneath her hood.

"I'd say I've thought of nothing but you these two days," he told her, "but that would not be true. Much as I delight in seeing you, Sarah, I must give you the news."

"What is it?" She looked up at him with apprehension.

"Our family is set on its ear. Stephen has returned."

She puffed out a breath that turned to white vapor in the cold air. "When?"

"Two nights past. I was doing my chores. Catherine saw him at the gate and thought he was a Pennacook."

"Oh, Richard! How wonderful. And after he'd told you that he wouldn't come."

He nodded. "We were all stunned." He struggled for the words with which to express to her his joy and turmoil. "Sarah, he told me that since he'd seen me he couldn't stop thinking about me. I'd told him how Mother prays for him every day. Indeed, we all do, but Mother especially, and that seemed to get hold of his heart. He says he began to wonder what a mother's prayers could do."

"God used it to turn his thoughts," Sarah breathed.

"Aye, you say right. He wept when Father took him in his arms. And the look on his face when first he saw Mother, I can't describe to you. But he's wild. He can't sleep in the house, and he's restless all the time. Wants to get out beyond the fence, where he can see a long way off."

"Have you put him in the loft, where he can see over it?"

"Nay, he insists on sleeping in the byre. I think the house constrains him. But he says for now he is comfortable with the cattle. Which is odd, don't you think?" He gazed down at Sarah's sweet face, searching for reassurance. "I mean, the Pennacook don't keep cattle, do they?"

"Seldom. But he probably wants to be where you can't see him. Or mayhap the sounds of others or the smells of cooking and such keep him awake."

"Did those things bother you when you came back?"

"Nay, truthfully, what bothered me most was a soft pallet to sleep on. Your sister's feather bed was even worse, but I enjoyed every moment of lying in it."

Richard laughed. "I hope he will be at our wedding."

"He will stay, then?" Sarah asked.

"We don't know yet, for sure. He hasn't said as much, and we're hopeful that he's not putting off a decision to leave us."

"That would be better than his deciding now to go."

"Aye, but. . .Sarah, I thought perhaps, in the spring. . ."

"What, Richard?"

He looked deeply into her eyes. "If you disagree, I shall not press the matter, but I thought we might offer him a room in our new home."

She nodded. "I don't mind. But I didn't think we would have such a large house to begin with."

"Father and I have been talking, and we think three rooms below and a large loft above. It's not safe to build a little cabin with no upstairs. You need to be able to look down on anyone approaching without. And we'll fence it all about, of course."

"Shall we live near your parents?"

Richard shrugged. "I had thought to build next to Father and extend the palisade, but a parcel of land is available between us and Gardner's. Our house would be between Father's and Charlie's. I suppose we could build closer to Father, on his land, but. . ."

"Nay, we should live on your property, if you are able to secure it," Sarah said firmly. "Richard, it will be good to have your brother with us, if we're to be one of the farthest houses out from the village."

"Aye, my thinking, as well. He told me he is glad to be home, but he feels a bit stifled. If he lives with us, he can come and go as he pleases. You would understand his discomfort better than my mother does."

"I am agreeable. But perhaps he would like to build his own wigwam, or a little cabin away from us."

Richard nodded. "I will tell him you suggested such. If he is content to stay, he shall always be welcome."

She smiled up at him. "Come. We have an errand to fulfill, and I see Goody Paine watching us closely."

"She's harmless," he said with a laugh, "but you are right. We must proceed, or I would stand here in the street all day talking with you and forget my business."

Epilogue

In the chilly little parsonage of Cochecho, Richard Dudley pledged his love to Sarah Minton in late November, and the Reverend Samuel Jewett solemnized their vows. All the young Jewetts stood gravely by, and Elizabeth sat in her armchair, alternately smiling and weeping. Jane Miller and Christine Hardin also witnessed the ceremony, both seemingly deep in thoughts of their own.

With Richard came his family. They had set out early that morning, the slow but faithful ox pulling his parents in the sled while Catherine, Stephen, and Richard plodded along through the snow behind.

It was Stephen's first appearance in the village, though the pastor had visited the Dudleys' home during the week. Few people saw his arrival at the parsonage that day, and fewer still recognized the tall young man. He looked much different than he had when he presented himself at the Dudleys' gate, for by his request his mother had cut his hair. She and Catherine had altered some of his father's clothing to fit him, and he now looked to be a respectable colonist.

At the conclusion of the vows, Richard bent down to kiss his bride, and all gathered close to wish them well. Jane and Christine began to serve the cake they had prepared and hot chocolate, a luxury provided by Richard's parents. Goody Dudley had brought extra dishes in the oxcart so that all could partake together.

Stephen stood aloof at first, but the parson drew him into conversation, and soon Ben and John approached, as well, eager to hear anything Stephen would tell about his former life.

After an hour of good company, the Dudleys prepared to make the journey back to the farm.

Jane came to hug her, and Sarah whispered to her, "Beware of the pastor and his wife's matchmaking."

"Should I? More than previous?"

Sarah smiled. "It's just that I saw a look pass between them."

"What sort of look?" Jane asked.

"You know the one I mean. One that says, 'We've done it! One safely home, and two yet unmatched.' "

Jane smiled. "Now that you speak of it, they do seem proud of this day's work. I shall be forewarned."

Richard brought Sarah's cloak and held it for her. "Well, wife, will you ride in the oxcart with my parents?"

"Nay," she said with a smile. "I shall walk with my husband, my sister, and my brother."

He reached for her hand and plunged it, clasped in his, into the deep pocket of his coat and whispered, "Homeward, then, my love."

A NEW JOY

Dedication

To Lydia,
my sweet granddaughter.
We delight in watching you grow and learn.

Chapter 1

December 1694

J ane Miller clung to the hands of a child on each side of her and stepped out into the parson's deep footprints in the snow. The biting wind tore at the shawl that partly shielded her face, and the only illumination came from the stars glimmering between clouds overhead.

"I don't want to go," four-year-old Constance Jewett whimpered.

Jane realized that while she stepped in the impressions made by their father's boots, the little girls had to wade through the unbroken snow. The new accumulation of six inches was too much for them.

"It's cold," said Abby.

Jane squeezed the child's fingers with her mittened hand. She could hear Abby's teeth chattering already. A gust of wind blew loose snow in a swirl around them, blinding her for a moment, and Jane stood still until it eased and she could once more make out the footprints in the eerie, blue-white landscape.

The Reverend Samuel Jewett turned and surveyed them. In his arms was his youngest daughter, Ruth, not yet two years old, wrapped in a blanket. His nine-year-old son, John, plodded on and managed to find the deepest drifts.

"Let me carry Constance, as well," the parson said.

Jane trudged the few paces toward him, pulling Constance along. Their long skirts brushed the heavy snow.

Constance let out a shriek. "My shoe! My shoe!"

Jane stooped to lift her. "I'm afraid she got snow in her shoe top."

Constance's layers of winter clothing and thick woolen cloak weighed her down. Jane stumbled the last step as the pastor came to meet her.

He hefted Constance against his shoulder and straightened. "There now, don't fuss, Constance. I'll do well to carry you and Ruthie all the way to Heards' garrison."

"I want Mama." Constance burrowed her face into her father's shoulder as the wind rose once more, cutting through their layers of clothing.

The parson threw Jane a sympathetic look. "I fear we're out on the coldest night of the year. No help for it, though. Keep Abby close." He turned and stalked off, taking slow, deliberate steps.

Jane squeezed Abigail's hand again. "Hold the edge of my cloak and come behind me, Abby. I shall try to stomp the path down for you."

Young John had plowed ahead, and Pastor Jewett called to him to wait. Even in the village, it wasn't wise to let a child run out of sight. Too many young ones had been captured by Indians and hauled off to Canada from the small villages of New Hampshire. Day or night, whether working the cornfields or walking to church, the colonists knew they were never safe. Though the biting cold this last week of December would probably keep the savages away, attacks had occasionally happened even in the dead of winter.

Jane shuddered at the memories triggered by her grim thoughts. Her own time in Canada was a part of her life she would rather forget. She turned her attention back to her task of making a path for the little girl behind her. The moon was down, and she thought they must not be more than an hour from sunrise, but she couldn't be sure.

As they neared the river, the pastor stopped, and Jane pulled up short behind him. A shadowy figure appeared before them, dark against the starlit snow. Jane's heart leaped into her throat. She held back her scream and felt quickly to be sure Abby stayed hidden behind her.

The two little ones in the pastor's arms stayed quiet, but the reverend called out, "Ho, there!"

"Good morn, Reverend," came a hearty voice.

"Oh, Gardner, I didn't recognize you."

The relief in the pastor's voice prompted Jane to peer around him. Her gaze settled on the tall man coming toward them, and she decided it was indeed Charles Gardner, whose farm lay on the outskirts of the village. His bushy beard, bulging pack, and thick winter coat and hat made him appear much bulkier than normal.

"Why are you afoot so early?" Jewett asked.

"I've a trapline along the river here. But where is your family bound?"

"My wife's time has come. I've sent my eldest boy, Ben, to fetch Goody Baldwin. Miss Miller and I are trying to get the other children to Heards' garrison to stay until after the birthing."

Charles Gardner's gaze took in the pastor and his double burden, young John hovering at his father's side, and Jane and Abigail in the rear. "But your wife—"

"Christine Hardin is with her," Jane said quickly then wondered if she should have kept quiet and let the pastor tell his own tale. But they must hurry and get back. Christine was no doubt terrified, being there alone with a woman about to give birth. Goody Jewett had assured her husband there was time to fetch the midwife and disperse the children, but still. . . Things didn't always go the way the mother anticipated.

"Let me help you," Charles said.

"There's no need—," the pastor began.

But Charles cut him off. "Nonsense. It's freezing. Let me carry one of the children, and we'll travel quickly to the garrison. Miss Miller can go back and help with your wife until Goody Baldwin arrives."

"If you're sure. . ."

Charles answered the minister by striding quickly to Jane's side and stooping to address Abby.

Jane wondered that the Reverend Jewett would allow the young man the villagers called wild and "half savage" to touch his daughter. Charles had spent two years with the Algonquin Indians in Canada, and people hereabouts still seemed to mistrust him. But the pastor made no objection.

"Good morning. Miss Abigail Jewett, is it not?"

Abby giggled. "Aye, sir."

"Would you permit me to lug you to the garrison?" Charles stood and let his pack fall to the snow. "I'll leave my catch here until I return, and you can ride on my back." He crouched beside her.

Jane helped Abby climb onto his back and wrap her arms around his neck. "Hang on tight." Then she adjusted the knitted scarf over Abby's ears and wrapped the ends around her face.

"Hurry," Abby said as Charles stood. "It's cold."

Her father barked a laugh but said no more.

"Thank you, sir," Jane murmured.

Charles nodded at her, and she fancied his eyes twinkled, but perhaps they only reflected the starlight.

The men set off with long strides. John trotted behind them.

Jane stood for only a moment in the cutting wind, watching the tall shadows grow faint. An icy gust enveloped her, and she turned her back to it. As quickly as she could, she plodded back to the Jewetts' little home near the meetinghouse.

◆

Christine met Jane at the door, breathless. "You're back so soon!"

Jane pulled off her shawl. "Charles Gardner met us and offered to help the Reverend Jewett with the children."

"Is Goody Baldwin on her way?" Christine asked.

"Not yet. I'm sure she'll come ere long."

Christine sighed and glanced toward the pallet in the corner where Goody Jewett lay. "I admit I was frightened to be here alone with her. In fact, I nearly ran across the way to see if Goody Deane could come. I've nursed women before, but not for this."

Jane smiled. Christine's nursing had no doubt been performed in the convent in Quebec City. The young woman had lived among the nuns for five years after her Indian captors sold her to the French.

"We shall be fine until the midwife gets here." Jane hung her wraps on a peg by the door and hurried to Elizabeth Jewett's bedside. "How are you?"

Goody Jewett smiled with clenched teeth. "Not so bad, but I expect I shall bleat and shout a bit soon. At least the children are not within hearing."

Jane smoothed the dark hair back from Elizabeth's forehead. "Christine and I shan't mind. We'll do whatever we can to help you."

Elizabeth caught her breath and braced against pain.

Jane eased down onto the edge of the featherbed and held her hand. Her only experience in midwifery was when her own child was born in an isolated farmhouse in Quebec. Although the villagers here in Cochecho knew she had been married to a French trapper, Jane had told no one in New Hampshire about her tiny, stillborn baby boy.

She could barely remember the things the neighbor woman in Quebec had done during the birth. Probably they wouldn't serve now, anyway. Jane's baby had been born too soon, and likely her labor was different from a normal, healthy childbirth. But she couldn't say any of that to Goody Jewett. She could only smile in sympathy and mop her brow with cool water while Christine brought fresh linens and kept the big kettle boiling.

She wished her friend Sarah Dudley were present. Sarah had recently married Richard Dudley, the young man she'd loved since childhood. Jane was sure that Sarah would know more about midwifery than she did.

A knock at the cottage door brought a surge of relief to Jane's heart.

Christine leaped up and admitted Captain Baldwin's wife and Ben.

"Well, so the babe is coming at last," the midwife said, bustling in and setting a basket on the floor.

"Aye, we thought to see this event a fortnight ago," Christine told her.

"Well, wee ones know their own best time."

When Goody Baldwin had warmed herself by the fire, Jane gladly gave place to her. The sun was up, and Christine allowed thirteen-year-old Ben Jewett only a few scant minutes to stand by the hearth. She passed him a biscuit and told him to go to the Heards', where all the children would stay until the baby had arrived and the arduous cleaning that would follow was completed.

Only minutes after Ben had left, his father returned, but Goody Baldwin instructed Jane to turn him away, as Goody Jewett's labor had progressed and a man was not wanted in the flurry of activity.

As the moment drew near, Christine retreated to their hostess's chair in a corner, her face pale. She sat still, with her eyes closed and her lips moving silently.

Jane wished she could also retreat to pray, but she knew her help was needed. Goody Baldwin kept her running for linen, water, string, a knife. . . . Jane was too busy to think about her own experience two years ago.

Suddenly it was over, and the baby was there in the midwife's hands. His first breath was a thin, broken wail.

Christine leaped to her feet and came to the bedside, staring down in wonder at the writhing, red little scrap of a boy. Before Jane even thought about calling his father, the door flew open, admitting the Reverend Jewett and a blast of icy wind.

"Well?" His pale face, lined with worry, and his intent dark eyes showed between his icy beard and his woolen hat.

"A fine little fellow you have, sir," said Goody Baldwin.

Pastor Jewett exhaled. "Praise God." He laughed and stepped forward to look at his third son.

"Not yet!" The midwife stood between him and the pallet. "Let us wash him up before you hold him."

Jane stepped forward. "Here, Pastor. You're freezing. Let me take your coat, and you sit near the fire for a few minutes. Melt the icicles out of your beard. When you've warmed up, you can hold the babe and visit with your wife."

The big man meekly obeyed her instructions, looking anxiously toward the bed as he peeled off his coat and handed it to Jane.

❖

Charles Gardner at last reached his cottage and stomped the snow off his boots outside the door. He hurried to the fireplace. The coals he had banked several hours earlier glowed only faintly. He stirred them and stripped off his mittens so he could break pine cones and bits of kindling into smaller pieces with his chilled hands. A few minutes' care and soft blowing on the tinder rewarded him. The blaze sprang up, and he held out his aching hands to receive its warmth.

Assisting the Reverend Jewett had kept him out in the frigid air an extra hour, but Charles couldn't help being glad he'd had the opportunity. Jane Miller, though she might be strong, could not plod through the snow as quickly as he and the pastor. By sending her back to the parsonage, he'd helped not only the Jewett family but Jane herself. He was glad to know she was warm and safe.

He'd first noticed her eight months ago, when the governor of New Hampshire commissioned him, Captain Baldwin, and two other men to go to Quebec and redeem as many captives as they could from the French. Though she'd been married in Canada to a French farmer, she'd also been widowed there. Captain Baldwin had negotiated long hours with the authorities for her return.

In the end, Jane Robataille had agreed to give up any claim to her late husband's estate in Quebec, preferring to return to the English colonies. She had no family here in Cochecho; that much he knew. He seemed to recall that she'd been close to fulfilling a period of indenture when she was captured during the massacre more than five years ago. She'd reverted to her maiden name, Miller, and stayed at the Jewetts' house since her return last May.

Charles's respect for the parson had grown when the Jewett family took in not just Jane but two other returned captive women without homes. Some others in the town shunned the redeemed captives, a disheartening attitude Charles had experienced when he returned from his own stint with the Algonquin.

But the mood seemed to be changing in the village. Sarah Minton, one of Jane's orphaned companions in the Jewett household, had married Richard Dudley just two months ago. The Dudleys were close neighbors of Charles, and he and Richard had been good friends for years. The newlyweds seemed to be accepted in the community, and Charles had heard no disparaging remarks about Sarah in months.

But Jane's marriage to the French voyageur—which he suspected had been performed against her will—put her in another category in the dour colonists' minds.

Of course, the third young woman at the Jewetts', Christine Hardin, was in even worse straits. She'd spent years in a nunnery in Quebec. No good Protestant wanted to associate with her, though the Jewetts treated her like a member of the family. She attended meeting every Sunday and seemed to listen intently to Pastor Jewett's sermons. Charles doubted she had renounced her Protestant faith, but that wouldn't matter to some people.

As the room warmed, Charles removed his coat and hung it on a peg, not too close to the fire. It soon began to drip, and the steam filled the cabin with the strong smell of wet wool.

He opened his pack and pulled out the carcasses he'd gathered before dawn—a beaver, two muskrats, and a mink. Too cold to skin them outside. His hands would freeze in minutes without gloves.

If his mother were alive, he'd have thrown them outside and waited to skin them later. But no women resided in the Gardner cabin now to chide him for making a mess of their floors.

He pulled his razor-sharp skinning knife from its sheath and set to work on the little mink first. The silky fur was so gentle on his calloused hands that he could barely feel it. Just the thing for a fine lady's winter bonnet and muff.

Jane Miller's face once more flashed through his consciousness. She would look lovely in furs and velvet. But a poor girl like Jane, a former indentured servant and captive, would likely never know such luxury. These furs would go on a ship to England in the spring, for some rich man to buy.

A firm rap on the door startled him, and he jumped, nicking his finger with the blade. He sighed at his own clumsiness.

"Ho, Charlie? Are you there?"

"Come in, Richard."

The door opened, and his friend came in, stamping his feet and shedding snow that lay unmelted near the door at the cold end of the room.

"Come and warm yourself," Charles said, concentrating on his job. "You're out early."

"Not as early as you, evidently."

"Aye, I had a good catch this morn."

"I came to see if you want to cut wood tomorrow."

"If it's warmer."

Richard nodded. "Not today, surely. But I need to finish cutting next year's firewood for Sarah and me, and for my folks, too."

"Aye. We'll trade work until it's done for us all." The skin of the little mink came free, and Charles set it aside.

"Sarah would never let me skin my catch in the house."

"Sarah doesn't live here." Charles tossed the tiny carcass into the fire.

Richard frowned at him and looked around. "You need a wife, Charlie."

"Ha! You're just saying that because you're still in the euphoric mist of new marriage."

"Yes, I am."

Charles laughed and pulled the large beaver onto the hearth before him. "Would you and your lady like a nice beaver tail for your supper?"

"Thank you, I'm sure Sarah would be delighted."

Charles severed the tail and set it to one side.

"I saw your eyes rest upon Jane Miller after the Sunday meeting. Of course, I wouldn't know, but my wife says Jane is looking rather pretty these days."

"Please, Richard." Charles slit the beaver's skin neatly up the belly, where the hide was thinnest. "I'm glad that you are happy, but I don't care to pursue the topic of marriage while I skin the bounty of my trapline."

Richard snorted a laugh. "You know you admire her."

"I do. I've told you so, and I make no secret of it. She's tough, she's deft with a needle, and she doesn't complain."

"And comely?"

Charles shrugged. "I couldn't say."

"Certainly you could."

"Not to you. It would be all over the village ere nightfall."

Richard's chuckle annoyed Charles. His friend had been married only two months, but already he thought himself an expert.

"You're worse than an old woman, Richard. Really. I never saw such a matchmaker."

Richard stooped and fed two small logs into the fire. "I went to the ordinary yesterday, and I heard a couple of young, unmarried men discussing Miss Miller in a favorable light."

Charles worked on in silence for a moment, but he couldn't keep still. "Who were they?"

"Oh, I can't tell you that. Every time you met them, your jealousy would rear up and make you dislike them. Can't have you being rude to decent fellows. Next thing, you'd be brawling."

"You're daft."

"Nay. I've no doubt one of them will seek to court her soon."

"It's none of my affair." But Charles wondered if perhaps he ought to approach the parson before one of the others did. Jane couldn't be much beyond twenty years of age. Though she had come to the village in May thin and bedraggled, she had gained flesh in the past few months, and she seemed to grow prettier as the weeks went by. He knew Richard was right. Several young men—and some not so young—watched Jane at Sunday meeting.

Richard glanced around once more. "You can't bring a wife to this sorry little cabin, though."

Charles bit his lower lip and concentrated on relieving the fat beaver of its fur. His father's plans to enlarge the little cabin into a fine farmhouse had come to nothing. John Gardner had died suddenly while his son was only half grown, and his widow was killed in the massacre, when Charles was taken captive.

"I can't complain about this farm," Charles said. "The town elders allowed me to inherit my father's land when I returned from Canada. Last year they admitted me as a freeman to the town's rolls. They didn't have to."

"Aye." Richard took another stick of firewood from the pile and tapped the edge of his boot with it. "It takes time to regain your losses when you've been away, especially the way you were. You're lucky this land wasn't given to someone else."

"It would have been if people weren't so frightened of Indian raids," Charles admitted. "But single-handed, I can never clear enough land to make this farm prosper. I have to fight the forest for every inch of ground I want to plant."

"I know. It's the same with us."

"But you have your father, and now Stephen is back."

Richard pressed his lips together and nodded. "True. My brother has been a help since he came back two months ago. But he's restless."

Charles looked up into his friend's eyes. "Do you think he won't stay?"

"I don't know." Richard leaned against the stone mantel. "I hope he will. Mother would be crushed if he left again."

Charles nodded. The same longing used to seize him. He'd think about leaving Cochecho and disappearing into the forest, walking northward and disappearing once more from the frontier community. But he'd left the savage life of the Algonquin. After he'd begun to think of himself as one of his captors, the governor's men came and redeemed him. He'd returned to civilization somewhat reluctantly. But God had worked in his heart. If Charles thought about it long enough he always put away those stray thoughts of returning to the wild life. Something kept him here. This land, this farm, these fellow Englishmen around him. But he wanted more.

He thought of Jane again. She didn't mingle much with the villagers, but he'd seen her laughing with the Jewett children and Sarah Dudley. Her pert nose and reddish-blond hair set off her solemn gray eyes. He always thought Jane looked like someone who had many interesting thoughts but kept them private. How he would like to hear them.

"Well, if I ever think of marrying, I'll have to build up this farm. I couldn't support a family the way it is."

"Yes, you ought to have a cow or at least a goat."

"And a dog to warn me if any Indians come skulking around?"

Richard laughed. "I think your knowledge of the brutes and their language protects you better than a dog could."

Charles resumed his work. "How about making us a little breakfast, Richard?"

Richard straightened and glanced toward the door. "I should get home. Sarah will have breakfast ready and wonder where I am. But I'll bring in some more wood for you and put some samp on, if you like." He turned to the shelf where Charles kept his foodstuffs and opened the crock of parched corn.

"Don't bother," Charles said. "I've got some Indian pudding left over from last night's supper in the kettle yonder."

"All right, then, I'll leave you." Richard settled his hat over his ears and pulled on his mittens. "Come by in the morning with your ax if it's warmer. You can breakfast with us, and we'll go into the woods together."

"Aye."

When his friend had left, Charles finished his task with painstaking care. He stretched the skins and hung them on the cabin wall outside then cleaned up the floor and the hearth. Finally, he brought in a bucket of snow to melt so that he could wash the blood from his hands. The cut on his finger stung, but it didn't seem to go deep.

A well was another thing on his list of improvements to make. In summer he hauled water all the way from the river. In winter he melted snow. He must dig a well come spring. Richard and his brother, Stephen, would help, if Stephen stayed in the colony. Then Charles would have water at his doorstep, like the Dudley family did inside their stockade.

That was another thing. Should he fence his dwelling? Would it really make him safer? Charles doubted it. Richard was probably right about that. Charles's own experience with the Indians probably protected him better than a dog or a stockade would. But a woman might feel safer with those amenities.

Once more he thought of Jane Miller. She'd been through tough times, but on the long march back from Quebec, he'd never once heard her complain. She knew how to work hard. But was she ready to marry again?

Chapter 2

The Reverend Jewett went to bring the five older children home from the Heards' garrison the next day. Jane dressed the new baby in fresh clothes while Christine helped Goody Jewett wash and change into her clean shift. Tears sprang into Jane's eyes at the thought of the little boy she had lost, but memories couldn't dim her delight for the Jewett family.

When the children entered, they all rushed to the pallet in the corner of the room. Constance and Abby snuggled up on each side of their mother and gazed adoringly at their new brother. John stared for a long moment at the little one, but Ben only gave the baby a glance and went to the hearth for the water bucket. He picked it up and went out the door without a word.

"What shall we name him?" Goody Jewett asked the other children as they crowded around. Her husband plopped Ruth on the coverlet beside Abby and pulled a chair over to the bedside. Ben brought in a bucketful of snow and dumped it into the large kettle on the hearth then went to stand behind his father's chair.

"Let's call him Samuel," said John.

"That's Papa's name," Abby objected.

"So?" John scowled at her.

"We can't have two Samuels."

Both parents laughed, and the pastor said gently, "Some families do, Abby. But what would you suggest?"

"David?" Abigail asked.

"I know," Constance cried. "Goliath."

Everyone laughed. During the family's time of devotions two nights past, her father had read the story of David and Goliath.

Jane loved watching the family together. The Jewetts epitomized the dream she'd had for many years. Some parents seemed reluctant to love their children, as many died early in life. But in spite of having lost two babies and feeling the cruel pain of grief, Samuel and Elizabeth Jewett never stinted their youngsters of affection.

When she was younger, Jane had longed for a loving family of her own. But her unfortunate marriage in Quebec had failed to bring her anything resembling the happiness she saw here.

Jane knew she couldn't stay here at the parsonage forever. The little house was growing more and more crowded. The nameless infant made ten in all. Jane and Christine shared the small loft with the three Jewett girls, while the parents and the two boys slept in the main room. Although Goody Jewett needed their help for now, Jane couldn't help feeling the parson's family would be better off if she or Christine left. Since neither of them wished to marry, Jane often thought one of them should hire out to another household.

After supper, the pastor stood and came to the hearth. "Let me pour that hot water into the dishpan for you."

"I can do it, sir."

"Nay, let me."

She stood back and watched him deftly swing the crane, bringing the simmering kettle of water off the fire.

"It's difficult to get a private word in this house, but I should like such with you," the pastor murmured.

Jane stared at him in surprise. "Indeed, sir?"

"Aye." He glanced about at the others. Christine was stacking the dishes at the table, and the other children had once more gathered about their mother. "A man approached me at the meetinghouse this afternoon as I was practicing my sermon. He mentioned your name."

"Mine?"

"Yours, Miss Miller. He asked if my wife and I would accept callers on your behalf. I told him that would be your decision."

Jane inhaled, feeling a sharp anxiety pricking at her lungs. "Well, sir, I. . ."

"You needn't see him if you don't wish to."

"Thank you." She knotted her apron between her restless hands. "Rather than marrying, I've thought of trying to find a place where I could work, though I have no wish to leave here in a hurry. Especially if your wife has need of me."

"Elizabeth is delighted to have your help and Christine's at this time," he assured her.

"Might I know who be asking, sir?"

He nodded. "It's Lemuel Given."

Jane frowned. "I cannot picture him."

"He's a widower. Lives on Dover Point."

"A sailor, then?"

"A fisherman," Pastor Jewett said. "He has five children. I expect he needs someone to take charge while he's at sea."

A rush of panic caused her stomach to lurch. She would be thrown into a strange family and expected to bring order while the head of the household was away. She recalled the long months in Canada while her husband went off to trade and the many trials she had endured alone. Was she ready to keep house for another man who was absent much of the time? Could she welcome him home at intervals and pretend gladness to see a man she hardly knew? What if he was cruel and she couldn't like him? What if the children were spoiled and rebellious? What if he despised her and treated her like a servant?

She looked up into the pastor's gentle face. "He's not looking for temporary help, is he?"

"Nay, Jane. He wants a wife."

"Ah." She sighed. "I do not wish to marry at this time, but if you think it expedient. . ."

"Far from it." He smiled. "You are welcome here for as long as you wish. You and Christine both. My wife and I are glad you consider this your home."

"Thank you," she whispered. "Then I shall decline."

She turned away and began to scrub the dishes. Could she really stay in this cramped, noisy cottage much longer? The parson seemed sincere in telling her that she could remain without arousing resentment. Did she still hope for a home of her own? She'd had that and found no joy in it. But was that home really hers? She'd worked from morning to night for Monsieur Robataille, and after his death she'd been forced to give up the farm.

No, that wasn't the dream she'd cherished as a girl. Even though she'd been wrenched from her own family and thrust into servitude at the age of eleven, and then captured by savages a few years later, she'd always assumed that one day she would marry a man of her choosing. A young man, her age or close to it. One she admired and perhaps even loved. They would work together and form a family and a homestead they could be proud of.

Jane realized that she had never given up that dream.

◆

After the sermon on Sunday, Charles waited at the back of the meetinghouse for Richard and Sarah to come down the aisle. In summer he'd have waited outside, but the temperatures, though somewhat moderated from the previous week, were still uncomfortable if one stood about for long in the open.

Sarah paused to talk to the Jewett children and Jane Miller. Charles assumed Christine Hardin had stayed at the parsonage with Goody Jewett and the new babe. Jane's face was more animated than usual as she and the children talked to Sarah. Even across the room, he could tell by their facial expressions and gestures that they were describing the baby. Richard moved on toward him, leaving his wife with her friends.

Jane seemed to be measuring the infant's length with her slender, delicate hands, and Sarah's smile brought an answering glint to Jane's eyes.

She's beautiful! Charles forced himself to look away lest anyone else witness his fascination.

"I believe you're smitten," Richard said at his side.

Too late. In spite of the chilly room, Charles felt heat flush his face beneath the cover of his beard.

"And I believe you're impertinent." He turned to face Richard squarely. "All right, I agree with what you said the other day. She would make a good wife. Do we have to talk about this here?" Charles glanced around to see if anyone else had heard his comment.

Richard leaned toward him and lowered his voice. "You'd best act soon if you intend to. I heard Lemuel Given telling Obed Bates earlier that he asked permission of the parson to call on Miss Miller."

Charles's heart sank. "Oh? What came of it? Are the banns to be read soon?"

"Nay." Richard chuckled. "Apparently he approached the reverend several days ago but only received his reply last evening. It was not to Given's liking."

Charles smiled. "The parson told him to stay away from her?"

"Given says the reverend told him she's not ready to remarry. But I also heard a whisper from another saying Miss Miller begged the Jewetts not to make her receive Given's addresses. She thinks him old and overly blessed with brats."

"She didn't say that!" Charles stared at him in dismay.

"I doubt she did, but you know the gossips in this town. They'll take what one man tells and twist it into something totally foreign. But I heard Given himself say that she thinks she's too good for an English farmer, now that she's been once wedded to a Frenchman."

Charles frowned at him in confusion. "Why would anyone consider marrying an Englishman a step downward?"

"Well, if the Englishman were Lemuel Given. . ." Richard's crooked smile brought Charles around to seeing the humorous side of the tale.

"Right." Charles looked over at the Jewett family again.

Sarah was still talking to Jane and had twined six-year-old Abby's hand in hers. Jane held the toddler, Ruth, and Constance clutched a fold of Jane's skirt, watching with large, round eyes as the two young women talked.

"Does Sarah miss living in the Jewetts' household?"

"Some," Richard said. "But she's going round to see the new babe and visit Goody Jewett tomorrow if the weather holds. She tells me the parsonage is a haven of blissful confusion, and she loves the family as if they were her own kin. But she prefers our quiet little nest now."

Charles smiled at his tall, rugged friend. He never would have believed Richard could become so besotted. "Your wife has made you mellow."

"You can be as contented." Richard gave him a meaningful grin. "Strike now, before some other hot-blooded young fellow asks for permission to court her."

"I thought you said she isn't ready to remarry."

"Not I." Richard nodded a return greeting to a couple filing toward the door of the meetinghouse. "The parson said that. Or rather, Given said that the parson said it. But he's twice her age and gone to sea fishing half the time. What's to become of her if she marries a man like that?"

"With all the youngsters at his house, she would probably become a drudge."

Richard nodded. "I suspect that when a charming young man with a good farm and no encumbrances comes around, Miss Miller will find that she is ready."

Charles didn't like to think Jane bided her time for an advantageous situation to come her way. Didn't character count. . .and feelings? Was love totally out of the question? On the other hand, why shouldn't a woman expect her husband to take care of her?

He looked toward the front of the room once more. The little group was breaking up. Jane was tying Ruth's bonnet under the little girl's chin, and Sarah hurried down the aisle toward Richard.

Richard leaned toward him and whispered a parting thought. "She's not skinny any longer, Charles. She's healthy and strong. Strike now."

◆

A few days later, the sun shone brightly on the settlement. Charles and Richard had finished putting up their firewood, and Charles walked to the village.

He found the Reverend Jewett huddled on one of the benches near a window in the bitterly cold meetinghouse.

"You're likely to freeze in here, sir."

The parson looked up from his open Bible. "Good day, Charles. I brought a warm soapstone with me"—he nudged a cloth-wrapped bundle with his stockinged foot—"but it seems to have lost its heat now."

"We ought to have built a hearth in here."

"Nay, folks bring their soapstones and rugs and warming pans of a Sunday. 'Twould take a prodigious amount of wood to heat this building."

Charles considered that and nodded. "In a way, sir, that's what I've come about. I wondered if you've plenty of wood for your house."

The parson cleared his throat and looked up at him. "Thank you for asking. We've enough for this winter, I suppose, if the weather doesn't turn icy again. I plan to cut some for next year soon. We've had so much going on at the house, with the new addition and all. . ."

"Yes, a fine little fellow, I hear."

"Well, he's not as sturdy as Ben and John were. Smallish child."

Charles nodded, wondering what constituted a smallish baby. "Well, sir, I'd enjoy helping you cut your firewood, if you'd like the company."

"Why, Charles, that's most good of you. Are you free later this week?" Jewett fumbled about with his feet until he found his shoes.

"Yes, sir."

The reverend closed his Bible, pulled the shoes on, and stood. "I should have this week's sermon ready by Friday. I could perhaps go into the woods with you that day, if the weather holds."

"That would be fine, sir."

"Will you take dinner with us now?" The parson picked up his soapstone bundle and moved toward the door, and Charles walked with him. "I come over here to study, even though it's cold. At home, with the children cooped up, there are just too many distractions. You understand."

Charles nodded. "I can well imagine."

"Yes, well, children underfoot and young ladies at work. Don't mistake my meaning—they are a big help, Miss Hardin and Miss Miller. But when you put six children and three women in a small house, and the baby cries and the loom thumps and the boys start their horseplay—"

"That reminds me, sir." Charles grabbed the topic quickly before it could get away. "You mentioned the young ladies in your household."

The reverend paused with his hand on the door latch. "Yes?"

"I. . .well. . ." Charles couldn't hold his gaze. He pulled in a deep breath and rushed on. "I wondered if perhaps Miss Jane Miller would. . .would take callers of an evening, sir. If you think I'm not too bold."

The pastor ran his fingers through his beard and scratched his chin. "I don't know, Charles. I had another inquiry last week, and she told me she'd rather not. But he was an older man, in a different situation than yours. I can ask her if you'd like me to."

Charles gulped, and it felt as though he'd swallowed a brick. "If you wouldn't mind, sir."

Jewett eyed him thoughtfully. "She's made it clear to both my wife and me that she prefers the single state for now. You know she had a bad experience in Canada?"

"Aye, sir. That is, I know she was married briefly, and her husband met an untimely end."

"Yes. And I understand he was much older than she. Perhaps that accounts for her aversion to. . .the gentleman I mentioned. Well, I'll put a word in for you. We'd like to see Miss Miller well settled, with a steady man."

Charles's chest expanded. The pastor thought him steady. That was more than most of the villagers would give him. "You can tell me Friday what she says, sir, when we go to cut wood."

Jewett tucked his burdens under his arms and pulled on knit woolen mittens. "Oh, why don't you just come by this evening? If she is against it, she can tell you."

Charles hesitated. He hated the idea of receiving a lady's rebuff in person. "I suppose I could."

"All right, do that. Now come have some dinner. I'm sure eleven won't matter more than ten for the stewpot."

"Oh, thank you, sir, but I need to stop at the trader's and then get on home. But I'll stop by this evening."

They stepped out into the dazzling January sun reflected from the snow. Charles waved and hurried across the packed snow of the village street. He was hungry, but he couldn't bear the thought of sitting at table with her, knowing the pastor knew his heart but Jane did not. He'd blush and stammer like a girl.

But even if he declined the dinner invitation, there was no getting out of the pickle he'd put himself in now. Jane would decide his future. Either she would say no and he would continue in his sorry plight, single and independent, a bit lonesome, but also too embarrassed to meet her gaze ever again across the village green, or—dare he think it?—she might say yes, and his life would never be the same.

Chapter 3

Jane stepped over Ruthie Jewett and carefully carried a cup of milk and a slice of rye bread to the toddler's mother, who was sitting in her chair. It was Elizabeth Jewett's favorite spot in the house—the only chair with a back. Her husband had labored many hours over it for her.

"What's this? Another supper?" Goody Jewett held up a hand in protest.

Jane smiled. "You need something extra to build your blood up, Goody Baldwin told me."

Christine paused in her sweeping of the hearth. "Aye. She said to feed you six times a day so you will regain your strength."

Elizabeth reached for the pewter cup. "You girls will spoil me, to be sure. Why, after Ben was born, I was up and doing all my kitchen work the next day."

"That were then, and this be now," Jane said firmly. "Drink all of that."

Goody Jewett meekly put the cup to her lips. A thin wail sounded from the low bed, and she stopped without drinking, looking toward the corner.

"You eat this morsel. I'll get the baby." Jane put the slice of bread in Elizabeth's hand and turned to pick up the infant. As she'd suspected, his clouts and gown were soaked. She took the small quilt he'd lain on, as well, and carried him over to the bench nearer the hearth, where they often changed him. The far reaches of the room were always cold, and she didn't want to chill the babe.

The little girls clustered around her. John and Ben stayed on their pallet on the other side of the room, where they were playing with a half dozen tiny wooden men their father had carved for them. The pastor was out calling on the sick, but a kettle of water steamed on the hearth so that he could have a cup of hot, brewed wintergreen leaves when he came home.

"Abby, would you fetch your brother a fresh gown?" Jane asked. Abigail scurried to the shelves near the bed to get one.

"There's a good girl," her mother said with a smile.

"I'm glad you named him Joseph," Jane told Goody Jewett as she untied the knot that held the baby's layered clouts together.

"I like it," she replied. Christine continued sweeping, but her lips turned upward, and Goody Jewett asked, "What are you smiling at, Christine?"

Jane and the Jewett girls looked up with interest. Christine never intruded in a conversation, preferring silence, but Jane was sure she had plenty of thoughts whirling about in her head.

"I only thought how much better it is than Hezekiah, as the parson thought to name him," Christine said, dipping her head and digging into the corner by the woodbox with her broom.

"Oh, Hezekiah," Elizabeth laughed. "I would have none of that. I don't think my husband was truly set on it, but suggested it to startle us ladies."

Christine stood the broom in the corner and untied her apron. "Come now, Constance, Abby. You, too, Ruth. It's time for you to get to bed. Gather up your things." She herded the three girls up the ladder to the loft. Ruth had lately been judged old enough to sleep up there, after the parson and Ben constructed a low railing across the front edge of the platform above the main room.

Jane deftly wrapped a small blanket about the baby and placed him in his mother's open arms. "Now, Ben and John, you strong boys must help me bring in enough firewood for the night."

"The boys can do it," Elizabeth said.

"Nay, 'twill be sooner done if I help," Jane replied. She knew the boys would stay at their task better if an adult joined them. John found it all too easy to leave off his chores and begin building a snow fort.

She took her woolen cloak from its peg and threw it over her shoulders and then wrapped a shawl about her head. As she donned her mittens, she noted with satisfaction that the boys were putting on their coats and hats. They were good boys and usually obeyed her and Christine now as readily as they did their mother.

The three of them went out into the glittering dooryard. The three-quarter moon reflected in sparkles off the snow in eerie beauty.

"Three good armloads each will do it," Jane said. "Load me up, Ben."

She stood by the woodpile with her arms outstretched, and Ben stacked five medium sticks across them. John stepped up and imitated her posture, and Ben loaded him, too; then he began to choose his own burden.

Jane turned toward the doorstone, but the crunch of boots on the snow made her look toward the street. She expected to see the parson arriving home, but instead Charles Gardner's tall frame loomed in the moonlight.

"Good evening, sir," she said.

Charles stopped and stood for a moment uncertainly then glanced toward the door. "The parson said I might come calling."

"He's not home this eve. Goody Branwell be ill, and he also planned to visit Mr. Otis and check on his injury."

"Yes, I heard Mr. Otis cut his leg badly. But I didn't really come to see the reverend." Charles glanced toward the small window covered with oiled paper. A faint glow spoke of the warmth within, the candlelight and a fire on the hearth, the children's laughter, and the closeness of a large family. "He told me he would ask a certain young lady within his house if she would receive me as a caller."

His words startled Jane. Charles looked decidedly uncomfortable, shifting from one foot to another. A certain young lady? The only young lady within the house right now was Christine.

"Be you coming to call on Miss Christine?" Ben asked, joining them with his arms full of firewood.

Charles opened his mouth and darted a look toward Jane as though asking for help. Of course. He was embarrassed and needed some assistance.

"I'll tell her you're here." Jane spun to open the door. A pang of disappointment struck her, but that was silly. A young man actually had his eye on Christine. How wonderful for her friend. Of course, Christine wouldn't think it was wonderful. She always tried to stay as far away from men as she could.

Jane managed to raise the latch without spilling her load. She dropped her wood into the box by the hearth, noticing that Christine had not come down from the loft. Jane heard her low voice as she spoke to the three little girls she was tucking in for the night.

She went to the ladder and scrambled up it. Below her, John and Ben came in with their firewood. Charles entered behind them, closing the door firmly to shut out the cold night air.

"Good evening," Jane heard him say.

"Good evening to you, sir," Goody Jewett replied.

At the top of the ladder, Jane hesitated. Christine was kneeling on the edge of the pallet shared by Abby and Ruth, listening to Abby's bedtime prayer.

"And help Mr. Otis's leg to get better, please. Amen," the little girl said.

"Christine," Jane hissed.

Christine looked around at her, with inquiry widening her hazel eyes. Her mousy brown hair was held back with a dark ribbon, but after a long day's work, wisps escaped and hung haphazardly about her face. Jane wished her friend would take more notice of her appearance. Now, of all times, she wished Christine were beautiful. But Charles must have looked beyond the tall young woman's plain features and lackluster hair and seen Christine's inner beauty.

Below her, Jane heard the boys dump their loads of firewood, and the door opened and closed as they went out for more.

"There's a young man here to see you."

"What?" Christine's eyes opened even wider.

"Charles Gardner is down below. He wants to see you. Did the pastor tell you he was coming?"

"Nay." Christine edged forward on her knees, just far enough to see down into the great room below. She caught her breath and sprang back into the shadows. "Make him go away."

Jane couldn't help smiling. She leaned forward and touched Christine's arm. "Surely wishing him a good evening would not be amiss."

"I can't. Please don't make me go down there." Christine's distaste seemed to border on fear as she shrank back beneath the eaves of the cottage. "Please, Jane. Tell him whatever you will, but I can't do it. You know I don't wish to marry. Ever."

"All right. I'm sorry I distressed you. But if you are certain—"

"I am."

Jane nodded slowly. "I'll tell him."

"Tell him graciously. I'm sure he's a nice young man. It's not him so much. It's just. . ." Christine bit her lip and looked away.

Jane noticed that Abby was watching them, bright-eyed, though the two younger girls had already drifted into sleep.

"You'll make him understand, won't you?" Christine pleaded.

"I shall do my best." Jane backed down the ladder, her knees trembling. What a dilemma she was in. From what Charles had let fall, she assumed the minister had agreed to speak to Christine, as he had to Jane when Lemuel Given approached him. But Christine had obviously heard nothing about a potential suitor.

Perhaps Goody Jewett knew something of the circumstances. Her hostess was conversing easily with Charles Gardner, who was now seated on a bench near her. Jane couldn't help but notice his pleasant features, neatly trimmed beard, and glossy dark hair. It was too bad Christine wouldn't give him a hearing.

Ben and John brought in more wood, and Ben joined Charles and his mother. "Sir, could you show me sometime how to set a fox trap? Father found a den at the end of our garden last fall, and we see them now and again. I want to catch them."

Jane sidled up to Goody Jewett, who held the new baby in her arms. "Would you like me to lay Joseph on the bed?"

"Nay, we're fine. Sit down by the hearth with Goodman Gardner."

"I?" Jane stared at her.

"He's come to call on you, not on Ben and me."

Jane turned just enough to see whether Charles was still talking to Ben. He threw a glance her way and stood when their gaze met. She leaned closer to Elizabeth and whispered, "I beg your pardon, ma'am. I thought he came to call on Christine."

Elizabeth stared back for a moment then glanced at Charles with a brief smile. "Won't you be seated again, Goodman Gardner?" To Jane she whispered,

"Did not my husband tell you?"

Jane felt a large lump rise in her throat. "Nay."

Elizabeth's smile seemed frozen on her face. After a long moment, she gave a nervous laugh. "Well, this is awkward. Goodman Gardner, please excuse our confusion. My husband told me of your conversation with him, but it seems neither of us mentioned it to Miss Miller. And she seems to suffer the illusion that you are calling on our other guest, Miss Hardin."

"Forgive me," Charles said, turning his hat about in his hands. "I failed to make my meaning clear outside, and I feared there was a misunderstanding. I hope no one is discomfited." His gaze swept the edge of the loft for an instant.

There was no sign of Christine above them, but Jane thought how relieved she must be, if she was listening. And how did she feel herself? She felt the blood rush to her cheeks.

Charles himself looked very uncomfortable. He gave a little shrug and attempted a smile that was only partly successful. "The reverend did tell me to just stop in tonight. Perhaps he thought we needed no intermediary. He said you would tell me if you objected to my presence."

He waited, and Jane could not quite meet his gaze.

"My dear, why don't you make some wintergreen tea for our guest?" Elizabeth asked. She turned to her boys. "John, you must get to bed. Ben, if you wish to read from Mr. Bunyan's book for a while, you may, but you must take the candle over near your bed."

The boys said good night to Charles.

Jane seized Elizabeth's suggestion and took the steaming kettle from the fire. She poured its contents into the teapot that she had earlier set out in preparation for the parson's refreshment then started toward the door with the empty kettle.

"May I help you?" Charles was suddenly beside her, and she jumped.

"I was only going to get more snow to melt for the pastor's tea when he returns."

"Allow me to fetch it."

Charles took the kettle from her hand and went out the door.

Jane turned at once to Elizabeth. "Goody Jewett, what am I to do?"

Elizabeth eyed her with some surprise. "Whatever do you mean, child? Be a courteous hostess."

"But I told your husband only days ago that I did not wish to receive gentlemen callers."

"Oh." The baby fussed, and Elizabeth lifted him to rest against her shoulder. "Does that apply to Charles Gardner, as well?"

"I. . ." The panic eased somewhat as Jane met Elizabeth's steady gaze.

"He's a nice young man and a diligent worker. Why not make him welcome and converse with him?" Elizabeth patted little Joseph's back, but he began to wail softly in spite of her attention. "It would only be fair to get acquainted with him a bit before you decide whether you wish to know him better."

"But if I let him stay and then decide to turn him away, it will be awful for him. And people will talk."

"People in this village will talk anyway," Elizabeth agreed. "Here, help me move my chair yonder so I can feed this babe."

The door opened as Jane helped her settle in at the other end of the room with the baby. Charles brought in the kettle full of snow and hung it over the coals.

"Shall I build up your fire, ma'am?" he asked.

"Yes, thank you," Elizabeth said. "It's getting chilly in here."

He worked at the hearth for a minute with his back to them.

Jane wondered if he was as embarrassed as she felt. She went to the cupboard and took down two pewter mugs. "Would you like tea, ma'am?" she asked Elizabeth.

"No, thank you. I'll wait until my husband returns and have a cup with him."

Charles stood and brushed the bark off his hands. "Shall I bring in more firewood? Or if you've buckets, I could get you water so you wouldn't have to haul it in the morning."

"We've ample now," Jane said.

Charles hesitated, looking from her to Goody Jewett across the room and back. "I. . .don't need to stay if you'd rather I didn't, Miss Miller."

She felt her color deepen. "Nay, it was kind of you to call, sir. Won't you be seated?" She carried the cups over, and they both sat stiffly on the bench holding their tea and staring into the fire.

Charles cleared his throat. "Captain Baldwin said last spring that you dwelt at Dover Point before. . .before you were taken by the Pennacook."

"Aye," Jane said, grateful the silence was broken.

"Were your people killed in the massacre? I thought most of the destruction was here at Cochecho."

She nodded. "My parents died nearly twelve years ago. I was destitute, and though I was young, my uncle indentured me to a family needing domestic help."

Charles nodded, obviously wanting her to go on.

"My master had come to Cochecho to do business with Major Waldron." Jane caught her breath as the memories of that awful night returned. It was only by chance that she and the couple for whom she worked were at the major's garrison when the massacre occurred. Her hand shook so that she thought she might spill her hot tea. She steadied the cup with her other hand and raised it carefully to her lips, taking just a tiny sip of the scalding liquid.

"It was a dreadful night," Charles said.

"Yes," she whispered.

"What were your duties for your employer?"

Jane sighed. "I served the lady and worked in the kitchen. They had another girl, Betty, working for them, as well, and she tended the children. But toward the last, when I was older, sometimes I watched them, too. When the master decided to bring his wife here with him to see the major, they left the young ones home with Betty. It was only to be a three-day journey, and they brought me to wait on the mistress. By chance, they arrived here the night the savages struck."

Elizabeth Jewett stirred. "You never told me that, my dear. I knew you were orphaned, but not that you were bound."

"My term of indenture was nearly over."

"How long was it?"

"Seven years. I had only one year left."

"That's a long time to serve another person," Charles said.

"Aye." Jane stood and walked across the cabin. It had seemed forever when she was told, at the age of eleven, that for seven years she belonged to Mr. Plaisted. She did not wish to recall those bleak and lonely years. "Is Joseph sleeping again?"

"Yes," said Elizabeth. "I think he'll rest now. If you'll just lay him down and put the coverlet over him. . ."

A stamping and bustle outside the door warned them of the pastor's return.

With the baby in her arms, Jane quickly flipped the edge of the blanket over Joseph's head to keep him from being chilled by the blast of cold air that entered with his father.

The moment he saw Charles, the Reverend Jewett burst out with a hearty greeting. "Well, Charles! I forgot you were coming. Welcome. I trust my wife and Miss Miller have made you comfortable."

"Hush, sir," Elizabeth warned him gently, a finger to her lips.

The baby wriggled, but Jane rocked him gently and held him close until he settled down again. His warm little body nestled against her, and she gazed down at the pink face, so sweet in repose.

Pastor Jewett hung up his wraps and went to sit with Charles. He launched into an account of his ailing parishioners' conditions.

Jane laid the baby on the bed after a few minutes and fixed tea for the pastor and his wife. Ben had blown out his candle and settled down next to John to sleep, and the four adults conversed in low tones for another half hour.

After the two men had confirmed their plan to cut wood together on Friday, Charles rose.

"Must you leave so soon?" the pastor asked.

"Aye, sir. It's late, and I must run my trapline early."

Jane sprang up and brought the coat Charles had earlier hung near the door.

"Come back again any evening," his host said. "I am usually at home, unless some ill folk need me."

"I should like to." Charles glanced at Jane and raised his eyebrows in question.

She realized he was asking her permission to call again. She was still a bit annoyed that the pastor had arranged this evening without consulting her. Still, it hadn't turned out so badly. She swallowed hard and managed to get out, "Please do, sir."

Elizabeth smiled in approval, and Charles gave her a nod that Jane construed as favorable.

A moment later he was gone, and Jane hurried about, putting away the tea tin and rinsing out the mugs.

"Mr. Jewett, I must tell you that you've been remiss," Elizabeth said to her husband.

He eyed her archly. "In what way, my dear?"

"You failed to tell Jane that young Goodman Gardner planned to call, and it set her all aflutter."

"Dear me, was I supposed to tell her? Forgive me, ladies. I trust his company was not too excruciating?"

Jane flushed, recalling her mistake. "I thought—"

Elizabeth laughed. "Jane is just fine, but I'm afraid poor Christine was a bit frightened."

"How so?" the parson asked.

"Why, Jane told her Charles Gardner was here to call on her, and Christine would have none of it."

Jane faced the couple squarely and straightened her shoulders. "It was all my fault, sir. I mistook his meaning when he told me and Ben he'd come to call on a certain young lady in the house. We were outside, you see, and Christine was the only eligible young lady within at the moment. I'm afraid I rather botched things."

Elizabeth chuckled. "I'll talk to Christine on the morrow. She must be quite pleased that he came to see you, not her, Jane."

The reverend nodded. "It did my heart good to see you treating him well. Charles is a steady lad. I do hope I didn't cause you any distress by telling him he might call and ask your opinion of the matter. My intention was only to let you make your own decision."

"Perhaps it was for the best, sir," Jane said, not quite looking at him. "Though she didn't wish to say so, she had found Charles Gardner's company to be tolerable. Of course, that didn't mean she was ready to get married again.

"Ah, yes," said the pastor. "If I'd forewarned you, you might have turned him away without a chance to learn his charms."

"Now, Samuel," Elizabeth scolded. "See how red Jane's cheeks are. You mustn't tease her so."

Jane was tempted to rebuke the parson herself but thought better of it. His wife handled the job creditably on her own.

She headed for the ladder and nodded to them both. "Good night, ma'am, sir."

Chapter 4

After a week of warm weather in mid-January, the snow shrank and patches of dry grass were laid bare on the village green. Jane packed her mending in a basket one clear day and persuaded Ben Jewett to accompany her in walking the mile to Richard and Sarah Dudley's new home.

Richard's house squatted beside the trail within shouting distance of his father's stockaded home, with only one cornfield between it and the forest. Jane still felt the ominous gloom of the vast woodland whenever she ventured out of the village. Strong memories of the massacre still assailed her. The weeks she had spent on the arduous trail north with the Pennacook Indians remained vivid in her mind. She and Ben quickened their steps without speaking of the past.

"I'm so glad you came!" Sarah took Jane's cloak and shawl and hung them on a peg as Ben hurried back toward home. "Tell me all that is going on at the parsonage. Is the baby well? Is Goody Jewett regaining her strength?"

"Yes, both are gaining." Jane looked around at the neat little room and inhaled the spicy scent of baking and dried fruit. Richard had built the cabin with a kitchen and a larger sitting room below and two rooms above, one on each side of the central chimney. "You have a fine home."

"Thank you. All the men of the village helped raise it for us, you know. Richard's father and Charles Gardner came every day for weeks to do the finish work. Sit here near the fire, Jane, and I'll fix us a biscuit and a cup of sweet cider."

Jane sat down on the settle and unpacked her mending, which consisted largely of the Jewett children's socks with holes worn in the toes and heels. "I brought extra darning floss in case you needed some."

"Oh, thank you. I do go through a prodigious amount, keeping Richard's socks in repair." Sarah fixed their refreshment and brought it over. She set the cups and a plate with two buttered biscuits on a stool within easy reach.

"You've butter in January. Hasn't your cow gone dry?" Jane felt hungry just seeing the fluffy white biscuits split and spread with yellow butter.

"Goody Dudley packed away several crocks last summer and fall in her springhouse. I don't expect it will last both households all winter, but we're enjoying it."

Jane accepted her offer of the plate and chose half a biscuit. She wasted no time sinking her teeth into it. "Mmm. I don't believe the Jewetts have had butter since before you left us."

"Well, you shall take some home with you." Sarah brought over a basket of raw wool and her wool cards and sat down near Jane. "I shall sit with you a few minutes before I begin to get dinner."

"I shall help you when the time comes," Jane assured her.

Sarah laughed. "It's nothing to get dinner for you, Richard, and myself after cooking at the Jewetts' for months."

"Never quite enough for all those hungry children," Jane agreed.

"And before that, in the Indian village, we never had much to work with. Corn, beans, squash, venison, fish. Times of plenty at harvest or when a hunting party returned, but mostly short rations for all, especially in winter." Sarah shook her head and looked about.

Jane noticed the strings of dried apples and slabs of pumpkin hanging from the rafters with bunches of onions and herbs. Several crocks and casks of meal, flour, molasses, and pickled meat and vegetables, along with sacks of salt and sugar, filled the shelves or stood about the edge of the kitchen floor.

Sarah continued, "We are blessed with abundance here. What I could not provide myself this fall, Mother Dudley gave me—cheese, bacon, preserves. Richard and I live very well. I'm afraid I'll soon be fat."

Jane laughed. "You look contented, indeed. I'm happy that you are so well fixed. But I know you didn't marry him for his pantry."

"That's true. And I've been trying to fatten his brother and Charles Gardner. Those two young men are still far too thin. Of course, Charles has not come round much of late."

Jane realized Sarah was watching her closely, and she studiously tended to her darning weave on one of John Jewett's stockings.

But Sarah was not about to drop the subject. "Charles tells Richard he's been spending two evenings a week at the parsonage."

"Indeed." Jane reached the end of her thread, knotted it, and snipped it carefully off. "It is true."

"Richard is of the opinion that he will marry soon."

Jane felt her cheeks flush. "Is he?"

"Of course we should love to see him settled," Sarah went on. "He's such a dear friend to Richard. And having you as a neighbor would be— Oh, Jane, I'm delighted for you both."

"Don't be premature, Sarah. He's only come and sat by the fireside for three evenings to date. That does not make a marriage."

"I expect all the village folk think it will, though."

Jane smiled. "Well, I admit I like him better than I thought I would."

"Charles is a good man," Sarah said.

"I'm sure of it. It's just. . .I wasn't thinking of marrying again. Not yet, anyway. But now it seems I will have to make a decision."

Sarah eyed her soberly. "You and Charles have many things in common. You've both lost your own families, and you were both taken by the Indians during the massacre."

"Yes, though when we were abducted, we were put in separate bands. I don't remember meeting Charles until he and Captain Baldwin redeemed me from the French. But we both made that grim journey, it's true, and we've both experienced shunning when we returned, as did you." Jane couldn't keep a tinge of bitterness from her voice.

Sarah reached over and squeezed her hand. "So many people have been in captivity and lived in Canada that I believe the villagers here are getting used to it. Everyone has treated me well these past few months."

"But you have Richard."

"Yes, that's so. And I know folks are still suspicious of his brother, because Stephen voluntarily stayed with the Algonquin when he could have come home. But Charles has been back several years, and I think most people like him. He's clever and diligent. He would make you a good husband." Sarah placed a clump of wool between her cards and scraped the two paddles across each other, untangling the fibers.

"I suppose Charles and I do understand one another better than some," Jane conceded.

"Is it the thought of marriage in general that distresses you?" Sarah asked. "I don't mean to probe, but I have wondered. I've thought sometimes you weren't happy as Madame Robataille."

"I wasn't. But I had no choice. Jacques Robataille arranged it somehow with the French authorities before I even met him. I was staying for a time with a family in Quebec. For four months, I scrubbed their floors and washed their clothes. It was hard work, but no harder than what I'd done while indentured. Then one day, I was told to gather my things, for a voyageur had come for me and I was to be married that day."

"How horrible."

"Yes." Jane laid her sewing down in her lap. "He took me to his farm, and three days later he left me there alone for two months while he went on a trading voyage. I was terrified, but I didn't dare leave. He'd told me to tend the fields and livestock until he returned. If I didn't, he said he would beat me. I believed him. After all, he'd beaten me our first night together." She stared into the coals in the fireplace before them and clamped her lips together.

"Oh, Jane, I'm so sorry."

Jane's eyes burned. Hot tears spilled over her eyelids and streamed down her cheeks. She dashed at them with the back of her hand. "I shouldn't have said anything. I never have before. . .to anyone."

"Did he ever strike you again?"

"Every time he was home. It was a regular thing. When he wasn't happy, he boxed my ears. When he was drunk, it was worse."

Sarah sniffed. "And to think I considered my lot in the Pennacook village a harsh one. I can see now why the idea of marrying again is distasteful to you. But I'm positive Charles would never treat you so."

Jane inhaled deeply and wiped another tear away with her sleeve. "You are probably right."

"Give it time, dear," Sarah said softly.

Jane managed a shaky smile. "I believe I shall. Who knows what the Almighty may have in store for me? Now what are we going to cook for your husband's dinner?"

———◆———

Two weeks later, Charles waited near the bottom of the meetinghouse steps for Jane to come out.

Ben Jewett had spread ashes on the icy steps that morning so the parishioners wouldn't slip on them, but the sun had been at work during the lengthy sermon and melted most of the ice from the treads.

Waiting for Jane to leave the building after services had become a habit, and she did not seem displeased when she came through the doorway and saw him standing there.

Goody Jewett came first, carrying the new baby. Jane and Christine followed her, herding the older children down the steps.

"Good day," he said to the pastor's wife, offering his hand to guide her down the stairs.

"A good day, indeed, Charles," Elizabeth replied with a broad smile.

"Miss Miller. . .Jane." He lowered his voice. "Might I call on you this evening?"

She stopped for a moment, holding Constance's hand tightly as the little girl tugged toward the street and home.

For an instant Charles feared she would say no. She could end his pursuit of her in a second. She had only to refuse his company, and he would not venture near the parsonage again.

She glanced about then spoke softly. " 'Tis lovely weather today. Perhaps. . . we could walk this afternoon?"

Gladness shot through him. This was progress. Evenings at the parsonage were not unpleasant, but with winter's cold came togetherness most of the time.

The parson had left off studying at the chilly meetinghouse, and the last time Charles ventured to call on Jane, all eight of the Jewetts and Christine Hardin had shared the great room of the cottage for two hours. It was impossible ever to speak a private word to Jane.

It would be nice to have the object of his admiration alone for a few minutes. Even if they stayed within the sight of the critical villagers, they could at least distance themselves from other people enough so that they could converse in private. "I shall come by in two hours' time, if that is agreeable to you."

She nodded but did not smile.

As she let Constance lead her away, he stared after her, regret and anticipation struggling in his heart. He wished she would smile more. Sarah Dudley smiled all the time now. He would have to ask Richard what he had done to put that gleam of happiness on Sarah's face.

Other people had passed him by, and the Reverend Jewett came last down the steps.

"Good day, Charles. Will you take dinner with us?"

"Thank you, sir, but the Dudleys have invited me." Charles fell into step with the pastor. "Sir, may I have a confidential word with you?"

"Of course."

Charles cleared his throat. "I've given it a great deal of thought, and I'd like to offer Miss Miller my hand in marriage, if that meets your approval."

"I have no objection, though we would miss her sorely. She's become a part of our family."

"Aye, sir, I can see that, and it's why I come to you as I would her father. She said she would walk with me this afternoon, and I thought to ask her then."

The pastor eyed him thoughtfully. "Then I shall tell her before you come that she would do well to accept. However, she can refuse you if she wishes. My wife and I do not mind if she wants to remain in our household awhile longer."

"I understand, sir."

"Good. Of course there will be talk—nay, there is already talk—in the village about the two of you. There be those who question your character and hers both, because of your time spent in Canada. Don't listen to gossip, Charles. Miss Miller is a fine young woman."

"Aye, she is diligent. I've seen that."

"And she is true to her faith," the pastor added, "despite what some may think. Her brief marriage to the papist. . .well, that is regrettable. I don't know if she's told you, but she explained to my wife that it was all arranged without her consent. A rather trying time she had, I'm afraid."

"Yes, sir. I understand." Charles left him to walk out to Richard's house for dinner, thinking all the while of what the minister had said. He had considered

Jane's status as a widow, and how that might affect her choice of a new husband. She seemed more independent and less eager to marry than most single women. He hoped his patient suit had overcome that tendency. However, he hadn't for a minute thought her religious past might keep them apart.

True, in Quebec she'd married a man of a different faith, but as the pastor had pointed out, that did not mean she had changed her own beliefs. And Pastor Jewett would never recommend that a man of his flock marry a woman whose faith was at question.

Nay, if she turns me down, it won't be for spiritual concerns. But she might find a hundred other reasons to reject me.

◆

The sunlight sparkled on the snow as Jane and Charles strolled toward the river. Although it was the third of February, Jane's cloak kept her warm in the balmy air. She let her shawl fall off her hair and rest on her shoulders. It was so good to get out in the fresh air after being cooped up through weeks of cold weather.

"I expect we'll get more snow before spring," Charles said.

"Aye," Jane agreed. "Winter's back is not broken yet. But it's nice to have a few warm days."

"I heard that a ship put in at Portsmouth with goods from England. The trader leaves at first light with his sled to go fetch some new stock."

"Ah. The trading post will be overrun when he returns."

Charles pointed ahead of them. "It's been so warm, the river's breaking up."

They had approached the riverbank, and Jane saw that already the ice had given way where the current was strongest, and a slash of dark water showed in the middle of the frozen stream. Likely another cold snap would freeze it again before long.

Charles kicked at the snow and stooped to pick up a stone. He threw it hard, and it flew out onto the ice.

"I'd like to marry you, Jane."

She caught her breath. The parson had forewarned her, but even so her mouth went dry and her heart pounded furiously. "This is rather sudden, Goodman Gardner."

"Forgive me. It does not seem that way to me."

"No?"

"I've thought of it for months."

She walked slowly along the riverbank, where other feet had trampled a path in the snow. Mixed feelings warred in her heart. She liked what she knew of him, but would he make a good husband? And did she want a husband at all? Not if he turned out like Jacques Robataille. She had long ago made that decision. She didn't want a mean man or one who would leave her to cope on her own for months at a time.

But Charles seemed unlike Monsieur Robataille. The first time she had met her Canadian husband—an hour before the wedding, she recalled bitterly—she had feared him, a feeling that never entirely left her until he was buried. She never wanted to be in a situation again where she could not control her own circumstances. Of that she was certain.

Charles was waiting for an answer, walking slowly along beside her and flicking an uncertain glance her way now and then.

"I. . ." She clamped her lips together.

"I admire you greatly, Jane, and I think we would suit."

"Do you?" She hated the way her voice cracked.

"Surely. We are much alike, you and I."

"How so?"

He stopped walking, and she did, too.

He stood looking down at her, a faint smile upon his lips. "We have both felt the stigma of being outcasts of sorts, because of the time we spent in Canada."

"That at least is true," she acknowledged.

He bowed slightly. "You know I was chosen last year to help negotiate for you and the other captives because I knew the language and culture of the savages. It was an advantage to the negotiators. But my skills, if you call them that, are not respected in Cochecho. The upright citizens still perceive me as half wild."

Jane knew he was right, even though many of the town's leading citizens seemed to accept Charles now. The elders had made a concerted effort to integrate him into the community when they granted him the status of freeman and allowed him to retain his father's land.

She looked up into his soft brown eyes. He waited patiently for her response, and she couldn't help feeling drawn to him. She had been skeptical at first, but after spending several hours with him during the past few weeks, she was beginning to know his mannerisms and opinions. She'd found no cause to dislike him. In fact, it seemed that the more time she spent with him, the better she liked him. But did she want to bind herself to him legally for the rest of her life?

She swallowed hard. "I will consider your proposal, Goodman Gardner."

His smile wavered, and he nodded. "Charles, please, or Charlie if you like. Thank you. That is all I ask. Please tell me when you have reached a decision."

As they ambled back toward the village, he unfolded to her his plans for his farm, and Jane listened eagerly. He was trapping furs to earn money for livestock and improvements to his property—property of which she might one day soon be mistress. The idea did not repel her. In fact, when he mentioned the possibility of purchasing foundation stock for a small flock of sheep, she entered into a deep discussion of wool culture.

"And do you spin and weave?" he asked.

"I do, sir. Not so well as Christine does, but I'm a fair hand at it."

"Richard and his father have pledged to help me expand my cabin as soon as the snow is gone. And I hope to add cattle soon. I'm a hard worker, Jane."

"Aye, so I'm told."

When they reached the parsonage, Goody Jewett invited him in for a cup of chocolate, a treat that Goodman Otis had brought them that morning, along with a joint of venison.

An hour passed quickly in lively conversation with the family. Even Christine offered a comment or two.

Jane realized how well Charles fit in with their little circle. She felt almost at ease with him here. But could she be comfortable with him alone in his remote cabin?

She pondered the topic for a fortnight. He came faithfully on Thursday and Sunday. After several more evenings spent with him by the Jewetts' hearth, Jane at last concluded that she knew her own heart.

Chapter 5

"Do you love him?" Sarah asked.

Jane frowned and took a few stitches in the apron she was hemming for Constance Jewett. "That will follow, don't you think?"

"Perhaps. Did it in your first marriage?"

Jane said nothing, for the only true answer would not be to her friend's liking.

Sarah's brow puckered. "I don't wish to see you wed a second time without love."

"How many women love the men they marry?"

"So speaks a woman who has never known true love."

Jane chuckled. "That is true. But I think love is rare. I see it between you and Richard, aye, and between Elizabeth Jewett and the reverend, when it comes down to it. They care deeply for one another. But I can't say that is the norm. Charles says we suit, and we are both diligent. We shall build up his farm together, and he shall strive to keep me in reasonable comfort. I've come to believe he is a decent man and will treat me kindly. That is all I hope for."

Sarah shook her head. "You aspire to so little. But I trust Charlie will teach you very soon how much more there is to marriage."

"I didn't come to hear you lecture me." Jane laid down her sewing and pretended to scowl at her friend.

"Indeed. You came to help me prepare dinner for my husband and his dearest friend and to deliver your answer to your suitor. Come. Let us start the corn bread baking. And I think we might make an apple pudding. Charlie is very fond of it. What say you?"

"I say I shall have to learn all his likes and dislikes." Jane stood and grasped her friend's arm. "Sarah, thank you for inviting me. I shouldn't like to have to accept his proposal under the eye of half a dozen or more chaperones."

Sarah hugged her. "You're most welcome. And I shall look forward with joy to the day you are my close neighbor. Come. Richard and Charlie have been hauling out logs for your new barn all morning, and they'll be here soon."

"*My* barn?"

"Of course. For the cow and sheep Charlie will buy you."

"Oh dear. I don't wish for him to think he must spend all his money to make me happy," Jane said. "It's not my intent to be a burden to him."

"It is a burden he will take on most gleefully."

Two hours later, when their dinner was finished, Charles offered to walk Jane back to the parsonage. She accepted, knowing this was the time they both craved for a private talk about their future.

Richard's detailed description of the projects he helped Charles undertake had sobered Jane. They were doing all this work for her—to make her comfortable should she accept Charles's suit. She couldn't turn him down now. He'd worked too hard to please her. Not that she wanted to reject him. But still, Sarah's prodding bothered her. What if she couldn't love Charles? What if they married and made a good effort, but she never knew that satisfaction Sarah spoke of—the knowledge that she loved her husband second only to God?

As they said their good-byes to Richard and Sarah, Jane couldn't keep back the dark thoughts. They were unworthy thoughts, she was sure. After all, Charles was a good man, and as such, he deserved more. She would give him unswerving loyalty and all the work her strength could give. But was it enough?

They walked along the path, past Richard's parents' stockaded house. The chilly air and low gray clouds told her that a storm was coming.

"I hope you get home safely, before the snow begins," she told him.

"Don't worry. I think it will hold off another hour, and that's plenty of time."

They walked on in silence for several yards.

"Goodman—Charles," she ventured.

"Yes, Jane?" He stopped in the path and drew her around to face him.

"I have considered your offer." She looked deep into his dark eyes, and she thought she saw anxiety that belied his outward calm.

"And?"

"If you. . .if you still feel the same way. . ."

"I do, Jane."

She nodded. "I'm not sure I can be the sort of wife you want. But I'll do my best. I'll work beside you, and—"

He pulled her into his arms, and she gasped as he engulfed her in his embrace. "Thank you. You've made me very happy, and you shan't regret it. Ever. I promise, dear Jane."

He held her for a long moment, and she kept her face turned away from his. She couldn't bear to look into his intent eyes again. He felt more than she did, and it made her feel guilty. Did he want to kiss her now? She hoped not. The thought of his cold lips against hers unnerved her, reminding her of Jacques's unwanted kisses. She shivered.

"It's cold," Charles said. "I'll take you home."

"Thank you."

He drew her hand through his arm and held it in the crook of his elbow. Through his leather mittens and her wool ones, a bit of warmth transferred from his fingers to hers.

"If you'd like, I shall ask the Jewetts to bring you out to my farm next week and look it over. You can tell me if you'd like anything done different before—before we—" He flashed a glance down at her. "When do you wish to be married?"

"At your leisure," she murmured.

"The first of March perhaps? Or is that too soon?"

The date he selected was only a fortnight hence. It startled her to think she would have only two weeks left with the Jewetts to prepare her meager trousseau and settle her mind to being a wife again.

"If you wish it," she managed.

He squeezed her hand. "If you'd rather, I can wait longer, but I'd like to have you settled before planting time. And if you want me to complete the barn or add another room to the cabin first, Richard and I can—"

"No, Charles. March the first is fine."

He smiled radiantly down at her, and she was glad she had answered as she did. A man so transparently happy couldn't be cruel. She'd never seen him angry, but didn't all men show rage at times? Her father had. Mr. Plaisted, her former master, had. Jacques Robataille had. Even the Reverend Jewett's eyes went steely hard the day Sarah told him how a villager had insulted her and Jane, and Richard had knocked the man down for it. There was no doubt in her mind that Charles Gardner had a temper, though she hadn't seen it yet. Still, Charles seemed a pleasant young man who did not anger easily.

Jane realized vaguely that the line between righteous ire and cruelty wasn't entirely clear in her mind. Best to think of other things. "You needn't buy a cow right away," she told him.

"Oh, but we'll want milk and cheese."

"A goat?" She looked up at him, and something stirred inside her when he smiled and patted her hand.

"Nay. We shall have a cow. Captain Baldwin has a fine heifer I've got my eye on. When I sell my furs, there should be plenty for that and the supplies we'll need to get through until harvest."

"And you'll be putting in corn this spring?"

"Aye, and we'll plant you a kitchen garden. You tell me what you want, and I'll trade for the seed."

By the time they reached the village, Charles's enthusiasm spread to Jane. She entered into the planning of her vegetable garden. They spoke of herbs for which she could get seeds from Elizabeth and Sarah and the special variety of beans Goodman Heard had grown last year.

Charles's gentle voice lulled Jane, and she thought it was a voice she could listen to willingly for years to come. Knowing he was happy brought her a measure of happiness, as well, and she barely noticed the tall figure approaching the parsonage from the river path.

"Someone's calling for the parson," Charles noted, nodding toward the Jewetts' front yard.

Only then did Jane focus on the man approaching the little house. In an instant something familiar about the figure struck her, and her steps faltered.

"Jane?" Charles stopped walking and looked down at her anxiously. "What is it?"

"It can't be."

The man raised his fist and pounded on the door of the parsonage. Ben Jewett opened the door, and the man's voice came to them from fifty yards away, through the crisp, clear February air. "I've business with the minister."

Instantly Jane recognized the haughty voice. She felt light-headed and grasped Charles's sleeve.

"I thought he was dead."

"Who?" Charles's faced blanched, and he shot a glance toward the stranger. "Surely that's not. . . No. Not Robataille."

Jane pulled cold air into her lungs. "Nay. Nay, not he. Jacques Robataille is truly dead. I saw him buried. But, Charlie! It's Mr. Plaisted, my old master."

———◆———

Charles stepped in front of Jane, instinctively placing himself between her and the stranger, blocking the man's view of her should he turn around.

The parsonage door was flung wide, but instead of admitting the caller as Charles had expected, the Reverend Jewett stepped outside onto the doorstone and closed the door. His voice was just low enough that Charles couldn't make out what he said, but when the stranger replied, there was no doubt.

"Where is she? Why was I not informed?"

The bits and pieces Jane had told him over the past few weeks came back to Charles's mind with a clarity that chilled him. *"I was indentured. . .seven years. . . I had only a year left to serve."*

He turned, keeping his body in the line of vision between Jane and the men at the parsonage door. "You must keep out of sight until I see what he wants." Her gray eyes were full of fear. Charles grasped her hands and squeezed them. "Goody Deane's cottage is near. Slip in there and visit with the old woman while I go and speak to Parson Jewett and your—" He couldn't bring himself to say *your master,* so he amended his words. "And this man. . . I will see what he wants, and when he's gone, I shall come and get you."

Jane swallowed hard. He thought for a moment she would argue. Instead, she turned swiftly, lifting her skirt a couple of inches, and dashed the few yards to old Goody Deane's door, across the snow-covered street from the parsonage.

Charles watched while she knocked. When the door opened and Jane was safely inside the widow's home, he squared his shoulders and turned toward the pastor's cottage.

He assumed a leisurely pace as he approached the two men. The pastor glanced up when he turned in at the path to the parsonage and nodded but kept on speaking to the stranger.

"I assure you, sir, Miss Miller did not willfully deprive you of her labor. When she came to us, she believed you and your wife were murdered at Waldrons' garrison the same night she was captured. If we'd known otherwise, our town elders would have sent word to you to come and claim her."

The other man shook his head. "I've made no secret of the fact I am alive. Apparently Miss Miller has lived here the better part of a year, when she ought to have been keeping house for me. I call that grounds to extend her indenture. Where is she? I shall take her back with me today, and she can begin serving out the time she owes me."

"Please, sir, be reasonable," Samuel Jewett said. "Miss Miller was only a girl when the massacre occurred, and she was in a strange place. She was carried off to Quebec and kept there five years. When she returned, we offered her sanctuary here, along with others who had no family to claim them. Her parents had died previously, and she had no idea her employer still lived."

"Nor I that she survived. My wife was killed that night, sir. No trace was found of Jane. I supposed the Indians took her, but whether she lived or nay, I neither knew nor, to be frank, cared for some time. My injuries were grave, and I grieved my wife. While the servant girl's fate concerned me, other things claimed my attention—my health, my children, my business."

"Of course, sir."

Charles eased around closer to the pastor so that he could observe the man's face while he talked.

Plaisted took a crumpled pamphlet from his pocket. "And then I read this history of Cochecho captives, and there is the name of my servant. I repeat, Mr. Jewett, where is my property? I expect we are in for some foul weather, and I wish to make it to Dover Point tonight so I can take a ship to my home in Gloucester tomorrow."

Pastor Jewett threw Charles a noncommittal glance before he spoke. "She is not here at the moment, sir. She went earlier today to visit with friends outside the village. If the weather does indeed turn inclement, I would expect her to stay with them overnight."

"What? Where is this house she's at? Tell me at once, and I'll go there and fetch her!"

"Calm yourself, sir." Jewett looked up at the clouds and frowned. "This be not a good night to travel, I fear. You had best go to the ordinary and bespeak a bed there. I can send to the farmhouse and see if Miss Miller plans to return this eve."

A snowflake landed squarely on Plaisted's beaver hat.

"Just tell me where it is," Plaisted said. "If you're not forthcoming, I shall find a constable to intervene in this."

"Please, sir," the parson said. "Miss Miller will do what is right, I'm sure. There's no need for legal action. Let me establish whether she is coming home tonight. I will find you at the tavern and let you know when you may see her tomorrow."

Plaisted eyed him coldly for a moment. "I suppose it would be too late to journey back tonight. I can depend on you to bring me word this evening?"

"You may," said Jewett.

Plaisted nodded. He glanced briefly at Charles but said not a word to him. He turned and walked to the street and off toward the ordinary near the river.

Pastor Jewett gave a deep sigh. "You heard?"

"I did," Charles said.

"And where is Miss Miller? I dared not speak to you whilst the man lingered. Is she safe?"

"Did you not see her duck into Goody Deane's cottage these ten minutes past?"

"Nay. She knows her old master has come seeking her, then?"

"As we came from Richard Dudley's house, she recognized the man who knocked on your door. When she told me who he was, I bid her pay a call on the Widow Deane until I tell her to come forth."

"Well done." Jewett smiled at him. "So what's to be done now, Charles?"

"I intended to step into your house this afternoon and ask whether you might perform a marriage ceremony March the first. But this could change things."

The pastor frowned. "March first. . .nay, that is too soon. I must read the banns two Sundays."

"I would say March the fourth, then, if not for this fellow who wants to steal Jane away from me."

"You did well to keep silent. I wish you all the best, but we must straighten this other matter out." Pastor Jewett glanced toward the house where Jane had taken refuge. "I'm thankful I did not see her, for I was able to truthfully tell the man she was a distance away. Let me speak to Jane and find how she was situated before her sojourn in Canada."

As they walked to Goody Deane's little house together, the pastor said regretfully, "When I penned that pamphlet last fall, I meant it only as a help to the young ladies, so they would become better understood by their neighbors. I never imagined it would bring harm."

"It's not your fault, sir. God knew your intentions." Charles knocked on the widow's door.

Jane opened it, peeking out timidly. "Where is he?" she asked.

"Gone to the ordinary for the night," said Charles.

The pastor stepped up beside him. "Come along home now, Jane, and we'll talk about this."

The widow's quavering voice came from within. "Parson, you can speak here without the distraction of the children. Miss Jane told me what's afoot. You ought to step in and thrash this out."

Jewett smiled at Charles. "Shall we?"

"If Jane doesn't mind, it would be more private, sir. Not that your family would matter, but. . ."

"But it might be easier for Jane if we keep this among us few," Jewett replied.

"Thank you, sir." Jane opened the door wider, and the two men entered. The snow fell thickly now, and they shook off the loose flakes as they passed through the doorway.

Goody Deane bade them sit, and she hobbled to a shelf. "Cider, that's what you need."

Charles glanced about the dim little room, which was nearly bare, and decided that offering cider to three callers would cut deeply into the widow's supplies. But they could not insult her by refusing. He tucked away a plan to bring her a bag of parched corn and some dried apples before the week was out.

"Now, Jane," the pastor said, "you told us recently that you were indentured as a girl. You saw the man who came to my house just now?"

"Aye, sir. That be my old master, Gideon Plaisted."

"You told us he and his wife were killed in the massacre."

Jane's lip trembled. "So I believed, sir. When Captain Baldwin redeemed me in Quebec, he asked if I had any kin. I told him about my parents' deaths and how I was bound to Mr. Plaisted. He recalled that Mr. and Mrs. Plaisted both were slain in the massacre. Indeed, I saw the savages hack at the master as they dragged me away, sir." Tears filled her eyes. "I never imagined he lived and that I owed him my labor. Please, sir, I speak the truth. You have treated me kindly, and I would not deliberately mislead you."

Charles's heart went out to her. He reached over and took her hand. She sniffed and did not pull away, but her gray eyes swam with tears.

Goody Deane set two mugs and a small firkin on the table and, with shaking hands, poured out the cider. They all thanked her and took a sip.

"Mr. Jewett," Charles said, "could we not get the town elders and talk to this man? Surely he must see that it would not be reasonable to ask Jane to go back and work another year for him now."

The pastor shook his head. "I don't think so, Charles. The man does have a legal right to Miss Miller's labor. And if the magistrate believed she intentionally withheld her whereabouts from her master, he might extend her term of indenture."

Jane stared at him, and tears coursed down her cheeks. "Please don't let me go back, sir. He is a cruel man. I was beaten for the smallest things. The girl, Betty, who watched the children, was whipped for letting the little boy run off. The child was found safe, but Betty was hurt so badly she kept her bed for near a month. Then the master took her to court and got the magistrate to add the lost time to her papers."

The pastor stood and paced the room.

The widow had retreated to her hearth, where she sat hunched on a stool, muttering and stabbing at the coals with a poker. "Not right, not right," said Goody Deane.

Charles cradled Jane's hand in both of his. "I shan't let him take you away, dear," he whispered.

Jane caught her breath, and he felt a slight pressure from her fingers. Her touch gave him joy, though he feared he might lose her. Whatever happened, he determined not to let Plaisted take her away with him.

The thought of taking her back to Richard and Sarah's house and asking them to hide her crossed his mind, but immediately he discarded it. The pastor would never agree to deception, and Charles knew he couldn't put forth such a plan to Richard, either. Whatever they did must be done honestly.

"Charles, the storm is like to grow worse," said the pastor. "If you stay any longer, you won't get home tonight."

"I shall not leave the village with this unsettled, sir."

"You've no livestock to tend?"

"Not yet, sir."

Jewett nodded. "You are welcome to sleep at my hearth with my sons."

"Thank you."

"Then let us take Jane home to my wife and seek out another man to go with us and speak to this Gideon Plaisted. The captain, perhaps. His authority might stand us in good stead."

"What shall you say to him?" Jane asked. She clung to Charles's hand, and he was not displeased.

"We shall reason with him," the pastor replied.

"What if he will not change his mind?"

"Fret not. Ask God to guide us, and if this Plaisted refuses to listen to us, the Almighty will put the needful words in my mouth."

Jane raised her chin. "I do not mind working when I should, sir."

"I know you don't," said Jewett.

"But if his wife be dead. . ." She shook her head. "He is a cruel one."

Charles stoked the widow's fire before they left, and the three walked in silence across to the parsonage. The pastor quickly told his wife their errand, and he and Charles left once more, going out again into the fast-falling snow. Dusk had fallen early, and there was no moon, but neither was there much wind. Charles felt that the storm would pass before morning.

They went first to Baldwin's house and asked the captain to accompany them. As they walked, Jewett again told the tale of Jane Miller's indenture and the arrival of her erstwhile master in the village.

"I can scarcely credit it," Baldwin said. "I was sure that man died. Ah, me. Perhaps I be partly at fault. I told the lass when we redeemed her that he had died. I'd no idea it wasn't so."

"He seems to have been gravely injured and took some time to recover," the pastor said. "And he told me when he first introduced himself that he no longer lives at Dover Point. He removed to Gloucester after he recovered from his wounds. Surely if he had not moved, he would have heard of Miss Miller's return last spring."

"Aye." The captain shook his head. "And she wishes not to go with him?"

"Nay, she implies he mistreated her when she was in his employ."

"She wishes to stay on with your family, then?"

Jewett smiled and nodded toward Charles. "In truth, she wishes to stay here and marry this stout young man, but we've not given Plaisted knowledge of that fact."

Baldwin grinned. "So! Going to settle down, are you, Charlie? We'll have to see that the bride stays in New Hampshire colony, then." He clapped Charles on the shoulder. "Don't worry, lad. I shan't let him talk round me. Your sweetheart has endured enough."

At last they came into the ordinary. Plaisted sat near the fireside in the public room, and Jewett made straight for him.

Plaisted stood. "Well, Reverend, what say you? Will Miss Miller be ready to travel with me in the morn?"

"Nay, sir, I think not." Jewett gestured toward Baldwin. "This man be one of our constables and captain of our militia. It is his opinion, having been instrumental in retrieving Miss Miller from the French, that she should be free now and her obligation forgiven."

"Nonsense." Plaisted's face darkened, and he glared at Captain Baldwin. "I have a legal right here."

"You do, sir," the captain said smoothly, "but the moral thing would be to release this young woman who has borne already much sorrow and hardship."

"Sorrow? Hardship? What of myself? I was injured. My wife was slain before my eyes."

"It is not up to Miss Miller to compensate you for your losses," Baldwin countered.

"You don't understand, sir," cried Plaisted. "This woman owes me a year's labor. A magistrate will find in my favor. She is my property for a minimum of twelve months. I have the document here."

Charles's heart sank as the man drew a folded parchment from his waistcoat.

"And the judge might well find that she should give me another nine months' work for the time she's spent here idle without my knowing it. Or even for the five years she spent in Canada."

Charles opened his mouth and closed it again. The man was mad! Could he hope to claim Jane's labor for years to come? He looked to the pastor for help.

"Sir," Jewett began, "it is possible for a master to sell a servant's indenture to another. Would you put a price on the year's contract Miss Miller left outstanding with you when she was captured?"

"A price?" Plaisted eyed him coolly.

"That is not a bad idea," Baldwin said. "State the value of her work, sir."

"I had not thought to sell the contract."

"But you could hire another maid with the money," Jewett said.

Plaisted scratched his chin. "Nay, I think not. Now that my wife is gone, it would be too hard to break in new domestic help. I had another hired girl, and she took sick last winter and died. Nay, Miss Miller is strong, and she's survived the hardships, as you put it, of captivity. She must be a tough one."

"But she has a new life here now," Pastor Jewett said. "Surely we can reach an agreement. There must be some way you can release her from this debt."

Plaisted looked the parson in the eye. "There be only one way, sir. If Jane Miller will marry me, then I shall forgive her debt."

Chapter 6

J ane went about her morning chores with a heavy heart. The pastor's report the evening before had chilled her to the bone. Marry Gideon Plaisted or go back and work for him for at least a year. She had lain awake most of the night, pondering the alternatives and begging God for a solution.

The fact that Charles Gardner was missing from his spot on the hearth when she rose at dawn hadn't helped ease her mind. No doubt he'd gone to check his trapline, but she had counted on having a word with him before the men went to settle things with Plaisted.

"I expect he'll be back ere long," the minister had told her. "But Baldwin has promised to go with me, and he thought to ask Mr. Heard to go with us, too. They'll come here, and we shall all go together to the ordinary. We shall do all we can to aid your cause."

Jane was not comforted. She had seen Plaisted beat Betty years ago, and he had even struck Jane at times, as well. It was all she had needed to teach her to be nimble and keep out of his way as much as possible. Marry the man? Never!

As she stoked the fire and cooked corn mush for breakfast, she prayed. Christine knew of her dilemma, and every time Jane looked her way, she saw that Christine's lips moved in silent prayer as she worked, tending the baby and dressing the Jewett girls. Together they put the last touches on the morning meal while Abby set the table for the first round of breakfast.

Pastor Jewett came in from outside with two pails of water from the river, poured the contents of one into the big kettle, and moved the crane into position over the fire to heat the water for dishes and laundry. In spite of her crisis, the routine of the family went on. Ben and John filled the woodbox, and at last Christine sat down with Mr. Jewett and his wife, Ben, John, and Ruth. Jane and Abby served them their meal, while Constance helped by wiping up the spills around Ruth's stool.

As soon as the boys and Christine finished eating, Jane quickly rinsed their dishes for the second sitting. She sat down with the girls to eat, but she had no appetite. Christine brought her a bowl of mush, a hot biscuit, and a cup of weak tea brewed from blackberry leaves. Jane sighed and forced down a bite.

Pastor Jewett lingered at the table, though Elizabeth went to the corner to nurse the baby.

"There must be a solution to this, Jane. I know you don't wish to marry this man." The pastor held up his cup so Christine could refill it with tea.

"I would die first." Jane stared down at her food. She could feel the parson's disapproving frown, but he did not scold her for speaking so.

"If you must go with him, I shall insist upon the terms being written out clearly. He can't keep you for more than a year."

"Can't he?" Jane felt tears spring to her eyes. "He is a cruel man, sir. If he wants to bind me longer, he will find a way." The law stated that indentures who ran away could have their terms of bondage doubled.

Beyond that, she dared not think or speak of the way Betty had been abused. When she was found to be with child, Betty was denied her freedom, even though her term of indenture had ended. The law said indentured servants who became pregnant must continue in servitude. Jane was a young girl when Betty's plight was discovered, and she'd heard Betty weep night after night in the attic they shared. Jane had never known who fathered Betty's child, but she had her suspicions. And Mr. Plaisted was widowed now. Perhaps marrying him would be better than being merely his servant once more. Jane shuddered at the thought.

A loud knock on the door announced the arrival of Captain Baldwin and John Heard.

"Morning, Reverend," the captain called. "Are you ready to go and straighten this out?"

"I suppose so." Pastor Jewett pulled on his coat. "I hoped Charles Gardner would be here when we went, but he left early this morning and hasn't yet returned."

"Got a personal interest in this case, has he?" John Heard asked.

"Well, yes, in a manner of speaking. I suppose it's no secret, and I was going to read the banns at meeting Sunday."

Jane turned away and busied herself by adding wood to the fire so the men would not see her flushed face.

"I pray you still can," said Baldwin. "Those two young folks deserve a chance at a quiet life."

"Aye. It would be a pity if this interloper spoiled things for them," Heard agreed.

"Miss Miller," the pastor called to her, "you keep close here with my wife. I shall return as soon as I am able to tell you the outcome."

She nodded and dropped a slight curtsy.

The door closed behind the men, and Christine came over and put her arm around Jane. "There now. God knows what is best."

"Aye, He does," Jane agreed.

"Come here, girls," Elizabeth called from her chair across the room. "Leave your work for a moment, and we shall pray together."

Jane and Christine gathered the children, and they all clustered about Elizabeth. The children sat on their parents' bed, and the two young women stood on either side of the mother. They had barely bowed their heads when the door burst open.

"Miss Miller! Jane!" The pastor surged through the door, followed by several others.

"What is it, Samuel?" Elizabeth asked, wrapping the baby's blanket closer about him. The small room seemed full of large men and overcoats.

"Wait until you hear. You won't believe it. No, wait. Charles shall tell it."

Captain Baldwin and John Heard stepped aside, and Jane saw that Charles Gardner had entered with them. She took a hesitant step toward him.

"Come, come," the pastor said, pushing Charles forward. " 'Tis a most marvelous answer to prayer."

The others stood in silence. Charles looked down into her eyes, and Jane felt her hope rising.

"Is Mr. Plaisted willing to release me?" Her voice squeaked, and she looked down, almost fearing to hear the answer despite the parson's excitement.

"Aye," Charles said quietly. "Jane, you owe him nothing."

Her heart skipped a beat, and she felt light-headed. She raised her eyes to meet his soft gaze.

"How can this be?" Elizabeth asked, looking toward her husband. "Last night he ranted that he would take her with him today."

"So he did. And yet he's already left for Dover Point and shall journey on to Gloucester alone. Speak, Charles!" the pastor boomed.

Charles cleared his throat. "It was very simple, really. After thinking about it overnight, he was willing to be compensated for your time, Jane. I bought your indenture."

---◆---

Jane opened her eyes. She was lying on Goody Jewett's pallet in the corner, and half a dozen people stood staring down at her.

"There, child. You're all right. Just rest." Elizabeth looked up at the others. "Mr. Jewett, could you take the children out to play in the new snow? Jane needs a moment to recover herself."

"I shall go with them," Christine said.

She and the pastor quickly bundled the little ones, all but the baby, into their wraps and hustled them outside. The men melted away, too, except for Charles. He and Goody Jewett knelt beside her.

"My dear, do you feel well?" Elizabeth asked.

"Yes. I. . ." Jane closed her eyes again. She must have fainted, something she never did, not even when she had seen savages tomahawking her mistress and they had seized Jane and dragged her from the burning garrison.

"Speak to her, Charles," Elizabeth whispered.

"Jane." His voice cracked.

She looked up into his worried brown eyes. "Is it true?" she managed. "Am I bound to you now?"

He frowned and shook his head. "Nay. You are bound to no one. You are free, sweet Jane."

She exhaled and thought about that. "But how did you pay him? You hadn't sold your furs yet."

"I routed the trader out of bed, and he agreed to buy them early this morning. Then I went to the ordinary and woke Mr. Plaisted—rather rudely, I'm afraid."

Elizabeth gave a short laugh, and Jane smiled. "And that was enough?"

Charles shrugged and looked off toward the fireplace. "Nay, his price was more than I had."

"Then how—"

"Richard and his father. I ran to them, and they loaned me enough money. They said we can take as long as we need to pay them back, but it won't be long, Jane. Another good week on my trapline or, failing that, a good corn crop this summer."

"But, Charles, I'll never be able to pay you back, even if you can pay the Dudleys."

"Hush, none of that." He took her hand. "You're going to be my wife, remember? At least you said yesterday you would."

She nodded. "If you still want me."

"Of course I do."

Elizabeth eased away from them and took the baby over to the bench near the hearth.

Jane struggled to sit up, and Charles stuffed the feather pillows behind her.

"Charles, you don't have to marry me, you know. By all rights, I should work for you now. If you want it that way, I can spin and weave and cook for you for a year. You needn't marry a servant if you don't wish to."

"Stop. That's foolish talk."

"Not so foolish. Many folk would never think of marrying an indentured girl."

"Nay. Don't think that way, Jane. Half the men and women in this village were indentured in their youth. I didn't buy you to own you or to make a slave of you."

"Then why did you put yourself in debt for me?"

"Need I tell you? I love you, Jane."

She shut her eyes once more, but it was too late. Her tears flowed freely. "Charlie, I. . .I don't know what to say."

"Say you'll let the parson read the banns on Sunday. That nothing has changed between us."

"You hold my indenture. That paper. . ."

"That paper is nothing. I hold it only so that I can prove you are no longer bound to Plaisted. If I thought him an honest man, I would burn it before your eyes. But I fear we must keep it until the term of your indenture expires. Be that as it may, I'll do something else, Jane."

"What?"

"Legally, I'm your master now. I'll write another paper saying you are free, and you can keep it yourself, to look at whenever you want. If ever I ask you to work harder than you're capable of, or if ever I'm mean or short with you, you can take that paper out and remind me that you are a free woman."

She sat still for a moment. It was a wonderful thought, and yet something about it struck her as wrong.

"But I'll be your wife." She felt her face redden as she said it. "A wife should never claim freedom from her husband."

He captured her other hand and held them both in his. "Jane, dearest, I shall try to be the kind of husband from whom you never want your freedom."

His eyes glittered, and Jane felt a giddy anticipation. She didn't deserve such devotion. And Charlie! He deserved far more than she could give him. She would work, yes, whether she was free or not. She would give her strength to help him.

If only she could learn to love him.

◆

On a bitterly cold March morning, Jane and Charles stood before the Reverend Samuel Jewett in his home. Jane wore a new white linen shift stitched lovingly by Christine. She fingered the rich brown overskirt that was a gift from her friend Sarah Dudley. She had never had such a fine garment as that skirt. Richard, Sarah, Christine, and the Jewett family crowded around while the pastor conducted the wedding ceremony.

"Do you, Charles Gardner, take this woman to be your lawfully wedded wife?"

"I do." Charles stood stiff as a poker beside her.

"And do you, Jane Miller, take this man to be your lawfully wedded husband?"

Jane looked up at Charles. His large brown eyes regarded her solemnly. "I do."

Her words were barely audible, but Charles's eyes leaped with joy. He smiled for the first time all morning and squeezed her hand. Jane felt light-headed, but she managed to smile back.

After the service, Richard and Sarah packed the bride and groom, with Jane's small bundle, into a sled pulled by Richard's father's oxen.

Richard's parents and sister, Catherine, met them at the gate of the Dudley family's stockade.

"You make a lovely bride," Catherine cried.

Jane kissed her and thanked her, but she felt out of place. Her unease increased as they sat down to eat the wedding breakfast with the Dudleys, including Richard's sixteen-year-old brother, Stephen.

The Dudleys' home, while not lavish, was three times the size of the parsonage and much more comfortable. These were her new neighbors, and Jane knew they would accept her with kindness, but her appetite fled. Had she made a mistake?

Charles knew about her background as an indentured servant and of her difficult marriage in Quebec. He had also gone through deep waters, but he seemed to have overcome past trials and was content now to go on with a quiet life as a settler on the New Hampshire frontier. Could she fit into that life with him and be the wife he needed?

Sarah must have read her discomfiture in her face, for after the meal, as the women put away the food and washed the dishes, she managed a quiet word with Jane.

"What is troubling you on this happy day?" she asked.

"Oh, Sarah, I fear I've wronged Charles. I should not have married him."

"Why ever not? He loves you."

"Aye." Jane ducked her head. "It isn't fair to him that he can feel that way, and. . ."

"And you can't?"

Jane said nothing.

"Charles is a gentle man," Sarah said softly. "I'm sure in time your feelings will catch up with your knowledge of him."

"But he's given all the money he saved and more—gone into debt to Richard and his father for me. I come to Charles with only the clothes on my back, an extra shift, skirt, and bodice, and a small sewing kit that Elizabeth Jewett gave me."

"And a quilt." Sarah turned to a chest behind her and lifted a folded patchwork quilt. "This is a gift from the Dudley women."

Jane stared at the colorful material and reached out to stroke the woolen patches.

"Such fine stitching!"

Sarah smiled. "My mother-in-law and Catherine and I sewed it for you.

Charles's cabin may be small, and it was stripped by natives during the massacre, but he has stocked it since his return. I'm sure you'll find adequate dishes and linens for the two of you. But if you need anything, do come and tell me. We shall share what we have until the two of you settle in and Charles's crops begin to profit you."

Jane nodded, still unsure she could be comfortable as a wife again, but this was not the place to express her doubts. Nor the time, two hours after her wedding.

Charles put the quilt with Jane's bundle into his pack, and the couple set out on foot with Richard and Sarah. The young Dudleys soon left them at their own house, and Jane trudged on behind her husband, feeling small and timid as they entered the forest.

The path between the two cabins was only a quarter mile but led through woods the men had not yet cut for firewood. Charles had mentioned to her that one day all his land would be cleared for fields, except perhaps for a narrow line of trees he would leave as a border to break the winter winds.

Jane had not left the village in ten months except for two visits to Sarah. Each time she got beyond hailing distance of the parsonage, goose bumps rose on her arms, and today was no exception. As they reached the tree line, Charles turned and smiled at her, waiting for her to catch up the few steps between them.

"Do I walk too fast for you?"

"Nay." Jane looked up at the bare limbs overhead. "Be these your trees or Richard's?"

"Ours." He shifted his musket to his other shoulder and held out his hand. "Walk beside me. The path is wide enough, and I want to watch your face when you see our farm for the first time."

Determined not to disappoint him, she plodded on, not pulling away from his touch. They broke out of the dim forest in a short time, and the wind caught at her cloak. Ahead lay a small, snug cottage of riven slab siding and a squat log barn with unroofed rafters rising against the gray sky.

"Richard and I will finish the barn before planting time," Charles said with evident pride. He looked at her anxiously. "What do you think?"

"It looks very fine."

He smiled and led her toward the cabin. "I banked the fire this morning, and it will be chilly inside, but I'll build it up for you straightaway."

Jane held her breath as he reached to open the oak plank door. She refused to make a mental comparison with the open fields and large outbuildings of the Robataille farm in Quebec. That was a place of fear and sorrow. This farm, however small and rough, would be a happier place if she made it so. Or so it would be, provided Charles did not reveal a darker side of which she was ignorant.

He threw the door open and stepped back, looking at her. She wondered for a second if he would pick her up and carry her over the threshold.

"Won't you come in, Goody Gardner?" His crooked smile almost calmed her, but then he pulled off his mittens and touched her cheek. "Welcome, dear wife."

Jane turned away to avoid his intent gaze and stepped up into the house. The one room was dim, lit only by the sunlight streaming through the door and that admitted by two narrow slits of windows in the side walls. The back wall was taken up entirely by a great fireplace.

She took a swift glance around. The room was neat, almost bare. She was pleased to see a rope bed frame next to one wall and a rectangular table and two benches in the center of the room. A rough settle stood by the hearth, and two kettles and a large skillet hung on pegs set in the stonework. At the other end of the room were a plain pine chest and a series of shelves that held dishes, boxes, small sacks, and crocks.

"Richard will help me add a room as soon as we can," Charles said.

Jane jumped at his nearness when he spoke and instinctively took a step away.

Charles rested his musket in a corner and took off his pack. He laid the quilt and her bundle on the bed. "I'll tend the fire."

She noted that a pile of wood filled a niche at one side of the fireplace, and a wooden bucket full of water sat near it.

She took a deep breath. "Shall I start dinner?"

"If you wish. You may hang your cloak and shawl here near the door." Charles went to the shelves and stored his pack away. "There be crockery here and linens in the chest."

She nodded.

He looked at her as though he would speak again then turned to the hearth.

Jane stood uncertainly, watching him stir up the coals and lay dry wood on them. The sticks began to crackle, and the flames flared.

Charles stood and faced her. He blinked, seeming surprised that she stood in the same spot where he'd left her. "I. . .have somewhat to tend to outside."

She wondered how many people she should prepare the mid-day meal for. "Be Richard coming today to work with you?"

"Nay. He will come tomorrow."

"Ah."

They looked at each other. Again Jane felt the uncertainty. She didn't belong here.

Charles turned and went out, closing the door behind him.

What on earth had she done? Tying herself to another man for the rest of her life had to be a mistake. She ought to have waited and insisted on more time to get to know Charles. And what if she conceived right away? Was she ready to undergo the rigors of childbirth again? On the other hand, what if she didn't? In the three years with Jacques Robataille, their only baby was stillborn. Was she capable of bearing a healthy child? Jane wondered if she had been remiss in not revealing this somber bit of information to Charles and letting him decide if he wanted a potentially barren wife.

She stood in the middle of her new house and slowly turned in a circle. It was no bigger than the parsonage, though the Jewetts had a bigger loft. She had expected this. It was dark, but that was probably because of the danger of living outside the village. Windows were only extra entrances for attacking savages. The slit windows in these walls would not allow any attackers to enter the house. Only the door would let them pass. That was reassuring. And the cabin seemed solid.

She took off her shawl and stepped to the pegs near the door. She hung the garment up and then put her cloak over it, leaving a peg free for her husband's coat when he came in from whatever it was he was doing outside. The room was still chilly, but the fire was gaining ground, and if she got to work, she would soon be warm.

A sudden curiosity prompted her to lift the latch on the only door and pull it toward her two inches. She peeked out through the crack but couldn't see a sign of Charles. She was about to close the door when she heard a quiet sound and looked toward the unfinished barn.

Charles came through the doorway carrying a huge reddish bundle. She gasped then exhaled slowly. A red fox carcass. His trapline, of course. He must be setting about to skin his latest catch. It would take many furs to make up for what he had spent to redeem her. Their plans to buy a heifer would have to wait.

Would he leave her here alone in the early mornings when he went to check his traps? And would he leave her a weapon to defend herself if savages came? Not that she knew how to use a gun.

She closed the door noiselessly and went to the bed. Untying her bundle, she shook out her extra clothes and laid the shift in the chest. Charles appeared to have an extra shirt and one extra pair of stockings there. She would see that he soon had more. Sarah had promised her some yarn.

She changed quickly out of the new wedding skirt. That would be her Sunday best. As she reached for the older, frayed, everyday skirt, her hand brushed the pocket tied about her waist. She reached into it and heard the stiff parchment crackle.

In the pocket were the three documents that determined the course of her life. Her indenture, which Charles had bought from Plaisted; the emancipation document he had presented to her that same day; and a copy of their marriage record, handed to her by the Reverend Samuel Jewett that morning.

She pulled on her gray wool skirt and smoothed its folds over her shift and pocket. As she tied her apron about her waist, she sent a prayer heavenward.

Almighty Father, I'm not sure I can be the kind of wife this man deserves. Please help me. Teach me all I need to know to be the best woman for Charles.

Chapter 7

Charles wrapped the chain around the butt end of the big maple log and signaled to Richard to start the oxen. The big beasts strained against the yoke and slowly began to walk toward his house. The snow was melting fast, and soon it would be impossible to drag logs or sleds easily. They would have to wait out the mud season until summer to haul anything heavy in a cart.

When they reached the back of Charles's cabin, he swiftly unhooked the chain, releasing the log beside several others they had already brought out.

"Shall we stop for dinner?" Richard asked.

Charles looked anxiously up at his chimney. Smoke poured from it steadily, but Jane hadn't come out to tell them the meal was ready. Usually if she heard them enter the yard, she came out to announce dinner.

"Perhaps one more twitch?" Charles asked.

Richard pulled off his cap and wiped his brow. "Charlie, we've been working dawn to dusk for weeks. Is it vital we get all the logs out now? It won't hurt you to wait and build the extra room later in the year."

"I want to give this to Jane. You understand."

Richard nodded, and Charles felt he did understand. But still Richard seemed ready to take a rest from their labor. "I'm tired, Charlie. That's the long and the short of it."

Charles pulled off his mittens and sat down on the log. "I'm sorry. I've asked you for more than a fair share of work."

"Nay, you helped me as much last fall, when I was trying to get a nice home ready for Sarah before our wedding."

"But we also gave two full days' work last week to help the other men haul out logs for adding rooms to the parsonage. You helped me put up a barn for livestock I don't have yet, and we've cut enough firewood for the coming year for us and you and your father's household. I've overstepped our friendship."

Richard sighed. "I don't begrudge the work. We all work hard. Such is our lot in life."

"What is it, then? Not enough time with Sarah?"

"Perhaps." Richard eyed him keenly. "You're quiet lately, and I wonder about you."

"How so?"

"For a man married a mere fortnight, you're awfully solemn. Are things all right between you and Jane?"

He'd struck home, and Charles couldn't meet his piercing gaze.

Richard came over and stood squarely in front of him. "Charlie? What's wrong?"

Charles shrugged. "I wish I knew. Perhaps I shouldn't have pressed her to marry me so soon. But I left it up to her. And now she barely speaks to me."

"Do you talk at the supper table?"

Charles scowled at him. "What about?"

"Anything."

"I tell her how much wood we've cut. But. . .we don't say much, either of us. I don't know how to talk to her."

"You both speak English."

"That's very clever."

Richard smiled. "Yet you have no trouble talking to me."

"You stuck your nose in and wouldn't leave it alone."

"Ah. Well, women like to talk, Charlie."

"Not Jane."

"Oh, I'll warrant she does. Do you talk about the farm?"

"A bit."

"Planned your garden?"

Charles shook his head. "Not yet."

"What about her housework?"

Charles gestured impatiently. "I let her run the house as she sees fit. I've tried not to make demands on her, so she could take her time settling in. She doesn't want to talk about sweeping and scrubbing."

"Maybe she does. My Sarah does."

That didn't seem right. Charles looked up at him. "Fascinating conversation at your house."

"No, really. I come in and wash up, and I tell her what I did that day. I tell her that the house smells lovely and ask her what she's been baking. And while we're at table, I ask her how her spinning went, and if she wasn't spinning that day, she tells me she was stitching or doing a wash or visiting my mother. It's all very nice between us. Leads to sweet talk."

Charles mulled that over. "Sounds delightful, but my Jane—" He broke off suddenly and jumped up as his wife stepped around the corner of the cabin.

"Dinner is ready." She didn't look at either of them.

"Thank you, Jane," Richard said with a smile. "We'll unhitch the oxen and wash up."

Jane disappeared silently around the corner.

Charles whirled to search Richard's face. "You don't think she heard, do you?"

Richard laughed. "No, I don't." His friend studied his face. "I'm sorry. I shouldn't have laughed. This isn't funny."

"No, it's not."

"Do you tell her you love her?"

Charlie winced. "I did once. When I bought her indenture. But she didn't answer me, and if she doesn't love me, I figure she doesn't want me to keep saying it. Oh, Richard!" He kicked at the log and jumped back in pain, hopping on one foot and holding the toe of his boot.

"Maybe she'd like to visit with Sarah more often."

"I've told her she can visit Sarah or her friends in the village anytime she wants, but she must tell me first so that I can escort her. I don't want her walking the paths alone."

"That's as it should be."

"I tell you, I will let her do whatever she wants, so long as she's happy as my wife. But she doesn't seem happy."

Richard nodded. "Come. She's waiting dinner on us. Bring her to visit Sarah tomorrow." He reached to unfasten the bowpin that would release the near ox from its yoke.

"All right, and we'll take the day off from hauling logs. You need to catch up on chores around your place."

The two men left the oxen inside Charles's barn to munch the feed Richard had brought for them. When they went in the house, Charles saw that Jane had laid out the soap and a towel and poured clean water into the washbowl. He allowed Richard to wash his hands first then took his turn.

As he returned from tossing the water out the front door, he was startled to hear Jane talking to his friend. "Yes, I should like to very much. I'd feel easier when Charles is off checking his traps or working in the woods with you."

"You'd like to what?" Charles looked from Jane to Richard and back again.

"Jane would like to learn to shoot."

"To shoot?" Charles sat down hard in his chair at the head of the table. Jane had never uttered a word to him about shooting. Was she even strong enough to heft a musket? And when he was off in the woods, he took his gun with him anyway.

"Do you still have that old gun of your father's?" Richard asked, as though reading his thoughts.

"Nay. I expect the Pennacook took it in the raid, or else someone came after and took it. This house was stripped when I came back from my two years in Canada."

Richard nodded. "I'm thinking of getting an extra musket to leave with Sarah when I'm gone. The stockade I'm building will give her a measure of security, but I'm sure she'd feel better if she had a gun."

Charles eyed Jane skeptically. "You. . .really want to learn to shoot?"

"I would like to, sir. We be far from help if trouble should find us here." She looked up at him. Her gray eyes held a somber, determined look.

He wondered if there wasn't more to her story than he knew. "Well, I suppose I could teach you." His mind totted up what he could get for the furs. There was no way he could afford another musket. And he couldn't leave his gun at home when he went traipsing about the forest. That would be suicide. There must be some other way he could help her feel safe when she was alone at their house.

"What if I bring Sarah the first warm day, and we'll have a shooting class?" Richard suggested.

"I suppose it couldn't hurt," Charles said. "If nothing else, they'll be better able to help us reload if need be."

Jane smiled. "I should feel much more competent if I learned that skill."

"All right, then." Charles threw Richard a baffled glance. "If you have no qualms about it, then we'll do it."

◆

The weather turned bitter in the night, and Jane was afraid Charles would refuse to take her to the Dudleys' the next morning. She rose early to fix breakfast and do her morning chores in the kitchen. When he asked if she wished to go in the cold, she stepped up eagerly. "I've looked forward to seeing Sarah. Do you mind awfully?"

"Nay. We'll go, then." He bade her bundle up warmly, and they swiftly walked the short distance.

Richard and Sarah welcomed them.

"It be too cold to work outdoors today," Richard said as Sarah took their wraps.

"Aye. The old year must go out with one last stretch of foul weather," Jane agreed.

"Let's hope April comes in with warmth," Sarah said. She went to the hearth and took a kettle of warmed cider off the fire. "Sit, Charles. You can help Richard fix my loom."

"Oh, I shan't stay that long. I've a score of beavers hung up in my barn to skin, and I need to rive more shingles. I'll come back ere sunset for Jane."

"Take supper with us, then."

"Well, perhaps." He shot an anxious glance at Jane.

"If you think it's safe to walk through the woods after dark," she said.

He nodded. "All right, then."

Sarah handed him a steaming cup of cider and prevailed upon him to sit for a few minutes with them before heading home.

Jane enjoyed the morning, sewing with Sarah while Richard worked on the loom in the corner. The pleasant conversation with her hosts soon lifted the gloom that had hung over her.

When Richard went out to check on his livestock, Sarah fixed her with a meaningful look. "All right, tell me. How does the married life suit you?"

"I think. . ." Jane took a few stitches then looked up at her. "I believe I'm lonely."

"Lonely? But you've got Charlie!"

"I know. It seems silly, doesn't it? But we hardly exchange a dozen words each day, and he's out working all the time. Being here with you today, I feel entirely different than when I'm over there alone." She clamped her lips shut and bent over her work.

"I know Charles and Richard have been working hard lately," Sarah said. "Perhaps they need to stop getting wood out for a few days and give you and Charles time to be together."

"Oh, we are together," Jane said, thinking of the long, silent nights in the cabin.

"Richard says you want to learn to shoot."

"Aye."

"Because of the Indians?"

"I won't be taken again, Sarah."

A shadow crossed Sarah's face, and she nodded. "Agreed. Richard's father has an extra musket. He told Richard he could use it to teach me. Can Charles come up with a weapon for you?"

"I don't know. I don't like to ask him to spend more, but I do get fearful when he's gone for hours."

"I know," Sarah said. "I try not to think about it, but we're more isolated out here than my parents' home was in the village. If Indians came here, no one would hear us scream. Do you keep the door barred while Charles is out working?"

"Aye. When I hear him return, I unbar it. And I pray a lot. I also keep a butcher knife near as I work about the house."

Sarah sighed. "It's part of life in this place. I'm glad our husbands have been working together of late. I know God doesn't wish us to live in fear, but experience teaches caution."

Jane set her jaw. She and Sarah both knew the horror of seeing loved ones killed and being forced to march off into the wilderness. "As I said, I will not be taken captive again."

"Let us talk of more pleasant things." Sarah settled back in her chair and picked up her knitting. "Knowing you are close by has made my days sweeter. Knowing Charles as we do, I expect he is kind to you."

"Aye. He's a very gentle man. He makes no demands on me, and he allows me to do just as I please."

"And this displeases you? You should be the happiest of women, I'd think."

Jane shrugged. "I don't know. I'm not used to it." She poked her needle through the material she held and sat back. "I've never been free before, except the months I lived with the Jewetts."

Sarah nodded. "We could have left anytime, but we didn't want to."

"I came to love them," Jane agreed. "Still, doesn't it grate on you as a married woman to be known about the village, not as Sarah Dudley or even Mrs. Dudley, but as Richard Dudley, his wife?"

Sarah frowned. "I've heard such things said. But it's just the way people speak. Women are part of their husbands' families. We bear their names and their identities."

"Doesn't that bother you? We can't own property."

"Do you want a farm of your own?"

"Nay, that's not what I meant."

"Then I misunderstand you. Jane, what is the trouble?"

Jane sighed and picked up her sewing. "I don't know."

"Is it that farm you lost in Quebec? It was bigger and grander than Charlie's, wasn't it?"

"That makes no matter. The price of being its mistress was higher than a woman should pay."

Sarah sat in silence for a moment. "I don't know all you suffered, to be sure. But I'm sorry. Sometimes I think my stay in the Pennacook village was an easy lot."

Jane shifted her position. Her own discontent rankled her. Sarah was right—she should be happy. She smiled across at her friend. "I am not ungrateful, and I don't say this to get your sympathy. But my present situation. . .I've gone from indenture to captivity to a miserable arranged marriage. Then I had a taste of freedom, though I felt I owed the Jewetts whatever labor I could give them. And now marriage."

"But marriage to a good man is not a bad thing," Sarah said. "I myself find it pleasant."

Jane sighed. "Sarah, keeping house for Charles is child's play. He's never in it, and his possessions are so few it's impossible to make a mess. He's out working all day, wearing himself out, and leaves me in there with nothing to do but tend the fire and cook a little. If I had a spinning wheel or a loom. . .but I can't ask him for that because he has no money, and that is my fault. I'd like to do something to help him pay off the debt and get ahead with the farm, the way he wants to."

"Give it time, dear. You're only just married."

"I know."

Jane bowed over her handwork. It was true her heart was restless. She felt she was a disappointment to her husband. But there were other things she couldn't express, to Sarah or to Charles.

"Surely you can find something else to put your hand to."

"I do. I bake and I sew, but I'm running out of flour and material. I hate to ask him for anything, after he gave every penny he had for me. Perhaps in the fall, when our crops are in, I can do something that will bring in money. Would you keep me in prayer, Sarah?"

"Of course. In fact, we can pray together right now." Sarah laid aside her knitting and leaned toward her friend.

Jane was taken aback at first. She felt the rush of tears flooding her eyes. "Thank you. I fear I haven't prayed enough. I do want to please Charles. I'm just not sure I know how."

"Then we shall ask that God will show you."

◆

The next evening, when Charles came to supper, he found Jane flitting about the cabin. The table was set, and she seemed to have cooked more dishes than usual. She'd stewed the rabbit he'd brought her that morning but also fixed pumpkin and biscuits and a spicy-smelling tart.

He tried to recall what Richard had told him as he went to the worktable. She had filled the washbowl with warm water for him and laid out a linen towel. "It smells delicious," he ventured, feeling a bit silly.

"Thank you."

Her warm response encouraged him. "Dried apple tart, is it?"

"Yes. Do you like it?"

"I'm sure I shall."

They sat down together, but still she seemed livelier, more eager than usual.

After asking the blessing, Charles mentally went over the bleak conversation with Richard again. "And how was your day? Do you have everything you need about the house?"

"Well. . .the flour is running a bit short." She peered at him almost timidly.

"I'm sure I can get some on credit from the trader."

Jane hesitated then said, "Sarah gave me more yarn yesterday, and I've started a new pair of socks for you."

He served out the stew, and they ate in silence. Jane kept looking at him across the table. He wondered if something had happened that he didn't know about.

After a few minutes she said, "Charles, I thought of a plan to help you earn the money back."

He winced. Apparently she persisted in thinking about his debt. He wished she would leave it be. He would earn the money and repay Richard and his father, and that would be that.

"I think we'll be fine," he murmured. "Don't trouble yourself over it."

"But I can help you—I'm sure of it."

He looked closely at her earnest face. Even though this was not the topic he would have chosen, she seemed more eager to talk than she had ever been with him.

"All right, then, what is your plan?"

"We could open our home to travelers."

He stared at her. "What?"

"Think of it! We'll have plenty of space with the new room you are building, and the village has no inn. There's only the ordinary. Ladies who travel don't like to stay at a tavern. But we could offer a quiet place and good food. Folks who come to Cochecho on business or who need a place to stay while building a house could stay here."

As he listened, Charles felt his world tilting. Strangers in the cabin? Let his wife cook and wash for peddlers and such?

"What do you think?"

Her gray eyes reflected the firelight, and he hated to dash her hopes. He allowed himself a brief moment to consider accepting her plan. Would it be so bad?

Yes, it certainly would.

He cleared his throat. "It's true I haven't much ready cash just now, but our farm will supply most of our needs, and I truly believe my late-season furs will fetch nearly enough to square things with the Dudleys. By harvesttime. . ."

Her face fell. "You don't like my idea."

He hesitated. "Well, it has merit, I'm sure, but. . .actually I see no need to earn money in this manner. It would only make more work for us both, and. . . and it would bring strangers into our home."

She blinked at him, frowning. "I only wish to help, husband."

"Of course. And I thank you. But you know, my dear, you don't even like to go to the trading post around strangers. I'm surprised you would want to open our private home like that."

"It wouldn't be the ideal, but if it would pay off our debt. . ."

"Let me handle that, please." He looked deep into her eyes. "Please."

She looked away first. "As you wish."

Charles reached for another biscuit. The atmosphere in the room had changed. Jane's features drooped, and she kept her eyes lowered. He tried to think how he could make things better without giving in to her suggestion. While he'd told himself—and Richard, for that matter—he would do anything to make Jane happy, this was beyond anything he had imagined she would want.

Her fork clicked against her pewter plate as she laid it down. "Would you like tea?" Her voice was stilted. He had hurt her feelings.

Charles forced a smile. "I should like that very much, thank you."

She rose and went to the hearth. He racked his brain for a way to keep her from closing up on him again. If they could keep talking, perhaps they could unravel this unpleasant incident and start fresh. Back to her excitement and eagerness. She'd worked extra hard to prepare a special meal for him; he knew she had. She'd set the scene before she presented her plan to him. And now he had shattered her hopes.

"Jane, please don't take me wrong. I do appreciate your willingness to help me out. I just think. . . Well, we live far from the village, for one thing. Travelers won't want to come all the way out here for a bed. And you might find yourself overwhelmed with work."

"I'm strong, Charles. I can work hard."

"Yes, but what if. . .what if you found yourself in a. . .a delicate condition, and you had to serve people anyway?" He felt his face grow scarlet at mentioning the possibility.

Jane stopped with her back to him and didn't move for several seconds.

He gulped air. *Now I've done it. How would you get out of this, Richard?*

Jane turned slowly with his cup in her hands. "What if I can't?"

"Can't what?"

"What if I can't have children, Charles?"

Her words silenced him as nothing else could. He realized he was staring at her and made himself look away. He picked up his knife and laid it down again. They'd only been married a couple of weeks, and she was talking about possibly never having children. Was there something he didn't know? He'd always imagined he would have sons. Was she telling him she couldn't bear children? Maybe they should have put the marriage off until they knew each other better and felt more comfortable in each other's presence. For the first time, he now wondered if he had chosen the wrong mate.

She brought the tea over and placed it on the table at his elbow; then she turned away and poured dishwater into her basin.

Charles couldn't think of a single word to say.

Chapter 8

When Jane rose the next morning, her husband had already left the house. She dressed quickly and put water and parched corn in a kettle over the fire; then she opened the door.

The temperature had moderated, and a steady *thunk-thunk* met her ears. Although the sun was not yet above the trees, Charles was already chopping away. Probably he was shaping the logs he would use to build the new room on the house.

He had his own well-ordered plans. Jane felt selfish for suggesting a different course that would add to his labor. He was doing something nice for her. Having a bedchamber would be nice. Their clothing and personal items would be out of sight when visitors came. Many colonists lived out their lives in one-room cottages, but Charles had bigger ideas.

She hurried back to her worktable, determined to present him in an hour with a breakfast that would fill him up with tasty food and strengthen him for a full morning's work. As she worked, she prayed for wisdom.

When all was ready, she went out to call her husband to come in and eat. She found him behind the house, shaping the end of a log that would fit with another to make a corner joint. The new room would perfectly match the cabin, a sturdy, graceful addition that seemed a part of the original, she was sure. Charles would not build anything that was not both beautiful and functional. She wanted to tell him that she knew this about him.

Before she could speak, movement on the path that came through the woods from the Dudleys' house caught her eye.

Ben Jewett trotted toward them.

"Charles," she said.

He lowered his ax and looked at her.

Jane pointed toward the boy.

Charles straightened. "Ben! What's the matter?"

Jane knew Charles was thinking the same as she—Ben wouldn't come so far this early unless with an urgent message.

The boy arrived panting and stood for a moment to catch his breath. "My mother. She's ill. Joseph and Abby, too. Father wishes Miss Jane to come if she is able."

"Of course I'll come," Jane said. "Did you break your fast, Ben?"

"Nay."

"I've food ready, and Goodman Gardner and I were about to sit down to eat. Won't you join us? Then I will gather a few things and come."

Ben pulled in another deep breath. "Father says hurry. He and Christine are doing all they can. He wanted to take Ruth, Constance, and John to the Heards', but they wouldn't have 'em."

"Why not?" Charles asked sharply.

"Smallpox."

Charles stared at Jane. "You can't—"

"Of course I can, Charles. I must."

"Nay. You are my wife, and I say you can't."

Jane glared at him. Just when she was softening and preparing to apologize for her selfishness, he would decide to bully her.

Charles breathed heavily, eyeing her with open disapproval. "Jane, I don't wish you to go into the sickness."

"But the Jewetts were so kind to me. No one else would take me in last year, but they showed true charity. I cannot refuse to go to Elizabeth now, Charles."

He stood still, his mouth set and his dark eyes narrowed.

"Come," she said, including Ben in her invitation. "Let us pray and eat together."

Charles offered the blessing for their meal and a heartfelt petition for the Jewett family. They began to eat in silence. Jane started to speak once but felt it best to hold her remarks.

When she had finished her portion, she rose and refilled the men's plates. Then she began to tidy her work area. She didn't have much to take with her that would help her patients, but she could offer her hard work. She tucked her extra shift, apron, and sewing kit into a basket.

When she fetched her cloak, Charles stood and watched her, his face set in displeasure. She pulled her shawl about her shoulders and over her hair before she met his gaze. "I must go to them."

A muscle in his cheek twitched. "Ben should stay here."

The boy looked up at him, his mouth open.

"What if he is already carrying the disease?" Jane asked.

"Then I am already exposed. If he takes ill, I'll bring him to the parsonage, and we shall all suffer together."

"Father told me to come back with Goody Gardner or Goody Dudley, whichever would come," Ben said.

"You stopped at the Dudleys'?" Charles asked.

"At Richard Dudley's. Goodman Richard wouldn't let me enter his house."

Charles frowned. "That's not like him."

"Perhaps it is for Sarah's sake," Jane suggested. Charles grimaced, and she looked away. Richard was protecting Sarah, but she wouldn't let Charles protect her. Again she had failed to meet his standard of what a wife should be.

As she left the house with Ben, she felt Charles's bleak stare. She did not look back for fear she would lose her resolve.

◆

Charles watched Jane go and felt helpless. What if she never came back? What if she decided she preferred the swarming Jewett household to the coldness between them? Worse yet, what if she caught smallpox and died?

Dear God, how could things go so wrong in such a short time?

He sat down hard on the bench at the table. The food she had prepared for him so skillfully still cooled on his plate. He looked around. She had taken all of her things, or nearly all. What if this bereavement was permanent? Already he was lonely, and she'd been gone three minutes. She had to return. He couldn't stand to go back to being a single man, living alone. He knew things could be better for him and Jane. They had to be.

Lord, please bring us through this. Show us how to work together in harness to honor You and build a godly home together. Please, Father, bring her back to me.

◆

The next day, Jane dressed Constance in her warmest clothing and prepared to walk with her and ten-year-old John to Goody Deane's cottage. Across the village, several families had been stricken with the sickness, and most quarantined themselves, refusing to open their doors to outsiders. The meetinghouse had remained closed on Sunday, and no services were held. But the widow had come across the road that morning and stridently told the parson to get whatever of his young ones were still healthy out of there and take them to her house.

Distraught at his wife's failing condition and the new baby's listlessness, the pastor agreed. Ruth, the toddler, had also presented a rash that morning and lay whimpering next to her mother on the pallet. Elizabeth lay flushed with fever, angry red spots marking her usually clear complexion, and the little baby labored with every breath. Abby, the seven-year-old, was fretful but still active. Christine had placed her on a straw tick near the hearth and given the loft over to the as-yet healthy boys. Abby seemed less ill than the others, and Jane had wrapped her hands in linen to keep her from scratching her pox.

"Do you wish the children to bid their mother good-bye ere I take them to Goody Deane?" she asked the pastor.

The Reverend Jewett looked up at her with dull eyes. "Nay. Bring them not near her. I know it is hard for them, but the old woman is right. Keeping them away may save their lives. Ben, you go, too. If I have need of you, I will fetch you."

"But, Father—"

"Nay, son, do not oppose me now. Go and help to occupy your brother and sister. If there is aught you can do for Goody Deane, then put your hand to it. Fetch wood and water for her, or whatever else she can find for you to do."

Constance began to cry, and Jane scooped her up in her arms.

Ben scowled but grabbed his coat and followed her and John out the door.

When she had safely deposited the three children at the widow's, Jane returned to the parsonage.

Christine was pouring water into the washtub. The parson still sat by Elizabeth's head, patting her brow with a damp cloth.

"Shall I bathe Ruth and Joseph again?" Jane asked Christine.

"Aye. I thought to put fresh linen on the bed and wash the soiled things."

Jane nodded and went about her grim tasks. An hour later she fixed corn pone and pumpkin sauce for dinner.

"Come, Pastor, you must eat and keep up your strength."

Christine set a cup of cider on the table for him. "Aye, you mustn't wear yourself out. Elizabeth and the children will need you."

He sighed and rose, stretching his long arms. "Is it Monday?"

"Tuesday, sir," Jane replied.

"I don't know how to thank you girls. When this is over, if you haven't succumbed. . ."

"Don't think of that now, sir. Just pray. The Lord has given us strength so far, and we are thankful we can help you." Jane handed him a small pot of preserves. She remembered making them last summer with Elizabeth, after she and Sarah and Christine had taken all the children out to pick blueberries.

Elizabeth moaned, and Jane hurried to her side just in time to hold a wooden bowl for her while she retched. Elizabeth lay back exhausted, and Jane rinsed a cloth and wiped her face. Her skin felt hot.

"There, dear. Rest now," Jane whispered.

Elizabeth sighed. "I don't know how I can heave when I've nothing in my stomach but a few spoonfuls of water my husband gave me."

"Easy. Let the sickness take its course."

Elizabeth's dark eyes focused on her face. "Jane."

"Aye, 'tis me."

"You should be at home with Charles."

"When you are better. Don't fret about him. He is used to fending for himself."

"You must love him, dear Jane. Do all you can to help him. Charles is a good man."

"Aye, he is that."

"Treat him kindly. He needs you, you know. Show him all your heart."

Jane nodded, not certain how she could do that. But she would not trouble Elizabeth with her turmoil. "I shall try."

Elizabeth's gaze darted about the room. "Samuel?"

"Here, my love!" The pastor leaped from his bench.

Jane quickly moved out of his way and took the slop bowl out to the garden behind the house. She hadn't paused for her shawl, and she shivered. Spring would come grudgingly in this harsh territory.

When she entered the house again, Christine drew her aside. "The baby is gone."

Jane gasped. "No!"

"Aye. But Goody Jewett knows it not. Her husband handed the little one to me and bid me place him on the chair. He says he will tend to him when his wife's crisis is past."

"Have you hope for Elizabeth?"

Christine lowered her eyes and shook her head slightly. "I doubt she is long for this world."

Jane threw herself into the drudgery of caring for the sick. She and Christine did all within their power to keep the invalids comfortable and the house spotless, but to no avail. Two hours later, Elizabeth Jewett breathed her last with her husband at her side. Jane's desolation nearly overwhelmed her, but she and Christine continued to care for Abby and Ruth, who seemed no worse as the day passed.

The parson went next door to break it to the other children that their mother was dead. He told Jane not to expect him home soon, as he must walk to the ordinary to find someone to build a coffin while she and Christine bathed the bodies of the mother and baby and dressed them in fresh clothing.

Jane thought her heart would break as they performed the tasks, but harder still was holding Ruth and Abby after their father returned and told them the news. Their sobs wrenched her, and Jane's tears mingled with theirs.

Later that day, the bodies were removed to a disused shed near the mill, to be stored there until the ground should thaw. The pastor sent Jane and Christine up to the loft in the evening, saying he would watch over Abby and Ruth, and they must sleep.

Jane looked down at him from the top of the ladder. He sat hunched in the chair by the hearth, as still as a statue.

◆

The next morning, the pastor staggered when he rose from the breakfast table. Jane seized his arm.

"Steady, sir. You must lie down."

The pastor stared at her with glassy eyes. Jane prayed he suffered only exhaustion. He rested a few hours but then insisted on rising again to help care for his daughters. By evening he was as feverish as little Ruth, though Abby seemed to be gaining strength. At Christine's insistence, he tumbled into bed once more.

Jane and Christine sat down at the table together for a bite of supper. All three patients slept fitfully for the moment.

"We must take turnabout nursing them tonight," Christine said.

Jane nodded. "And I think we should bring Ben over to tend his father."

"But what if Ben takes ill?" Christine's eyes filled with tears. "We mustn't let any more of the children into this. If the pastor survives, we don't want to see him bury any more of his kin."

"I know, but. . ." Jane looked over at the pallet where the big man lay. It would be difficult for the two young women to care for him properly, and propriety was another question. She looked at Christine again and saw beads of sweat standing on her friend's brow, yet the room was chilly.

"Christine, be you ill?"

"Nay, I'm tired, is all."

"Are you sure?"

Christine pushed away from the table. "Aye. But if you'll take the first watch tonight, I shall lie down for a bit." She stood and clutched the edge of the table. Jane saw her shudder, and then Christine sat down again.

"You *are* ill." Jane rushed around the table. "Come, let us remove your skirt and stays. Lie down with Abby."

"Nay, I can go to the loft."

"I shan't let you climb the ladder, shaking as you are." Jane supported her as they hobbled across the room toward Abby's pallet.

It took her half an hour to help Christine undress and situate her for the night. Before they were done, Christine began to shake with chills, and Jane scrambled to the loft for extra blankets.

As she descended the ladder, the pastor moaned and turned over, groping for the slop bowl.

God, help me! I cannot nurse four people alone.

A knock sounded at the door. Jane set the blankets on the table and hurried across the room. She was surprised that anyone would come near a house known to be infected with smallpox. When she raised the latch and opened the door, she caught her breath. Never had an answered prayer looked so good to her. "Charles!"

"Aye, I'm here. I heard Goody Jewett is dead."

" 'Tis true, and now her husband has sickened. Christine, as well. Oh,

Charles, I'm so glad to see you." Tears flooded her eyes. "I don't want you to get sick, but I need help."

He stepped inside and shut the door. "I've brought you a rabbit so you can make some broth. Tell me what to do, and then get some rest."

She sobbed and put her hands to her face. The next instant she felt his strong arms about her. She couldn't stop her weeping, but Charles held her with her face against his cold woolen coat, stroking her hair. For a moment she let herself lean against him and feel his strength and support. God had speedily answered her prayer.

At last she took a deep breath and straightened. "I'm so glad you came."

He touched her cheek. "So am I. And I shall stay with you as long as there is need."

Chapter 9

April blew in wet and gray. The snow in the village street melted, and the ground beneath it oozed with mud. Jane and Charles worked side by side. They hardly stepped outside the little parsonage for nearly a week except for wood and water or to empty the slop bowls.

One morning when Charles came in with two buckets of water, he told Jane the river was clear of ice. "The snow is nearly gone, and the breeze is warm."

The patients had passed the feverish, nauseous stage of the disease and seemed likely to recover. After their rashes appeared, Jane knew they would be weak and uncomfortable for several weeks. Abby, however, seemed much better by this time, though she still rubbed at her scabs and fussed about the itching.

News began to trickle in from the community. Charles exchanged greetings with others when he went for water, spreading the word that the pastor was still very ill but likely to survive.

On Sunday morning, a service was held for the few who came out, with one of the deacons leading a time of scripture reading and prayer for the sick.

Because of their close association with the patients, Jane and Charles stayed away, lest they even now begin to show signs of disease and spread it to others. But Charles stood in the front yard when the meeting was over and gathered news from all who passed.

The Dudleys were spared, but Heards' garrison was hit hard, and three had died there. A fisherman and his wife both died, and the trader's son was ill and not apt to recover.

As the patients at the parsonage improved, Jane spent less time cleaning and laundering and more time baking, for Abby's appetite had returned, and Ruth began to eat solid food again. Several of the parishioners brought gifts of food to the parsonage door. Jane shared this bounty with Goody Deane, who still kept the three healthy children.

Late one evening, Charles took Jane's arm and steered her gently into Elizabeth Jewett's chair. He sat down on one of the benches by the table and faced her.

"I shall leave you in the morning, if you think you can manage now."

The thought of his going saddened her, but she realized he had left much undone at home while helping her. "All shall be well here now, I think. Thank you for coming and for working so hard with me."

"Aye, well, don't bring the other children home until all your patients have lost their scabs."

Jane nodded. This advice had been given by the parson himself before he took ill. "I fear Ben and John have tired of living with the widow Deane."

"So do I. I walked over this evening and told the boys they could go home with me in the morning if they wished. They can help me and Richard get on with the new room we're building."

"If you wish to take them, I'm sure it would be a help. Pastor is starting to fret about them and fears they'll wear out the old woman with their restlessness."

Charles's dark eyes were fixed upon her, and Jane wondered what he was thinking. In the past ten days, she'd had little time to meditate on the advice Elizabeth had given her. "Love him," her friend had said. How did a woman go about that? Jane was still not sure she knew how to love her husband. But she had a new conviction that she wanted to.

He reached out and touched her hand with his warm fingers. "When you are ready, send me word, and I will come for you."

"All right."

He nodded. "Get some rest, then. I'll wake you in a few hours, and I'll sleep until dawn."

Jane rested better that night than she had in a long time, though the lumpy straw tick in the loft was uncomfortable. She woke when he came and touched her shoulder gently. In the near darkness, she pulled on her overskirt, stays, and bodice. By the time she found her shoes, Charles had taken her place in bed and was breathing softly.

He came down from the loft at first light without her calling him. After he stoked the fire and filled her woodbox and water pails, she fed him well on the plain fare the parsonage afforded.

Christine and the pastor were stirring as he donned his coat and picked up his musket. "Step outside with me, Jane."

She took her shawl from its peg and followed him onto the doorstone.

Charles took her chin in his hand, turning her face up toward his. "I know it might be a couple more weeks, but. . .you will come home?"

"Aye."

He smiled then, and his features softened. He stooped and kissed her softly then stepped back.

Jane watched him stride across the street toward Goody Deane's cottage. Warmth flooded her.

Dear Lord, are You answering my prayer? Because I think I am beginning to love him. Thank You.

Charles turned in the street and looked back at her.

Jane waved, and he lifted his hat with a tired grin before approaching the widow's door.

◆

Two weeks later, Jane helped Christine to dress, and they fixed breakfast together. Abby seemed as healthy as she had ever been, with only a couple of dark scars on her cheeks revealing her prolonged illness.

The pastor came to the table for the first time in weeks. "I'm still a bit shaky, but I believe I shall stand in the pulpit this Sunday." He sank onto the bench and sighed.

Jane poured his cup full of hot tea. "Give yourself time to recover, sir," she counseled.

After he said the blessing, Jane brought a kettle of corn mush from the fire and ladled out the portions for the others. "Here, Abby. Goodman Dudley brought some nice milk yesterday. Have some on your samp. And there's a bit of maple sugar Mrs. Otis sent over."

Abby wriggled in anticipation. "Can Connie come home today?"

"Not yet, child," her father said. "Your scabs are gone, but Ruth and I are still peppered, and Miss Christine is not quite well yet."

"I feel stronger each day," Christine said. "Before you know it, Abby, you'll be helping me do the Monday washing."

Abby smiled up at her, but suddenly the little girl's face crumpled. "I miss Mama."

The pastor said nothing, but he looked as though he might cry, too.

Jane slipped her arm around Abby's shoulders and pulled her close. "We all miss her sorely. I shall never forget how kind your mother was to me."

"Nor I," Christine said. "She was a dear friend, and a blessing to many."

The pastor pushed back from the table. "Forgive me, ladies, but I feel the need for some fresh air."

Jane eyed him warily, knowing his full strength would not return for some time. "Do you need company, sir?"

"Nay. I shall not be long."

He paused briefly at the door to take his coat from a peg then hurried outside.

Tears bathed Abby's face as she stared at the closed door. "Will Papa die?"

"Nay, child," said Christine. "He is getting well, as are you and I. Ruthie, too."

As though she had heard her name, the two-year-old let out a wail. Jane jumped up and hastened to her pallet. "Well now, Ruth, are you hungry? I thought you would sleep the morning away." Quickly she changed the little girl's clothes and carried her to the table, where she sat down with Ruth on her lap.

Christine, meanwhile, had risen and brought a fresh portion of samp to the table.

Jane dipped a spoonful of the cooked corn dish and held it to the little girl's mouth.

Ruth pushed the spoon away and burrowed against Jane's bodice. "Mama! I want Mama."

Abby's tears began to flow again, and both girls sobbed.

"Oh dear," said Christine. "What shall we do?" Her own eyes glistened.

Jane pulled in a deep breath. "I suppose we shall all cry together, and many times before we are through." A firm knock sounded at the door, and she rose to answer it.

Charles stood outside carrying a burlap sack. "Good day." His somber brown eyes searched Jane's face. "I've brought the boys back."

She looked past him toward the muddy street. "Where are they?"

"We met the parson in the dooryard, and they've walked out back with him." Charles shook his head. "He looks to have lost half his flesh."

"Aye. They're all thin. It's only by God's grace they survived."

"All are gaining strength now?"

She nodded. "Did the boys wear you out?"

"Nay, they're good boys. They helped me a lot, and you shall see the results of their labor when you come home. But they were restless, wanting news of their father. I had them bring their stuff and told them they could stay if he allowed it."

"I expect he will. He misses having them all about him now that he's up again. And the house seems very empty without his wife." Jane stepped back. "Won't you come in?"

"Yes, I'll wait to see what he says about the boys." Charles pulled his hat off and ducked beneath the lintel, blinking in the semidarkness. "What of you, Jane? Are you well? You look thin, too."

"I'm fine. A bit tired."

"I should think so."

Still at the table, Christine stood. "How good of you to come, Goodman Gardner."

"Oh, please. Call me Charles."

She nodded.

"I trust you are on the road to recovery?" he asked.

"I believe I am," Christine said.

Charles held the sack up. "I've not had much success hunting lately, but James Dudley butchered a yearling ram. He sent a hindquarter for the parsonage."

"Wonderful." Jane took the heavy sack and carried it to the worktable. "We haven't had meat here in a week. I'll make a nice soup for tonight's supper."

Charles turned his hat about in his hands. "I hoped you might come home with me, Jane."

She turned and eyed him anxiously. "I daren't leave yet, Charles. Christine is too weak to lift Ruth yet, and if the boys stay, I suppose Constance will come home, too."

He nodded at the obvious implications. More people to cook for, more washing and scrubbing. "When you are able, then."

"I shall."

"It won't be long, sir," Christine said. "You've been most kind to let us have Jane so long."

"Well, I. . ." Charles looked everywhere but at his wife. "You needed her," he said at last, crumpling his hat in his clenched hands. "This were her home for many months, and you needed her."

"Charles! Charles!"

The door crashed open, and Ben Jewett catapulted inside. Jane almost scolded him for speaking so familiarly to Goodman Gardner, but she checked herself. Charles showed no annoyance, and they had just lived two weeks together. Besides, Ben stood only a couple of inches shorter than Charles now, and no doubt he was finding his way into manhood. Perhaps Charles's acceptance and friendship would ease the way for him.

"Father says John and I may stay," Ben said, his eyes gleaming. "We are to take over all the heavy chores, and Miss Jane may go home with you."

"Nay," Jane said quickly. "I shall stay a bit longer, until your father and Christine are stronger. But we are making good progress, and we shall be glad to have you and John here to haul the water and wood."

Charles looked at her and nodded slowly. "That's right. A few more days, perhaps. She must stay. And when you don't need her anymore, then my wife shall come home."

◆

The steady spring rains took the last of the snow and mired the village so that walking to the meetinghouse taxed the most patient souls. But only three days after the boys and Constance returned, the sun shone and the wind blew gently up from the river.

Christine urged Jane to go back to her husband. "You've been away from home a month. Charles needs you more than we do now."

Jane put her hands on her hips and surveyed the cluttered work area. "I don't know, Christine. You're not fully recovered yet. This large brood is a handful."

"Nonsense. Even Ruth is getting about again, and the pastor is back to his preaching. I've two strong boys to help me with the chores, and Goody Deane comes over every day to help me watch the girls and bake."

Jane nodded, knowing it was true. The old widow across the way seemed happy to take part in the household's recovery, and Christine made sure she went home each day with a portion of the baking. The arrangement would benefit both households.

"All right, then. I suppose you're correct." Jane pulled at the strings of her apron and took it off, rolling it into a small bundle. She went to the corner and tucked the apron into her basket with her sewing kit and extra shift. The thought of going back to the farm at the edge of the forest seemed odd. *That's my home,* she reminded herself.

"Take Ben with you," Christine said.

Jane considered that. "He would be all-over mud when he returned, and that would be more work for you. I shall be fine. The savages will wait for better travel conditions before they bother us again."

Abby and Constance stared at her. "You're leaving?" Abby wailed.

Jane went to her and embraced her and Constance. Ruth toddled to them and wriggled into the hug, too.

"I shall come again soon." Jane kissed each one's shining hair. She and Christine had bathed all the girls the day before and combed out their tangled tresses. "You must be good and help your papa and Miss Christine."

"We will." Constance's lips trembled.

"Will you come for—" Abby stopped, and tears trickled down her cheeks.

"What, dear?"

"For when they bury Mama and baby Joseph? Papa says it won't be many weeks now."

Jane pulled her close. "Aye. Send Ben with word when the service will be held. Goodman Gardner and I will be there."

Ruth clung to her with her arms locked about Jane's neck.

Jane held her for a long moment then gently disentangled the little girl's arms. "I'll see you at meeting anyway. That's only four days away, if we're able to get there."

"The streets are so sloppy," Christine said.

"Aye, but we'll manage, unless it rains violently." Jane passed Ruth to her and looked about the little house once more. "I'll stop at the meetinghouse a moment and tell Pastor and the boys I am going."

◆

Charles worked steadily across the back roof, adding course after course of shingles. The new room he and Richard had built was actually two and doubled the size of his house. A roomy pantry nestled between the original cabin and the spacious new bedchamber.

Not only that, but with help from John and Ben Jewett, Charles had built a clothespress. That and the rope bed were the only furnishings in the new room and left it looking bare. But he knew what he would tell Jane. There was plenty of room in there for a spinning wheel and a loom. After harvest next fall, when the cold weather came again, he would build her a loom. He thought he could copy Sarah's. And if he couldn't trade for a wheel, he'd figure out how to build that, too. His hands seemed to have a way when it came to working with wood.

And Jane, he was sure, would find other ways to brighten the room. She was clever with a needle. Maybe she could make some rugs and curtains like Sarah had in her cozy house.

If Jane came back.

The wind had a cold edge. He turned his collar up and tried to drive away the dark thoughts that crept at the edge of his mind. She'd assured him only a few days ago that she would return, and he would cling to the promise.

He reached for another shingle and saw that he'd used nearly all that he'd brought up to the roof in a bushel basket. He would have to go down for more soon. A snowflake landed on his sleeve, and he looked up. The sky had clouded over and a halfhearted, late-season snow was falling. Taking the next shingle, he laid it in place and held the nail to it. Would winter never end? If the snow thickened, he'd have to stop work.

She might want to stay and keep house at the parsonage and never come home.

He cast that thought aside and concentrated on the task at hand. A soft thump came from below, just as he was about to strike with the hammer. He hit his thumb and jumped, pulling his hand up to his mouth. His sudden movement almost overbalanced him, and fear shot through him for an instant as he wobbled on his perch.

Don't do anything suddenly on a roof, you fool, he told himself.

He sat still for a moment and took a deep breath. Suddenly he froze. He had definitely heard a muted sound. Someone was in the house.

Several thoughts ran through his mind. Indians, rifling his foodstuffs? Or Richard, come calling? A scraping sound reached him, and the stone chimney belched a big puff of smoke.

Charles smiled. Could it be? He didn't dare hope, and yet. . .Richard wouldn't build up his fire. He'd have heard him pounding and come around back first thing. Indians would steal what they could and get out. Anyone else would have knocked. It had to be Jane!

With care, he held the last shingle in place and drove the nail in. Cautiously he stood up on the board he'd temporarily fixed along the side of the roof for a brace and walked along it to the edge of the roof, where his rough ladder stood.

He put his hammer in the basket and tossed it down to the ground then swung over to the ladder.

He put his tools away in the barn before going to the house door. The few minutes tortured him sweetly. His disappointment would hit hard if he was wrong. He stood in the barn doorway for half a minute, staring across the yard at the cabin.

She wouldn't have come all the way out here alone, would she? Only last summer, the congregation at another village was ambushed while leaving its Sunday meeting. Jane well knew the dangers of walking about alone and unarmed.

He sniffed the sharp breeze. Someone was cooking dried apple tart in his house.

Charles smiled and strode toward the door.

Chapter 10

C harles closed the door loudly enough so there was no doubt Jane heard it. He removed his coat and hat and hung them near the door.

She stayed bent over her kettle at the hearth, stirring what he assumed was to be their dinner.

"Welcome home."

She turned toward him and nodded soberly; then she went to her worktable and measured some rye flour into a crockery bowl.

Charles took off his boots and hesitated. Should he speak again? Or let her go about her silent routine? "How be the Jewetts?"

"All gaining."

"The boys are pitching in?"

"Aye." She frowned over her concoction and added a teaspoon of something white. "Ben says thank ye for having them and he'll come when you plant."

"Good. I can use him." Charles carried his boots nearer the fireplace, but not too near, to dry out. The fire had burned down to coals. He nearly threw a log on, but perhaps Jane didn't want him to. "Do you be using these coals?"

"Aye."

He took a piece of oak down from the mantel and drew his knife; then he sat down on a stool beside the hearth.

Jane eyed the stick in his hand but went back to her work without speaking.

Charles couldn't help drawing an unfavorable comparison to Sarah Dudley. If Richard sat down to carve on a piece of wood, Sarah would ask him what it was. Richard would probably tease her and make her guess, but Sarah would badger him playfully until he told her. Not Jane.

Ask me. Let me tell you it's for your loom, sweet wife. Please ask me.

Five minutes later, Jane carried her Dutch oven to the hearth. She took down the small shovel, pulled a bed of red coals onto the stone hearth, and positioned the oven precisely over it. Then she scooped hot coals onto the lid. She straightened and hung up the shovel. "We shall eat soon. I'm sorry I didn't have it ready when you stopped work."

"Nay, I stopped because of the snow. And. . .I'm pleased to find you home, Jane."

She seemed to mull that over for a few seconds; then her lips twitched, but she said nothing. She returned his gaze.

He wished he could smooth out the fine crease between her eyebrows. "Have you seen the new chambers?"

She blinked. "Nay, not yet."

Charles rose and put the oak stick and his knife on the mantel. "Come, then."

He'd kept the doors to the bedchamber and pantry closed to conserve heat. Though he'd moved the bed into the new room, he had yet to sleep in there. Instead, he had thrown his pallet down near the fire the last two nights, unwilling to claim the new room as his own. He had built it for Jane. Let her decide.

She'd been away so long, he was no longer sure she would welcome him again into her bed. They'd spent far more of their short marriage apart than together, and perhaps she preferred it that way. She didn't seem any too pleased to be back here with him.

He walked to the pantry and paused, waiting for her to step over near him. When he opened the door, she gasped. "Oh, Charles."

He let her pass him, and she stepped inside then stood gaping at the shelves he had fitted. A long board at waist height held her kneading trough and dishpan. "You did all this while I was gone?"

"Aye. Richard and his father helped me, and then Ben and John."

"I didn't expect anything so fine." Her gray eyes glittered in the dim light afforded by the one narrow window at the end of the pantry.

Charles felt a knot in his shoulders come loose, and he leaned against the door frame. She had smiled—just a little smile, but it was enough. "I'm glad you like it. When I sell my furs, I'll bring you some supplies. And at harvesttime, we'll fill these shelves."

She nodded.

He turned away and waited for her to come out.

She stepped into the main room and carefully shut the door, testing the latch.

What would she think of the new bedchamber? He wished suddenly that he'd gone to the trader and taken credit for more furniture. But no, that would only upset her again, and she'd be scheming to earn money for his increased debts. Best to pay things down slowly as he'd been doing and get the things that would make them comfortable when they could afford them.

He swung the door open. Her skirt brushed against him as she entered the room. She stood in silence so long that he walked around her and studied her face.

"It's so large," she said softly.

"Aye."

She walked to one of the windows and looked out at the woods behind the cabin.

"We can put up the shutters inside to keep the cold out," he said. No need to mention that the shutters would also keep the Indians from firing into the house. "The fireplace isn't as large as the other one, but it will take the chill off at night. And I. . .I thought you'd want your loom and wheel in here later." Still she said nothing. "Or we could partition it off separate, if you'd like that. But I thought you might like to keep it one large room."

"I can make rugs," she said.

His relief was so great, he almost laughed.

"Aye, and curtains if you like."

She nodded, and he grinned.

"It's a fine room." She turned slowly, and her gaze fixed on the new clothes-press. She threw him a look that was almost inquisitive, and his pulse quickened. Slowly she approached it and opened the doors.

He was glad he hadn't put anything in it yet. "You can arrange your things however you like. Oh, and Sarah sent this over for you." He went to the bed and lifted two lengths of material he had left folded there.

"What is it?"

"Some worsted and flannel. Richard's father took a boat to Boston and came back with a lot of stuff for his wife and Catherine and Sarah. Too much stuff, Sarah said."

Jane nodded. Sarah loved to give simple gifts, now that she was able. "That's kind of them."

He laid the cloth down and stepped away.

Jane reached out and felt it.

Charles renewed his resolve to take their marriage at her pace. Jane was his wife until death should part them—that much he had settled with God. He would do all he could to make a go of it. Even if that meant keeping his distance.

He pulled in a deep breath. "Jane?"

She looked toward him, a question in her eyes.

"I. . .well, I thought if you. . .if you preferred it, I could stay out yonder." He jerked his head toward the main room.

"For what?"

"I mean. . .I could sleep out there if you want me to."

Her features froze.

Charles felt suddenly empty. He leaned against the stone fireplace and waited for her to say something—anything.

Instead, she turned to look out the second window.

"Jane?"

She didn't turn.

He sighed. "I'll bring some wood in here and make up a fire so it will be warm if you wish to work in here this afternoon."

As he headed for the door, she spoke. "Charlie."

He spun around. "What?"

"We be wed."

"Aye."

She nodded. "So don't be daft." She brushed past him into the main room and began to scrub the table.

He stood in the doorway, uncertain how to take her words. Was he daft to build a fire and burn extra wood when it wasn't needed? Or to. . .

He stared at her straight back and her thin shoulders, at her dark blond hair that glinted red, pulled up on the back of her head, at the curve of her neck above the edge of her bodice.

Lord, I shall take this as a sign of hope.

◆

In early May, the breezes wafting off the river warmed the village. The maples, oaks, and beeches uncurled tiny leaves. And the sexton dug graves in the churchyard for those who had died during the winter.

Charles and Jane made the trip to the village.

The muddy paths were drying out, and the entire Dudley family walked with them. James and his wife, along with Catherine, Stephen, Richard, and Sarah, carried gifts for the Jewett family: parched corn, a jug of molasses, bacon, and a large sack of wool for Christine to spin.

Charles carried a cake Jane had baked and a pair of small wooden dolls he had carved for Ruth and Constance. Jane added a few scraps of flannel for the girls to use for doll clothes. Charles wasn't sure the little girls would find his dolls appealing, but Jane assured him that anything new would catch their attention for at least a short time and keep their thoughts from dwelling on their grief.

Nearly all the villagers gathered in the churchyard for the occasion. Though it saddened them to bid a last farewell to the departed, it also cheered them to stand together in the sunshine and see all who had survived the cruel winter. Parson Weaver had come all the way out from Portsmouth to preach the funeral sermon for Elizabeth Jewett and the other smallpox victims.

Charles thought Pastor Jewett looked stronger. His step was certainly steadier, but his large frame was still too spare, and new lines etched his forehead.

After the graveside services, Jane and Charles went with the Dudleys to visit the trading post. By unspoken agreement, Charles and Jane bought nothing, but he noted the pleasure Sarah and her sister-in-law, Catherine, took in picking out notions for their sewing projects. He wished he could tell Jane to purchase whatever she liked. Someday he'd be able to do that.

She glanced toward him just then, over the tables of merchandise, and smiled. It was almost as though she'd spoken to him. *I have all I need, husband.*

The next evening, Charles sorted his sacks of seed. Jane had traded shell beans for pumpkin seeds with Sarah.

"This be the seeds I promised Christine." She set aside a small pouch containing a selection of vegetable seeds.

Charles nodded. "We've plenty."

"She has some Goody Jewett saved, but I want her to have plenty to plant in the garden at the parsonage."

"We can take them to her Sunday."

"Thank you, Charles."

He shrugged. It was a small thing. And yet he felt that they grew closer each day, and their purposes converged as they learned to know each other better. They seemed to talk more now, though it was usually of inconsequential things.

Jane's growing contentment soothed him, and he was happier than he'd been since the day she agreed to be his wife.

———◆———

Jane set off one pleasant morning toward Sarah and Richard's cabin. The men had widened the path through the woods, and from their yard Charles could see the peak of the Dudleys' roof and watch her nearly all the way to the neighbors' house. Jane was permitted to make the short walk unescorted, so long as he knew she was going. This small added freedom cheered Jane. She and Sarah made the journey one way or the other nearly every day.

In Jane's basket was a baby's gown she was stitching for Sarah. The glad news of a coming child was not unexpected. When the smallpox struck two months earlier, Jane had wondered if that was Richard's reason for not allowing his wife to go into the disease-ridden Jewett household. It gave the two young women much to talk about these days.

As she came to the corner of the stockade Richard was building, she saw two smaller figures skipping about in the yard between the fence and the house. "Abby! Constance! How delightful to find you here," she called.

As the girls turned toward her, their faces lit with joy. "Miss Jane!" Abby ran to her with Constance only a step behind. "We came to call."

"What a treat." Jane embraced them both. "May I assume Miss Christine is inside?"

"And Ruthie, too," Constance said.

"Indeed! Did Ruth walk all this way with you?"

"Papa carried her," Abby told her. "He had to see Mr. James Dudley, and he said Miss Christine might as well take us for a visit to the younger Dudleys. So here we are."

The cottage door opened, and Sarah grinned at her. "I thought I heard your voice. Come in, Jane. I found some new wintergreen leaves yesterday, and we're just about to have tea."

Jane greeted Christine with enthusiasm and allowed Ruth to climb up on her lap as she sat at Sarah's table. The little girl clutched the wooden doll Charles had made her, and it was now dressed in a tiny linen shift and flannel overskirt. Jane recognized Christine's meticulous hemstitching. "What fine clothing your dolly has."

Ruth smiled and held the doll close.

Christine lifted a linen napkin from her basket on the table, disclosing a plate of small raisin cakes. The little girls' eyes grew large as she placed it on the table. "There now, young ladies, one cake apiece."

The three Jewett girls quickly claimed their treats, and Jane also accepted one of the cakes.

"Christine was just giving me the village news," Sarah said. "She is living with Goody Deane now."

"Is Goody Deane ill?" Jane asked. "Does she need your nursing?"

"Nay," said Christine. "It's for propriety."

"To quell the gossips," Sarah said in a low voice. "You know how it is in Cochecho."

"Aye," said Jane. Only the Indians inflicted more harm on the village than did the wagging tongues of its residents.

Christine leaned toward her and murmured, "One of the deacons told the pastor it was unconscionable for him to keep me at the parsonage any longer. It struck him to the heart, poor man. He's been so diligent since his dear wife died, trying to do all he can for his people and yet be at hand for the children when they need him."

Sarah clucked her tongue. "It must have shocked him to learn his people could think ill of him."

"Unfortunately, that is the way folks think," Christine said. "Now I fear he's sunk into his studies. Spends all day at the meetinghouse poring over his books, since the weather took a turn for the warmer."

"How sad. He was very fond of Elizabeth." Jane looked down at Ruth, but the little girl seemed to be concentrating on her raisin cake.

Sarah refilled her kettle and stirred up the fire. "I suppose that some folks would consider it improper for you to stay there, even with five children in the house."

"They do," Christine said.

"So you sleep at Goody Deane's across the way and go back and forth?" Jane asked.

"Aye, both of us. I think the widow enjoys it tremendously, doing for other people. She sweeps and spins and plays cat's cradle with the girls. She's good company for me, now that you two have deserted me."

Jane stared at her. "Well, Miss Hardin! I don't think I've ever heard you speak so much before."

Christine chuckled.

"Goody Deane is large on conversation," Abby Jewett said. "She doesn't believe in keeping silence all day."

A smile tugged at Christine's lips. "She says the nuns taught me that, and I must get over it."

"Perhaps she's right." Sarah sat down with them and sipped her tea.

When the three little girls had finished their refreshments, Sarah allowed them all to go out again to play.

"Stay inside the stockade. Abby, you'll watch Ruth closely? You know the fence isn't finished yet, and I don't want her wandering off."

"I will, Miss Sarah."

When Sarah rejoined the others at the table, Jane said, "Charles tells me that as soon as the men have their corn planted, they'll put up the new addition to the parsonage."

"It can't come too soon," Christine said. "Though it will be bittersweet for the pastor, I suppose. Elizabeth so looked forward to having more space. Now it will be just him and the children."

"But they need privacy for the girls, and a quiet place for the pastor to study in winter without shivering over at the meetinghouse," Jane said.

Christine nodded. "Aye. The boys will have the loft again, and they can get all the bedding out of the keeping room."

Sarah smiled. "The church folk will be able to visit the parson without stepping on quilts and babies."

They all sat in silence for a moment, remembering the little boy who was buried with Elizabeth just a few days earlier.

Jane wiped a tear from her cheek. "I do miss Elizabeth."

"Poor Pastor." Christine lifted her apron and wiped her eyes with the hem.

Sarah lifted Jane's cup to refill it with tea. "Come, let us talk of more pleasant things."

"All right," Christine said. "I've a bit of pleasant news. It means less work for me. Ruth has stopped wearing clouts."

Jane and Sarah laughed.

"That is good news," Jane said.

"Aye. I've washed them all, and on Sunday you and Richard can stop in after meeting and get them. A present for your little one."

"Oh, that is very generous," Sarah said.

"Well, the Jewetts shan't be needing them anymore, and Parson said to give them to some as can use them. Of course I thought of you, though some are worn quite thin."

"Thank you. I shall be glad to have them, but our baby won't be here until November." Sarah's face went a becoming, delicate pink. "If anyone in the village needs them before, you may pass them along."

A half hour later, the pastor came to collect Christine and the children. He greeted Jane cheerfully, but she noted the drawn look about his eyes. He invited her and Sarah to visit Christine and the children at the parsonage whenever they wished. Both promised to come soon.

"So tragic," Jane said as she and Sarah watched the figures stride down the path toward the village.

"He'll not soon leave off grieving for Elizabeth," Sarah agreed.

"She told me I must love Charles, you know, just before she died." Jane glanced over at Sarah to catch her reaction.

"Oh? And how are you doing? I've been praying for you all this time, since you told me how much you wanted to please him."

"I try. But I'm not sure I give him all he needs. He doesn't seem truly happy."

"Then you must figure out what more he needs."

Jane smiled. "I know what he *wants*. He's hinted it a couple of times."

"And what is that?"

"A child."

"And is that so impossible? Surely if I can do it. . ."

Sarah's coy laugh almost lightened Jane's heart, but her memories squelched the possibility. "Perhaps."

"Ah. I see. Your marriage in Canada. I should have realized. Three years with Monsieur Robataille and no babies."

"Actually—" Jane bit her lip, but it was too late. She'd already snagged Sarah's attention. "Actually there was a child," she whispered.

Sarah's features drooped. "It's cold out here. Come inside and tell me about it." She drew Jane back into the house and stoked the fire once more.

Jane pulled her chair close to the hearth and kept her shawl, for the brief time outside and her dark thoughts had chilled her.

"So"—Sarah placed a fresh cup of tea in Jane's hand—"what happened?"

Jane sat for a long moment, looking into the blaze. It was something she didn't want to dredge up, but Sarah was a woman and her best friend. And she knew part of it now. Jane couldn't very well back down and refuse to confide in her.

She started to sip her tea, but it was too hot, so she set it over onto the table and folded her hands in her lap. "Monsieur Robataille was not present when it happened. He went away, you see. He always went in spring, on a long voyage. And before he left, he told me all the things I must do in his absence, just as he did the year before. I must tend the gardens and the livestock, arrange for men to get the harvest in, and so on. And if I couldn't hire men to do it, I must do it myself."

"Did he know you were expecting a child?"

"He knew." Jane bowed her head and fought the stinging sensation of tears trying to escape. "He had one hired man to tend the sheep. But the shepherd was old, and he was not able by himself to do the heavy farmwork. It was up to me to find someone. The year before I had hired three boys, and I thought we did well, but when Monsieur Robataille returned in the fall, he was not pleased. We were late getting some of the crops in, and they were past prime."

"What happened?"

Jane reached for her tea and took a drink. Still Sarah waited. Jane did not look up at her, but she said, "He struck me."

Sarah drew a deep breath. "I'm so sorry."

Jane nodded. "It was not the first time, nor the last. And so I was determined to do it right the second year. He told me that when he came back, he wanted to find the baby in the cradle and the crops in the barn."

"Charming man, wasn't he?" Sarah raised her cup to her lips.

Jane sat still, feeling the welcome heat of the fire on her face. She let her shawl slip down from her shoulders. "I couldn't get enough help, and in August I spent nearly every day in the fields. All day we worked, bringing in hay, harvesting corn. And then one morning I woke up, and I knew something wasn't right. I was bleeding, but it wasn't time for the baby until October." She sobbed. "I sent the old shepherd for the midwife, but it took hours for her to get there. Or so it seemed. I don't really know how long it took. I was out of my mind with fright."

"And the baby?" Sarah whispered.

Jane's tears spilled over. She swiped at them with a trembling hand. "When Madame Couteau saw him, she shook her head and said he was dead before my pains started. 'This one was never meant to breathe,' she said."

Sarah leaned over and tucked a handkerchief in Jane's hand.

Jane wiped her cheeks with it. "She asked me if I wanted to send for the priest, and I said no. It was too far, and anyway, I didn't like the thought of having him come around." She shivered. "He always made me feel worthless. He knew that in my heart I kept my 'heretical' beliefs, I suppose."

"Heretical?" Sarah's eyes widened.

"I would not give up being a Protestant."

"Ah."

"The midwife took the baby. . .took him out of the room. I just cried until I went to sleep. Later I woke up, and Madame Couteau told me she had buried him. And so far as I know, she never told anyone, nor did I. It was considered very bad, to bury him without the priest. But I prayed at his grave many times and asked God to forgive me if I did wrong."

Sarah left her chair and put her arms around Jane. "My poor, dear Jane. You didn't do wrong."

"I hope not."

"So Robataille found out when he came home?"

"Yes. He thundered and screamed. He'd been drinking, of course. He always stopped in town with his friends on the way home and had some liquor. He was very angry, and he said it was all my fault that his child was dead. I ought to have kept myself strong enough to bear a healthy child. Not only that, but I hadn't seen that his son had a Christian burial."

"Oh, Jane."

"And of course, the crops weren't in. I'd been ill for weeks afterward, and I couldn't work. The old shepherd had got some men to come for a few days, but it wasn't nearly enough. The wheat was rotting in the field."

"And your husband misused you again."

"Aye. I was so bruised I could barely get about to make his meals. And I never. . . There were no more babies after that. I wondered if things had gone so wrong inside me that I couldn't. Of course, Monsieur Robataille railed about it now and again. He'd made a bad bargain and got a lazy, barren wife. But the next spring he went off again, and he never came back."

"He died on his voyage?"

"Aye. They told me he was drunk and fell overboard and drowned. I believe it. They brought him home to the village, and I let the priest bury him in the churchyard." Jane rested her head against Sarah's shoulder. "I've never told anyone how it was with him. No one. Only you."

"But you must tell Charlie."

"No, I can't." Sobs wracked her body.

Sarah held her, smoothing Jane's hair as she cried.

Jane let the misery of those weeks and months alone take over for a few minutes, feeling guilty even as she cried. Jacques Robataille was not a man worth crying over, and she didn't regret being ransomed from that bitter life. So why was she weeping now? She had landed in a much better situation, and she ought to rejoice. But she couldn't stop sobbing.

When she quieted at last, Sarah said, "You don't think Charlie should know all this?"

Jane drew a ragged breath and squared her shoulders. "I suppose you think it wasn't fair of me not to tell him before we wed. But I didn't. And now. . ."

A fresh wave of guilt washed over her. Had she married Charles under false pretenses? Of course a young man like him wanted children and expected to have them. She met Sarah's gaze. "If it looks like I can't carry another child for him, I will tell him. But I hope. . ."

"What, dear?"

"Well, I wonder if I'm not with child now."

Sarah drew back and stared at her. "Now? But, Jane! This is good news."

"Is it?" Jane felt a new tear trickle down her face. "I'm frightened, Sarah. What if I can't carry a healthy child?"

"But Charlie won't work you to death or hit you! Of course you can have a healthy baby now."

"Maybe." Jane dabbed at her eyes. "But. . .it might turn out like the last time. There's a lot of pain in childbearing anyway, but there's more pain, and sorrow, too, if things don't go right." She couldn't help picturing the little grave in the windswept pasture back in Quebec. "Forgive me. I'm just so fearful that perhaps I can't give Charles what he wants most. But if I can—" She darted a quick look at Sarah's trusting face. "You mustn't tell him yet. Or Richard, either. Not until I'm sure. Please, Sarah."

"All right. But I hope it's true, and we'll both have babies next winter. Jane, you have to promise me. . ."

"What?"

"That if something goes wrong, you will tell him, so he can fetch me right away for you."

Jane nodded, feeling a bit nauseous just to think of the agony she'd endured that other time. "I pray that I don't go through that again."

Sarah grasped both her hands. "So do I. But if the worst happens, I'll be at your side. And Charlie won't be hundreds of miles away with a bateau crew, trading and drinking while you suffer. He'll be there with you."

Jane sobbed, and Sarah hugged her close again. "I'm sorry. I shouldn't have said that."

Heavy footsteps sounded outside, and Sarah leaped up. "Oh my! Richard is here for dinner. Where has the morning gone?"

"I must go. Charles will want a meal, as well, and I've overstayed my welcome." Jane bounded out of the chair and pulled her shawl on as Richard and his younger brother, Stephen, came in. She hoped they wouldn't notice her puffy red eyes.

Chapter 11

A week later, Charles sold the last of his furs from the season. He sent them with the trader on a ship to Boston. Four days after that the trader brought him his profit.

Charles left Jane at the Dudley garrison while he went to the village with Richard. All morning, Sarah and Jane quilted with Goody Dudley and Richard's sister, Catherine.

When the men returned, Catherine ran out to open the gate for them at Richard's shout.

Charles came in grinning and handed a small leather pouch to Richard's father. "I thank you again, Goodman Dudley. You helped Jane and me at a time when we needed it sorely."

James weighed the pouch in his hand then set it on the mantel. "Thank you, Charles. I could wait a bit, if you've need of the money for other things."

"Nay," Charles said quickly. "This squares my debt, and now Jane and I are able to go on unencumbered." He looked Jane in the eye and nodded.

She felt her face flush, and she looked down, crumpling her apron in her hands. The furs had sold for enough to discharge the debt. She never should have doubted Charles.

"Come, wife," he said. "My pack is outside. I've brought you a few things. We'll live small until harvest, but we'll get by and be happy."

"Of course we shall," Jane said. She wove her needle into a scrap of cloth and put it in her basket, with the half dozen fresh eggs and small cake of maple sugar Richard's mother had pressed upon her. "Thank you so much, Goody Dudley. Catherine, come visit me soon."

Sarah kissed her cheek. "I'll see you tomorrow."

Richard opened the door and held it for Jane, grinning as though he knew something hilarious.

She eyed him and sidled past him down the step. Charles came behind her, and she felt his steady hand on her elbow as she descended to the yard.

Yip! Something brown and furry jumped up from the ground beside his pack and let out a fierce bark.

She jumped back, and Charles's arm clamped about her waist.

"What, scared of a half-grown puppy, wife?"

She stared at the little brown dog. Its nose trembled, and its tail curled high over its back. It stood with all four feet planted, glaring at her and snarling menacingly in its throat, as though it would guard Charles's pack with its very life. She laughed. "He's only a baby."

"Aye. And needs some training. Are you up to the task?"

"I'm not sure. Will you help me?"

"Of course. I couldn't buy you a musket, but Captain Baldwin let me have this pup for a song. Perhaps the dog will bring you a little measure of security. Oh, and I've bartered for a few chickens, too. I'll fetch them home tomorrow."

Charles untied a rope from the strap of his pack, and Jane saw that the other end was fixed in a firm loop around the dog's neck. Her husband turned and waved at Richard and his family. "Farewell, Dudleys. And beware when you approach our cabin that we now have a fierce protector."

◆

Two days later, Charles answered Richard's call to help him raise the gate in his new stockade. Stephen also came to help with the chore.

The gate was made, and the hinges set on it. All the three needed to do was hoist it into place.

"Be sure you fix some sort of lock on it," Charles said, "else the enemy would be able to remove the gate as easily as we put it in place."

"Aye," said Richard. "I've iron bolts to drive into place above each hinge, once we've raised it."

They put their strength into lifting the gate of heavy oak and positioning it. Then they let the pins on the hinges fall into place. Richard placed his ladder next to the gatepost and climbed it. Charles stood below to hand him his tools.

"You've finished this none too soon," Stephen said when his brother climbed down again.

"I know it."

"You think the Algonquin tribes will molest us again this summer?" Charles asked.

A dark look passed between Richard and Stephen.

"What?" Charles asked. "You know something."

"I was hunting yesterday," Stephen said. "Two warriors surprised me in the woods, up near the falls."

"Have they come down to fish?"

"Aye. But more than that."

Charles passed the hammer from one hand to the other. "All right. What?"

"These were two St. Francois men," Stephen said.

"That's the tribe you were with last, up in Quebec?"

"I spent nearly four years with them. They are closely related to the

213

Pennacooks Sarah lived with."

Charles nodded. The Pennacook and Saco tribes of the Abenaki confederacy had united to burn the village of Cochecho in 1689 and had killed nearly half the inhabitants. About thirty whites were carried off captive, with himself, Stephen, Sarah, and Jane among them.

"Sarah was adopted by a Pennacook woman," Stephen went on. "The tribe is dwindling. They sold some of their captives to the French. I ended up with their cousins, the St. Francois, farther to the north."

"But you came back." Charles well recalled the desperate trip he and Richard had made into Canada to try to find Stephen.

"I did. But they were not happy. I had pledged to stay with my Indian family, and I fully intended to do so. But after seeing Richard again. . ." Stephen cleared his throat. "I had to sneak away, or they would not have let me leave."

"And now they've found you again."

"Aye. They know I'm living here with my parents again."

Charles took a deep breath and turned to Richard. "Are we all in danger?"

"Perhaps."

Charles nodded. "Have you told Sarah?"

"Not yet. I wanted to finish the stockade first. I'll tell her tonight."

"You say they're camped at the falls. That's only twelve miles from here." Charles looked toward the river, but the intervening woods hid it from view. "What can we do?"

"I told my father," Stephen said. "He doesn't wish to fort up in the village. He thinks we can defend his garrison if necessary."

Charles shook his head. "They burned five garrisons that night."

"We know," Richard said. "Do you think we should all move into town? Take up residence at Otises' or Heards' garrison until they've left?"

Charles considered that. It might be safer to stay for a while at one of the larger compounds, but he didn't want to neglect his farm and sit idle in another man's house. "No. Unless. . ." He looked keenly at Stephen. "These warriors were men you knew?"

Stephen nodded.

"What did they say to you?"

"That I had betrayed their family. Their aunt had adopted me, and they said her heart was broken when I left. They said they could have killed me right then, but that would only make her grieve more."

"Did they ask you to go back to the tribe?"

"Not in so many words."

Richard picked up the ladder. "Come, boys, let's put these things away. I'm sure Charles doesn't want to leave Jane alone long."

"They didn't seem in a warlike mood," Stephen said, swinging the gate shut behind them. He put the two bars in place.

"They wouldn't come after you, would they?" Richard asked.

"I don't think they would force me to go back."

"I don't like them being so close," Charles said.

Stephen shrugged. "They come every year."

"I know."

Stephen chuckled a bit sheepishly. "I came with them once, three summers ago."

"What?" Richard dropped the ladder against the inside wall of the stockade and stared at him. "You came that close to home, and we didn't know it?"

"Just that one time. I was tempted to come over here, but they watched me. And at that time I was confused. I didn't think I was, but now I can see that it's true. I thought the Indian way was better, and I didn't wish to live the white way again."

Charles refused to dwell on that or to wonder what the lad would have done if the Indians had raided his father's house that summer. "But now?" He eyed Stephen anxiously. "You wouldn't go back to them now, would you, Stephen? Your mother—"

Stephen shook his head. "Nay, I am here for good. I have made my peace with God. And I shall not hunt anymore while the tribe is at the falls. I've no wish to meet them again."

Charles pondered that. Should he tell Jane? He didn't want to alarm her. They were about to plant their crops. He would be extra careful and not let her work in the field alone. He would stay closer to home than he had been of late. Uneasily, he glanced at the sky and saw that the sun was high overhead. "I must go home."

"You can take dinner with us," Richard said. "I'm sure Sarah has cooked enough."

"Nay. Thank you, but I don't think I'll leave Jane alone any longer."

◆

Jane's back ached as she bent to drop bean seeds in the furrow. Charles came behind her with his hoe, covering the seeds over and tamping the earth. All afternoon he had trudged along the rows with his musket slung over his shoulder and his hoe in his hands.

The dog, which Jane had named Samson, trotted about the field, sniffing here and there, snapping at bugs, but he always returned to Charles. As they neared the end of a row, he galloped toward them and plopped down in the loose earth at Charles's feet. He stared up at his master, tail wagging, with a pathetically wistful expression on his face. Charles laughed aloud and stooped to pet him. Samson woofed and ran off again to explore the brush pile at the corner of the field.

Jane feared Samson was too friendly to make a good watchdog, but somehow Charles seemed to have gotten across to him that Gardners were good and anyone else approaching the homestead was suspect and therefore worthy of much noise and ferocity. The dog had scared Sarah when she visited, jumping toward her with his teeth bared, halted only by the chain that held him tethered to the barn wall. But inside the house he was gentle, and Charles encouraged Jane to spoil him just a bit so that he would love her.

"You be the one to feed him," Charles had told her. "If you pet him regularly when you give him his feed, he'll be your slave. He'll go with you when you want to go to Sarah's or Catherine's, and if you meet anyone, he'll stand and protect you."

"What can he do?" Jane had asked. "He's only a youngster."

"He'll grow yet. And don't let his size fool you. If you win him over, you'll have his loyalty, and he'll defend you tooth and nail."

And so she did as Charles said. She fed Samson special treats but didn't urge him to befriend the neighbors.

At the end of the row, she straightened, shoving her fists into her lower back and watching Charles finish covering the seeds with soil.

"What now?" she asked. "More beans?"

Charles squinted up at the sky. The sun had sunk behind the trees edging their field. "You've done enough for one day. I shall plant another row while you go and put our supper on the table."

She nodded. "It shan't take me very long. I left the stew simmering."

Charles had killed a feral pig a few days earlier, and they'd dined on pork and shared a roast with the Dudleys. It pleased Jane to be the one giving the portion of meat. Sarah had come to help Jane try out the lard, a job the women usually did at fall butchering time. But Jane didn't mind. The nights were still cool enough to keep the meat from spoiling quickly. Having fresh meat in late May was a luxury, and she could see that her husband enjoyed it, too.

Her sore muscles protested as she plodded to the house. She couldn't think of it as a cabin anymore. It was too fine for that now, with the two large rooms and the luxurious pantry, though most of its shelves were still bare.

The small barn was complete now, too, and Charles was confident they would soon be able to buy a heifer and a few sheep. The half dozen chickens he had bartered for tottered about the yard, scratching for insects, as she approached the door. Their farm was on its way to prosperity.

And their family would increase. She was almost sure now. Not that she would let herself rejoice until she felt the baby kick. That would be the sign that all was well, and then she would tell Charles. She knew he would be pleased.

She could almost see his contented smile as he sorted through the hardwood logs he had cut and set aside to dry, hunting for just the right wood from which to build his son's cradle. And she would stitch a flannel gown for her own babe and embroider it all over with rosebuds.

Samson came and thrust his nose into her palm. She petted him, and he turned and ran back toward the garden where Charles still worked.

Jane went into the dim house and hung up her shawl. She found herself humming a psalm as she swung the crane out from the fireplace, getting her stewpot out of the way, and poked up the fire. Charles had been so good to her, she would like to give him the gift of a child. A son he could teach to hunt and fish and farm.

Yesterday she'd almost told him when he came in from planting corn and found her napping in the middle of the morning. She was so tired all the time. Today she'd made an effort to hide her fatigue and keep up with Charles as they planted the garden. She didn't want him to feel she couldn't work at his side when he needed her.

Their relationship was entirely different from the one she'd had with Jacques Robataille. She'd felt like a slave those three years. Monsieur Robataille told her what to do then went away. If he returned and found things weren't done to his satisfaction, he made her pay for it.

Charlie, on the other hand, borrowed James Dudley's oxen to plow his field. He put the bag of seeds in Jane's hand and followed her step by step down the rows, covering the beans and peas that she dropped, watching over her all the time. And at night he came in for his supper exhausted and thanked her for cooking it.

Yes, things were very different with Charles than they had been on the farm in Quebec. Could things get any better, she wondered? More to the point, was there anything she could do personally to make things better for the man who treated her so well?

Aye, she told herself. *You can tell him he'll be a father next winter, and that will make him the happiest man in the colony.*

But if I tell him, and then I find out it isn't really so. . .

No, it was so. It had to be. The morning nausea she'd only just overcome, the aching muscles, the chronic fatigue, the missing cycle. Sarah insisted it was true. A child was growing inside her. Sarah also badgered her to tell her husband.

Nay, better wait a little while longer, just in case.

Jane stirred up the dough for fresh biscuits. The new lard would make up for the lack of milk and the flat taste of last year's flour. She hurried to get the biscuits cooking in the Dutch oven.

Her heart lifted as she heard Charles's firm step at the door. While he came

217

Chapter 12

Jane gasped and ducked inside, slammed the door, and groped for the bar. "Charlie! Quick!"

Charles leaped from his chair. "What is it?"

"Indians!"

Her husband was at her side, sliding the heavy bar into place and slipping the two iron hooks he'd installed at the top and bottom of the oak door into their staples. As soon as the door was secure, he stepped to the corner where he had left his musket leaning a few minutes earlier. "Where are they?" he asked.

"I only saw one, just beyond the east corner of the barn. He's killed Samson, I fear."

"Get my bullet pouch and powder horn."

Jane rushed to grab them from the shelf beside his leatherworking tools.

"Now put up the shutters in the bedchamber." Charles slung the strap of the powder horn over his neck.

Jane ran to the other room and quickly raised the shutters, turning the wooden blocks that held them in place. The room became pitch-dark, and she groped her way back to the doorway.

Charles had closed all the shutters but one in the keeping room and was staring through the slot that looked out on the barn.

"Do you see them?"

"Nay." He glanced at her. "That dog saved our lives, I've no doubt."

Jane gritted her teeth. "Well, they aren't saved yet."

"Are you certain of what you saw? I mean. . .it couldn't have been Stephen Dudley, could it?"

"He wore buckskins, and his hair hung down in a long lock. Stephen cut his hair and has put off his Algonquin clothing."

"Aye, it's true."

"Besides, Samson would still be barking if it were Stephen come to call. And Stephen would have come to the door by now."

"I fear you are right. I only hoped there might be a mistake."

A sudden *thunk* on the roof caused both Charles and Jane to look upward.

"Something hit the roof," Jane said.

Charles tightened his grasp on the stock of his musket. "Pray that it's not a fire arrow."

"The shingles. . ."

"Will not catch as readily as thatch would, but those on the front of the house are seasoned and dry."

"Charles!" She stepped toward him and stopped. Panicking would not help. "Think you they will burn the house around us?"

"They might."

She shivered. "Why are they so quiet? When they attacked Major Waldron's, they shrieked and howled."

"He saw you when you looked out. They've lost the element of surprise. But still—"

A missile whizzed in through the window slit, narrowly missing Charles's ear, and tore through the air between them. It struck the stone fireplace opposite and clattered to the floor. A scream stuck in Jane's throat as she stared down at the shattered arrow.

Charles looked at her in the dimness for an instant; then he whirled once more to the narrow window and peered out into the twilight.

"Charles, don't!"

He flattened himself against the wall beside the aperture. "Would you have me put up the shutters and wait for them to burn us out?"

She gulped and nudged the arrow with her toe. "Is it Pennacook? Can you tell?"

"Bring it here."

She picked up the end with the fletching and took it to him, staying clear of the line of fire through the window.

Charles held up the broken shaft, examining the feather work. "One of the Algonquin tribes, anyway. But they're all kin. The tribes could join together, as the Saco and Pennacook did at the massacre six years ago." He shook his head. "Either the archer was right outside the window, or that was an incredibly fortunate shot. The opening is only three inches wide." He drew Jane closer to the wall and held her against him for a moment. "I'm sorry, dear wife."

Breathing was suddenly a chore, and she wished she could stay sheltered in his arms forever. But she pulled away from him and straightened her shoulders. "Can't you speak to them? Tell them you are a friend?"

"Am I?"

She hesitated, not sure of his meaning. "You lived with them. You know their language."

"I don't think they consider me their friend anymore, dearest. I left them and turned back to my own people. When Richard and I went looking for Stephen, we were not treated as friends."

"But still, Charlie! Might it not give them pause to hear you speak in their own tongue?"

Still he stood unmoving.

A chilling scream split the night. Jane dove into his arms.

"These may be men I hunted and raided with a few years ago," Charles said softly, his lips against her hair. "What would I tell them? I'll never go back to their ways. And I shall not open the door and invite them to supper, Jane."

"Do you wish me to go into the bedchamber and look out the back?"

"I should hate for you to expose yourself."

Another arrow thunked against the wall outside the window.

Jane raised her chin. "I won't be captured again, Charles."

He nodded. "Then we need to know how many they are and where. I'll let the fire die out. If you see any flicker of light outside or smell smoke or hear a crackle of flame, you tell me."

"Aye. They couldn't come in through the chimney, could they?"

"Nay, it's too small. There's one loophole up in the loft yonder. I'll climb up and see if I can see anything from there. Mayhap they won't look up and I can surprise them."

"Do be careful." She crept through the bedroom door and cautiously lowered the shutter on the window nearest the bed, crouching beneath the casement. When nothing happened, she straightened beside it and leaned over for a quick glance outside. It was now so dark that she could see little. The trees at the edge of the clearing waved, and a breeze soughed through the branches.

Jane shivered. She wished she had grabbed her butcher knife as she left the kitchen. She stared out into the night, keeping to one side just in case a savage should fire point-blank at the window slit.

She heard Charles moving in the other room, then a rustling behind her. She turned. A shadow filled the doorway, and he spoke.

"I couldn't see them from above, and I've put up all the shutters for now. Can you see anything?"

"Nay. But it's windy, and I can't tell for sure. They could be out there at the tree line."

"Then we may as well shut this one." He raised the plank cover and fixed it in place. "Jane, there's something I must tell you."

"What?"

"Stephen told me yesterday that there were Algonquin at the falls."

Her heart stopped for a moment; then it raced. "Why didn't you tell me? We spent the whole day out planting!"

"I thought we were safe. He said they were a Canadian tribe, come down to fish."

"Were they the ones he knew?"

"Aye."

"He spoke to them?"

"Two of their men surprised him in the woods."

She caught her breath. "They didn't hurt him?"

"Nay. But they let him know they were not pleased he had left them."

"I wish you had told me."

He sighed. "I didn't wish to alarm you."

She nodded. "Well, it seems they want something now."

"Probably food and other plunder."

Suddenly a loud thumping came on the door, and the whole house shivered. She threw herself into his arms.

"Charles! We mustn't let them break through! I tell you, I shall not go with them, whatever it costs me."

Slowly he pulled her arms from around his waist. In the dim light, she saw his grim expression.

"Here. Take my skinning knife." He pressed the hilt into her hand. "Get into the pantry and lock yourself in. I shall go up into the loft again. It overhangs a few inches above the door, and there is a small hole in the floor. If they're at the door, I might be able to shoot one of them."

"I shall come with you and reload for you."

"Nay, Jane. Lock yourself in. Do not open the door for anyone but me. But please, my love, if they burn the house. . ."

"Go quickly," she gasped.

He left her.

She squeezed the bone handle of his knife and drew in a deep breath. It was only a few steps to the door of the bedchamber. She felt along the wall to the door of the pantry. Inside the small storeroom, she fumbled with the latch. She hadn't noticed before that he had put two sturdy bars on the inside of the door. Jane struggled to fit them into place.

In the darkness, she knelt on the floor. *Please, dear God, save me and my husband!*

◆

Charles bounded to the ladder and up again into the loft. His father had added it over one end of the main room of the cabin years ago. The upper part of the house stuck out over the front door. It wasn't as pronounced as in the larger garrison houses, but it gave enough leeway for him to cut a hole in the floor just over the front door. Most of the garrison houses in the area were built with the chimney in the middle and the upper story jutting out over the lower one all around, enabling the inhabitants to fire down on people outside. The Gardner house was not nearly so convenient, but Charles was thankful for what little advantage he had.

As he gained the loft, the front door shuddered again, and he was afraid for a moment the hinges would give. He ducked his head and hurried across to the one narrow window. Lowering the shutter, he looked out but couldn't see what was going on below. He had a clear view, however, along the path toward Richard's home. No light was visible. The new fence around the Dudley house might obscure illumination from within the building, he thought. At least the place wasn't on fire.

He felt along the edge of the wall and located the hole his father had made in the floor. Peering through it, he had an impression of confused movement, and another loud thud jarred the house. He'd thought they were ramming the door with a log, but now he wasn't so sure. Perhaps they were attacking the oak planks with a hatchet. A sickening thought hit him. He'd left his ax in the barn, and they might be using his own tools against him.

He stuck the barrel of his musket into the hole and waited. He could barely see past it, and he didn't want to waste his shot. He might get only one. It would take him a minute or two to reload. That delay might be enough time to let them gain entrance to the house. The first shot had to count.

There came a pause in the chopping sounds. He heard them muttering, and then the *thud-thud* resumed. He thought the movement he saw was the ax, swung by a dusky arm. He didn't want to hit one of them in the arm. He wanted a clean, fatal shot. And so he waited, holding his breath.

Suddenly a light flared, and he knew they had ignited a torch. A loud crack told him one of the planks of the door gave way, and a dark body shoved against the door. Charles pulled the trigger.

At once he wished he'd put wool in his ears. The report of the gun in the enclosed space deafened him for several seconds, and acrid smoke brought tears to his eyes. He crawled to the window loop and put his face to the slit, gulping in fresh air. Slowly his hearing returned, though his ears rang with an ongoing tone that muffled the sounds from below. A soft glow told him the torch still burned, and the Indians were yelling in outrage.

He groped his way back to the hole in the floor and peeked through it. Nothing. He put his mouth close to the opening and yelled, in the Algonquin language, "Go away! I shall kill you all if you do not go away!"

He jumped back away from the hole and fumbled in the darkness to begin the reloading process. He hoped Richard had heard his musket fire and received a warning. Or was it too late? Was this small raiding party one of many?

He couldn't help remembering that awful night six years ago, when four hundred warriors had attacked the settlement, killing or capturing half the colonists. Everyone in the colony measured time by that event. "The year before the massacre. . ."

He dropped a bullet and felt about for it in the dark. Rather than waste more time searching for it, he reached into his pouch for another.

The chopping at the door began again.

Chapter 13

In the dark pantry, Jane huddled in a corner and prayed. She jumped when a gun fired. That had to be her husband's musket. The repercussion rang in her ears, but she had heard no firearms outside.

All was quiet for a minute, and she heard voices. Then the pounding began again. *They must be battering the door.* How terrible this waiting was!

She remembered that other time, when her mistress had yanked her out of bed. *"Quick! Put your skirt on. There be savages at the door."*

Jane hadn't even had time to don her overskirt that night. The roof of Waldrons' garrison was already ablaze. She grabbed her clothing and ran. Indians had caught them as they fled from the fire. Her mistress was tomahawked on the doorstep. Jane had hung back in terror, but strong hands had seized her and pulled her from the blazing building. Instead of killing her, they had dragged her outside the stockade and bound her with several others to await the end of their captors' bloody business. Then the long march began.

She shivered and hugged her flexed knees, holding tight to the knife's hilt. *God, help us! Help my Charlie! Send us aid, Lord!*

What would she do if they killed Charles and discovered her hiding place? The idea was too terrible to consider. Feverishly she renewed her prayers.

Crack! The musket fired again.

She jumped and stared toward the door she couldn't see. Charles was still fighting them off. She needed to be beside him. If they killed him, her life was worth nothing. She and their baby would die or be herded off to Canada again, and sold to the French or made to live with the savages as Sarah and Stephen had been.

She scrambled up and groped for the door. In the darkness, she threw off the bar at waist level then reached for the one above.

The stillness stopped her. No one was yelling. No one was pounding on the front door. No gunfire. No *thwack* of arrows against the stout walls.

She heard a muffled thud then unmistakable footsteps. Her husband? Or the enemy? Indians would not wear hard-soled boots. Her heart pounded, but she dared not open the door.

"Jane?"

She almost collapsed, so great was her relief. She grasped the upper bar and stood on tiptoe to throw it out of its niche. The end of it fell down and whacked her forearm. She let it fall to the floor with a clatter and stood clutching her bruised arm.

"Jane?"

The door creaked open.

"Charlie!"

He pulled her into his embrace, resting the stock of his musket on the floor. "Are you all right?" he asked.

"Yes. Are you?"

"Aye."

"Are they gone?"

"I think so. I saw shadows retreating toward the woods."

"Did you reload?"

He laughed and hugged her tighter. "Aye, wife. I'd have been here sooner, otherwise."

She squeezed him with all her might. She would rather have died here and now than to carry Charles's baby into Canada and give birth there. But this third option was far sweeter.

"What happened?"

"I haven't opened the front door, what's left of it. But I'm pretty sure I hit two of them. The rest gave up."

Her hairpins had come loose, and her hair had come unbound and spilled over her shoulders. Charles held her and stroked her long tresses and planted a kiss on the top of her head. "Come. We must warn Richard and the others."

"You can't leave me here alone!"

He hesitated. "Nay, I shan't. They perhaps heard my shooting. But, Jane, we can't take the chance that the warriors left here to attack another house."

"Then fire your gun out the window. Charlie, you mustn't go out! You'll be killed."

"It's possible," he acknowledged. "Would you really mind so much being widowed again?"

She stared at him, able to see only his glittering eyes. A huge sob worked its way up her throat. Did he think she cared nothing for him? She threw herself back into his arms and wept.

◆

Of all the crackbrained things he'd ever said in his life, this had to be the worst. Charles held his wife, not knowing what else to do. It seemed her crying would never end. Her tears soaked the front of his linsey-woolsey shirt.

"Jane, my love, I'm so sorry. Forgive me."

She sobbed harder. Her arms circled his rib cage, squeezing the breath out of him. He managed to lean the musket against the shelves in the corner and slid down to the floor, taking her with him. He pulled her onto his lap, leaned against the door frame, and let her weep.

At last her sobs slowed, and she gulped great gasps of air between them. Her lush hair swirled about her face as her shoulders heaved.

He patted her back with one hand and pushed her hair away from her face with the other. "I'm sorry," he whispered. "That was thoughtless of me. Can you forgive me?"

She nodded vigorously and sobbed again. He cradled her into a more comfortable position, sheltering her in his arms.

After a long moment, she sat up, wiping her eyes with her apron. "If you must go to see if Richard is well, Charlie, so be it. I shall barricade myself and wait for you to return. But I warn you, I shall never forgive you if you leave me here to raise your son without a father."

Charles sat very still. He wished desperately for a candle in that moment so he could see her face. "My. . .son?"

"Or daughter. Girls need their fathers, as well, you know."

"Is this. . .something I should know, wife? Or are you merely hypostatizing?"

She sniffed. "If I knew what that meant, I would answer."

He chuckled. "I heard the parson say it. It means you're advancing a theory."

She laid her head on his chest. "I assure you, sir, this baby is not theoretical. It's early, but I'm sure I felt him kick as the savages beat on our door."

Charles inhaled deeply, letting the joyous warmth creep over him.

Her small, warm hands crept up about his neck once more. "Are you pleased, husband?"

"More than I can tell you."

She ran her fingers into his beard and stroked his cheek.

He pulled her to him and kissed her.

A sharp rapping on the door startled them apart.

Jane clenched handfuls of his shirt in her fists. "They're back!"

"Nay. They would not be so polite. Hear that?"

They both listened and heard an anxious voice calling, "Charlie! Charlie! Are you in there, man? Open up if you are!"

"Richard," Jane breathed.

Charles stood and braced himself against the doorjamb so he could pull her to her feet.

"Let me get a candle," she said.

"No time."

Charles hurried across the dark keeping room. "Hold on, Richard!"

227

Jane groped about the pantry for a candle as she heard him unfastening the door. Her hand closed on a tin holder with the stub of a tallow candle in it. She seized it and hurried out to the fireplace in the other room.

"Charlie, we heard you shoot, and Stephen and I thought we'd best come make sure you were all right. What happened?"

As her husband explained their brief siege, Jane probed the ashes in the fireplace with the poker and found a few red coals. She held her candle stub to one and soon had a light. She used the flame to light two more on the mantel and carried one to Charles.

He took it from her and raised it to aid him in examining the damaged door.

"A few more blows, and they'd have been in the house," Richard said.

"Aye. So it seems." Charles ran his hand over the broken planks.

"They nearly had you. Why did they leave?"

"I shot a couple of them. See that?" He held the candle over the doorstep, and they saw a dark smear on the flat granite stone. "That's blood. I've a little hole in the loft floor. It gave me just enough room to shoot through. I believe I seriously wounded or killed two of them."

"They've taken their friends away," Richard observed, peering about the yard.

"Come in." Charles stepped back and let the brothers enter.

Jane hurried back to the hearth, took some pinecones from her tinderbox, and laid them on the coals. By adding a few small sticks of kindling, she soon had a good blaze going.

"You must stay at our house tonight," Richard said.

"It would be better if you all, including Sarah, come over to Father's," Stephen said.

"You think they will come back?" Charles asked. "Could they have gone for reinforcements?"

Stephen shrugged. "I doubt it. The encampment at the falls was a small one. But you never know, and it's many hours until daylight."

"Safety in numbers," Richard agreed. "Jane, grab your cloak and a blanket or two."

"We've not even had our supper," she protested. "I was about to feed my husband when the attack began."

Richard laughed. "Then cover your stewpot, and we'll bring it along."

"Hold, now," said Charles. "I'm not sure I want to go and leave my house unprotected. If I'm not here to defend it, they could return and plunder everything."

"How many did you see?" Stephen asked.

"I didn't actually see much, I tell you. I wasn't about to open the door, and my windows don't afford much of a view, unfortunately. But from the sound of things—"

"It sounded like a legion of them," Jane said.

Charles chuckled. "Nay, there weren't many, or they'd have been all around the house and shooting faster. I think there were only a few. Certainly not more than half a dozen of them, perhaps fewer."

Stephen eyed the scarred door again. "Maybe in the morning we should gather a delegation of men from the village and go up to the falls. Pay them a visit and let them know we won't put up with this sort of thing."

"I don't know," Richard said. "When they came six years ago, they had four hundred warriors. What if they gather a swarm like that again and retaliate?"

"Well, we can't just live out here on the edge of the wilderness in terror every minute," Jane said. She fitted the cover on her stew kettle and handed it to Charles.

He studied her face. "Perhaps we should move into the village—for the summer, at least. A lot of people do that. Live in town and walk out here to work their fields."

But Jane raised her chin. "Nay, husband. We'll not let them run us off. Your father claimed this land, and Gardner land it shall be. As you said, if we leave the house empty, they are more apt to pillage. And you've just built me that fine new addition. I'll go with you this one night to Goodman Dudley's garrison, but tomorrow morning we return."

Pride swelled in Charles's chest at her words.

"You speak well. But I think my next building project should be a stockade." He turned to the Dudley brothers. "Are you willing to help me?"

Richard and Stephen gave their assent, and the four left the little house.

As they walked toward the path that led to Richard's house, Jane stared about at the starlit yard. "Charlie! I believe they stole our chickens."

"That would not surprise me. I believe they got my ax, as well."

"Impudent scoundrels!"

Charles reached for her hand. Indeed, he had chosen the right woman.

◆

Jane was grateful for her neighbors' hospitality, but by morning she was anxious to return to her own home. At first light she was up and helping Goody Dudley prepare a hearty breakfast for them all. But she was to be disappointed. The young men insisted on walking to the village to enlist the aid of the elders in dealing with the Indians. Sarah and Jane stayed with Richard's parents and his sister, Catherine, while Charles undertook the mission with Stephen and Richard.

"You are restless, Jane," Goody Dudley said an hour after the young men had left. "Did you bring your fancywork?"

"Nay, I didn't think to bring anything but my kettle and a quilt," Jane said.

"Then put your hand to the spinning wheel. You shall have all the woolen yarn you can spin this morning."

"Oh no, that is too generous, but I shall spin for you." Jane approached the large wheel in the corner of the main room.

"Nonsense." Her hostess came over and opened a large sack of carded wool. "James and Richard have finished the first shearing, and we look to have a good crop of wool this year. In fact, Charles was speaking to my husband about bartering for a couple of lambs."

Goodman Dudley nodded. "After your Charlie has a stockade built, I'll let him have some ewe lambs to start you a flock."

Sarah had brought her knitting, and she sat down near Jane to work, while Catherine and her mother began to set the dough for their week's baking.

"I'll warrant you'll need lots of wool this year to knit wee things, won't you, now?" Goody Dudley said with a smile.

Jane gasped and eyed Sarah suspiciously.

"I didn't say a word. My mother-in-law is canny about these things."

Goody Dudley laughed. "Ah, so my hunch is true. Two new babies on the frontier next winter. Well, I shall stitch you a flannel gown for the babe, Jane."

"Thank you. No one's embroidery is as fine as yours, ma'am."

"And I shall make you a little blanket," Catherine said.

Sarah leaned toward Jane. "Did you tell Charles yet?"

"Aye. Last night, when he proposed leaving me alone to go and warn you about the savages." Jane felt her face flush.

"Good, because my mother-in-law is not known to be close-lipped."

Jane smiled.

An hour later, Richard returned alone.

"Captain Baldwin has mustered thirty men to go with him to the falls," he reported as he took off his coat.

"But where be Stephen and Charles?" asked his father. "Did they go with the captain?"

"Aye, he wanted them to translate."

"Do you think those savages will attack again?" his mother asked.

"What if they have more men than Stephen thought, and they force a confrontation?" Sarah asked in alarm.

Richard shook his head. "Charles's house seems to be the only one they menaced last night. It's distressing, yet if they intended widespread mischief, I think they would have gone elsewhere when Charles ran them off. The captain agrees. He thinks they were a small band out to see if they could make a quick raid for whatever they could plunder."

"You don't think Stephen was the cause, then?" Catherine asked as she lifted a loaf of rye bread from the Dutch oven.

Richard scowled at his sister. "Why do you say that, Cat?"

"You know what he told us. They stopped him in the woods the other day. They know who he is and that he lives nearby. It occurred to me that perhaps they thought Charles's house was his."

Richard looked toward his father. "I don't think so, do you, sir?"

James Dudley frowned. "If they wanted revenge on Stephen, they could have killed him in the woods. Ambushed him anytime they pleased. Nay, I lean toward the captain's notion. Perhaps their fishing has been poor, and they thought to steal some corn and livestock."

"I agree." Richard pinched a small piece of bread from Catherine's loaf, and she swatted at his hand. "This was not a war party. Just an ill-advised venture by some hot-blooded young warriors. Be thankful they didn't burn us all out."

They stayed within the stockade all day. Richard and his father tended the stock and the kitchen garden but did not venture out to the fields.

At last, as the sun dipped behind the trees to the west, Charles and Stephen came to the gate, and Richard let them in.

"They are few," Stephen told them. "Only twelve or so men and their families. They were packing to leave when we got there."

Charles nodded. "One man lay inside a hut. They said he was sick, but I figure he was one I wounded last night."

"And I think you killed one, as well," Stephen said. "They were frightened when they saw our numbers. Of course, the captain told them we have many more men in reserve if they want to make war. They assured us they are peaceful."

"Denied coming near my house," Charles said, "but we know better. I saw the feathers from our chickens, Jane."

"They ate them already?" she cried.

"I'm afraid so."

"They thought they had an easy target at an unfortified house far from the village," Richard said.

"But they've gone now," Stephen said. "We stayed until they broke camp and headed off north."

Jane took their wedding quilt from the chest by the door. "So we shall be safe at our house tonight?"

"I believe so. Are you ready to go?" Charles picked up her kettle and his gun.

No persuasion from Richard's mother could convince them to stay, for Jane was eager to be back in her own house. She realized as they trudged along the path that the farm on the edge of the forest had become her home.

As they came into the dooryard, a hen cackled and flew up from almost beneath Charles's boots.

"What do you know?" he cried. "At least one of our chickens escaped them."

Jane looked around. "I don't see Samson."

"I stopped and buried him on the way back from the falls."

"Good." She'd tried not to think that Indians might have taken him.

"Richard and Stephen shall come in the morning," Charles said as he opened the door to their house. "Perhaps James, as well. They are all agreed we must have a stockade here."

"Charles, you want to stay here, don't you?" She hung her shawl on its peg and hung the kettle on the crane over the cold hearth. "Because I don't want you to do it if you'd rather not."

"Aye, abandoning this place would go against the grain with me. My thoughts were only to keep you safe, Jane."

"Then it's settled. We shall stay."

He smiled and reached inside the front of his shirt, drawing out a small doeskin pouch. "This will help us."

"What is it?"

As he handed it to her, his dark eyes twinkled.

She could tell by its weight and firmness that it held coins. "Where did you get it?"

"Captain Baldwin."

"Whatever for?"

Charles flexed his shoulders as though somewhat bewildered himself. "He gave this to me before we left the village. Said he'd written to the magistrate in Portsmouth about our situation, and the court declared that since Gideon Plaisted had profited from selling your papers to me—and he set a very high value on your labor, you know—why, then, he should reimburse the governor for the ransom that the colony paid for you."

Jane gasped. "They made him pay?"

"Aye, and the governor sent part of the money here, since the village of Cochecho raised much of the ransom. The elders apparently felt some of that should come to me. To *us*, that is. Baldwin said there was an air of justice about it."

She laughed and loosened the thong at the neck of the pouch and poured the coins into her hand. "Why, we could buy the captain's heifer!"

"Yes, we could. I wanted to show you the money first and let you decide how to spend it. Would you like a heifer, wife? And perhaps a spinning wheel and a sack of wheat flour?"

She trickled the coins carefully back into the little sack. "Do as you think best, Charles. I know you will be wise in your dealings."

232

He smiled and knelt to build the fire up. As the kindling caught and began to crackle, he said, "It's good to be home. Tomorrow we'll begin building the fence. But my evening job for the next few weeks shall be another building task."

"What is that?" Jane tried to think what he would build next. "Do you mean repairing the door they've chopped to pieces? Or the loom you spoke of making for me?"

"Nay, not those, though I shall fix the door straightaway. But I was thinking of another project. I cut a big cherry tree last fall, and it's drying in the clearing. I didn't know what it was for then, but now I do." His dark eyes gleamed as he stood and reached for her.

"What?" she asked, but she thought she knew.

"A cradle, sweet wife."

She let him kiss her and twined her arms about his neck, inviting him to linger. "I meant to tell you about it when all was sure and safe," she whispered. "Not when we were like to be killed."

"It's all right." He squeezed her. "I'm glad, no matter how you told me."

"There's something else. I know I should have told it to you before, but I didn't."

He leaned back, a stab of concern in his face. "What is it?"

"Only that I love you, Charlie."

His smile returned, brighter than the glow from the hearth. "Another answered prayer. I love you, dearest Jane."

ABIDING PEACE

Dedication

To my aunt, Joyce Page Whitney, and my uncle, Robert Page,
who are also descendants of blacksmith Richard Otis.

Chapter 1

C hristine Hardin sat up straight on the backless bench in the meeting-house as the Reverend Samuel Jewett finished his sermon with a stirring benediction. The congregation rose to blend their voices in the final hymn. Christine glanced sideways, along the line of Jewett children—all five of them, from three-year-old Ruth up to Ben, who was nearly as tall as his father now. At the far end of the row sat the widow Deane. All eyes stayed forward, except Ruth's. The little girl swiveled her head and looked up at Christine. She smiled and raised her arms in a gesture she used many times a day, begging Christine to pick her up.

Christine couldn't help smiling back at the sweet child, though the reverend wanted his children to be sober in church. She tousled Ruth's dark curls, which were the exact shade of her dead mother's. As she turned toward the pulpit once more, hoping Ruth would follow her example, Christine let her hand rest lightly on the little girl's shoulder. All five of the children grieved their mother, and Christine mourned her dear friend. Each time she looked into the minister's eyes, the emptiness there tore at her heart.

"You may be seated," the Reverend Jewett intoned, and the children stirred and looked to her with confusion. Wasn't it time for dinner?

Christine sat down quickly and pulled Ruth against her side, nodding to Abby and Constance to sit, as well.

The congregation quieted, and the parson raised his voice once more. "Hear ye, hear ye, the marriage banns of Mordecai Wales, a freeman, and Parthenia Jones."

A soft murmur rippled through the congregation.

"A fortnight hence, on the twentieth of August, in the year of our Lord, one thousand, six hundred and ninety-six, the marriage shall take place, if so be the will of the Almighty."

Christine saw ten-year-old John Jewett start to turn his head, but his older brother, Ben, elbowed him. The Jewett family occupied the front pew in church, and the children learned very early that they must never, never look behind them during services. But she recognized how tempting it was just then.

Most of the congregants must be staring at old farmer Wales. He had buried his second wife a mere month ago, and now it seemed he intended to marry a third—and much younger—woman in two weeks' time. Parthenia Jones was also widowed, and she had two small children. It would no doubt be a good match for her, as Mr. Wales would provide for her and the little ones. She, in return, would take over management of his household and the half-grown offspring of his second marriage. She would tend him in his old age. And, if she didn't succumb in childbirth first, she would be well taken care of after he died.

Still, Parthenia couldn't be more than eight-and-twenty, Christine calculated, and Mordecai Wales must be all of sixty. Ah well, the farmer probably wanted a stout young woman who could work hard and perhaps bear him more children. Christine felt her cheeks redden just for thinking it.

People behind them rose to their feet and shuffled toward the aisle, and she realized the pastor had dismissed them.

On the common outside the stark meetinghouse, Christine's friends, Jane and Sarah, waited for her. Their husbands, Charles Gardner and Richard Dudley, stood off to one side, talking with Richard's brother Stephen. Charles held his little son, who was eight months old, on one arm, his musket in the other hand. The baby tugged at his father's beard, much to Charles's delight. Ben Jewett, the pastor's eldest son at fourteen, joined the men and was welcomed into the circle.

Christine kept a close hold on Ruth's hand and drew her over to where Jane and Sarah stood. Sarah held her little girl, Hannah, who would soon be a year old. Constance Jewett followed Christine, but Abby flitted off to spend a moment with her friends.

"What did you think of the announcement at the end?" Sarah Dudley asked with arched eyebrows. She shifted Hannah to a more comfortable spot on her hip. Hannah promised to grow up to be as lovely as her mother. Christine was happy that her two friends had found loving husbands who treated them well.

"He didn't waste any time picking out a new wife," Jane noted.

Sarah chuckled. "True. But the marriage will be an improvement in situation for Parthenia, even though he is so much older than she."

"I'm surprised he didn't come courting you, Christine." Jane smiled at her impudently.

Christine shuddered. "Please. You ladies have convinced me by your example that marriage is not necessarily all bad. But to a man of Goodman Wales's years? I think not."

"Aha! You witnessed what she said." Jane turned eagerly to Sarah. "Christine is open to the idea of marriage at last."

"I didn't say that."

"Of course you did," Jane said. "And we must look about for a *young* man for her."

"Or at least one not yet in his dotage." Sarah seemed perfectly willing to enter into Jane's teasing.

"Miss Christine." Constance tugged at her overskirt.

Christine felt a pang of contrition. Here she was gossiping with her friends and setting a poor example for the parson's daughters, who were in her care.

"What is it, Constance?"

"Are you getting married?"

Christine stared down at the six-year-old's innocent face, at a loss for words.

"Not yet," Jane said, reaching out to tweak Constance's braid. "But we shan't stop trying to find a match for her."

"A match?" Constance's brown eyes widened.

"A husband," Sarah said. She glanced at Jane and Christine. "I think this conversation has gone about as far as it should for now."

"I agree. I implore you ladies to put it out of your minds," Christine said. She had long maintained that she had no desire to marry. Indeed, she cringed at the very thought.

Pastor Jewett came out onto the steps of the meetinghouse carrying his musket, which he had traded for in the spring. Renewed threats of Indian attacks had prompted the peace-loving minister to make the purchase. Only two weeks had passed since some of his congregation had been attacked by hostile savages as they left the church service. None of the men went about without their guns these days. He rested it against the wall and spread out a sheet of parchment against the church door, then pulled a hammer from his coat pocket.

"Come, girls. Your father is posting the marriage banns."

"Ah, he'll be wanting his dinner," Jane said.

"Yes. Time to go home." As she turned to look about for Abby and John, Christine noticed a portly woman approaching her. She usually tried to stay out of the path of Mahalia Ackley, who was known for her sharp tongue. Indeed, her reckless gossiping had sent the goodwife to the stocks on more than one occasion. This time there was no avoiding her, however.

"Miss Hardin."

"Good day, ma'am."

The older woman pulled up before her, panting, with her skirts swirling into place. "My hired girl left me last week. Her father moved his family to Cape Cod."

"I heard that." Christine sensed what was coming, but she waited out of courtesy.

"I be looking for a stout girl to do for me. Cleaning and washing mostly, but I hear you're a fair hand with spinning and weaving, too."

Christine forced a smile. She had lived with the Jewett family for nearly a year before the pastor's wife died and still worked for them more than a year after Goody Jewett's death. Her position made her privy to all the secrets of Cochecho, and she knew that Goody Ackley had run through the list of available domestic help in the village.

"I'm sorry I can't accommodate you, ma'am. I've all the work I can handle at the Jewett house."

"Surely the parson's children are old enough to do for themselves."

Christine had the distinct feeling the woman was chiding her. She sought for an appropriate reply. "The children are a big help with the work about the parsonage, to be sure, but the girls are very young yet. They can't do the cooking and washing themselves. Goody Deane and I go across the road nearly every day to help them."

Mahalia Ackley looked furtively about.

Sarah Dudley had joined her in-laws' family and handed Hannah to her husband, but Jane Gardner still stood by Christine, listening with apparent interest.

Goody Ackley took Christine's sleeve between her plump fingers and tugged her aside. She leaned close and said in a confidential tone, "Surely the parson can't pay you much."

Christine felt her cheeks color. She wanted to end this line of conversation firmly, but she couldn't embarrass the pastor by flinging a rude retort at one of his parishioners. She cleared her throat. "I receive adequate compensation, and since Goody Jewett died last year, I feel the family needs me more than ever. You understand."

Goody Ackley's dark eyes snapped with displeasure as she pulled back slightly. "Oh, yes, yes. The poor, motherless children. Some people don't understand that as folks get older they need more help than the able-bodied young ones." She gathered her skirts and whirled away, stirring up dust in the dry churchyard.

Jane stepped closer to Christine. "Good for you. You stayed calm. I'd have spat in her eye."

Christine gave her a rueful smile. "I felt tempted to say what I thought, but. . ."

"I know. It's not in your nature, and it *is* Sunday."

"Their children are all dead or moved away, and I suppose she does need help."

"My husband is waving at me," Jane said. "I suppose we and the Dudleys shall all take dinner at the Heards' today, so the men can discuss building the new pews with Brother William. Of course you mustn't tell the parson they are talking about work on the Sabbath."

Christine chuckled, but Jane seemed to take the matter seriously. She left Christine and joined her husband. The neighbors living close to the meeting-house opened their homes on Sunday afternoon to the farmers from outside the village, so they would have a place to eat their Sunday dinner in relative comfort. Then all would return to the meetinghouse for the afternoon service, which sometimes went on until the supper hour. Christine waved and gathered the pastor's three little girls about her.

◆

"Goody Deane, be you joining us for dinner at the parsonage today?" Samuel Jewett called to his elderly neighbor, who was saying good-bye to a knot of other ladies.

"Aye, if ye want me," the wrinkled old woman replied.

"Of course we want you."

"Especially if you've baked gingerbread," the impish John added.

Samuel swatted playfully at his younger son. "Here now, be polite. The lady will think you a greedy pig."

"He is that when it comes to gingerbread." Goody Deane cackled as she hobbled along toward the street.

Samuel and Christine matched their steps to hers. John, Ben, and Abby ran ahead, but Ruth toddled along holding her father's hand, and Constance stuck as close to Christine's skirts as a cocklebur.

The two women set to work getting the meal ready as soon as they reached the parsonage. Samuel helped little Ruth change out of her Sunday dress and watched with approval as the children helped carry dishes and set the four pewter plates and mismatched mugs on the table.

He sat down at the table with the two boys and Goody Deane for the first sitting. When they had finished, Christine and Abby quickly washed their dishes and set the table again for themselves, Ruth, and Constance. It was the regular routine of the family. Samuel wished he could afford more dishes, but they got along. Elizabeth had never complained, and he had carved wooden bowls enough to go around. Perhaps he could purchase a couple of tin mugs from the trader. But there were so many other things they needed, and his small stipend was paid only if the tithes amounted to enough to cover it. Members of the congregation occasionally brought his family a load of wood or a sack of meal, it was true, but the pastor's family was one of the poorest in the community.

He saw Christine cast a wistful glance at the loom in the corner of the room. Samuel gave her free use of his deceased wife's loom and spinning wheel.

Christine had shown a talent for weaving soon after her arrival two years earlier. She had learned the craft from the nuns at the convent in Canada where she'd lived for four years. Of course, they both knew she wouldn't be weaving on Sunday.

Samuel turned his attention to the meal—a simple stew, corn bread baked yesterday, and the promise of gingerbread after. The spicy smell of ginger tantalized them all from beneath one of Goody Deane's threadbare linen towels.

He didn't like to recall Christine's background or the events that had brought her into contact with his family. A number of the village's residents had been captured by Indians, either at the massacre of 1689 or in other raids. Several members of the Otis and Dudley families, as well as Charles and Jane Gardner, were survivors of captivity. Busybodies set rumors flying about the conditions under which the captives had lived and the state of their souls as a result. But none of the others had lived in a nunnery for years, as Christine had. The people of Cochecho had accepted most of the redeemed captives back into their ranks, but he knew a few still looked on Christine with suspicion because of her years at the convent.

He saw growing acceptance as Christine attended church faithfully and performed good deeds with a self-effacing humility. Most of the prominent women of the community now treated her well. Samuel's close contact with her had taught him that her faith was firm, and her love and tender care for his children was exceeded only by that which their own mother had bestowed. Christine was indeed a blessing to their family.

"Will you have some greens?" Goody Deane stood at Christine's elbow with a wooden bowl of boiled greens the girls had gathered at the edge of the woods on Saturday.

"Aye, thank you." Christine held her plate up.

"We'll be eating corn from the garden soon." Pastor Jewett set the kettle of steaming water for the dishes aside and raked the coals into a heap on the stone hearth. He covered them with ashes, banking them. They didn't want to keep burning wood all afternoon since it was now very warm in the house, but they would want the live coals later, when it was time to cook supper.

"Yes, and cucumbers, too." Goody Deane put a small portion of greens on each of the girls' plates.

"I can't wait for fresh corn." Constance rubbed her tummy.

They all laughed.

"Me, either," Christine said. All that was left of last year's crop was dry ground corn and a barrel of parched corn kernels, and those supplies were dwindling. "It will be a little while longer before we get corn, though." The summer garden supplied them with plenty of green beans, leaf lettuce, and tender carrots and beets. This time of year, the Jewetts ate as well as most other families in Cochecho.

Samuel sat down and opened his Bible on his knees. He wanted to refresh his mind for the afternoon sermon.

When Christine and the girls had eaten and washed and put away their dishes, Goody Deane threw out the dishwater, and Christine put Ruth on her pallet for a nap.

"There, now," Christine said to Abby and Constance, "Goody Deane and I shall see you at worship. We'll go home now for a short rest. Be good girls, won't you?"

"I be going to call on Richard Otis after the service this afternoon, to see how he is recovering from his wounds," Samuel said.

Christine straightened and looked at him. "Do you wish me to stay with the children then?"

He hesitated. Richard Otis, the blacksmith whose father had been killed in the massacre six years earlier, was one who had suffered grievous wounds in the attack two weeks ago. Since that fray, the elders had posted a lookout on the meeting-house steps during each service. But the parsonage lay in the middle of the village, and he would not be gone long this evening. If the service did not run overly long, he could be home before dark. "Nay. You've done so much. There's no fire hazard, and Ben is a responsible enough lad to watch his sisters for a couple of hours. Eh, son?"

Ben grimaced. "Yes, Father."

Samuel stood and ruffled the boy's hair. "Good lad."

Christine hung up her apron and glanced once more toward the loom. She couldn't work at her weaving today. In fact, scripture bade them do no more work than they found absolutely necessary on Sunday. Samuel strictly enforced the Sabbath rest in his household. He knew Christine understood this, but still, her plain features took on a wistfulness when she regarded the loom.

"Let me walk you ladies home," he said. "I'd like a word with you, Miss Hardin." He was not usually so formal with her except in public, but the matter he needed to discuss was a serious one.

Christine raised her eyebrows but said nothing.

After the three had crossed the road together, he paused on Goody Deane's path.

Christine halted as well and waited for him to speak.

"Constance tells me Goody Ackley asked you to work for her," he said.

Christine looked down at the ground. "Aye. But I declined her offer."

Goody Deane swung around near the doorstone. "I'll be stretching out yonder if you need me, Christine. Thank you kindly for the vittles, Parson."

"And thank you for bringing the gingerbread, ma'am. It added a festive note to our Sabbath-day dinner."

"Ah, well, a bit of gingerbread never went down wrong, I say." Goody Deane nodded and went into the cottage.

Samuel cleared his throat and met Christine's gaze. "If I could pay you in coin, I would. You know that. Your labor in my house has been worth much more than I've been able to give you. But I expect the Ackleys would give you a fair wage, and if you—"

Christine's hazel eyes grew large as he spoke, and her brow puckered. "Please, Pastor, do not speak of it. I do not wish to go to the Ackleys', and I'm happy with our arrangement."

He exhaled and smiled. "Bless you. But the Ackleys would give you room in their loft, I'm sure. The last hired girl had a place there."

"I enjoy living with Goody Deane, and I think I do not boast to say she likes having me."

"Oh, to be sure," he said quickly. "I've thought it good for her since the beginning. I'm certain you are a great help to her, and she seems in much better spirits since you've boarded with her."

Christine nodded. "A pleasant situation and a congenial employer go further than a generous wage, sir. And I'm not sure how generous the goodwife we speak of would be."

Samuel couldn't refute that. He'd heard Goody Ackley wrangled over the last ha'penny with the trader, and her husband, Roger Ackley, was well known to be a skinflint. But even the stingiest couple in Cochecho would probably pay Christine more than he could. He rarely gave her a coin. He did allow her to sell cloth that she wove on his loom and keep the profit, but most of the textiles she produced seemed to find themselves clothing his own children.

"When it comes down to it, I don't give you much for your labor."

"Ah, well"—she looked down once more, and her cheeks flushed—"you give me all I need, sir. My food and any other necessities. And you've allowed me to be a part of your family, which is a great boon."

They stood in silence for a moment. Samuel tried to imagine the family now without Christine. A brief image of domestic chaos and wailing children flickered across his mind. "You truly do not wish to go to the Ackleys' farm, then?"

"I do not." She looked up and gazed at him earnestly, her plain features less serene than usual. "If you are happy, I should like to continue things as they are."

"We agree then. I shall see you in half an hour, at meeting."

Samuel tipped his hat and turned toward the street.

Chapter 2

A week later, Christine spent a good part of Monday morning working in Goody Deane's garden. The pastor had suggested in the spring that they plant enough vegetables at the parsonage for Christine and Goody Deane as well as the Jewett family, and Tabitha Deane's small plot was now given over to herbs. Christine had invited the three little girls to help her weed the small garden and pick mint, yarrow, and basil leaves for drying. Ruth and Constance took to the work eagerly.

"Why don't you sit in the shade now with your dollies?" Christine asked when they had picked all the herbs she wanted for the present. "I shall finish placing stones along the path here. You girls may play for a while, and then I shall fix us a cup of mint tea."

The two girls retrieved their rag dolls from the back stoop. Christine had fashioned Ruth's doll from scraps, modeling it from the design of the ones Elizabeth Jewett had stitched for her two older daughters. Now Ruth's doll, Lucy, was never far from her. She had cried the first time her father told her that Lucy could not go to church with her, but Abby had calmed her and whispered to her that their dolls would go to "doll meeting" while the real people were away. Ever since, Ruth had happily dressed Lucy in her best gown and shawl on Sunday mornings and left her sitting on Mother's chair beside Abby's and Constance's dolls when they left for the meetinghouse. Stories about "doll meeting" were now favorite bedtime tales.

After a quarter hour's hard work on the stone walkway, Christine looked up to see Goody Deane and Abby Jewett returning from their excursion to the trading post. While Christine disliked going out among people, Goody Deane enjoyed socializing. When her joints didn't ache too badly, she would happily undertake errands while Christine dealt with cleaning. Christine had permitted Abby to accompany her on her excursion that morning.

"Miss Christine," Abby cried when she spotted her in the garden. She ran up the path, clutching the handle of the small basket Goody Deane had entrusted to her. "We got the black buttons you asked for and a bottle of ink for Father!"

"Lovely." Christine straightened and pressed her hands to the small of her back. Being tall had its disadvantages. "You two are just in time to join us for a cup of tea."

The widow had by this time reached them. "Bless you. I can use it." She pulled a snowy handkerchief from the sleeve of her brown linsey gown and wiped her brow. "I shall remember this heat next winter when I'm shivering. Remind me if I complain about the cold."

Christine laughed and gathered her tools. "Come, Ruthie. Constance, time for tea."

They all went inside, and Christine stirred the embers in the fireplace while Goody Deane hung up her bonnet.

"There, now," Christine said. "I'll fix the tea, and you can get a loaf of that new bread, Abby. We'll all have a slice."

The girl headed for the worktable near the window where two loaves of crusty brown bread awaited her. The widow had risen early, set her bread, and had it baked and cooling before she ever left for the trading post.

"Goody Deane?" Abby's voice rose in uncertainty.

"What is it, child? I shall fetch the knife, is that it?"

"Nay." Abby turned and looked at Christine and the widow. "Were there not three loaves when we left this morn?"

Christine and Tabitha Deane stepped toward the table.

"To be sure," said Goody Deane. "Miss Christine must have put one away."

Christine shook her head. "Not I."

"Well. Isn't that strange? I'm sure we had three. But sometimes I get addled."

"Nay, you remember correctly." Christine looked on the floor and at the shelves on the nearby wall. "Where do you suppose it got to?"

Constance and Ruth came over to stare at the two remaining loaves.

"Perhaps it's with Mr. Heard's shirt," Abby offered.

"How is that?" Christine glanced at her keenly.

Goody Deane waved a hand through the air. "Ah, she heard it told at the trader's how Mrs. Heard missed her husband's second-best shirt off the clothesline last washday." The widow drew in a quick breath. "Perhaps there's some sense in that, though, Abby. After all, when Mrs. Heard told it, Goody Ackley chimed in with a tale of a missing roast of lamb."

Abby nodded solemnly, her wide brown eyes still on the loaves.

"Well, come on," Christine said briskly. "Let's have a slice of this good bread before it walks off on us."

She poured hot water over the crushed mint leaves, and Goody Deane set about cutting the bread. Christine took down the only two cups in the house, a chipped saucer, a small pannikin, and a custard dish. The girls wouldn't mind drinking out of the odd assortment of dishes. At last each was settled about the table with a thick slice of the good rye bread before her, slathered in butter that

Sarah Dudley had brought them on Sunday.

"I believe young Mrs. Dudley makes the best butter I've ever tasted." Goody Deane smacked her lips.

"Aye, Sarah has a fair hand with it. She says it's because of all the clover in the field where their cow grazes." Christine reached over to tuck a linen towel securely in the neckband of Ruth's dress.

"Goody Ackley was rude today." Abby licked a smear of butter off her fingers.

"Really, Abby. Let us be kind," Christine said gently.

"She be honest," Goody Deane said. "That woman was rude, indeed, but it were nothing new."

Christine inhaled slowly, wondering how she could teach the girls not to gossip if their hostess encouraged it.

"Who did she rude to?" Ruth asked.

"To whom was she rude," Christine murmured.

"Aye." Ruth nodded vigorously, and Christine had to smile.

"Goodman Ackley." Abby took a big bite of her bread and butter.

"Her husband?" Christine eyed Abby then shot a glance at Goody Deane.

"As I said, nothing new in these parts." The widow sipped her tea. "Roger Ackley was with her, and she kept needling him about this and that, things she needed that he seemed reluctant to buy. I heard him say once that something could wait until after harvest, but the wife went on about how she always has to wait, wait, wait. So he put it on credit." Goody Deane shook her head. "And she treats the trader's clerk shamefully. She as much as accused him of cheating her this morning, but when the coins were laid out and counted, the clerk was in the right."

"Well." Christine didn't know what else to say.

"Aye. But did she apologize?" the widow asked.

"She did not," Abby cried, her eyes glittering. "She scooped up the pennies and said, 'Hmpf.'"

Christine held back a giggle. She reached for her cup to give herself a chance to recover her decorum. After a sip, she said, "Well, perhaps we should introduce a new topic."

"Do you be going over to the parsonage today?" Tabitha asked.

"Aye." Christine glanced at the window and noted how the sunlight shone through from nearly overhead. "It's getting on for noon. I must go over and get dinner on."

"Father will be home from church soon." Abby jumped down off her bench and ran to fetch her doll.

"He could do his studying at home, now that they have the two new rooms," Christine said.

"But people would talk if you spent the day there while he was home," the widow reminded her.

It was true. She couldn't stay at the parsonage all the time, especially when the master of the house was in it. Though she had lived there while Elizabeth was alive, that was no longer acceptable. When the pastor's wife died, Goody Deane had offered her a bed in her cottage across the way, and she often accompanied Christine to lend an added air of propriety.

"I can go with you," Goody Deane said.

"You are far too kind. Don't you have things you wish to do here?"

"Nay. You keep this little place so tidy, I've naught to put my hands to. But the children always have washing and mending to be done at the parsonage, and one can never bake enough cornpone to keep those boys sated."

Christine patted her hand. "Thank you. If you wish to come over later and do some mending and perhaps stir up some biscuits, I might put an hour in at the loom. I'm nearly done with that length of linen, and I'd like to warp some black woolen soon."

"The boys be outgrowing their togs?"

"I'd like to weave enough for new trousers for both John and Ben, and their father's winter coat is disgracefully shabby. I hope he'll have a new coat before snow falls again in New Hampshire."

Goody Deane brushed the crumbs off the table into her apron. "Be Sarah Dudley giving you the wool?"

"Aye, she traded me a great quantity for Ben's work at planting time. Well, she traded with the pastor and Ben, that is."

"She's a good soul." Tabitha frowned as she covered the remaining bread in a towel. "I do wonder where that loaf of bread got to. We might have to bake again before the week is out."

◆

"Move along, John. We haven't all day." Samuel hastened to fill the woodbox, while the boys carried water and fed the few chickens that scratched the backyard bare.

When he returned to the house with his last load of firewood, Christine was tying Ruth's skirt on over her diminutive cotton shift. Constance sat on the bench by the table. Abby knelt before her, wielding the buttonhook.

"Almost ready, Father," Abby called as he dropped his wood into the woodbox.

"Good girl."

Christine caught his eye, and he smiled at her over Ruth's head. They *were* good children. Well behaved and diligent. Since their mother's passing, Christine had proved trustworthy to continue their training. She even did a bit of spelling and ciphering with Abby and Constance on mornings when John and Ben joined him at the church for their lessons. He would have to talk to her before harvest to see what she thought about the dame school Mrs. Otis planned to start. It would ease Christine's burdens a mite to have the two girls out from underfoot a few hours each day. Still, she didn't seem to mind having them about.

"We're ready," Constance cried, jumping off the bench. She stumbled forward, toward the hearth, and Samuel reached out just in time to catch her.

"Careful, now. Even though the fire's banked, you could get hurt badly if you fly into the hearth."

"Yes, Father."

He locked eyes with her and nodded sternly before releasing her. Cooking and scalding accidents accounted for many deaths among the women and children of the colony, and he demanded caution in the kitchen. In his capacity as makeshift healer, he'd seen too many charred bodies. If he could help it, his children would never be among them.

"Will we get to see Catherine?" Abby asked as they left the parsonage.

"Perchance," Samuel said. His girls had a fondness for Catherine Dudley, Sarah's young sister-in-law, who often told them stories and brought them treats. "My purpose is to visit her parents today and see what their needs be and to make arrangement with Goodman Dudley about the work he needs from Ben."

"And we ladies shall call on Sarah Dudley and Jane Gardner as well," Christine said.

The searing August sun already baked through Samuel's clothing. He rarely went about without his coat, but the weather had given him pause. Would he rather be thought a proper parson and risk taking ill from the heat, or seem informal to his parishioners and live to tell about it? He had compromised on a waistcoat over his best linen shirt. He hung his powder horn and bullet pouch over his shoulder, hoisted his musket, and swung Ruth up with his other arm. "Come, littlest. We shall make better progress if I carry you."

As they traversed the path between the village and James Dudley's palisaded compound, he considered the progress his family had made since Elizabeth's death and that of their infant son at the end of March the year before. The rift was still fresh in his heart, but they had fallen into new routines and habits, made easier by Christine's ministrations.

She was a capable housekeeper and a gentle caregiver for the children, though she exacted obedience from them. *Too bad she doesn't wish to marry,* he mused. Christine might make a natural mother. But she had voiced her disinclination to marry and bear children several times to his wife, back when she lived at the parsonage. He was sure her captivity and her years in the nunnery had strengthened those feelings. She seemed content to work for a family not her own, to the point of exhausting herself. He recalled how ill she had been after she and Jane cared for his family during the smallpox epidemic.

Although most grateful for her selflessness, he desired to make things easier for her. He supposed the best thing he could actually do to lighten Christine's burdens would be to remarry. Then she could go and work for someone else for real wages. Or, if she preferred to stay on, she could at least share the labor with the mistress of the house.

The thought made his head swim. Some men remarried quickly after being widowed, with Mordecai Wales a case in point. But the idea of taking another woman as his wife repelled Samuel. Elizabeth had been his joy, and she was gone little more than a year.

I'm nowhere near ready for that.

No, it was not to be considered. He squared his shoulders, relieved to have faced the thought.

All in Your time, heavenly Father.

As they passed Roger Ackley's farm, he heard the goodwife's shrill voice through the open window of the house.

"Mr. Ackley! Mi–i–i–ister Ackley! Where be that tub of water you promised to fetch me for washing?"

Christine looked askance at him, and Samuel shrugged.

"I hear Alice Stevens is going to start working for the Ackleys soon." Privately, he questioned how long that would last. If Mahalia Ackley treated her maids the same way she treated her husband, it was no wonder she couldn't keep domestic help.

They trudged on, and when they were past the house, he could see Goodman Ackley toiling toward the side door, pushing a wheelbarrow that held a squatty barrel Samuel assumed was full of wash water.

If the children had not been along, he would have stopped to have a word with the couple, but he had no desire to expose his family to the farm wife's critical eye. He had heard the damage her tongue could do all too often. He wouldn't want her telling others, for instance, that Abby's skirt was scandalously short. Why hadn't he noticed before how tall she was getting? Perhaps Christine could make over one of Elizabeth's old skirts for his eldest daughter.

James Dudley and his sons were in the hayfield when the Jewetts and Christine approached. James and Richard sliced the tall grass with sweeping cuts, while Stephen stood guard with a musket.

Samuel had no doubt the other two had guns lying close at hand as they worked. He lowered Ruth to the ground and let her walk with Christine and the older girls toward the gate in the fence surrounding the garrison house. He walked into the field with John and Ben. The smell of the newly cut hay hung in the hot air. "A fine crop you'll have," he called to James as he neared his host.

"Aye, thank ye. That we shall, if the rain holds off."

"The Lord willing, it shall come when needed," Samuel said with a smile. "We're later than I'd planned. Forgive me. But Ben brought our scythe along."

James shrugged. "It takes a big family time to pack and remove. I should be shocked if you arrived at dawn with all the young'uns in tow." He leaned for a moment on his scythe handle and wiped his brow with a kerchief. "I allow Catherine and my wife will be glad to see all your womenfolk."

Samuel waved to Stephen, who waved back and returned to scanning the edges of the field. "Any sign of Indians?"

"Not since that fracas after meeting a fortnight past," James Dudley replied.

Samuel nodded. "They usually come at night or early morn. You're probably safe."

"But you never know." Dudley lifted his scythe and swung viciously at the tall grass.

———◆———

By the time they left for their walk back to the parsonage in midafternoon, Christine's fatigue oppressed her. She had spent much of the day on her feet at Jane's house, spinning wool and churning butter. Catherine and Sarah had joined them, and all had shared in the cleaning and baking. At the end of their visit, Jane had two pounds of fresh butter—she sent one back with the Jewetts—two skeins of fine gray woolen yarn, two berry pies, and enough newly baked bread to last her and Charles a week.

The smell of the baking loaves had prompted Abby to tell the ladies about the disappearing bread at Goody Deane's house. Christine had confirmed her story.

"Likely Goody Deane was confused," Sarah said. "She is getting on in years."

"Nay, she baked three loaves, of that I'm certain." Christine shook her head. "I hate to think someone stole one."

"It wouldn't surprise me," Catherine said. "I had a row of beans almost ready to pick last week, in the bed just outside the palisade. I went out one morning to pick them for dinner, and what think ye? Someone had stripped the vines before I came. Fair tasting them, I was."

"You didn't tell me," Sarah said, her blue eyes narrowed.

"Someone picked them off before you?" Jane asked.

"Aye. I asked Father and Mother and Stephen, but none of them had done it."

"Perhaps a deer got them," Christine suggested.

"Nay, they would have eaten the plants right off. These were very neatly picked. Father said to be watchful for savages, but we never saw any."

Christine kept a sharp eye during their walk home, but no mishaps befell them.

"You needn't tend our supper tonight," the pastor said as they approached the village. You're fatigued. Go home and enjoy the rest of the day with Goody Deane."

"Who will feed us?" Constance asked, staring up at her father.

"I shall do it. Even a man as clumsy as myself can build up the fire under the stewpot and set out the biscuits Miss Christine put by last night. And you and Abby shall help me."

"And there be mince pie left," said John, licking his chapped lips.

"We can fend for ourselves," Samuel said with a smile.

Christine returned his smile. "I'm sure you can, but I'd like to come and weave for a while, if you don't mind, before the light is gone."

She did just that, managing to finish the linen that she and the pastor had agreed she could sell.

"That's nice work, Christine," he said as she carefully folded the material. "You have a buyer already, I believe?"

"Mrs. Heard told me last spring she would take any linen I could give her, after she saw the sheeting I wove for Mrs. Otis."

The pastor nodded. "Aye. And you shall keep the price."

"Nay, sir. You supplied the flax and the loom."

"We have had this conversation before. Without your labor, there would be no linen."

She inhaled deeply. "Then, sir, if you insist, we shall split the profit." She glanced at the children and lowered her voice. "I don't like to say it, sir, but Ben at least will need new boots in the fall. All of the children are growing quickly, and—"

"I fear you are right. I noticed today how tall Abby is getting. Think you that one of my wife's skirts could be cut down for her?"

It was the practical thing to do, of course. "Certainly. I'll see to it tomorrow."

He nodded. "Very well, then, we shall go halves. My portion of the linen money shall go to the cobbler and to the trader for whatever foodstuffs you think we need. But your part is yours to keep and do with as you wish."

She could see that he would brook no further argument, so she lowered her chin. All too stubborn that chin had become lately, she supposed. Sometimes it felt as if these were her own children she championed. "We agree, sir."

"Good. Now, you must be on your way. I insist that we shall make our own supper tonight."

She opened her mouth to protest, but Ben chimed in with, "I'll make up the fire, Father, and John will help Abby set the table."

John threw a dark look at his brother, but the pastor's features relaxed.

Christine decided it might be well for him to have a calm evening alone with his children. She had left the stew ready to heat in the iron kettle, and there really wasn't much to do. "Thank you," she said. "I expect Goody Deane and I shall retire early." She gathered her things and crossed the dusty street to the widow's cottage.

As she opened the door, Goody Deane startled in her chair, and Christine greeted her softly. "Good evening. The pastor says he and the children can take care of themselves tonight."

"I been looking for ye to come back," the old woman said. "If I'd known ye weren't eating at the parson's, I'd have put supper on."

"Don't stir yourself," Christine told her. "It looks as though you've made a lot of progress on your knitting today. I'll build the fire up and fix us a bite."

"Oh, do we need to heat the house up? It's just now getting bearable. I have hopes of a restful sleep tonight, but not if we get the fire up and heat the house to a simmer."

"Very well." Christine opened the tin box where they kept bread and remnants of food. "I think there's enough lamb here to eke out a meal with bread and butter, and I spy a morsel of seed cake. I'll fetch a bucket of cool water, and we'll sit down."

She took up the nearly empty water pail and dumped the little that was in it into a pitcher. The cottage had no well, but the walk to the river was a short one. It took her only a few minutes to reach the bank and fill her bucket.

The trader's daughter had also come to fetch water, and they greeted each other cheerfully.

Christine trudged alone back to the little house, thinking about her place in the community. When she first returned from her captivity in Canada, she had felt like an outsider and was shunned by many of the villagers. But time and contact had softened their attitudes, and she now felt a part of Cochecho. Her pleasant days divided between Goody Deane's cottage and the parsonage filled her with contentment.

She was nearly to the cottage door when she saw a dark figure flit across the garden in the twilight, toward the back of the house. Christine halted so quickly that water sloshed over the rim of the bucket, soaking the bottom of her skirt. She set the pail down quietly in the path and tiptoed to the corner of the house.

A man in ragged clothes was peering in Goody Deane's kitchen window. He turned toward her, his eyes wide.

Before she could speak, he gestured threateningly. "Quiet, miss. If ye give alarm, I'll kill ye."

Chapter 3

S amuel served his children supper and was about to sit down to his own plate of food, when a peremptory knocking sounded on the door.

Edward Chapman, one of the fishermen who lived along the riverbank, stood outside, panting as though he had run all the way from his house. His rapid breathing and unsteady gaze told Samuel immediately that something untoward had happened.

"Edward! What's the trouble?"

"Parson, can you come? The cow kicked my boy, Philip, and I think his knee is broken."

"The poor lad. I'll come take a look." Samuel looked around, swiftly taking a mental count of the children. "Ben, I shall be gone for an hour or two. Read a chapter with the children and send the girls to bed. Abby, you will have to help Ruth undress."

"Might I stay up with Ben, Father?" John asked.

"Aye. And if you need any help, run over the way for Miss Christine."

Ben picked up Ruth and her doll from the rag rug. "We'll be fine."

"Here, Father. Take this with you." Abby ran to the table and plucked a biscuit from his untouched plate.

Samuel smiled and accepted it from her. "Thank you, Abby, dear. Be good and help put the dishes to rights, won't you? But let Ben pour the hot water."

He went out into the dusk with Chapman, shoving the biscuit into his pocket. As they walked, he sought to calm the worried father. "Be Philip in sore distress?"

"Aye, sir. He bellowed like a cow moose. Awful pain."

Samuel shook his head. "I'm sorry, Edward. I hope one day a physician will feel called to settle here among us. My ministrations are far from expert."

"You've a better touch than anyone else in the village, and twice the heart."

Samuel bowed his head and sent up a prayer for wisdom beyond his skill. Lately it seemed his theological studies were interrupted more and more often. Of course, summer brought more accidents with all of the farming activity.

Word had gotten about the first year he and Elizabeth moved to Cochecho, after he stitched up a man's gashed scalp. The new preacher was as good as a doctor, some insisted. Samuel knew better. He acted because someone had to, and so they believed he had a special aptitude for it. As the village grew, so did the calls for his medical assistance. When he could, he steered people to Captain Baldwin's wife, who acted as midwife and herb woman. But serious injuries were beyond her, she'd told him early, though she often helped nurse Samuel's patients after he had done what he could.

Chapman seemed calmer by the time they came in sight of his cottage near the river. "I expect the boy will be fine once you set his leg," he said.

Samuel nodded. "Let us pray so. If it needs setting, I'll have you fetch me the splints."

"I can do that."

"Good. How has your catch been this summer?"

"The Lord has been quite generous," Chapman said. "I've been out on the boat much of the time. By chance I was home tonight when the boy went to milk the cow."

"God knew you would be needed," Samuel said.

They reached the path to the house. "Well, he's quit screaming," Edward noted. "I made sure I was home ere nightfall. The wife says there's been pilfering in the neighborhood. Like as not, some Indians are skulking about, she says."

"I've heard as much from some others," Samuel admitted. "I have no explanation. . .but I've heard of no raids or attacks since the one at the church. Just small things gone missing. Food, mostly."

As Chapman opened the door, he heard weeping, and the fisherman's wife cried, "Bless you, Parson! Our boy is in bad straits. I told him you would come and make it better."

Samuel winced, wishing he had a stock of medicines and a physician's manual. But God had called him to be a minister, not a doctor. He closed the door firmly and smiled at Mrs. Chapman. "I will do my best, ma'am. Have you any comfrey or boneset?"

"What do you want?" Christine's voice croaked. Her heart drummed as though it would leap out of her chest.

The man stood in shadows, with his bearded face muffled in darkness. The pale skin below his eyes stood out, and as he shifted, she caught a metallic glint in his right hand.

"Don't you yell."

"I won't." Christine bit her bottom lip to still its trembling.

He raised the knife just a bit, making sure she saw it. "If you squawk, you've had it, that's all."

She nodded.

"Good, then. Bring me something to eat."

in and hung up his hat, she poured hot water in the basin and added some cold; then she laid the pannikin of soft soap and a linen towel beside it.

The small tasks she performed for her husband added a sweetness to the day. She was tired, yes, but she didn't mind that. Being here with Charles in their home and knowing their labor would produce food to sustain them through the year brought her a great satisfaction. In fact, her present contentment was deeper than any she had known before.

He smiled at her as he dried his calloused hands, and Jane found herself smiling back at him.

His eyes glinted and he leaned toward her, across her worktable, and tucked a wisp of her hair behind her ear. "I like to see you happy, wife."

"I *am* happy, Charles."

A smile of true delight spread over his face, making her glad that she had told him.

"I think we shall have a good year together," he said.

"Aye, we've made a good start on our garden, and you say we shall have some stock soon."

He nodded thoughtfully, and she realized he spoke of things less tangible than the crops. But it was still difficult to talk about those things. She would work on it.

"Is everything ready?" he asked.

"Aye."

He went to the table. Jane followed, carrying a dish of butter that Richard's mother had brought on her visit a few days past.

Outside, Samson began to bark. Jane looked at Charles in inquiry.

"Did you hitch him by the barn?"

"Nay, he was chasing a squirrel when I came in. He probably wants his supper."

Charles started to rise, but Jane was already on her feet, so she strode toward the door. She passed one of the tall, narrow windows and peered out to see if she could catch a glimpse of the dog. But Samson was out of sight, still barking. She opened the front door and looked toward the sound.

As she leaned out, his barking stopped. She saw a dark figure in the dusk. At once she recognized the hairstyle and buckskin garb of an Algonquin warrior. Her heart seemed to stop for in instant as the Indian bent over the body of her little mongrel dog. The warrior looked up, his dark eyes settling on her.

"Where shall I bring it?"

"Christine?" The widow's quavering voice floated through the window and across the sultry air. "Is that you, Christine Hardin?"

"Answer," the man hissed.

"I'm coming."

"When she's abed, you come," he said. "Take it out back, near the necessary. I'll be waiting." He faded into the twilight.

Christine hurried to where she had left the bucket of water. She hefted it and bunched up a handful of her skirt, lifting the hem a couple of inches. She hobbled into the house as quickly as she could without spilling more water.

Goody Deane stood just inside the door, holding the poker in her hand.

"What kept you, child? I thought I heard a man's voice."

"Oh, a man did greet me in passing." Christine turned away from her and hid her face while she poured water into the teakettle. She drew the muslin curtains, wondering if the stranger was watching and listening. She wished she dared put up the shutters, but Goody Deane would complain about the heat.

"What man?"

Christine froze for an instant. She couldn't lie. But what could she say? She made her hands resume their labor. "Oh, it was. . .just a man passing by."

"Did he want to call?"

"Oh, no, no, nothing like that." How awful if Goody Deane had the mistaken impression that Christine had a suitor and tried to hide it from her. "Trust me, dear lady, I shall tell you if we have gentleman callers."

Goody Deane smiled. "You never know. Now, what will it be? I baked a little honey cake today."

"Lovely. But we must have some cheese first and a slice of bread." Even as she spoke, she wondered if she could save the small portion of lamb for the stranger.

She sat down at the table a moment later with Tabitha Deane and managed to choke down her supper.

If only she could tell someone. But whom? The Reverend Jewett seemed most logical. His children were the ones threatened by this criminal. Did she dare? If she told anyone, the outlaw would retaliate. She mulled over his words, his tone, his manner, and decided she indeed believed he would carry out his threats.

When at last the widow was abed and snoring gently, Christine tiptoed to the tin box and removed the small amount of meat left there and two generous slices of bread. They had no fresh vegetables in the house, but she had no doubt the man was helping himself to those from her neighbors' gardens as quickly as they ripened.

She lit a candle in a pierced tin lantern and carefully opened the door. She ought to have put some grease on those hinges.

Outside on the flat stone before the door, she waited half a minute, listening. She almost wished Tabitha would start up and call to her again, but all was silent within. The cricket choir chirped, and the warm breeze rustled the leaves of the maple trees.

She set out slowly along the path through the herb garden, around the side of the house. Each step seemed more difficult. Madness, meeting a violent man alone in the night.

Lord, give me safe passage there and back!

The little building stood just within the tree line, a discreet distance from the cottage, but too far for Christine's liking. If she screamed for help, would her voice penetrate the widow's slumber?

She stopped, eyeing the tiny shed. The door was off the latch. He wouldn't be inside, would he?

"So, ye came."

She jumped and whirled to face a black shape emerging from the trees.

"Y–yes. I said I would."

He gave a snort of a laugh. "So ye did. Ye can be sure I was watching to see if you went out again tonight. If you'd gone anywhere but here, I'd have known."

She shivered, wanting nothing more than to get away from him. "Here." She held out the tin plate with the food on it. "It's all I could get. It's not much, and the widow might question me about it even so."

He took the plate and shoved a piece of the meat into his mouth. "You've saved a man's life, miss." She could barely make out the words, garbled as they were with his chewing.

"I doubt that," she said. "You'd have found sustenance somewhere. I only made it easier for you and less likely you'd be caught."

"That's right. This ain't stealin', now, is it? You gave me these vittles."

She didn't deign to reply.

"I'm not so bad. Truly, I'm not. I'm innocent, you know?"

"Of what?" She wished she hadn't responded, but he'd piqued her curiosity.

"They run me out of Haverhill, they did. Said I done something terrible, but I was innocent. I went to trial, and they couldn't prove anything on me, but they still made me leave. The magistrate banished me from the township. I went to Portsmouth, but they heard about me from folks in Haverhill, and they said the same. 'Go peaceful, or we'll lock you up for vagrancy.' But I'm innocent of the charges, I tell you."

She wanted to ask what the charges were but decided she might be better off not knowing. She turned away.

"Wait!" he called, his mouth full again.

She paused and turned back unwillingly.

"You'll need the plate."

"Leave it on the step. I'll get it in the morning."

"Oh, I can do better than that. The old woman might go out early and step on it there. Nay, I'll set it up on the window ledge, behind those pretty white curtains. When you get up, you can reach out and get it ever so easy. And bring me a blanket. Sure, it's warm tonight, but it might turn cool tomorrow."

She eyed his dark silhouette for a moment. He picked up a slice of bread and folded it, sticking half of it in his mouth. She left him, walking quickly down the path without looking back.

Chapter 4

In the morning Christine found the plate, as promised, on the window ledge. She took it in, washed it, and used it in setting the breakfast table before Goody Deane was finished dressing. The old woman's gnarled hands made it difficult for her to button and tie her clothing, but she didn't want to give up trying. Usually she managed, albeit slowly.

"I believe I'll go over to the Jewetts' with you today," the widow said.

"You'll be welcome. I plan to do a wash and begin weaving that wool. If there's anything ready in the garden, you and the children can pick it."

"Aye, and pluck a few weeds." Tabitha eyed her hands. "As long as God allows, I'll keep on being useful."

Christine was thankful that Tabitha had decided to go. Otherwise, she probably would have fretted all day, wondering if the stranger hung about and Tabitha was in danger. Of course, with the cottage empty, he might go in and help himself to whatever he could find. She refused to dwell on the unwelcome thought.

By the time the two women arrived at the parsonage, Pastor Jewett had already left with John to take Christine's linen to the Heard garrison and visit his patients at the Chapman and Otis houses. Christine set to work with a sense of relief. His absence settled the nagging question of whether or not to tell him about her encounter with the outlaw.

"You should have fetched me last night," she said, when Ben told her about Chapman's call for his father the evening before. "I could have come back."

"Nay, we were fine. Except Connie cried because there was no more mince pie."

"What? I thought half a pie was left."

"So we thought, but when John went to get it down, there was only one small piece left." Ben shrugged. "Of course, we had to leave it for Father."

"Of course." Christine walked to the pie safe on the shelf and opened it. The tin box was now empty.

"Father said when he came home that mayhap you—" Ben stopped and looked away.

"What?"

He winced. "He said mayhap you took it home for you and Goody Deane."

"I did no such thing."

"We had a cake of our own yesterday, and no mince pies," the widow chimed in, glaring at Ben.

"I didn't really think it." Ben kicked at a piece of bark on the hearth. "Do you want the fire built up?"

"I think we'd better," Christine said.

Goody Deane nodded, her eyes snapping. "Aye, it sounds as though we'd best make some mincemeat pies for this rabble."

"Oh, you don't need to—"

"Hush, Ben," Christine said with a smile. "She's only teasing you. Fetch some good, dry wood and get a new crock of mincemeat from the root cellar."

"There be only one left."

"Ah, well, soon we'll have apples to make more, won't we?"

"Not for a good month," Goody Deane said.

"I know where there be blackberries," Abby piped up from the corner where she sat with her sampler. "May we go and pick some, Miss Christine?"

The thought of the outlaw crossed her mind. "Oh, I think not."

"They're only out behind the church," Ben said. "I'll take the girls, if you like."

She turned that over in her mind. They would be easily visible from the common, and easily heard if Ben called for help. Still, she had no doubt the thief had been inside the parsonage while the family was at the Dudleys' the previous day. "Very well, but leave Ruth here with me. Ben, you must watch the girls, and beware of strangers, won't you?"

He cocked his head to one side in a gesture that imitated his father exactly. "Aye."

She helped them get ready, wondering if she was making a costly mistake. She tied Constance's bonnet strings firmly and put a small pail in her hands.

"You will be careful of them, Ben?"

"You can be sure of it, Miss Christine."

She leaned toward him and whispered, "All this pilfering, you know. There may be someone lurking about."

His eyes widened. "You mean—the pie?"

"Well, we don't know, do we?"

He nodded gravely and hustled the two girls out the door.

While they were gone, Christine went through the parsonage larder. She thought there were fewer raisins than there had been, but John was known to sneak a handful now and then. The height of the beechnuts in their jar seemed lower, but she couldn't be sure. She simply couldn't tell if the outlaw had stolen more than two or three pieces of pie, but she had no doubt in her mind that he had rifled the Jewetts' stores while they were gone. He had certainly had more to eat than that loaf of Goody Deane's bread on Monday.

She looked about the main room. He knew the arrangement of the house now and where the children slept. It made her skin crawl. "I shouldn't have let them go."

"What?" Tabitha Deane asked.

"The children. I should have made them wait until their father returned."

"It's only behind the meetinghouse."

"I know."

"Go with them, then. They'll pick their berries quicker and be home in half an hour. I'll watch Ruth and start preparing the crust."

Christine untied her apron and hung it up. "You think I'm silly, don't you?" She grabbed an iron kettle with a bail handle.

"Nay. You speak as a mother would."

She dashed out the door and through the knee-high grass between the parsonage and the meetinghouse. Rounding the corner of the stark building, she slowed and made herself calm down. There were the children, picking around the edge of the berry patch that had sprung up where the men had felled trees several years earlier. They were fine. They laughed together in the sunshine, and the smell of the leaves and the warm, plump berries encouraged her. She walked onward, swinging the kettle.

"Miss Christine!" Constance let out a squeal and ran to greet her.

"I thought I'd help you, and we'd finish picking sooner." Christine gently pulled up the bonnet Constance had let fall back on her shoulders. "You must shade yourself from the sun, dear."

Ben looked askance at her but kept picking without comment, and soon they had more than enough fruit for two pies.

"We could pick more and make jam," Abby suggested.

"Why not?" Christine also gathered blackberry leaves to dry for tea.

As they headed home at last, John and his father came ambling along the village street.

"Hello," the pastor called. "I see you are all out foraging."

"Aye, sir," said Christine. "You shall have fresh blackberry pie when you sit down to dinner."

"I look forward to it with pleasure." He handed her a small leather pouch. "Your share of the linen money."

"Oh. Thank you." Christine felt the blood rush to her cheeks. She tucked the pouch quickly away, in the pocket tied about her waist beneath her overskirt.

"Mrs. Heard was most pleased, and she says if you have time to make more, she'd be delighted to get it."

"My next project is already begun. Dark gray woolen for the boys' new trousers."

He nodded. "Well, I appreciate that, but I don't begrudge you to earn more if you can."

"Thank you."

Ben and John carried the bundles the pastor had purchased at the trading post, and the minister left them to enter the meetinghouse and study for his Sunday sermon.

Christine headed for home with the children. She wished she could unburden her heart to the pastor. But if she did, what evil would come to the family?

A sudden thought chilled her. The outlaw had demanded a blanket. But Goody Deane had no extra blankets, and surely if she took one from the parsonage it would be missed. All day she thought about it.

In the afternoon, she sorted through Elizabeth's clothes and selected an everyday linsey-woolsey skirt that she could make over for Abby. With care, she could probably make a dress for Ruth from the material, as well. Samuel had offered her his wife's Sunday skirt and bodice, but she had turned him down. It would not be so long before Abby was big enough to wear them.

As an afterthought, she examined the bed linens in the trunk kept in the loft. The family didn't need many blankets at present, and three quilts were neatly folded there. But she couldn't give one of those to the stranger. Elizabeth had stitched them with her own hands. Not only would the family need them in cold weather, but they would be heirlooms for the three girls. Beneath them, in the bottom of the chest, she found a tattered woolen blanket. That might do. Surely no one would miss it for months, and if she worked hard, she might be able to weave some thick, blanket-weight wool after the trousers and Pastor Jewett's new coat were finished, though those projects would take her the rest of the summer.

When she descended the ladder, Goody Deane picked up her basket. "I shall go over to my house now and lay supper on for the two of us, unless you plan to eat here tonight."

"I'll be there to dine with you," Christine said. She hated the thought of the old woman's possibly encountering the thief if she ventured about alone. "Would you like Master John to walk you home?"

"Me? Nay, I can take myself across the street."

Christine almost protested further but could see no logical reason to do so. She had never been overly solicitous of the old woman in such matters. After all, Tabitha had fended for herself for years. If Christine began to fuss over her, she would get suspicious. "Very well, but do let us know if you need help with anything."

While the children gathered the clean laundry off the clothesline behind the house, she managed to smuggle the old blanket outside and hide it in the woodpile, where she could get it when she left. And what would she take the man for sustenance? If she came with no food, he would no doubt rant at her. She wrapped two biscuits in a napkin and set them aside. She didn't like to take him anything that required dishes. Returning them would be too obvious. And the Jewetts were already watching their food supply since the disappearing-pie episode.

And so it was with only the biscuits and blanket that she headed out that night after dark. She told Goody Deane she would make a quick trip to the necessary. When she reached the edge of the woods, she waited for a minute in the spot where the man had accosted her the night before, but all was still. She laid the blanket down, with the biscuits on top. An animal might get the food. But if the blanket was gone in the morning, she would know he had come for it. And if it remained where she left it? She prayed it would. For then she could assume he had moved on.

After evening prayers on Thursday, the parishioners stood about the green in the balmy evening air. The Dudleys and others whose homes were a mile or two away set out, but those who lived close lingered. The hour after Thursday meeting was the social time of the week, more so than on Sunday as the people had more freedom on weekdays to laugh and jest. The talk this week reverted to the rash of purloining suffered by the villagers. Samuel Jewett stood to one side discussing with William Heard the work to be done on the meetinghouse, but he kept one ear tuned to the conversation behind him.

"I think it's just folks not paying attention and then blaming the imaginary thief," said Mr. Lyford, who owned the gristmill.

"Nay, not so," said Joseph Paine, the trader, who also served as the town's constable now. "There be too many reports of things missing."

"That's right." Daniel Otis, the blacksmith's son, stepped forward. "I was smoothing the handle of a pitchfork I was making last week. I laid it by at milking time, with my knife beside it. When I came out of the byre and went to take it up again, my knife was missing. Clean gone. I looked all about and asked my family, but we've not found it yet. I'm afraid an Indian took it. With what designs, I won't speculate. We're locking up our tools, day and night, you can be sure."

"Young Stephen Dudley goes about as quiet as an Indian," Mahalia Ackley said.

Her husband smiled sheepishly. "Aye, he scares me. Came up behind me in my cornfield t'other day. I'd no idea the lad was about, and when he spoke to me, it startled me so I dropped my hoe on my foot."

The other men and their wives laughed.

"That Stephen's a sly one, that he is," said Lyford.

"It comes of his living with the savages all those years." Goody Ackley nodded emphatically. "I wonder if he's not the pilferer, I do."

Otis huffed out his breath. "What makes you say that? He's a good lad."

"But he's so stealthy. Them Indians taught him to skulk about, and no doubt he learned to steal, too." Goody Ackley glared at Otis, as though daring him to contradict her.

"Careful, ma'am," said Pastor Jewett, and all heads turned toward him. "Speaking ill of someone without a shred of evidence to support the accusation can bring you trouble."

"That's right," said the trader.

"I meant no ill," Mahalia Ackley said quickly. "I only said how furtivelike he moves. And it's the truth he stayed with those Indians long after he had a chance to go home to his folks. We all know his brother went to find him in Canada, and he wouldn't come back. He—"

"Enough." Samuel's steely voice silenced her. He advanced a step toward the couple and looked into her eyes. "I tell you, madam, such talk does not become you."

Constable Paine took up a rigid stance beside the parson. "Indeed. This is gossip of the worst kind that can ruin a young man's reputation."

"Aye," said Otis. "If there is indeed a thief among us, Stephen Dudley be an unlikely candidate. Why would a young man whose father owns a thriving farm steal a knife? Why would a lad whose mother can outcook all the goodwives in Cochecho steal a few biscuits and a dish of sauerkraut?"

"Goody Ackley, desist from this train of conversation or you shall find yourself in the stocks tomorrow," Paine told her.

"Hmpf." Mahalia lifted her skirt and turned toward her husband. "Husband, I believe it is time we went home."

"A truer word was never spoken," William Heard muttered as the woman marched toward the street with her husband trailing behind her, his chin on his chest.

Paine clapped his hand to Samuel's shoulder. "Thank you for that, Parson."

Samuel shook his head. "I should have spoken to her privately first."

"Nay, she's let her tongue run too many times in public. You'd think she would learn after the times she's spent in the stocks."

Samuel couldn't help a pang of guilt. Paine represented the law, and he would have put the woman in her place without his own interference. As minister, he needed to stay neutral in local wranglings. Still, he'd felt a compulsion to stand up for Stephen and put a stop to Mahalia's vicious talk.

"Well, time to get my children home and into bed." He looked about for them and noticed Christine. She had the three girls and John clustered about her, waiting a short distance off. Ben had edged into the fringe of the knot of adults, but he detached himself and walked toward the family, reaching them just as Samuel did.

"Shall we be off?" Samuel asked Christine.

"Aye, sir."

They turned toward the parsonage in silence. When they reached the house, Christine entered without asking whether he wanted her presence and helped the girls prepare for bed. Samuel placed his Bible on the shelf and hung up his coat. When he turned, Ben and John were standing by the loom, watching him.

"To bed, boys."

"Father," Ben said, "people can't accuse Stephen of stealing like that, can they? He wouldn't do such a thing."

"Nay. There's no evidence of such a thing. Goody Ackley is a malicious gossip, that is all. No one puts store in what she says. I say that to you in private, however. It is not something I would wish you to say among others."

"Even if it's true?" John asked.

"There be times, John, when we ought to keep silence—especially young people. I perhaps should not have spoken out tonight. There were others present who could have done the job better than I, and as pastor, I must be particularly careful."

Ben nodded, but his face still held a troubled expression.

Samuel walked over to him and touched his arm. "Don't brood on it, son." He gave John a quick hug. "Good night, John."

The boys climbed the ladder to the loft just as Christine came from the girls' bedchamber.

"Thank you, Christine. Allow me to escort you home."

"There's no need."

"I don't like you to go about alone at night, especially with all this talk of thievery."

He thought her cheeks flushed, but in the poor candlelight he might be mistaken.

"Thank you, sir," she said softly. They walked across the way together.

"I hope Goody Deane feels better tomorrow," Samuel said. Christine had made the widow's excuses earlier, telling him she had a catarrh.

"She thought it best to stay away from the children for a few days, and I agreed. She'll be better off to stay home and rest than to come over to the parsonage and wear herself out with scrubbing and cooking when she's ill."

They reached the cottage door, and she paused. "Thank you, sir."

He looked down at her plain face in the moonlight. A year ago she would have averted her eyes in his presence and tried to avoid his notice at all cost. How far she had come in a year. She was still markedly reserved, but no vestige of fear remained. What a blessing she had been to his family.

"Christine, I appreciate all you've done for the children. For myself, as well."

After a moment, she looked away. "I enjoy doing for your family."

He nodded. "I thank God for you every day. Good night now."

She put her hand to the latch, and he turned away.

◆

Christine stood inside the little cottage, her back to the door, listening. Goody Deane's labored breathing broke the stillness. The poor woman's nose was clogged, no doubt, which made her snoring more pronounced.

Christine had not encountered the outlaw tonight. Perhaps that was due to Pastor Jewett's presence. If she stayed with other people and didn't give him the opportunity to catch her alone, perhaps she could avoid ever talking to him again.

Or maybe he had left the area. She didn't really believe that, with all the reports in the village. And if he left Cochecho, he would work his evil somewhere else. Did she really want him to go about threatening other people and stealing from them?

The old blanket she'd left at the edge of the woods had disappeared. He had at least taken that last night.

She walked to the kitchen window and pushed the muslin curtain aside. A bank of clouds obscured the moon, and she thought it likely to rain before morning. The wind stirred the branches.

Was he out there, even now, watching the cottage? She shivered and turned away.

Chapter 5

Friday was the scheduled workday at the meetinghouse, and Samuel planned carefully so that he could spend the day with the men of the parish, who would give of their time to make improvements on the building.

For years the church folk had talked about building better pews inside—enclosed seating for each family, rather than the rows of plain benches they now used. Constructing a fireplace at one side of the building had also been bandied about, with the conclusion that they could get along as they always had in winter—with their foot warmers and soapstones and hot bricks wrapped in sacking. Some members even brought their dogs to church in winter and persuaded the animals to lie on their feet and keep them warm, but this sometimes resulted in disruption of the service.

Samuel had tried not to take sides in the debate, though in his mind a fireplace would have done them all good. As it was, they retired to nearby houses at noon to get warm on winter Sundays, returning to the frigid meetinghouse for the second sermon. Of course, attempting to heat such a large, open building would take a lot of fuel, which meant the men would have to give more labor toward providing wood. As it was, the parsonage sometimes went short of fuel in winter. He didn't like to ask them to do more, especially as the nearby supply of firewood was dwindling and the settlers went farther each year to furnish their woodpiles.

But the pews were another thing. The elders had agreed that the boxlike pews with four-foot partition walls were what they needed. These would give each family privacy and prevent the churchgoers from the distraction of eyeing their neighbors during the service. These enclosures would be built around the edge of the room, and William Heard's plan allowed for six more in the middle. The pulpit would be raised on a small platform, enabling all the people to see the minister while they were seated.

James Dudley arrived early, while the grass was still wet from the rain, with his cart loaded with lumber. Samuel heard the cart creaking up the street and called to Ben and John to join him. James and his son Stephen walked beside the cart, and Samuel hurried to help them unload.

"My brother and Charles Gardner be coming, too," Stephen told the pastor. "Richard and Charles are carrying the babies, so that the ladies can take them to visit at the parsonage today."

"Splendid," Samuel said. He looked back down the street and saw the two young men, their wives, the elder Mrs. Dudley, and her eighteen-year-old daughter, Catherine, approaching along the track that led to their outlying farms. "The ladies will have a good day together, and I'm sure they'll put on a toothsome luncheon for us."

William Heard and two of his sons arrived next, bearing tools and a small keg of sweet cider. "Richard Otis be bringing plenty of nails," Heard reported. On top of the stack of wide boards, he unrolled the plan he had drawn to guide them in their work.

"Do you plan to have a boys' pew?" James Dudley looked over Heard's shoulder at the meticulous diagram.

Heard glanced at Samuel. "What say ye, pastor? Methinks we decided not."

"That's right, Brother William. I know they do it some places, but in my opinion, boys will behave better if they sit with their own families. Let the fathers keep them in line."

Heard nodded. "So be it. The deacons will have their places here, and the pews we have planned will accommodate all of the regular parishioners and visitors, with room for a few new families."

"Aye, our village is growing." Samuel made a mental note to visit a new family that had taken up residence within the township, upriver toward the falls. "But we shall leave it to the deacons to assign the pews."

He could picture his five children, with Christine Hardin and Tabitha Deane, of course, in the front, center pew, sitting straight and listening attentively as he spoke. What would he have done without those two ladies this past year? The thought of Christine moving to another family's pew—whether as a maid to one of the church ladies or as the wife of another man—disturbed him. He shook off the thought and picked up his hammer.

———◆———

At the parsonage, the women gathered with great joy. A day together was a treat for all, though they would spend it working hard. Christine especially enjoyed cuddling her friends' babies and helping Constance and Abigail take turns holding the little ones.

"You shall have to come out to the farm again soon, Christine," Jane Gardner said. "Charles has finally finished my loom, and I wish you would help me to warp it the first time."

"I'd love to."

"Good," said Sarah Dudley. "Richard says the sheep have grown their wool back prodigious-fast, and he plans to shear them again next week. We'll have an abundance of wool this year."

Goody Dudley set a heavy basket on the table. "I brought extra dishes, and I'd like to leave a few here for the pastor. You have church folk to feed fairly often, Christine, and with all the children. . .well, I thought giving the parson a few extra plates would not be amiss, and I put in a couple of tin cups the children can use."

"Bless you," Christine said. "Those will be most welcome."

She directed her guests in preparing a huge pot of bean soup and another of mutton stew for the workmen. Goody Dudley and Catherine had brought the ingredients for a prune pudding, and they started it cooking. As the morning waned, Goody Deane offered to bake a batch of biscuits on her own hearth across the street, and Goody Dudley went with her. The younger women contributed to the preparation of another batch of biscuits and a large pan of corn bread at the parsonage.

While Jane's baby boy napped, Abby and Constance played with Hannah Dudley and Ruth.

With the little ones out of earshot, Jane turned the talk to a more sensitive matter. "You know the Wales wedding is Sunday."

"Aye." Christine shaped the biscuits with a round cutter and laid them in the pan. "Pastor Jewett is performing the rites at noon. If the weather is fine, we're to take food and eat in the churchyard. Parthenia's family is providing cake for everyone afterward."

"It will be strange to call her Goody Wales," Catherine said. "But since Goodman Jones died, I suppose she is taking the best course for herself and her children."

"I don't know about that," said Jane. "The second Mrs. Wales didn't live long after she married him. Only five years or so."

Sarah shrugged. "And the first one less than ten. Are you saying the Wales women are short-lived?"

"If I were her, I'd be cautious," Jane said.

Sarah chuckled. "Really, Jane, you're so droll."

Jane, who had experienced an unhappy marriage and widowhood, shrugged and went on with her task of measuring the ground corn. Christine felt that Jane took the matter more seriously than Sarah did but saw no profit in pursuing the topic.

The urge to tell them about the threatening stranger rose in Christine's mind, but she checked the impulse. What good would telling them do? And she had heard nothing from him in two days, nor any fresh stories of thievery. Better to forget it and let others forget it, too.

"I'm giving Parthenia a set of two linen towels," she said.

"I'm embroidering an apron for her." Catherine cracked two eggs into her mixing bowl while Sarah greased a large pan for her.

The baby began to cry, and Jane hurried to fetch him.

"So, Christine," Catherine said as she stirred the batter for the corn pone, "I heard Goody Ackley asked you to work for her."

"I declined."

"Which was probably your best choice," Catherine admitted, "though I'd love to have you closer. If you were at the Ackleys' farm, I'd doubtless get to see you more often."

"I would like that, too," Christine said, "but I am happy with my position here. I've grown to love the children dearly, and I think the Jewetts really need me." She felt her face flushing and feared the others would misconstrue her words. "That is, they need *someone*, and. . .well, the Lord put me here."

"That's right." Sarah smiled at her. "The Lord put all of us here two years ago—you, Jane, and me. I know you're a blessing to Pastor Jewett and his family."

Jane's eyes twinkled as she returned with little John Gardner held against her shoulder. "So perhaps you'll be best off to stay here, as Sarah and I did, until the Lord brings along a husband for you."

"Oh nay," Christine returned with a laugh. "No husband for me. I'm content in the state I'm in. My employer may not be so well fixed as Goodman Ackley, but I believe the atmosphere here to be more congenial."

"You speak truth," said Jane.

The day flew by. When the ladies had served dinner to the men and cleaned up the remaining food and dishes, they sat down at the parsonage to do their handwork, whether knitting, mending, or stitchery. All too soon, the Dudley men returned to take their womenfolk home. Goody Deane went to her own cottage while Christine prepared supper for the Jewett family. It was short work, with all the food left from the nooning.

Christine stayed until sunset, straightening up the main room while John and Abby did the dishes.

When they had finished, she carried the pan of dirty dishwater around to the garden behind the house. With the hot, dry weather, the vegetable plants could use every drop of moisture the household could give them. She sloshed the water out along a row of parsnips and was about to return to the house, when a tall, thin man appeared between the shoulder-high cornstalks.

She gasped and stared at him, knowing at once that he was the outlaw. She had never seen him in good light before, but his lean form, unkempt beard, and ragged clothing left no doubt.

"You've not brung me anything these two nights." He stayed within the line of the nearest corn row, and his eyes flickered toward the house.

She swallowed with difficulty. "I thought you'd gone."

"Nay."

"You've been eating, though." She looked into his flinty gray eyes.

His lips twitched. "Aye, short shrift it's been. But you've cooked a great heap of food today. I saw the men eating in the churchyard. I says to myself, 'You'll eat tonight, you will.' Bring me a plate. I'll wait here."

"I can't fix a plate and carry it out now that the family is done eating. Everyone would want to know what it was for."

"Tell them it's for the widow."

Christine's heart clenched. He knew so much about them. She could probably do that, and the Jewetts would accept her word. But she wouldn't lie to them. How could she ever look into the reverend's kind blue eyes knowing she'd lied to him?

"Nay."

His eyes narrowed. "Be you forgettin' what I said? You'd best bring me a plate, out back of the widow's house, at full dark."

"I won't."

He looked toward the house again. "Then I'll get it myself and not care who I slash to get it."

"No. You mustn't." She gripped the tin basin tightly. "I'll. . .I'll bring you something."

"Good. And I need a pair of trousers."

Christine felt as though the breath had been pummeled out of her. "How do you expect me to come by those?"

"The parson. I can fit his togs."

"Nay. He is a poor man. You can't steal his clothing."

"Would you have me go about indecent? 'Twill soon come to that."

Involuntarily, she glanced down at his ragged trousers. Both knees were torn through and a large tear gaped in the side of one pant leg.

"Can't you get them elsewhere?"

"I've tried, but I have to be careful, you know."

She gritted her teeth. "Oh yes, I know. You're such an honest man you must stay hidden from all the law-abiding people hereabouts."

His expression darkened. "Enough. Bring me food, and plenty of it, and a pair of trousers with no rips." He disappeared into the cornfield.

Chapter 6

Christine returned to the parsonage with a heavy heart. It was true, the man's clothing was in tatters from his weeks of skulking about. A small part of her felt sorry for him. But his gruesome threats hardened even the most tender spots in her heart.

I should have told Samuel!

The thought shocked her, because she never thought of the Reverend Mr. Jewett as Samuel. He was Pastor, or Mr. Jewett. But he was also her friend, and now his family was in danger. If she followed her impulse to tell Samuel about the outlaw, what would he do? At once she knew he would organize a search for the criminal. But what if the man was crafty enough to elude them? He'd gone uncaught for some time now. She didn't know where he was getting his food on nights when he didn't demand it from her. Perhaps other women in the village were as frightened as she was and handing over rations to him, too.

He has to be stopped, Lord!

Her prayer seemed futile. If she revealed the man's demands, he would know it, and he would do something horrible to the pastor's children.

Stealthily she took the pastor's workday trousers from the clothespress. He had two other pairs, his best for Sunday, and the pair he wore most days, when going about the parish to visit his flock. She ran a finger over the neat patch on one knee of the oldest pair. His dear, dead wife had stitched that patch on with love.

Forgive me, Father. I don't know what else I can do. I must protect the children. If there is a better way, then show me.

———◆———

He was waiting when she took the food and folded trousers out that night. She sensed his presence before she saw him. Was it an odor, or an influence of evil?

"What took you so long?"

"I had to make sure Goody Deane was asleep."

He snatched the bundle. "I like to have perished waiting."

"Please, I don't know how I'm going to explain to the parson about his trousers."

"You'll think of something. Just remind yourself that if I get to looking decent, I can show myself and look for work. You're helping me become an honest man, that you are. I do want to be honest."

She wanted to believe him, but his manner and his past actions prevented that. She had managed to get out of the parsonage undetected with a covered dish of stew. He pulled the linen napkin off and dropped it on the ground, then he tipped the bowl up to his mouth.

"I brought you a spoon."

He lowered the dish, wiped his lips with the back of his hand, and reached for it.

Christine shuddered as she put the spoon in his hand.

"Why ain't you got a husband?"

She stiffened. "I beg your pardon?"

"You heard me." He took a bite of stew and kept talking as he chewed. "It's true you're homely, but you seem a fair cook and a hard worker. That counts for a lot."

She stared at him for a moment, scarcely able to believe he had spoken to her in that manner. "Put the dishes on the window ledge when you are finished." She turned and stalked into the house.

◆

After the eventful weekend, Samuel needed a rest. All of Friday and a good part of Saturday he had spent helping William Heard and the other men build the new pews. Samuel left off on Saturday afternoon to put in more time on his sermon preparations.

The men had finished the work inside the church by Saturday night. The next morning, the parishioners seemed suitably impressed by the accomplishment. Elder Sawyer had assigned the pews. Of course there were a few minor squabbles over which family should have which box, but Samuel left that entirely to the elders. Roger and Mahalia Ackley tried to corner him to complain about their pew's position after the service, but he quickly excused himself, since he had to prepare for the marriage ceremony.

After the morning's sermon, he performed the marriage rite for Mordecai Wales and Parthenia Jones. This was followed by the usual nooning hour and then the afternoon service, which lasted three hours.

By sunset on Sunday, Samuel was always wrung out. Christine had prepared a cold supper for him and the children Sunday night and then left them to a quiet evening and early retirement. He slept through the night, hardly stirring from the moment his head hit the feather pillow.

But now Monday had dawned, and he longed to stretch his muscles and do some physical labor. He climbed out of bed, knelt to pray for his family and congregation, then arose and went to the pine chest where he kept his clothing.

His shirts, all but the one he'd worn yesterday, were folded neatly inside.

"We. . .don't have much."

"Oh, I know. I've seen you go back and forth to the house over yonder. But you keep food here, too. Here, where there's no kids snooping around. That's why I came here and not there. I thought I had a better chance to get somewhat to eat without anyone seeing me."

Christine shivered, though the evening breeze was warm. "Did you steal our loaf of bread yesterday?"

He smiled, and she could see his white teeth grinning ghoulishly in the fading light. "Aye, and good bread it were. I know you ladies can cook, that I do. I says to myself, 'This 'ere loaf will last a long time.' But it was so tasty, and I was like to starve. I ate it all yesterday, that I did."

"I can't steal from Goody Deane. She's a poor woman and she doesn't have much."

"She's got more than me." His lips drew back in a snarl, and he moved the knife. "Bring me some vittles, woman. You hear?"

Christine gulped for air. Would she ever be able to draw a full breath again? Her lungs felt as though a giant squeezed them. "I'll try."

"See that you do. And don't you tell the old crone." He laid a hand on her arm, heavy and warm through her sleeve.

Christine yanked away, and he chuckled.

"Think about it, now. If you tell that old woman—or anyone else—I'll see that you regret it."

"I'm not afraid of you." She threw back her shoulders, hoping he hadn't caught the tremor in her voice.

"Oh, you're not? Well then, I'll have to see that you are. You need to respect me because I will act if you don't do as I say."

"What will you do?" She meant it to come out strong and sneering, but her dread was all too apparent in the low, shaky words.

He smiled again and held the knife up, trying the edge of its four-inch blade with his thumb. "Those pretty little girls what live yonder. . ." He jerked his head toward the Reverend Jewett's home. "I'll make one of them not so pretty. Y'hear?"

She jumped at his growl and stepped back. "Y–yes. I'll bring you something."

"That's a good lass. Bring me some of that cake I smelt cooking earlier."

"I don't know about any cake. I've been gone all day."

"Oh, I know, I know. But there was cake, and she won't have eaten it all."

A shiver snaked down Christine's spine. How close had he ventured to where Goody Deane worked? Just beneath the window? And for how many days had he spied on them? She had no doubt that he would make good his threats if she did not do as he asked.

life, never knowing the joys of marriage.

The sweet companionship of his wife, Elizabeth, had carried him through many a painful situation. He missed her terribly. She'd been gone more than a year now; again the idea flitted through his mind that perhaps it was time to consider marrying again. This was not the first time the concept had occurred to him, but still the thought stabbed him with a dagger of guilt. And yet, scripture allowed it.

"Ah, Lord, Thou hast said it is not good for man to be alone. Yet whenever I think of replacing my dear Elizabeth, it pains me so much I cannot contemplate it."

The sun beat already on his shoulders, foretelling another sweltering August day. He reached his doorstep and went inside. Ruth and the boys were up, and Christine had them seated at the table eating corn pone and bacon.

He glanced toward the loom and saw that her new weaving was of fine charcoal gray worsted, a mixture of fine linen thread and wool. For him and the boys. She wouldn't be able to sell it if she used it on clothing for them, and he would have nothing to pay her this month. She didn't seem to mind.

She met his gaze, and he noted a slight apprehension in her hazel eyes.

He smiled as he set the buckets down. "I neglected to say good morning, Christine. Forgive me."

Her expression cleared.

"And good day to you, sir. Will you break your fast now?"

◆

After breakfast was over, Ruth was changed out of her nightclothes, the hearth swept, and the dishes cleaned, Christine began her washing. Ben carried the kettle of hot water out behind the house and emptied it into the washtub. He and John brought several buckets of cold water to add to it, and she wound up with a lukewarm bath for the family's clothing and linens.

Constance and Abby helped her. After Christine had scrubbed a garment on the washboard, she tossed it into the tub of rinse water. The girls' job was to retrieve it, dunk it in a bucket that held a second rinse water, wring it again, and hang it on the clothesline. She kept the two little girls busy running back and forth. Constance couldn't reach the line, but she handed the wet clothes to Abby, who was a head taller and proud that she could perform this task.

Meanwhile, the pastor and his sons weeded the garden and picked the vegetables that were ripe. The peas were gone by, but beets, lettuce, Swiss chard, green beans, carrots, turnips, and onions would liven up their meals. Last year's root vegetables were nearly exhausted, and what was left had gone soft. The new harvest cheered everyone.

Christine attacked the pile of soiled clothing with a vengeance. She had brought her own and Goody Deane's laundry over, to save time and resources. If she finished this daunting task by noon, she would do the ironing after dinner and perhaps snatch a couple of hours at the loom.

Such a shame that the reverend had discovered the loss of his old trousers so quickly. She should have expected it on a Monday, she supposed. Samuel often took that day to catch up on chores around the parsonage. The worsted suit she now intended to sew for him would be suitable for Sunday best, however. It wouldn't actually replace his work clothes. He could wear the older breeches, as he did today, but she knew he preferred his comfortable long trousers for dirty work.

As she scrubbed, she racked her brain for a way to get him some serviceable trousers. Perhaps Jane or Sarah could help her, but if she asked them, she might have to reveal what she had done with the old pair. And making Samuel an entire new suit would delay weaving the thicker wool cloth she needed to make him a new winter coat.

She sighed and wrung out Ruth's nightdress, the last of the light-colored clothes. Stooping, she lifted an armful of darker clothing into the washtub. As she straightened, she looked out over the garden and corn patch. Was the outlaw watching them, even now, from the edge of the forest?

He had come the past three nights, and she had taken him small amounts of food. It had become her routine. They met in darkness, while Goody Deane slumbered. Once the old woman had woken in her absence, and Christine had dodged her questions, feeling guilty. Each time she met the outlaw, he told her that he wanted to do honest work. Yet he continued to intimidate her into feeding him.

Where was Ruth? A sudden panic seized Christine, and she whirled about. Ah. There she was, playing with her dolly, Lucy, near the woodpile.

"Abby, bring Ruth closer, where I can watch her. She can sit in the shade of the rose bush." Christine looked once more toward the line of trees beyond the cornfield. Perhaps it was her imagination, but she felt him watching.

Chapter 7

Christine asked Ben to escort her and his three sisters to the Gardners' farm on Tuesday. Leaving them there with Jane, he went to spend the day working with Richard Dudley and Charles Gardner, who were gathering hay from Charles's field, within sight of the house.

"What's that you're working on?" Jane asked as Christine pulled a roll of linsey-woolsey from her workbag.

"It's material Goody Dudley gave me last spring. I was hoping there would be enough to make some everyday trousers for the reverend, but I fear there's not."

"He needs clothes?"

Christine hesitated. "Well, I'm weaving some nice worsted for a new Sunday winter suit for him, but he really needs something to work about the place without fear of ruining it."

"Ah. Well, I might have something."

"Your Charles is taller than the pastor."

"This is none of his clothing."

"Well, don't give me anything you and Charles will need."

"Nay, 'tis a piece of cloth he picked up for me on his trip to Boston last month. He brought home a bolt of serge, for which I was grateful, and two pieces of flannel for the baby, and a bit of blue silk." Jane smiled, her cheeks going a becoming pink. "He said I should make myself a bodice from the silk, but I don't know as I'd dare wear it. The women of Cochecho would think I was putting on airs."

"I think it would be lovely, and it would please Charles."

"Perhaps. Anyway, there's this piece of coarse cotton. He said he thought I might use it for pillow ticking, but it's not near so fine as I'd like in a pillow." Jane went into the next room and returned with a folded length of cloth.

Christine ran her hand over it. "That would do. If you're certain. . ."

"Oh, I am."

Christine nodded. "I'll spin for you in exchange."

"Nonsense."

"Nay, you do far too much for me."

The baby cried, and Jane smiled. "There's Johnny, awake from his nap. After I feed him, I'll help you cut out the pieces."

Christine went out to check on the little girls. They played inside the fence that surrounded the house, barn, woodshed, and yard.

"We're building a house for the dollies." Constance took her hand and led her to where they had formed a little stick house from twigs they'd gathered in the yard.

"Goodman Gardner has a baby calf yonder. And we got to pet it." Abby pointed to the small barn. "Do you want to see it?"

Christine caught a glimpse of color through a slit between the upright posts of the palisade. "I should love to, but I see young Mrs. Dudley coming along the path. Shall we go meet her? We can help her carry some of baby Hannah's things, perhaps."

"I'm so glad to see you," Sarah called as they approached. "Richard doesn't like me to walk even this far alone, but I could see him and Charles working almost as soon as I left my own doorstep, so I knew he wouldn't mind." She handed a basket to Abby and a small sack to Constance. "Thank you, my dears. Hannah is eager to play with you."

Sarah provided not only a store of anecdotes to entertain them but a pudding for the dinner she and Richard would share with the Gardners and their guests. Jane and Sarah set about preparing the noon meal while Christine took out her mending, and the little girls settled to play with Hannah and John on a blanket on the floor.

"Richard's mother paid a call on Goody Ackley yesterday." Sarah chopped scallions while Jane punched down her bread dough and set it to rise a second time. "Mahalia had asked her if she had any rye flour left, so Mother Dudley took over a small sack. She found Alice Stevens rather put upon."

"Oh?" said Jane. "Isn't that a maid's lot?"

"Aye. But Mother thought Mahalia treated her ill. Whatever the girl did, the goodwife complained in front of Mother until Alice was so nervous she dropped the plate of biscuits she was serving."

"Oh, dear."

"What did she do?" Christine asked.

"Mahalia screamed at her and told her to go and finish the washing. Mother Dudley said Alice was crying when she left the house."

"It's too bad." Christine knotted her thread and broke it off.

"Aye," Sarah said. "Alice was always a pretty and pleasant girl, if a bit timid. I fear she'll turn into a cowering ninny if she stays long at the Ackleys'. After she went out, her mistress told Mother Dudley she was a sly, sniveling girl and not nearly so good at cleaning as the last one."

"Well, I'm glad it's not me." Christine took out one of Ben's socks and her darning egg.

"You did well not to go there." Sarah wiped her hands on her apron and sat down on a bench. From her basket, she took a hank of soft lavender woolen yarn.

"Oh, how lovely," Christine said.

"How did you ever get it that color?" Jane came around the table to peer at it more closely.

"Mother Dudley did it. She's a clever one. Boiled it with the paper that came wrapped around a sugar cone. Isn't it the prettiest color? I thought to knit a wrap for Hannah to wear when the cooler weather sets in."

"She'll look darling in it." Jane set her bread pans on a shelf. "Come, Christine, let's lay out that cotton and cut it. We've time before dinner."

As they walked home later, Ben carried his littlest sister, Ruth, on his shoulders, and Constance held tight to Christine's hand. Abby walked alongside, carrying her diminutive basket with her rag doll and sampler tucked inside.

Christine let her thoughts wander to the late afternoon conversation she and Jane had held, after Sarah left them.

"How do you know you can trust a man?" It was the closest she dared come to asking Jane's opinion about the outlaw. But Jane had jumped to the wrong conclusion.

"Who is he?" Her face had lit with excitement. "Christine, don't tell me that at last you're in love!"

"No! Not that. I was only asking. You know I've never lived around men much."

"Until the reverend."

"Well. . .yes, but I wasn't thinking of him. Truly."

"Ah." Jane turned sober then, bouncing the baby on her lap. "Well then, I suppose you must spend time with him and talk to him, until you feel you know him quite well."

Christine wanted to protest. Spending time with the shadowy thief was the last thing she would do. But looking across the room at the three little girls playing so placidly with Hannah, she knew she couldn't reveal the truth. No palisade surrounded the parsonage in Cochecho. Samuel Jewett had bought a musket only when he felt it absolutely necessary because of the frequent Indian raids. If the outlaw struck at his children, he would be hard pressed to protect them. Let Jane think what she may, Christine must keep her secret.

And so she left embarrassed and confused. Jane had automatically assumed that her affections were set on the minister. Given the circumstances, the entire village probably thought as much. But Samuel. . . Christine shifted the heavy basket on her arm. What *were* her feelings for Samuel?

❖

Two nights later, by sitting up and sewing by candlelight, Christine finished making the new work trousers for the pastor. She put the last stitch in the hem late. As she stood and folded them, every muscle ached. Somehow she had to rid herself of this anxiety.

Her prayers seemed to have become vain repetitions—*Father, show me what to do. Lord, keep the children safe.* Mindlessly, she went about her daily work to make them comfortable. And every night she took their potential assailant sustenance so he could come back again tomorrow and threaten them again.

Something thunked against the side of the house, just below the window. She blew out the candle and stood in the dark, her heart racing.

Plink.

It sounded like a pebble had hit the boards outside. He had returned. He expected her to bring him food, and she hadn't gone out yet tonight. If she didn't go, he would keep up the racket, possibly awakening Tabitha.

With shaking hands, she carried the candle to the fireplace and relit it from the dying embers. She hastened to gather a scanty meal for him. There wasn't much, but she had deliberately put aside a small portion of dried fish, not admitting to herself at the time that it was for the lurker. And she had left half of her Indian pudding uneaten to sneak it into a covered dish when Tabitha looked the other way.

Another pebble hit the side of the house as she lifted the latch. Carefully balancing the earthenware dish, she slipped outside and closed the door behind her.

"Thought you'd forgotten me."

She jumped, almost dropping the dish. "Hush! You mustn't come so near the house."

He edged away, into the herb garden.

She still held the dish, and so she followed.

He went to the shadows beneath a large maple and turned toward her. "Well, lass, bring it here."

She hesitated. Why had she even bothered to ask Jane about trust? She didn't trust this miscreant one whit. "Nay. I'll leave it here." She stooped to set the dish on the ground.

"What, afraid of me?"

"Should I not be?"

"I'll not hurt ye, Christine."

She shuddered. He had never used her name before. Had he asked someone in the village the name of the young woman who worked at the parsonage? More likely he'd heard the children call out to her weeks ago. Or perhaps he'd heard Goody Deane use her name the night she called out when she'd heard his voice. Christine couldn't remember, but it disturbed her that he acted so familiar.

"Leave us alone." She swallowed, hoping she could keep her voice steady.

"This be the last time I will bring you anything."

"What? Ye cannot let me starve."

"Oh, but you can make us all live in fear."

He laughed. "I don't see anyone acting fearful. Anyone but you, that is."

Her anger simmered. In the darkness she thought he smiled. "You say you'll stop stealing, but you don't. I've given you food and clothing and a blanket that were not mine to give. You've made me steal for you. Do you hear me? You've made a thief of me. This must stop."

"Can you help me stop?"

"How would I do that?" she asked. He was toying with her, she thought, keeping her here in the shadows for his own purposes.

"You could speak for me to one of the gentlemen of the village. Tell them to hire me."

"Whom could you work for?"

"Anyone."

"The master at the brickyard?"

"Perhaps, though it's sorry work."

"Have you sought to hire on with the fishing captains?"

He flexed his shoulders. "Seasick, I fear. Debilitating."

She nodded. He would make excuses for any real job possibility, she calculated. "Harvest will soon be upon us. I know farmers who could use a hand at haying and grain harvest. Shall I speak to them for you?"

His momentary silence confirmed her assessment. He didn't want to work. Not really. At least, not hard, sweat-inducing, energy-sapping work.

"Certainly. But I shall need decent shoes and more food than you've been bringing me if I'm to slave all day in the sun."

"You new employer can feed and clothe you. I'll spread the word tomorrow. What is your name? How shall they find you?"

"Well, I. . ."

Again his hesitation emboldened her. She stepped toward him. "Speak, sir. Shall I put it about the village that a strong laborer will go to the ordinary at noon seeking employment?"

"Ye're a bit hasty, miss. I've not eaten well for many a week. I've not the strength you seem to think I have."

"Oh, haven't you? I've been kind to you. You know I have. Leave us. Just leave us. I won't tell anyone you were here."

"Nay, I think not." He stepped forward, and his face became clearer in the moonlight.

"I tell you now, sir, I cannot provide for you any longer."

He moved swiftly, another step forward. Suddenly they were toe-to-toe, with a glinting knife blade between them.

"You'll do as I say," he spat out in a low, raspy tone. "If you don't, you'll be nursing one of those little dark-haired girls tomorrow. See if one of them don't meet with an accident."

"Christine?" Goody Deane's sharp voice startled them both.

The man glanced toward the house, over Christine's shoulder, and melted back into the shadows beneath the tree.

Christine drew in a ragged breath and turned around. "I'm coming, Tabitha."

"Who was that man?" The widow peered toward the garden. "Shall I run for the parson?"

Christine reached her side. "Nay. He is. . ." She struggled to pull breath in past the heavy weight on her chest. "Oh, Tabitha, you cannot tell Reverend Jewett."

Goody Deane's eyes glittered as she frowned up at Christine. "What are you saying, girl? You've formed an attachment you're ashamed of."

"Nay. Oh please, don't think that!" Christine let out her breath and reached for Tabitha's hand. "I see I must tell you all."

"And about time, I'd say. Come inside. I'll stir up the fire, and we shall have blackberry tea and a bit of that Indian pudding you put by."

Christine stared at her. "You saw that?"

"Of course I did. You think I don't notice what goes on at my own hearth?"

Glancing behind her, Christine realized that the outlaw had managed to grab the dish of food as he retreated. "Then you'll soon realize we won't be eating any pudding. And we may be out one dish as well, if he doesn't return it. But I expect I'll find it on the window ledge at dawn." Tears streamed down her cheeks, and she felt the absurd urge to laugh. "I'm relieved, actually, that you know."

Tabitha squinted toward the dark expanse of the garden. A breeze ruffled the maple tree's leaves. "Come inside, my dear. I think this is a night to bar the door and bare your soul to God and a human friend."

Chapter 8

Samuel set four math problems for John on his slate Wednesday morning and immersed himself in the scripture for the Thursday evening sermon. So many distractions in summer. Ben was off working for James Dudley today, and John fidgeted. Every sound that reached them through the oiled paper window of the meetinghouse called to the ten-year-old boy. The oppressive heat found them, even inside the big building, though it was cooler inside than out in the scalding sun. It was a wonder the boy learned anything at all.

He thought of Christine and the girls, no doubt baking today, poor things. He'd told Christine she needn't build the fire this morning, but she insisted that if she didn't, they'd have no bread tomorrow and their fish would be presented raw at supper. He would keep himself and John away from the house all day so that she and the girls could work in their shifts. Even so, they were likely to swelter in the little house. Did they have plenty of water for their cooking and washing needs?

It took determination to put his household out of his mind. He had only another thirty hours before evening worship, and he had much work to do on Sunday's two sermons as well.

"Father."

Samuel looked up.

John stood beside him with his slate ready.

"Ah. Finished your problems, have you?"

"Aye."

"Good lad. Let me check them." He took the slate from his son and put his mind to work on the arithmetic. "Excellent. Now, study your Latin."

"Father, be we going home for dinner soon?"

"I told Miss Christine she could send Abby over with a cold luncheon for us. I don't wish to add to her work in this heat."

John nodded and wiped his brow with a kerchief. They had both stripped off their jackets and vests hours since, but even so, the back of Samuel's linen shirt stuck to his skin.

"May I get a drink now, Father?"

"Aye. Let us both." Samuel stood and set his Bible on the pew next to his ink bottle, quill pen, and two sheets of thin birch bark on which he'd been jotting notes for the sermon. Parchment was too expensive, and his scant supply of locally made paper was nearly gone. Perhaps he could replenish it when he received his quarterly salary, though many other needs seemed more pressing.

The door of the meetinghouse flew open, and Roger Ackley stood blinking in the doorway, panting for breath. He held his shabby coat in one hand, and his clay pipe was stuck in the band of his shapeless hat of beaver felt. "Reverend?"

"Aye, Brother Roger. How may I help you?" Samuel walked down the aisle between the new box pews.

"Ah, there ye be." Ackley stepped inside. "It's cool in here."

"Is it?" Samuel asked.

"Sir, I've come about my wife. Goody Ackley left for the trader this morning. She said she wished to go while the air was still bearable. She ought to have been back by half past nine, but she weren't. I sent Alice, the girl what be our maid now, to see if she were coming, but Alice didn't meet her. She went all the way to the trading post, and Paine said she came in early, just as she planned." He pulled in a deep breath and shook his head. "But it's past noon now, sir, and she never came back. I'm on my way to see Paine, and I thought you might be of help."

Samuel laid his hand on the older man's sleeve. "I'm sorry, Roger. We'll find her, I'm sure. I'll send word around the village. Perhaps she decided to visit one of the other women while she was in town."

"Perchance you're right, Parson, and I wouldn't fret most days, but you know we've had Indian trouble already this summer. This time of year, they come down out of Canada and worry us. You were there, sir, when they came at us after meeting last month, and Richard Otis was shot before we ran them off."

"Yes, I understand." Samuel turned to look at his son. "John, get Goodman Ackley a dipper of water. Then I want you to run home and tell Christine—oh, never mind! Here's Christine with our dinner. I'll tell her myself. Then we'll walk over to the trading post and speak to Mr. Paine."

"Can I go?" John asked eagerly. He scooped water out of the bucket near the door and handed the dripping dipper to Goodman Ackley.

"Aye, I'll let you go along, but you must stay with me." Samuel smiled at Christine as she mounted the steps, and he took the basket from her. He lifted the corner of the linen napkin to peek inside. "Thank you, Christine. That looks delicious. Are you suffering from the heat?"

"Prodigiously, sir."

He chuckled. "Well, we're thankful for the repast."

"I thought to speak to you, sir, if you've a moment."

Samuel wondered what her errand was. Probably something about household affairs. He stepped to one side, so she could see that he was not alone. "I'm afraid John and I must go straightway to the trading post to speak to Mr. Paine. And I want you to keep the little girls close. Mrs. Ackley is missing, and until we find her, I want to know you are all safe at home."

Christine's hazel eyes widened, but she nodded without comment.

"Is Goody Deane with you at my house?"

"Yes, sir."

"That is well. Go now. I'll watch to be sure you get home safe."

He handed the basket of lunch to John and stood on the step until he saw Christine enter the parsonage next door.

"Here, Father. Biscuits, cheese, and baked fish."

"Ah. Loaves and fishes, as Christ gave to the five thousand. We must give extra thanks for the cheese." Samuel smiled. "Have you eaten, Brother Roger?"

"Nay."

"Then you must share what we have. Let us ask God's blessing, and we shall eat as we go, for I know your wife's well-being lies heavy on your heart just now, and we must not delay."

"What is your plan, sir?" Ackley asked.

"Constable Paine first. I expect he'll start an organized inquiry throughout the town."

"And if we do not find her?"

"Why, then I suppose we must search elsewhere. But let us not borrow trouble."

———◆———

As men arrived on the common before the meetinghouse, Christine stood in the parsonage doorway and watched.

Joseph Paine had taken charge. He assigned each new cluster of arrivals an area to canvass.

"Surely they'll find she stopped to have dinner at a friend's house," Christine said.

Tabitha sat in the late Goody Jewett's chair, playing cat's cradle with Constance. "I don't know about that. Would you invite her to stay for a meal if she came by your house?"

Christine gritted her teeth together. She couldn't deny the truth—not many women in Cochecho liked Mahalia Ackley. Her venomous gossip had long since put her on the outs with all of her neighbors. Even the most tolerant ladies of the church avoided her. "Mayhap she felt ill because of the heat and took refuge at some house," Christine suggested.

"Aye, that could happen. Should we bake this afternoon?"

"I hate to. It's so hot. But if the men are kept searching all day, they will need to be fed this even." Christine turned from the doorway and assessed their staples. "We've plenty of ground corn but not much rye flour. The wheat flour is gone."

"Be there any meat left?" Tabitha asked.

"Nay. And we used up the fish Ben caught yesterday at luncheon."

"I've a strip of bacon in my root cellar, if that ne'er-do-well didn't get it."

Christine caught her breath and glanced at the widow, then looked pointedly toward Abby and Constance.

"Don't fuss at me," Tabitha muttered. "You should have told their father first thing this morning."

"I wanted to, but he was all in a hurry to get Ben off to the Dudleys'. He and the boys were going out the door when I arrived. And when I took his luncheon to the meetinghouse, Goodman Ackley was with him and I couldn't say anything."

Tabitha sighed and pushed herself slowly up from the chair. "Well, I'll go raid my own larder and bring over anything I think would be useful. I know there be plenty of dried beans. The Jewetts have fed me often enough this past year that I can contribute to their offering."

"Probably the other women will help as well," Christine said. "I don't like you to go over there alone."

Tabitha leaned in close. "Well now, you can't leave the children alone with that ruffian lurking about, can you?"

"Nay." Christine shuddered. She had told the outlaw she wouldn't provide for him. Leaving the Jewett girls unsupervised would be just what he needed—an opportunity for retaliation.

"Well, I know one thing, it ain't Indians has got Mahalia Ackley."

"How do you know that?"

"Ha. We've had more Indian raids than most villages, and we always know it within a short time. They're quiet until they strike, but once they begin their perfidy, there's no silencing their howling and whooping."

Christine shivered, recalling her own experience six years earlier when her home had been attacked. She well remembered the bloodthirsty screams of the savages as they wrought their destruction, killing and burning all before them. Her family had lived down the coast, near the mouth of the Piscataqua River, where her father worked a saltwater farm. The Indians had attacked and plundered several farms in the neighborhood, and Christine saw her parents and three siblings hacked down. Only after many years of prayer in the quiet convent had she found herself able to give thanks for her survival.

Sometimes she still thought it might have been better if she, too, had died that night. But nowadays, Samuel Jewett in his sermons echoed what the gentle nuns had taught her. Only last Sunday he had preached on thankfulness.

Whatever my lot, whatever my position, God has placed me here. And I thank Him.

"Take Abby with you if you are going across to your house."

Goody Deane frowned. "If you truly believe that man means to mend his ways, then you must also trust him not to carry out his threats."

"I've never said that I trust him. I only spoke to him and gave him what he asked for fear he would do violence."

The old woman nodded grudgingly. "I'd not be able to do much to protect Abby in time of need. But if I see that rascal, I'll tell her to run back here quick, and you raise the men."

"I shall."

"Abby, come with me to get a few things from my house, child. Put your shoes on."

Christine forced herself to stay away from the doorway but instead opened the barrel of parched corn and prepared to cook a mammoth kettle of samp. Goody Deane and Abby soon came back with a bit of bacon and a small sack of dried beans, which they put to soak in cold water.

"Peter Starbuck came by while we were at the cottage," Tabitha said. "I invited him to search my property if they think it needful."

Christine leaned against the frame of the loom. "I really thought they'd find her by now."

Tabitha nodded grimly. "You may as well weave. I'll watch the wee ones and the kettles."

Christine sat down and picked up her shuttle. Usually weaving brought her peace, with its monotonous movement and quiet sounds. Seeing the fabric slowly grow beneath her hands brought satisfaction. But not today. Instead she could think only of the farm wife the men searched for and the shadowy outlaw they didn't know existed.

"Lord, give me wisdom."

It flashed over her mind suddenly that in not telling Samuel about the outlaw, she had done the entire village a disservice. What if the man she had aided was responsible for Goody Ackley's disappearance?

"I must tell him." She laid her shuttle down and stood.

The doorway darkened at that moment, and Samuel Jewett entered the house. "I'm leaving John here with you, Christine. I want you all to stay inside. We fear there's foul play been done, and I don't want to risk anything happening."

John came in, stiff-legged, his lips puckered in disappointment. So his father had drawn the line. The situation had turned grim, and he had decided the boy was still a boy and shouldn't be part of this.

"Is Ben back?" she asked.

"Aye. He and the Dudley men and Charles Gardner all came into town after a runner went to ask if they'd seen Goody Ackley. I'll keep him close to me." He looked at Tabitha. "You stay, too, Goody Deane, though I know you be capable and fearless. Stay here with my family, won't you, until this is resolved." He lowered his voice. "Paine has men looking in the river now and all along the banks. The men are forming search parties. Take care, Christine. I'll see that you get word as soon as we know anything." He turned to go out.

"Samuel, wait!" Christine realized she had used his Christian name, but she hadn't time to think about that. The blood rushed to her cheeks as she stepped briskly toward him. "I must speak to you alone, sir."

His eyebrows drew together. "Is it urgent?"

"Aye. I don't think it bears on this event, but it may, and if I don't tell you and you find out later that it did, why, I shall be desolate."

He eyed her carefully then nodded. "Come outside then." He stood aside and waited for her to go out. As he followed her onto the doorstone, he closed the door behind them. "What is it? Do you know something about the good-wife's doings?"

"Nay, sir, but I know something else. Something I should have told you sooner. I would have, too, except I feared that in so doing I would endanger your children."

He turned his head slightly as though not sure he'd heard her correctly. "I don't understand."

"Forgive me. I'm rambling, but that is because I so dislike to tell you what I must. There is a man hovering about these parts. Lurking, one might say."

"A man?"

"Aye. You've heard folk say how they missed things. Foodstuffs. . .a knife. . ."

"A pair of trousers?"

She forced herself to look into his rich blue eyes. *Don't hate me, Samuel! Lord, make him understand.*

"Aye, sir. I hate to say it, but you strike true. This. . .criminal—I cannot call him less—has accosted me several times in the evening."

"How is this possible?"

"He watched the house. Both our houses. He knew our situation. The first time, I caught him peering in Tabitha's window at twilight. After that, he lingered in her garden or at the edge of the woods. He. . ." She swallowed with difficulty and looked up at Samuel.

He waited with the patience she had often seen him exercise with his children, but his eyes had a somber cast.

"He told me to bring him food. . .and other things. . .a blanket, a pair of trousers. . .and if I did not oblige him, he threatened. . ." She choked, and tears flooded her eyes.

Samuel grasped her wrist and drew her closer to him. "Christine, what are you saying? My dear girl, did he hurt you?"

She gasped and shook her head. "Nay, I promise he did not. But I was afraid, Samuel. . .Pastor." She looked away.

"Ah, Christine." He tugged gently at her arm and drew her around the corner of the parsonage where the wall and the woodpile would hide them from view of the people on the common or coming up the street. "Tell me everything, my dear, but make haste. I must tell Constable Paine about this. The man you describe may have skulked about and harmed Goody Ackley."

"I don't think he would sir. But, then. . ."

"You said yourself you would have told me about him had you not feared him."

"Aye, it's true. He said he would hurt the children if I didn't bring him sustenance. Oh, Samuel, forgive me. I should have told you at once. I see that now, but I thought he would do it. He made these dire threats, and I took him at his word."

"Then we must assume he might harm another innocent person, namely Mahalia Ackley."

"But why?"

"Who knows? She had been to the trader. Several people saw her there this morning. Perhaps he thought to rob her of the stores she had bought, and she wouldn't give them up."

"Oh no."

"She is a stubborn woman." Samuel rested his large, strong hand on her shoulder, and the warmth of his touch comforted her. "Let us not assume the worst, but what you tell me makes me very uneasy. We will concentrate our search along the road from the trading post to the Ackley farm. Can you tell me what this man looks like? Though any stranger would be suspect under the circumstances."

"I mostly saw him in the dark, but I did get one good look at him. His beard and hair are sandy colored. He's tall. As tall as you, perhaps, and a bit thinner. His shoulders are not as broad."

Samuel gave her a bittersweet smile. "So, my gardening trousers fit him?"

"I believe they did. He might have tied them in closer than you with the bit of rope he wore for a belt."

"If he still loiters about the village, we shall find him. When did you last see him?"

"Last night. Tabitha saw him, too, though not clearly. She discovered us talking. He must have wakened her when he threw pebbles at the wall to summon me. I was telling him that he must cease and that I would not continue to do his bidding, when Tabitha came to the door and warned him off."

"She knows then."

"Aye. I told her all about it last night, and we agreed I should tell you today, but you left in such haste this morning, and then Goodman Ackley was with you at noon. . . ."

"Yes, I see. Christine, I must leave you. There is no time to be lost in searching for this woman. We shall speak more of this later."

A fresh rush of tears burst into her eyes, and she raised the hem of her apron to wipe them away. "Can you forgive me? I was foolish not to tell you right away, but I truly thought I must keep silence for the children's sake."

He touched her cheek gently, and she looked up at him. "You have nothing to fear from me. Keep close with the children, as I said, and wait for word that all is well." He hesitated a moment, then took her hand in his and pressed it. "Do not torture yourself over this. You did what seemed best."

"Father?" came a voice from the front of the parsonage.

Christine flinched, and Samuel stepped away from her.

"Father? Where are you?"

"Here, Ben." The pastor strode around the corner of the house.

Christine followed, dabbing at her damp cheeks with the apron.

"Father, come quick to the Ackleys'."

"What's happened?"

Ben stood tall as a man, but his lips trembled. "They found her. Goody Ackley is dead."

291

Chapter 9

B en, you stay here." Samuel turned around and found Christine close
behind him, her eyes red rimmed from weeping. "You heard?"

"Aye. Let me go with you, if Ben will stay with Tabitha and the
children. Goody Baldwin will need help to prepare the body."

Samuel nodded. "Son, do they know what happened to her?"

Ben shook his head. "I heard only that she was found and they were carrying
her home in a cart. Mr. Heard told me to run and find you."

Samuel and Christine walked the mile to Roger Ackley's farm in silence.
People had gathered as the word spread, and a score of men and women milled
about the yard. Captain Baldwin's wife came forward to meet them.

"My husband be out back, with the constable and Brother Ackley. I be
waiting for the word to tend the body, poor woman. They told me to send you
around there and no other, sir."

Samuel nodded grimly. "Miss Hardin came to help, if you need assistance
when the time comes."

Goody Baldwin nodded at Christine. "I can use a level-headed woman in
times such as this. I expect Mrs. Dudley will be here soon, too."

Samuel left the ladies and walked around to the back of the house. James
Dudley stood by his oxen, with one hand on the near ox's shoulder. Behind the
team was his cart, and Baldwin, Paine, and Ackley all stared down over the side-
board, into the bed of the cart.

As Samuel approached them, Captain Baldwin looked up. "Ah, Pastor.
Good. You're the man we need. Take a look, sir."

Samuel joined him beside the cart and looked down at its grisly burden. "It
appears to me this work was not done by savages."

"Aye, sir," said Baldwin. "My first thought. See the wound on her temple?
An Indian would have brained her with a tomahawk and scalped her."

"This looks more like a blow from a club or some such thing," Samuel
agreed. "And do you see the mark around her neck?"

The men crowded in closer.

"Aye," said Paine.

"I am not a surgeon," Samuel said, "but I should think something was tight
about her neck that is not there now."

"You think she were strangled?" the constable asked.

Samuel reached out and gently probed the discoloration beneath Goody Ackley's chin. "It seems likely."

Roger Ackley turned away from the sight and put his clenched fists to his eyes as though to rub away the terrible sight. "Ah, my poor, poor wife! I should have gone with her this morning."

Baldwin laid a brawny hand on his shoulder. "Easy there, Brother Roger. You cannot blame yourself."

"Can I not? She wished me to go with her to the trading post, but I told her I was too busy. If she wanted me to finish getting the hay in, she could go alone. That is what I told her. And she went."

Joseph Paine straightened, a faraway look in his eyes. "She was there when I opened this morn. She came in with a big basket, the one she often brings."

"Aye," Ackley said. "She totes things home in that, or rather, usually I do the toting."

"But where is the basket now?" Paine asked.

The men looked at each other.

"Perhaps if we find the basket, we shall know more," Baldwin suggested. "She was found in the woods, not far off the road. I shall have the men fan out from the place where she lay and see if they find her basket or any of the things she carried in it."

He left them. Samuel said to Paine, "There is nothing we can do for her but carry her inside and let the women lay her out."

"Aye. Where do you want her laid, Brother Roger?"

They mustered two more men to help them transfer the body.

Ackley ran ahead of them into the house and threw a clean sheet over the rope bed. "Place her there. I shall have to get someone to build a coffin. I would do it myself, but I am all at a loss, gentlemen." Ackley sank onto a stool, his shoulders sagging.

"I expect Charles Gardner would be willing to make the coffin," Samuel said. "Shall I speak to him for you?"

"Aye."

Christine, Goody Baldwin, Sarah Dudley and her mother-in-law, and the maid, Alice Stevens, entered the house.

"Oh, my poor, poor mistress," Alice cried when she saw the body stretched out on the bed in the corner. "I asked if she wished me to go with her this morn, but she said, 'Nay, you must finish your spinning and churn the butter.' "

Christine put an arm around her shoulders. "Mayhap you wish to go home to your mother, dear. We can tend to her."

"Nay, I must help. It is the last thing I can do for her. She were mean

His Sunday breeches and second-best pair likewise. His stockings and drawers occupied a corner. But his workaday trousers—the ones he wore when gardening or helping one of the farmers with haying—were nowhere to be found. He looked around the room in confusion then put on his second-best breeches, his oldest, most worn shirt, lightweight stockings, a leather waistcoat, and shoes. Then he emerged into the great room.

Christine had already arrived, and she knelt by the hearth to kindle a cooking fire.

"Christine."

"Yes, sir?" She swiveled on her heels to look at him.

"Where are my old trousers?"

She hesitated a moment, and her face colored.

Of course, under ordinary circumstances it would be considered vulgar for a man to mention his trousers in the presence of an unmarried female. But after all, Christine did his mending and laundry. Indeed, she had sewn some of his clothing, and she handled his most intimate garments almost daily. They ought to be able to discuss them.

"I am stitching a new pair for you, sir." She ducked her head and seemed inordinately concerned with coaxing her pile of tinder to catch a flame.

Samuel cocked his head to one side and considered that. "Did you take the old ones to use as a pattern?"

After a long moment, she said without turning around, "I might have."

"Ah. Then I suppose I must garden in such as I wear now. Permit me to tend the fire for you."

"It's going now. But if you'd care to bring in more water, I won't say nay. This be my washing day."

"Of course."

Samuel picked up the two water buckets and emptied them into the largest kettle he owned. As he walked the short distance to the river for more water, he went over the brief conversation in his mind. It didn't make much sense to him, but he was certain Christine had a purpose. His old trousers weren't that bad, but they did bear a couple of patches. Neat patches, it was true, but perhaps she felt it an embarrassment to have the minister go about in patched trousers. Still, he wouldn't wear the old ones if he were going around the village.

He gave it up and raised a quiet prayer as he dipped the buckets full of water. "Thank You, Lord, for trousers, and for shirts and shoes and hose. Thank You for Christine and the labor she bestows so willingly on our family."

Yes, Christine was a blessing to be thankful for. She would make some man a fine wife, if only she were willing to marry. Of course, if she did, he and the children would be lost without her. What a pity for Christine to live a solitary

Samuel peered where he pointed, bending closer than before. Constable Paine leaned in, too. Samuel did see a few short, fine threads clinging to the discolored skin.

The physician took a pair of tweezers from his bag and plucked one of the fibers. "That may tell you with what she was suffocated."

◆

Christine waited in the yard with the other women.

The physician was inside not ten minutes when Goodman Ackley rushed out the door and around the corner of the house.

Goodman Otis followed, more slowly. "Where is Brother Roger got to?" he asked.

Christine pointed, and Otis followed the bereaved husband.

A few minutes later, the doctor, Captain Baldwin, Paine, and Samuel emerged. Samuel headed straight toward her, and Christine felt her color rise.

"I shall go home and be with the children," he said. "Plan you to stay here all night?"

Christine looked toward Goody Baldwin, who nodded. "Aye."

"Then I shall come for you in the morning." He hesitated then said, "Walk with me a moment, Miss Hardin. I've something to say to you."

Christine walked a few steps away with him.

"My dear. . ." Samuel seemed to find inhaling difficult. "Christine, say naught to the others, but I fear the man you described to me, the outlaw who bade you feed him, is the killer."

Her lips trembled as she drew in a deep breath. "What leads you to this conclusion?"

"Nothing, except I cannot imagine any one of our own people doing this foul deed."

She also found the idea inconceivable. But still, it was hard to think that the man who had proclaimed his innocence would murder for a few groceries. Was it possible that in refusing to help him, she had condemned Mahalia Ackley to death? "Oh, Samuel, I'm afraid."

He reached toward her then let his hand fall to his side. "I'll see that the captain posts at least one man here to watch through the night. Do not try to leave here alone."

"I won't, sir."

He nodded. "I told Paine and Baldwin about the outlaw. It is time to gather the men of the village, warn them, and plan how we shall find this felon."

"You will be sure he is not harmed, won't you?"

Samuel looked at her strangely, his forehead wrinkled between his brows. "Christine, you cannot believe him innocent of this."

"But I can. He at least should have a fair trial. No one has proven him guilty of anything. I myself would testify that he has pilfered and manipulated and intimidated, and, yes, stolen. But I do not say he has killed. Not until I see proof."

"You seem certain. If you fear him, as you told me you do, how can you think him incapable of this act?"

"I cannot fully answer that." She tried to picture the man's haunting face once more, and a shudder ran through her. "I'm not fully persuaded that he is innocent, but neither am I positive of his guilt."

Samuel closed his eyes for a moment. When he opened them, he nodded. "As you wish. I shall speak for him because you ask me to. It is right for him to be fairly tried, as you say. 'Vengeance is mine,' saith the Lord. I shall admonish the men not to mistreat him if they catch him. But I tell you, it stirs my wrath when I think of what he said to you—when I remember he swore to mutilate my dear little children." His voice cracked, and he looked away.

Christine's heart wrenched. "Oh, Samuel." She longed to touch him, but several people still milled about the yard, and there was no surer way to ruin a minister's reputation than to let him be seen touching—or being touched by—a woman not his wife. "My dear Samuel," she whispered, "thank you. I shall pray that God will bring this all to rights."

"Your faith is stronger than mine at this moment, though I know you speak truth." He turned and took the road to the village.

Christine watched him go, her heart aching.

◆

The Dudley men stopped by the farmhouse in the morning just after sunup on their way to the village. Christine and Goody Baldwin went with them, leaving Alice Stevens and Goody Dudley with Roger Ackley and the corpse.

As Christine had feared, the constable raised a posse to beat the forest all about. Christine watched them come and go on the common. The Jewett children fretted to go outside and play, but she would not let them.

Goody Deane was nearly as bad. She sat in the chair, darning stockings and muttering all morning. At last she called to Christine, "Do something, lass! Weave or bake or scrub, but don't stand there in the light of the doorway."

Christine turned and saw all four children—Ben had gone with the men—staring at her. Tempting as the loom was, she knew she hadn't the right to please herself that day. If she retreated in solitary brooding and weaved the hours away, the children would suffer.

She forced a smile. "Come, children. Alice Stevens bade me bring a cheese and some dried apples back with me. Let us see what we can make special for dinner. Won't your father and Ben be surprised if we have dried apple tart waiting for them?"

Too late she remembered they had no wheat flour, so they crumbled maple sugar and oats over the apples instead of a crust. "A sprinkle of cinnamon and a bit of lard." She let Constance cover the Dutch oven. "There now. Stand back, and I shall cover it in coals." Once it was baking, she was hard pressed to come up with another project.

Goody Deane finished her darning and coaxed Abby and Constance to sit with her and try to knit. "You shall make your dollies a fine new coverlet," she promised them.

John got down his wooden soldiers and animals. He even let Ruth play with a few, and so the hours passed.

All the while, Christine's thoughts roiled round and round. Was the outlaw guilty of murder? How would they ever know for certain, unless he confessed? Had her hesitation to expose him brought about Mahalia Ackley's death? She sent many prayers heavenward, until they all seemed to run together.

Father, keep Samuel and Ben safe. Let justice be done. Forgive me if I did wrong.

But she knew not whether to pray they found the outlaw or not.

———◆———

Samuel and Ben tramped through the woods between the gristmill and the brickworks. They penetrated every thicket and peered up into every tree. They could hear other men not far away doing the same.

Paine and Baldwin had done a good job of organizing the search, Samuel thought. As well as any man could do. Every structure in the village had been searched, from the meetinghouse on down to the lowest root cellar. No trace of the man had been found. One man had gone so far as to suggest Miss Hardin's outlaw was a phantom, made up to let them give up looking for the murderer among themselves.

Samuel had silenced that talk quickly, saying Miss Hardin was as honest and as staunch as they come. Baldwin, Paine, and the Dudley men backed him up, and the search resumed.

As he hunted the elusive man, Samuel wondered if Christine had told him all. She had met the outlaw at least half a dozen times, he judged. Did she sympathize with him? Had she gone so far as to set her affections on him? It was unthinkable, and yet the inkling was there. Samuel raised his corn knife and slashed viciously at a thicket of brambles.

Lord, calm my spirit.

With a sudden start, he realized that a man crouched in the bushes, his hands raised before his face.

Samuel froze with his arm over his head, ready to strike the brambles again.

The man roared and leaped at him.

297

Chapter 10

Wait!" Samuel cried.

His adversary plunged forward.

Samuel swung the corn knife downward at the man's arm. His breath whooshed out of him as his adversary's body hit him, knocking him to the ground. Samuel lost his grip on the corn knife and grappled with the man, rolling over in the thicket.

He heard yelling, but he didn't dare pause to make sense of it. As he continued to struggle, the man's grip seemed to weaken. After a moment, Samuel felt strong hands tugging at his arms, lifting him off his opponent.

Stephen Dudley and Charles Gardner jumped on the stranger, hauling him to his feet.

Samuel realized that Richard Dudley had pulled him away from the man and was supporting him as they watched. "Are you well, Parson?"

"Aye, Richard. Thank you. He had a knife in his hand."

"Looks like you got the better of him." Richard stooped and picked up Samuel's long corn knife.

"I regret that," Samuel said. "I had only a moment to act, and I struck hard, I fear."

The captured man bled profusely from a deep gash on his forearm, where Samuel had slashed through his sleeve.

He fumbled with the knot that tied his handkerchief about his neck. "Here, Charles. Hold him steady, and I'll wrap his wound."

The man snarled as he approached.

"Easy, now," Charles said, yanking him up straighter. "The parson is a healer. Let him see to your arm."

"He like to ha' cut my arm off!"

Stephen picked up a bone-handled knife. "And you never planned to hurt him with this, I suppose."

Richard put his own kerchief in Samuel's hand, and the pastor moved in warily and pulled the man's sleeve up. The cut went clear to the bone.

"You'd best let him sit," he told Charles. "I'll wrap it tight and try to stop the bleeding, but he needs to be sewn up."

"Should we fetch that doctor back from the Point?" Stephen asked.

Samuel swallowed hard. He was a little light-headed. "Perhaps so. I could do it, but I fear my hands are not steady now, and I wouldn't do so neat a job, I'm sure."

"Reverend?" Captain Baldwin shouted from fifty yards away through the trees. "You faring well over there?"

"Come on over here, Captain," Richard bellowed. "We've got a prisoner for you."

Samuel felt a timid touch at his elbow. He turned and found Ben staring at him with glassy eyes. "Father! Are you hurt?"

"Nay, son." Samuel realized he was shaking all over. He pulled Ben toward him and gave him a swift hug. "I'm fine."

"I didn't see him," Ben choked.

"Neither did I until it was too late."

The captain arrived with half a dozen other men from the search. "Well, now, what have we here?" Baldwin asked with a pleased air. "Caught a skulker, have you, Preacher?"

"He was hiding in the thicket," Samuel said.

"Aye, he went at the pastor with this." Stephen held up the stranger's knife.

"Hey!" Daniel Otis stepped forward. "That's my knife that I lost a couple of weeks ago. . .or rather my knife that someone stole."

Richard clapped Samuel on the shoulder. "You'd best get home and rest, Pastor. We'll lock up this worthless excuse for a man."

"Aye," said Baldwin. "Let's march him over to Heards' garrison. We can lock him in the smokehouse there until a magistrate tells us what to do with him."

"I didn't do anything," the man cried. "This barbarous preacher tried to cut my head off, and I didn't do anything!"

"Nothing?" Baldwin grasped the front of the man's shirt and pulled him up close, nose to nose with him. "What about the goodwife who was throttled yesterday, hey?"

The man's lips trembled. "I know nothing of that. I swear."

"Be careful what you swear to," said Charles. "Now, come along."

◆

The door latch rattled. Christine jumped up from the bench by the loom, her heart racing. She had laid the bar in place before sitting down with Abby to give her a lesson at weaving. It seemed odd to bar the door in the daytime, but with the men out looking for the killer, she would not have been surprised if the outlaw tried to take shelter there.

Tabitha and the children all stared toward the door. A loud knocking resounded through the house.

"Who is it?" she cried.

"It's I, Christine. Let me in."

She sprang forward at Samuel's voice and grabbed the bar. The door flew open. She felt tears spring to her eyes as Samuel and Ben entered.

"We found your thief." Samuel headed for the water bucket and helped himself to a dipperful.

Christine put one hand to her lips. "Is he. . ."

"He's alive."

"Father sliced him with his corn knife," Ben blurted.

The girls gasped.

John jumped up and ran to his brother. "Really? Did you see it? Tell us what happened."

"There, now. Hush, John." Samuel sank down on the bench at the table.

Christine noticed blood on his hands and sleeve. "Sir, are you wounded?"

"Nay. The blood is not mine." He ran his hand over his eyes. "If I weren't so tired, I would get up and wash."

She stepped toward him and stopped, wanting to ask all sorts of questions. She crumpled her apron between her hands. "May I bring you something, sir?"

"Aye. There's no chocolate, I suppose."

"Nay, sir, but I can fix you some strong mint tea."

"I suppose that will do."

While the tea steeped, she brought a basin of warm water and a facecloth. Samuel looked up at her and murmured his thanks then began to rinse the blood from his hands. She set a plate of samp with a slice of cheese and a portion of boiled cabbage before him and fixed one for Ben as well. The boy sat down and began to eat ravenously.

Samuel looked up at her, his eyelids drooping. "Thank you. I'm about played out, I fear, with all that's happened these last two days. And tomorrow we shall bury Goody Ackley." He sighed and reached for his spoon.

She bit her lip and forced herself to keep silence.

"Did Father really catch the murderer?" John sidled onto the bench next to Ben.

"Keep your peace, John," Samuel said. "We caught a man lurking in the woods, but we know not whether he killed Goody Ackley. That shall be determined when the magistrate comes."

Christine cleared her throat. "When will that be?"

"I don't know. Captain Baldwin took charge of the prisoner. They're taking him to the Heards' to lock him up. I expect to hear more tomorrow."

Goody Deane pushed her knitting into her workbag and rose. "And tonight you should rest, sir. Now that the blackguard is in custody, I shall go home."

"Nay, you and Christine must have your supper first. You've stayed here all day, and I doubt you had much rest with these four children cooped up here with you."

Christine could see that Tabitha moved slowly, as though her stiff joints ached. "Sit down now with the men, dear lady. Have some food, and as soon as I've fed the children I shall take you home. Abby and John can do the washing up tonight, if I pour the hot water for them. Can you not, children?"

John nodded somberly, and Abby hurried to her side. "We can do it, Miss Christine. Will you let me weave some more tomorrow?"

Christine smoothed Abby's hair and smiled. She was glad the girl was more excited about weaving than about the man whom Samuel had apparently injured. "Of course I will. If you like it, you'll soon be making material for your own petticoats and skirts."

The next morning, Samuel ate his breakfast and prepared to go over to the meetinghouse for an hour or two's study before Mahalia Ackley's funeral service. He paused in the doorway with his Bible in his hand and watched Christine place several biscuits and a dish of gruel in a basket. "May I inquire your purpose this morning?" he asked.

She looked up and paused. "I thought to take something to the prisoner."

Samuel stepped away from the door and stood for a moment, regarding her in confusion.

"Mrs. Heard will prepare something for him to eat, I'm sure. The captain will have set a watch over him. You needn't trouble yourself on his behalf."

Christine stood still, her eyes downcast. "Forgive me. I should have asked your permission first. I only want to be sure he is being treated well. It was cooler last night than it has been in many weeks, and I thought he might need a blanket tonight. And I wondered if they let him wash, or whether anyone will tend his wound, which you—" She stopped abruptly and turned away, her hand at her lips.

"Which I caused." Samuel stepped toward her, acutely aware of his children watching. "Christine, do you think we would let him languish unfed, untreated? I shall go myself to dress his wound after the service if need be, but it was Baldwin's intention yesterday to fetch the physician back again to tend him and stitch up his arm."

Her shoulders jerked.

Samuel stepped closer and lowered his voice. "Christine! Think you that I injured him on purpose? He tried to kill me, lass. I struck in self-defense. I regret it turned out this way, but that is what happened. Do you care about this felon so much? Please, do not imagine that I gladly maimed him."

"You are angry with me." She turned, and he saw a tear clinging to her lashes.

"Nay. But I shall be if you go to the Heards'. Would you leave the children alone to go and comfort the prisoner the morning we bury his victim?"

She caught her breath. "How can you say that? You forbade John to call him a murderer until such is proven, yet you say it yourself."

He stared at her. Something twisted in his heart. Could she possibly have formed an ill-advised attachment to the man who bullied her and perhaps strangled her neighbor? "I forbid you to go to him."

She straightened her shoulders, and her eyes flashed. For an instant he feared she would challenge his right to speak so and go anyway.

Dear God, how have we come to this? Meek Christine defying me! Please, let us not show ill will before the children.

He swallowed hard and tried to frame a gentle overture, but Christine opened her mouth first. "Very well, sir." Her posture drooped. She took the food out of the basket and folded the napkin.

He stood unmoving for a moment. The children still watched. The quiet in the room bespoke their attention, and he could feel their stares. He cleared his throat. "Thank you for that. I shall go at once to the garrison and inquire whether the prisoner needs food or medical care."

Leaving his Bible on the table, he set out with long, purposeful strides.

◆

Christine sent all of the children but Ruth to the river to fill the water buckets. Mr. Dudley did not need Ben's labor this morning, since all of the villagers would attend the funeral service. Ben would watch John and the girls, and the brief excursion would do them all good.

As soon as they were out the door, she crumpled into the chair by the hearth and pulled her apron up to cover her face. Her sobs came unbidden, shocking her. She must stop weeping before the children returned.

After a few minutes, she felt a small, warm hand on her wrist.

"Why you cryin', Miss 'Stine?"

She raised her chin and wiped her eyes. Ruth stared up at her with wide blue eyes, as troubled as her father's.

Christine clasped the little girl to her. "I'm sorry, dear. Your papa is right. There is no need to worry."

Did she weep for the outlaw or for herself? She could not tell. Perhaps it was for the straining of the fragile tie between her and Samuel.

Things had changed between them. Two days ago, when she told him about the outlaw, he had responded considerately, almost tenderly. But now his tone had hardened. He thought her foolish to have acted as she did, aiding the thief and concealing his existence. Once, she had felt Samuel respected her and counted her a friend. Had that changed? Would she ever enjoy his high regard again?

She managed to smile at Ruth. "Come, let us set the bread to rise while we are at the service."

◆

Samuel returned to the parsonage just long enough to retrieve his Bible before the funeral procession reached the common. Christine had all the children scrubbed and turned out in their Sunday best, and Goody Deane had come to walk over to the meetinghouse with them.

"You needn't worry about McDowell," Samuel said.

"Who?" Christine stared at him.

"The prisoner. The Heards will feed him. He is well taken care of, and the physician dressed his wound this morning."

"Ah." She ducked her head and untied her apron.

So. . .she hadn't known even his name. Somehow that lightened Samuel's spirit.

He went out and hurried to the meetinghouse steps. James Dudley's cart carried the coffin, and all of the neighbors who lived in that direction followed slowly behind. Elder William Heard cut across the green past the stocks. Samuel greeted him. Heard went inside and brought out the large conch shell they used to call the people to meeting and began to blow.

Other people came from up and down the village street, walking with somber, measured steps. Samuel waited until all the people had gathered on the green before the meetinghouse. The pallbearers lifted the casket out of the cart. Roger Ackley, his face set like stone, joined him on the steps, and Samuel led them into the building.

After the service and the burial, the villagers melted away to their farms and businesses, with no prolonged socializing. Many had already lost two days' work due to Goody Ackley's death and could not afford to give up more.

Ben went home with the Dudleys, and Samuel walked home with the children and Christine for his dinner. While she put the food on, he walked about the garden, observing the abundant crops brought on by hot, steamy days and occasional gentle rains.

When Constance came out to call him to the dinner table, he took her hand and walked in with her.

"We have corn to pick," he told Christine, "and a few cucumbers."

"The children and I can do it this afternoon."

"I'll stay a short while and help." He made the decision as he spoke. Working together in the garden might give him a chance to speak to Christine again out of earshot of his offspring.

To his surprise, he had no need to make an opportunity. After dinner, she put baskets in the children's hands and sent them into the garden, then she turned to him as she tied the strings of her bonnet. "I fear this business has caused a rift between us, sir, and I do not like it. Can you forgive me?"

He stepped closer and looked into her serious hazel eyes. "As I told you two days past, there is nothing to forgive. You acted as you thought best. Indeed, you may have saved the family from tragedy."

A flush stained her cheeks, but she did not look away from him. "I meant, forgive me for my ill-considered actions. . .and my words. . .this morning. I was wrong to put this man—McDowell, you call him—ahead of you and the children."

"Nay, not so remiss. It is only Christian charity to see that the lowest— widows, orphans, prisoners—are cared for."

"But—" She bit her lip.

"What is it, Christine?"

"I did feel animosity this morning when you spoke to me. Perhaps it lies beyond my right to mention it."

Samuel sighed. "Nay, I hope you will come to me with anything that concerns you. And you are not far off the mark." He looked out over the field, where the children raced to fill their baskets. "I fear I misconstrued your actions today. It is I who needs pardon."

"Pastor, you cannot think I imagined. . .that I cared for him in any but the most humane way."

He smiled as the bittersweet reality struck him again. She was right. A new formality that had not been there before separated them. "You called me by my Christian name not so long ago."

Her color deepened. "Forgive me. I spoke in haste and agitation."

"I do not wish to forgive that slip, Christine. It was pleasant to hear. . .and to think we were friends."

She couldn't look at him then, or so it seemed. Had he spoken too plainly? For he could no longer deny that Christine, who had come to them a shy, tall, awkward girl with the plainest of features two years ago and more, had become a responsible, caring woman who had found a place in his heart.

"If you count me as a friend," she said softly, watching the children, "then please take my word. I sympathized with him, it is true. At times he almost convinced me he was innocent. But even if he were the vilest of men, he ought not to be locked up and left unattended while he bled and suffered. My faith in our people was small that day. I had seen them go out vowing to find the murderer and flay him alive."

"That is true. I spoke to several of the men, in an attempt to calm them. I'm glad it was I who stumbled upon the fugitive. I should hate to think what some of the men would have done if they had found him first."

"But we still don't know if he had anything to do with Mahalia Ackley's death. Yet today at the graveside, I heard murmuring that the prisoner should be taken out and hung at once."

Samuel drew in a deep, uneasy breath. "You are right. There is unrest in the village. Captain Baldwin has posted a double guard at the Heards' smokehouse to be sure the man is not molested. And I. . ." He watched her closely. "I have agreed to go to Portsmouth as one of the delegation that seeks to bring a magistrate here to try McDowell."

She was silent for a moment; then she looked up at him. "You agree with me then? That the truth must be uncovered?"

"Of course. I would want nothing less. But McDowell refuses to admit to anything, even stealing Daniel Otis's knife, which we found in his possession. Are you willing to accept the truth if it be not to your liking?"

She nodded. "The thing that would upset me would be injustice—condemning a man before his case is proven."

"Then I promise you I shall do all in my power to see that the truth is found and upheld. And will you make a promise to me?"

Her brow furrowed. "What is it?"

"That you will never lie to me or hold back information that will affect this family again."

Tears sprang into her eyes. "Oh, yes."

He reached out and wiped away the single tear that rolled down her cheek. "I know you went to great lengths not to tell an outright lie, my dear. I see that now."

"Yes, but you are right. I did deceive you about it. The trousers. . ."

He chuckled. "Aye. McDowell was wearing them when he jumped on me. I never noticed until Paine and Baldwin marched him away."

"I've made you a new pair, from some cloth that Jane Gardner gave me. It's coarse material, but they will make good workaday trousers."

He felt his smile growing, and he didn't try to hold it back. "Do you assure me that you could never have tender feelings for a man like that?"

"I do, sir."

He arched his eyebrows. "Do you recall that you have many times told me you couldn't feel that way for any man and that you wished to remain unmarried?"

A cloud descended on her brow. "Aye, sir."

They stood looking at each other for a long moment. Her trust and championing of the outlaw might be misplaced empathy but surely not affection, Samuel mused. Still, he mustn't assume that she had developed deep personal feelings for himself. He was her employer—of sorts—and the father of the children she cared for. He had exercised the utmost discretion to show her nothing beyond Christian love.

But someday, he would ask her if she still held to her declared purpose of remaining single. Because he was beginning to hope she would not.

"Father! I've filled my basket. Look!" Abby ran toward them.

Ruth ran along behind her, holding up her smaller basket. "Me, too! Look, Miss 'Stine."

Christine knelt and gathered Ruth into the curve of her arm. "Well done, girls."

Samuel smiled. "Here we've stood idle while you children worked. I shall stay and help Miss Christine husk the corn."

"You shall do no such thing." She stood and brushed off her skirt. "You shall go and study, and we shall husk the corn."

Chapter 11

The next day, the minister and Ben left with William Heard and Joseph Paine for Portsmouth, pledging to bring back a magistrate or the promise of one's soon arrival. Christine took her quilt and her few extra garments and moved into the parsonage, expecting the pastor to return by Saturday evening.

The pilfering in the village had ceased, but gossip ran rampant. Tabitha and Jane brought Christine reports of what was whispered at clotheslines behind the cottages. The outlaw the Reverend Jewett had captured was behind it all. Goodwives cudgeled their memories and pulled out anecdotes describing items they had lost over the past few months and ascribed them to McDowell's evil doings. Christine had to laugh when she heard old Mrs. Squires say McDowell had surely stolen her hoarded pouch of coins. The woman's savings had disappeared more than a year earlier, long before McDowell came to Cochecho, and on the same day, as it happened, that her knave of a son had run off.

Christine, ten-year-old John, and the three Jewett girls spent a quiet day on Friday, working in the garden and about the house. Abby had a weaving lesson in the afternoon, and Goody Deane came over to partake of supper with them. Christine urged the old woman to spend the night with them, but she refused, saying she would sleep better in her own bed.

In truth, Christine was anxious about where she would sleep that night. No matter what the reverend had said before he left, she could not stay in his room. The very thought made perspiration break out on her brow. His chamber and that occupied by his daughters were built the year before, added on to the parsonage by the men of the parish. The cramped family had sorely needed the extra space. However, Christine was sure the parson must feel quite lonely now, with a fine bedchamber all to himself. She thought it a pity that he and his dear wife had slept on a pallet in the great room, and the new chambers were only constructed after Elizabeth's death.

John solved her problem when bedtime neared. His tone held a note of jest, but Christine felt he half meant it when he said, "I shall miss old Ben tonight. What shall I do, tossing about all alone up there in the loft?"

"What, afraid of the dark?" Abby asked.

"Nay."

Christine said, "I expect he feels as you would if Constance and Ruth were elsewhere tonight." She smiled at John. "I tell you what. Would you like to sleep down here by the hearth, as you and Ben used to do when you were younger? We shan't keep a fire tonight—'tis too warm. You may set up your wooden soldiers on the stones, and I shall climb the ladder and sleep above."

"You, Miss Christine?" Constance asked, her eyes round with wonder.

"Aye. Not much more than a year past I slept up there every night with you and your sisters. Have you forgotten?"

Constance's face darkened. "Aye. When Mama was with us."

"That's right." Christine infused her voice with cheerfulness. "And I shall do it again tonight."

"May we sleep up there with you?" Abby asked eagerly.

"Me, too," Ruth cried.

Christine caught her breath. Would the pastor approve? She had feared that the funeral they attended the previous day had reminded the children strongly of their mother's service last year. The diversion of sleeping in the loft would certainly keep the little girls from thinking about the morbid events they had witnessed lately.

"All right. And when we've settled our bedding up there, I shall tell you all a story, and then John shall come down and blow out the candles, and we shall all sleep well."

It happened just that way, and even Christine did not lie awake long. After a sincere prayer for the safety of the men who went to Portsmouth and a petition for the outlaw's soul, she drifted into slumber.

She had barely dressed and got the fire going the next morning, when a quiet knock came at the door.

John scurried to open it and admitted Stephen Dudley, who was now seventeen years old and living quietly with his parents and sister. However, from his tenth year to his fifteenth, he had dwelt among the Algonquin in Quebec and had made the choice to return on his own a few months after Christine had come to Cochecho. "Good day, Miss Hardin."

"Good morning, Stephen. You're about early." Christine noticed that he carried a large basket. "May I help you?"

"Be the pastor at home?"

"Nay. He's gone to Portsmouth with Mr. Heard and Mr. Paine and Ben to fetch the magistrate."

Stephen's mouth tightened. "I'd best go to Captain Baldwin then, I suppose."

Christine's curiosity was piqued. "Is there anything I can do? The pastor will return this evening, I expect."

"Some of us poked about yesterday afternoon, near the place where Pastor

Jewett flushed out the knave, and we found a camp."

"A camp?"

"Aye. Someone had stayed there. Built a fire and made a bed of pine boughs." He pulled a dirty, ragged blanket out of the basket. "This were nearby."

Christine drew in her breath. Filthy though it was, she recognized the old blanket she had left for the outlaw.

"And this." Stephen lifted the basket toward her. "I found the basket beside his fire ring. Think you it belonged to Goody Ackley?"

Christine grasped the corner of the table to steady herself. The basket indeed resembled the one she had often seen the late Mahalia Ackley carry about the village.

"It may well be hers. Perhaps you should take it to her husband and ask him." Stephen hesitated. "I could do that."

Christine sensed that, in spite of his adventures and his solitary travel for hundreds of miles through the woods, the young man was reluctant to face Roger Ackley alone. He had probably hoped the minister would accompany him.

"I could go with you," she offered.

Stephen's expression cleared at once, telling her she had assumed correctly. Stephen disliked the thought of confronting the bereaved man and perhaps suffering further disparagement from his acerbic tongue.

"John," Christine said to the boy, who had hovered near and listened to their exchange, "run yonder and fetch Goody Deane, if you please. Your sisters will be rising soon, and I don't like to leave you four alone while I run this errand."

While John ran across the street, she hung up her apron and fetched her shawl. Though the sun was well up, the air promised to be less stifling than it had been lately. She wished she had some fresh baking to take to the widower, but she had none.

"Shall I ask Captain Baldwin to accompany us?" Stephen asked.

It would take him time to go to Baldwin's house and back, but it sounded like a wise idea to Christine. "Perhaps you could go now and speak to him. I shall stay until Goody Deane is here, and then I'll meet you on the path to Goodman Ackley's. Oh, and Stephen. . ."

He had turned to leave, but swung around to look at her.

"You needn't take the blanket. That came from this house."

"Ah." He held it out.

She took it with distaste and wadded it into the corner where dirty laundry awaited her ministrations.

Stephen left, carrying the basket, and Christine set about cooking cornmeal mush for the children's breakfast. John soon came racing back, with Tabitha Deane hobbling along behind him.

Christine stood in Goodman Ackley's house a half hour later with the owner, Stephen, Captain Baldwin, and Alice Stevens. Christine was surprised that they found Alice there, with the mistress of the house dead and buried, but on their arrival Alice left her work in the garden and joined them inside.

Baldwin handed the basket Stephen had found to Goodman Ackley. "Be this not the market basket your wife always carried to the trader?"

Alice gasped and covered her mouth with her hand, staring at the basket.

Ackley appeared to study it with care, fingering the woven reeds. "It might be that," he said at last.

Baldwin fixed his gaze on the maid. "What say you, Miss Stevens? Be this your late mistress's basket?"

"Aye. The mistress had it on her arm the day she left here." Alice looked away.

"Young Dudley found it in a thicket near where we caught the prisoner," Baldwin said. "There were a blanket and the remains of a fire near it."

Goodman Ackley's eyes took on an interest. "Then he did it. That man, McDowell. It were his camp, where he lurked. And he went about his nefarious business from there, no doubt."

"But your wife's body was found at least a mile from there, much nearer this house."

"He stole her basket of provisions," Ackley said, nodding eagerly. He looked again at the basket, peering inside it. "Yes, it's Mahalia's. Don't you see? She'd been to the trading post, and he attacked her as she made her way home. He took what she'd bought. Ye didn't find any packages of food lying about, did you?"

Baldwin looked at Stephen, and he shook his head. "I'll go with Stephen and examine the spot myself," the captain said. "But whatever foodstuff the thief didn't use may have been ravaged by animals."

Stephen said nothing.

Christine hoped this evidence would not hang McDowell. It seemed rather thin to her, when a man's life was at stake. As they were leaving, she said to Baldwin, "Mayhap we should keep the basket as evidence for the magistrate?"

"Aye, you may be right. Do you mind, Ackley?"

The farmer shook his head.

They set out along the road to the village. When they were out of sight of the Ackley farm, Stephen said to the captain, "What think ye, sir?"

Baldwin frowned. "I'm not sure yet, Stephen. Let us wait and see what the future brings."

Christine looked at them in confusion. "I don't understand."

The captain stopped and eyed her soberly. "Stephen told me that he and his brother went over that area in the woods yesterday, after the funeral service.

They found the outlaw's camp then."

"But. . .Stephen only came to us this morning with the basket."

"Aye. The basket were not there when they went yesterday."

"I only went back this morning at dawn to be sure we hadn't overlooked anything," Stephen said. "We'd found the blanket, but it was an old rag." He hesitated, throwing her a look of embarrassment.

"Aye, so it was," she said. "That is why I gave him that one when he demanded a blanket, and not one of the parson's or Goody Deane's good quilts."

Baldwin nodded. "When Stephen came to me this morning with that basket, I knew something was up."

"It was lying right beside the blanket," Stephen said. "We'd have tripped over it if it had been there yesterday."

Baldwin fixed them both with a somber look. "Let us keep this among the three of us. We shall let the parson and the constable be privy to it when they return, but none other, saving the magistrate. Agreed?"

Stephen and Christine nodded gravely.

◆

Samuel strode swiftly with his son along the dusty road toward Cochecho. Paine and Heard had elected to stay in Portsmouth over the weekend in order to do some business on Monday, but Samuel had to be back in time to preach his sermons on Sunday. He and Ben had taken a boat to Dover Point but had to walk the last few miles to the village. They should reach home before sunset.

Home. Thoughts of the humble parsonage now included Christine, and the knowledge that she and the other children waited there for his return. He knew she took good care of John and the three girls in his absence, just as he knew she prayed for his safety. She had perhaps done a washing today, or maybe she had baked. She had surely prepared the meals and supervised the children in sweeping the floor and washing the dishes. If nothing pressing called her attention, she might be sitting right now mending, or more likely, weaving.

Christine. The parsonage would not be home without her.

And yet, he might lose her soon. Samuel felt keenly the possibility that she might leave his employ. She had said nothing to that effect, and yet. . . He had promised to help find the truth in McDowell's case. If the outlaw was proved innocent, would Christine champion him and perhaps set her affections on him? It was unthinkable. . . . The man was a thief, if nothing more. And yet Samuel still considered it.

On the other hand, if McDowell was found guilty of Mahalia Ackley's murder, Christine might be angry. In spite of her meekness yesterday morning, did she resent Samuel's role in capturing the outlaw? Would she deny his guilt even if the magistrate and a jury declared it? If so, she might not wish to be around the pastor anymore.

The thought caused him to slow his steps. Christine now held a firm place in his heart, as well as in his home. He didn't want that to change, unless. . . How good it would be for the children if she were his wife!

"Father?" Ben was eyeing him carefully.

"What is it, son?"

"You seem distracted, Father."

"Aye. Long thoughts. Let us hasten. I long to be home with my family."

Ben seemed to have no objection, and they hurried forward.

An hour later, they reached the village. Samuel's steps were slower. It had been a long and tiring day. But his spirits rose when he saw Constance and John come running around the corner of his house. Beyond, Christine followed more slowly from the vegetable patch with Ruth clinging to her hand.

Samuel swung Constance up into his arms with a grunt. "You'll soon be too large for me to pick up, young lady." He kissed her and set her on the ground. "Did you children behave?"

"Yes, Father," said Constance.

"Of course!" John fell into step with Ben. "What did you see in Portsmouth?"

As Christine and Ruth approached them, Samuel slowed and let the children go into the house. "Good evening." He stooped and hauled Ruth into his arms. "Where's Abby?" He straightened holding the child.

Christine smiled. "She's at the loom. I fear I've taught her almost too well. She has a good touch for it, and I can barely coax her from her weaving at mealtime."

"That will pass when she's woven a few yards of cloth," Samuel said. "All is at peace here?"

"Aye. I've somewhat to tell you, though."

They reached the doorstone, and Samuel set Ruth inside the doorway. "There, now, tell Abby that Father would like some tea." He turned back to evaluate Christine's sober expression. Her hazel eyes held suppressed excitement tinged with anxiety. "What is it?"

"Stephen Dudley found Goody Ackley's market basket near the outlaw's camp in the woods. But he and Richard had been there yesterday, and he's certain the basket was not there then."

Samuel inhaled deeply and looked out over the village. The outlaw again. Christine must care more for McDowell than she had admitted, if she could think and speak of nothing else. He had been gone a day and a half, yet the first topic she broached when he returned home was that worthless thief.

He sighed. "Well, the magistrate will come as soon as he can."

"When?"

sometimes, but I want to do a kindness for her if I may."

"Miss Stevens," Samuel said, "pardon me for asking, but wasn't your mistress afraid to walk a mile through forest and field alone?"

"She declared that she wasn't, sir. It be not far to the village. Oh, how I wish I had pressed her to let me go. But I was afeared she would call me lazy."

Roger Ackley rose and stumbled toward the door. "My wife was a sharp-tongued woman, but she didn't deserve this horrid end."

Baldwin cleared his throat. "Reverend, I've heard that a physician now lives at Dover Point. Shall I send a man or two to fetch him?"

"Aye, that might be good." Samuel said to Goody Baldwin, "Perhaps it is best if you ladies do not wash or dress her until we see if the physician can come. He may tell us more of her passing."

Goody Baldwin nodded. "I'll sit with her, then. If Alice wants to stay, she may. We can prepare for our duty and bake toward the morrow."

Alice sniffed. "Thank you, ma'am. I expect all the village will want to view her tomorrow. We must have gingerbread and journey cake."

Christine insisted on staying with them.

Samuel went home and ate supper, then he took his Bible to the church and studied for a scant hour.

Daniel Otis found him there at twilight. "The leech is come, sir. He's headed to the Ackleys' now."

Samuel hurried along the path beside Daniel. The physician was already in the farmhouse when he got there, and he and Daniel entered and stood in silence by Captain Baldwin and Joseph Paine to one side, while the doctor examined the body. Roger Ackley sat in a corner, declaring that he could not look on as the doctor completed his task.

The physician finished and pulled the blanket up to Goody Ackley's neck. "I do not think she was carnally defiled."

The men let out a collective sigh.

"But she was struck in the face. See how bruised her cheek is? And strangled, that is certain. You see how her eyes have ruptured."

Samuel walked across the room and leaned over the body. He could see the fine red blood vessels in the eyes. The sight repelled him, but who knew when he would need this knowledge again?

Ackley stood and rushed outside.

"I shall go to him," said Daniel Otis.

"Reverend, you are the one they tell me tends the sick and injured?" the physician asked.

"Aye, sir. It is not my choice, nor my calling, but I do what I can in need."

"Just so. You may wish to note the white fibers in the crease of her neck."

Chapter 12

On Sunday morning, since Brother Heard had not returned from Portsmouth, Samuel allowed Ben to blow the shell and call the people to worship. They came from the farms, from the fishermen's cottages, and the garrison houses. Samuel preached with passion, although his hours for preparing the sermon had been severely curtailed that week. His words on justice thundered through the rafters.

Christine sat very straight and still in the new boxed-in pew, center and front, just below the pulpit. Her eyes were fixed on him so intently that Samuel had to force himself not to look down there too often. When he did, though, he saw that John was wriggling, and Christine paid the boy no mind. Half of Samuel's mind hoped Brother Wentworth would see and rap John smartly on the head with his staff. The other half hoped he wouldn't, and thus save him the embarrassment of having the entire congregation know that his son had misbehaved in church.

At the noontime break, he shook hands with each of the church members and greeted them. Several of the men asked about his journey to Portsmouth and when the magistrate would arrive.

At last he left the church doorway and found Christine on the green with the children about her. "Why don't you invite your friends to eat their dinner at the parsonage today?" he asked.

"Oh, Father!" Abby cried with shining eyes. "We'll get to play with the babies again."

"Hush now." He looked only at Christine. Her hazel eyes met his gaze with confusion.

"But this is a quiet hour for you, sir, when you can eat your dinner in peace and meditate on your message for this afternoon."

"I thought you might like to ask the Gardners and the Dudleys over. You've not had a chance to visit with them lately."

"Only if you wish it, sir. I can wait."

"I wish it."

She did not bounce about laughing, like Abby and Constance, or giggle in glee, like Ruth, but he thought her quiet smile showed a pleasure he seldom saw on her face. Why did he not more often seek to please her?

"Thank you. I shall invite them."

Fifteen minutes later, he found himself at his table surrounded by Richard Dudley, Charles Gardner, and their wives. The mothers held their babies on their laps while they ate the food they'd brought in their baskets, and his own children waited for the plates to be washed. When Christine began to serve them, Samuel said swiftly, "Sit down, Christine, and enjoy the company. Let Abby and Constance do that."

The unaccustomed fellowship brought a glow of pleasure to her face. He had not always been so stern that his family thought it ungodly to enjoy the company of other believers on Sunday, Samuel reflected. When Elizabeth lived, they used to have large groups of people into their home for Sabbath-day lunches, especially in the cold winter. But lately he had pleaded the need to rest or study.

Seeing the three young women together again brought back memories of the days they had all lived in his home. And now two of the young captives were settled, with good, God-fearing husbands. He smiled as he thought how Elizabeth had despaired of ever finding a husband for Christine. She had been so withdrawn, so aloof, to the point of being prickly. And women like Goody Ackley had whispered that no man would ever offer for the tall, homely girl.

Odd how one's perspective changed. He no longer noticed how tall Christine was, except perhaps when she stood beside one of the young children. When he spoke to her and their eyes were not more than a few inches off being level, it didn't bother him. And would anyone call her homely now? She seemed to have softened somehow.

Perhaps it was the more becoming hairstyle she had adopted under Jane Gardner's urging, or the gentle manner she exhibited with his children. She seldom scowled, and when she smiled, her features smoothed into lines, if not pretty, then at least agreeable. He only knew that lately he'd begun to think she had improved her appearance. Her deportment was almost regal. Her features. . .why, a man could look at that honest, straight nose and those thoughtful eyes every day and not tire of it. In fact, he did!

Richard Dudley nudged him with his elbow. "That right, Pastor?"

"What?"

Richard chuckled.

"I'm sorry," Samuel said. "I was lost in thought, I fear." He hoped they did not see the flush he felt reddening his face beneath his beard. A sidelong glance at Charles Gardner told him otherwise. He'd been caught, no question. Caught staring at Christine.

She jumped up suddenly. "Let me get the teakettle."

Samuel thought her ears had gone quite pink. Yes, she had a most interesting face.

As they walked back to the meetinghouse after dinner, Sarah Dudley caught Christine's elbow and leaned close to her.

"The parson seemed quite preoccupied at dinner."

"I expect he was thinking of his sermon," Christine said. "He usually studies during the noon hour." She felt an annoying blush returning to her cheeks. Of course she had noticed that Samuel, in his reverie—whatever the topic—had stared at her while he let his thoughts roam. And her friends assumed they were centered on her. How awkward for the pastor. Jane and Sarah wouldn't gossip about it, though. At least she hoped not.

"Somehow I received a different impression," Sarah said.

"Hush. You mustn't put about such a whisper. It would damage the reverend's reputation horribly."

Sarah squeezed her arm. "Oh, my dear, forgive me. I was only teasing. I do love the pastor. We all do. And we've felt so miserable for him this past year. It would cheer us all to think he might be ready to. . ."

"Don't even think it!" Christine glanced quickly about to be sure none of the others had heard. "Sarah, please. It would be painful for me and for Samuel if you entertained such ideas."

"Oh, for *Samuel*." Sarah smiled. "Very well, I shall be quiet. But you must come and see me on a weekday, when there are no listening ears about, and tell me straight to my face that you have not thought of this."

"I don't know what you are talking about."

Sarah stared at her in mock horror with innocent blue eyes. "My dear Christine! I've never known you to lie before, and on the Sabbath!"

Christine's face went scarlet, she was sure, as she passed through the portal of the meetinghouse and into the welcome shadow of the pew.

The opening prayer gave her twenty minutes to calm herself and turn her thoughts heavenward. This was followed by the singing of a psalm. When Samuel at last began to preach, she found her mind riveted to his words.

"Our God is a God of great mercy." Samuel's text was 2 Samuel 24:14. "And David said unto Gad, I am in a great strait: let us fall now into the hand of the Lord; for his mercies are great: and let me not fall into the hand of man." Samuel pleaded earnestly with his congregation to exercise God's mercy toward one another and to all creatures.

Christine felt a tight kink in her chest slowly loosen and unknot. Samuel truly did want to see McDowell treated fairly. To see justice done, yes, but not to see punishment meted out where it was not deserved.

As they left the meetinghouse again two hours later, her heart was full. She hoped for a chance to talk to Samuel in more detail about the implications of the scriptures he had expounded.

She passed a small group of men who clustered outside at the bottom of the steps. Roger Ackley was in their midst, and his angry voice came clearly to her.

"I tell you, the parson's too soft on that evil man. He wants us to go easy on the man who murdered my wife!"

◆

Samuel walked to the Heards' garrison in the late afternoon. He could not stop Roger Ackley from spouting hatred among the people, but he could show an example of charity. He'd stopped at his house only long enough to see the children settled under Christine's care for a few more hours. He'd promised her that he would return ere nightfall and left again carrying a couple of her soft, light biscuits wrapped in a scrap of linen and a pair of his own clean stockings. Let it not be said that he hadn't been evenhanded in his sermons this day. Justice in the morning, mercy in the afternoon. Surely none could find fault with that.

Yet Roger Ackley did.

Samuel petitioned God for wisdom and entered the gate at the garrison. "Is the prisoner still in the smokehouse?" he asked William Heard's son, Jacob, who met him in the fenced yard. His voice was hoarse from speaking most of the day.

"Aye. We just took him his supper."

"Ah. I should like a word with him."

Jacob led him to the small building between the barn and the woodshed.

McDowell sat with his back against the wall, with an empty pewter plate on his lap and a corked jug beside him. His feet were fettered, though where Goodman Heard had come up with the irons Samuel couldn't imagine. He'd never seen a man chained in Cochecho before. Perhaps Captain Baldwin had supplied them, or maybe the blacksmith had made them specially for this man. Another chain, stout enough to hold a yearling calf, ran from the anklet to a ring in the wall. The man's shoulders slumped, and his spine curved in dejection, his chin resting against his chest until he raised it to see who might be opening the door of his cell.

Samuel thanked Jacob and stepped in. The confined space smelled of bacon and wood smoke and unwashed humanity. He remembered Christine saying the prisoner ought to be allowed to wash. Had they offered him a basin of water, soap, and a towel? "Good evening," he said.

McDowell shifted, and Samuel saw that his hands were linked, too, but with a chain at least two feet long so that he could move them about.

"You be the preacher." McDowell's eyes glinted for a moment.

"Aye." Samuel then stood in silence, seeking God's leading in how to proceed.

"Why'd you come? I suppose she told you what I said I'd do if she gave me away." McDowell squeezed back against the wall, as though afraid the enraged father would beat him for the threats he had made against his children.

"She did, if you mean Miss Hardin," Samuel said. "But that is not why I'm here."

"Why are you here then? Come to save me?"

Samuel sat down on the straw opposite the prisoner. The dim light gave him a poor view of McDowell's face, but the man was watching him warily. "I couldn't do that if I wanted to," Samuel said. "Only Jesus Christ has the power to do that."

McDowell looked away and raised his hands, with a clanking of the chains, in a gesture of futility. "I suppose they're going to hang me t'morra. Sent you to tell me to repent."

"I hope you *will* repent. But no one sent me. No one but the Almighty."

"They're saying I killed a woman."

"Yes, they are."

They sat in silence for a long time.

"Thought I was in here for thieving," McDowell said at last.

Samuel peered at him. "Only that?"

"When you all came after me, I thought she'd told, and you were going to drive me out of your township." The man ducked his head and changed his position again. "That girl they call Christine—she brought me food, you know."

"I know."

"That weren't stealing. She gave me things."

"Because you threatened her and those she loves."

"Not I."

Samuel stood. It was no use trying to reason with him.

"Wait, Parson!"

He turned back. "Well?"

McDowell raised his hands in supplication. "I never meant it. I only said it so she'd bring me enough victuals to keep me alive, and I wouldn't have to go and rob someone. I were desperate, you know."

"You could have asked the elders of the village for help. You could have come openly to the parsonage when I was at home. I would have given you sustenance."

"We can't undo what is done, now, can we?"

"Nay, we cannot. But you can still have forgiveness. Even the vilest can repent and experience God's mercy."

"I didn't kill no one."

Samuel sighed. *Lord, show me what to do.*

He sat down again. "You say you didn't kill the woman we found murdered."

"Not I." The prisoner's eyes narrowed. "It weren't the homely girl, were it? She treated me nice, mostly. She got mean at the end and said she wouldn't bring me no more. But she'd given me enough to get by on for a week or two."

Samuel stared at him in disbelief. Was it possible he didn't know who the victim was, or was he cleverly seeking to gain Samuel's trust? "Nay, it was not Miss Hardin. But. . ."

"What?" McDowell asked.

"She wasn't nearly so tall as Christine, and she'd darker hair." That at least was true when Mahalia Ackley was younger; he did not mention that her raven hair had lately been cloaked in gray. "She'd been to the trader, and she carried her purchases home. Are you sure you didn't attack her and steal the bundles that she carried?"

"Nay, sir. I'd remember that, surely I would." His furtive, dark eyes skewered Samuel, and his upper lip curled. "Were she pretty?"

Samuel felt ill. He wanted to flee the felon's presence, but he felt the Lord's leading to stay put. "McDowell, you need Christ, whether you killed that woman or nay."

"You think God Almighty would forgive the likes of me?"

"I know He would."

Again they sat without speaking.

Samuel felt drained of energy and emotion. Did he really want the man who had said he would mutilate his precious little daughters to repent? If he was honest, he would have to admit he wanted the man to hang. But would he wish to see even such an evil person condemned for eternity?

Chapter 13

Three days later, Christine sat at the loom, throwing the shuttle back and forth through the threads of the warp. Ben and John had both hired out to help with the corn harvest at the Gardners', and John was excited to leave that morning with the prospect of earning half a shilling. She had packed lunch for both of them in a tin pail, which John carried, and Ben took a jug of water for them to share. Samuel had seen the boys off and then gone to the meetinghouse, as usual, to study for his next sermon.

Christine went about her tasks methodically, but her thoughts flitted here and there. She knew that later in the day, Samuel would go to the garrison to visit McDowell. He had gone every day since Sunday. He told her almost nothing about these visits, but Abby had confided to her that in the evening, after she had left, when he read scripture to the children, he instructed them to pray for the prisoner.

She kept praying for McDowell as well, though she had not been told to do so. She prayed for his soul and the magistrate's speedy arrival, and she persisted in asking that justice be done.

While the girls sat on the front step—Abby and Constance with their samplers and Ruth with her doll—Christine wove. The length of gray wool grew daily. Most afternoons, she let Abby put in an hour or two. But the cloth must be finished soon so that she would have time to make all of the clothes the men of the family needed before winter. Her hands flew, and in comparison to Abby's pace, Christine produced material at lightning speed.

While she wove, she brooded. She knew she shouldn't do that, but her thoughts drifted often to Samuel and his somber mood. Was he sorrowful because of the evil McDowell had done or because the man would not repent? Or perhaps it was because of her own part in the drama.

Christine wished she knew what she could do to lighten his heart and take things back to where they had been a month ago, before the outlaw first appeared, before she had accommodated his demands, and before Samuel had ever called her "my dear."

That was it, she realized with a start. Not once, but twice, the minister had spoken thus to her, and each time her pulse had raced. She had allowed herself to imagine that he was conscious of his choice of words, not accidentally using in those moments of tension an endearment that he formerly had bestowed on his wife.

Of course, he called his daughters that as well. He might call any female acquaintance "my dear" in a moment of affection or even out of respect, she supposed. Aye, she had heard him call Tabitha "dear lady." So why should she have felt so giddy when he used the term toward her? But she had.

For the last week, he had gone about with a grave face, never laughing and hardly even playing with the children, something he'd always loved to do. It was almost as if they'd regressed to the weeks after Elizabeth died, when Christine feared Samuel's heart would break with sorrow.

She had been at the loom an hour and was beginning to think she should stop and begin supper preparations, when the girls rushed inside.

"Miss Christine, we have company," Abby called.

"Oh?" Christine rose and hurried to the door.

"It's Miss Catherine," Constance said.

Stephen and Richard Dudley's sister was always a welcome guest. Her youth and enthusiasm couldn't help but lift Christine's spirits.

As she and the little girls spilled out onto the doorstone to meet the caller, Christine saw that Ruth had not stood on ceremony but had run to fling herself into Catherine's arms at the edge of the street. Catherine laughed and stooped to hug her, while juggling her parcels.

Christine walked out with the two older girls to meet her and carry Ruth back. "I'm glad to see you, Catherine! Surely you didn't come into town alone?"

"No, Richard was coming on an errand, and I begged him to bring me to see you. Ever since you told me Abigail was learning to weave, I've been meaning to give her this." She held out a wooden frame about a foot square, laced with heavy thread, which Christine recognized at once as a small hand loom.

"Oh, that's perfect for Abby!" Christine took it and placed it in Abby's hands. "You can weave belts and kerchiefs and all sorts of things on this, my love. Not a large piece of cloth, but small lengths big enough for doll clothes, or towels, or. . .well, anything, if you piece them together."

"Yes, I made pockets and dolly skirts and all sorts of things with that when I was your age," Catherine said. "But I never use it now, and I thought perhaps you would like it."

Abby looked up at Christine, her eyebrows raised so high that the skin of her forehead wrinkled like rows in a plowed field.

Christine laughed. "Yes, you may accept it. I doubt your father will object, and if he does, we'll explain that you are merely borrowing the loom."

"Well, you needn't give it back, so far as I'm concerned," Catherine said as they walked toward the house. "When you outgrow it, Abby, you can pass it on to Constance or Ruth. And this"—she patted the basket that hung from her arm—"is our refreshment. Seed cakes and a packet of chocolate. Father bought the chocolate, but mother doesn't like it. She says it is too bitter to drink. She prefers her sassafras or raspberry tea. Anyway, I wanted you to try it."

"Perhaps if we put sugar in it," Christine said with a frown, though she wasn't sure it would be a good use of the little maple sugar in the parsonage pantry.

"Well, I find it tolerable, but Father is the only one at our house who really likes it," Catherine said. "We'll have fresh cider in another month, and glad we'll be to get it again."

Christine arranged a chair near the doorway for her guest so that Catherine would not get too warm when she stirred up the coals in the hearth to heat their tea water. They spent a pleasant hour talking while Catherine showed Abby how best to thread the hand loom and Christine stirred up fresh biscuits for supper. She hadn't felt like laughing much lately, Christine noted. But with her young guest in the house, merriment was inevitable. She even found herself humming a psalm as she stoked the fire, although perspiration dripped from her brow onto the hearth.

When they'd shared their cakes and chocolate—which they all agreed was better with a scant spoonful of sugar in it—they went to the garden and picked a few carrots, which Christine sliced and added to the stewpot. By the time Richard Dudley came to collect his sister, she realized that Samuel would soon be home for supper. He'd no doubt taken his journey to visit the prisoner, and she hadn't thought about either of them for quite some time. With a guilty start, she sent up a quick, silent prayer as she waved good-bye to Catherine and Richard then herded the Jewett girls back inside to set the table.

◆

Samuel returned home for dinner on Thursday. His sons were both at home that day, as a light rain that morning had put a stop to all harvest activity.

"You boys come over to the meetinghouse with me for an hour after dinner," he said. "I fear you'll forget your Greek and mathematics if we don't continue lessons soon."

"Do you plan to visit the prisoner today?" Christine asked.

He looked at her in surprise. She had not mentioned McDowell for several days, and he'd hoped her preoccupation with him had lessened. "Why, yes. Probably a brief call, after the boys do their sums and grammar. I'll want to study a bit more before evening worship."

"Might I go with you, sir?" Christine's eyelashes stayed low over her expressive eyes, and he couldn't tell from her carefully neutral voice what her mood was.

He hesitated. McDowell was still chained, so she would be in no danger if she kept her distance. William Heard saw to it that he was washed and properly clothed. But still. . .

If he denied her this, would she resent him? And would she find a way to see McDowell without him? Better to take her there himself, he decided. Perhaps if he witnessed the meeting, he would better understand her feelings for the man.

"Shall you come to the meetinghouse in one hour? I'll send Ben home to mind the girls then. Or you could ask Goody Deane to come over for a bit."

"Thank you, sir." She did not smile, nor did she look at him, but went about gathering up the dirty dishes.

She arrived punctually an hour later with a basket on her arm. He had expected that and made no comment. Goody Deane was at the house, she reported, and since the rain had stopped, he allowed the boys to go to the river and fish until suppertime.

The gate stood open at the Heards' garrison, and the men were preparing to go into the fields. William greeted them, eyeing Christine in surprise.

"My wife be inside, making jelly," he told her.

"I shall be glad to see Mrs. Heard," Christine said, "but my real errand is to visit the prisoner."

"The lady comes on an errand of compassion?" Heard asked Samuel. "Well, go along then, but my advice to you is that you go in first and make sure the prisoner is presentable before you admit the lady. He's a hard'un, miss, though lately he's seemed less surly."

"I believe his attitude has changed," Samuel murmured.

Heard nodded. "Well, please do bar the door of the smokehouse from the outside, as usual, when you leave, Parson. I like to think he's secure here, though we haven't posted a guard these past two days."

Samuel followed his suggestion and left Christine outside while he entered the small, dim building.

"Well, Parson"—McDowell sat up straighter on the straw with a crooked smile—"I wondered if you'd forgot me today."

"On the contrary, I've brought someone with me."

"Oh?" The outlaw cocked an eyebrow at him. "Be the magistrate come then?"

"Nay, not yet. This is someone from the village. Someone you've met before."

"Wh—" McDowell peered toward the open door. "Not the girl."

Samuel was glad he hadn't said "the homely girl," for he was certain Christine could hear every word.

"Aye, it's Miss Hardin. She requested to see you."

"Well, now." He smiled and put one hand up to his beard. "I don't make much of a sight for young ladies." His expression changed to a frown. "She don't be come to spit on me and rail at me, does she?"

"Nay, I assure you she would not do so."

"Good. 'Cause that man who came t'other night, I thought he'd kill me. The master had to throw him out of the stockade."

"What man?" Samuel asked.

"They told me it was the husband of her what was killed."

"Roger Ackley was here?"

"That's the name. He ranted and shrieked like a savage. Said they'd ought to string me up. Heard said he'd been hitting the rum, but it gave me a start, I'll tell you."

"Well, you needn't fear a mob coming after you. William Heard and his sons would prevent it, and if need, we would protect you—the captain, Constable Paine, and I, and several other members of my flock. But I shall go and see Roger Ackley and make sure he doesn't do that again. He is distraught, of course."

McDowell shrugged. "I might be guilty of some things, sir, but I should hate awfully to be strung up for something I didn't do."

"I knew it." The doorway darkened, and Christine stood there, her dark skirts blocking much of the sunlight. "Pardon me, but I couldn't help overhearing. I've told the Reverend Jewett several times that you could not have done such a deed."

"There now, miss." McDowell lowered his hands as though to conceal the chains and smiled up at her. "Think of it! Ye've come to see me, after I treated you so mean and all."

"I've forgiven you for that. I wanted to see you for myself and make sure you were well. You must pay for your crimes, sir, I don't deny that, but you must not be made to pay for those someone else committed."

McDowell looked up at Samuel. "Here now, Parson, mayhap I should have this young lady represent me at court."

Samuel did not find the suggestion amusing. "We must not stay long. Christine, say what you wish, and I shall see you home."

She knelt in the straw before he realized what she was doing and pulled the napkin off her basket.

"Here, I've brought you some biscuits and baked fish. I know they are feeding you, but I thought a bite or two extra would not be amiss. And I've brought ink and paper. I wondered if you wished a letter written to anyone. Do you have family you'd like to notify, sir?"

McDowell blinked and looked up at the pastor with a baffled expression. "Nay, who would I send a letter to? I've never thought of such a thing in my life."

"Well, that's fine," said Samuel. "I'm sure Miss Hardin means well."

"I do," she said. "I tried to think if there was any service you might need while you are here."

McDowell sighed. "Nay, but thank ye kindly, miss. And if you'll allow it before you go, I'd like the parson to pray for me again."

"Of course." She looked up at Samuel, her eyes wide now and shining in the reflected light that streamed through the doorway. She sat back a little away from McDowell.

Samuel bent his knees and lowered himself to the floor. "Shall we pray, then?" The three bowed their heads, and he offered a plea for a swift and just end to McDowell's confinement.

At his amen, the prisoner began a faltering petition. Samuel was not shocked, but he heard Christine's sharp intake of breath.

"God above, look down on this sinner," McDowell said. "Deliver me from my sin, Lord. I do not ask You to deliver me from my bonds, for they are just. Amen."

When he finished, Samuel rose and held out his hand to Christine. She took it and let him pull her to her feet. She sniffed and turned to the prisoner.

"Good day, sir. I shall continue to pray for you daily."

"Thank ye, miss. And you, sir."

Samuel nodded. "Shall we go?" He hopped down the high step to the ground and offered his hand to Christine again. When she stood on the ground beside him, he carefully swung the door shut and put the bars in place.

"Do you wish to see Mrs. Heard now?" he asked.

Christine was patting her cheeks with a handkerchief. "I don't feel like visiting, if the truth be told, but we told her husband I would, so I must."

They paid a brief call at the door of the house, declining to go inside, then set out for the parsonage.

They were halfway there before she spoke. "Does Mr. McDowell pray with you every day when you go to him?"

"Aye. Since Sunday. I believe he truly repented then and came to the cross."

She inhaled deeply. "I'm glad. Thank you for letting me see him."

"Perhaps I should have told you, but. . ." Samuel eyed her carefully. "I did not want you to think I believe him totally innocent."

"Nay, he has admitted he is not. Of the murder only he claims to have a clear conscience."

"Yes, he's confessed other things to me."

She looked up at him, her brows furrowed. "What sort of things? Stealing from us?"

"From us and other people. Dan Otis's knife, Brother Heard's shirt, Goody

Deane's loaf of bread. Other things, here and in other villages. Christine, you would not be safe around that man."

"But if he's repented. . ."

Samuel sighed. "Yes. And I believe he means it. But I would want him watched, if he were set free, and made accountable. Sincerity must be proven."

She considered that for a minute as they walked along and then nodded. "What you say is true. If John stole an apple tart and then said he was sorry, I should always watch him on days when I baked."

"Exactly." They went on together, and Samuel felt they were more in tune than they had been all week.

When they were within sight of the meetinghouse, she spoke again. "I understand your concerns, Samuel. McDowell did frighten me, and I'm not sure I'm over that yet. I did see his quick temper and a threatening side to him that I'll not soon forget. But I'm willing to believe he can change, or rather, that God can change him. Still, I don't say he has changed. You're right about that. Time will show whether or not he is the same man who threatened me."

Samuel paused and looked down at her. "I'm glad to hear you say it. I was surprised that you could feel such sympathy for him. For any man, for that matter. You always seemed to distrust men and to avoid them."

"So I did." She hesitated then added, "If it is not too forward, I should like to tell you that I credit your teaching with my change in attitude."

"My. . . You mean from the pulpit?"

"Aye, sir, and in your daily life. You have shown me that we must be open and willing to forgive."

Samuel spotted a cart coming up the street and a man heading toward the ordinary. "Let us walk," he murmured. He must take care still of the village gossips and not be seen lingering with a single woman. "I am glad the Lord has used me to help you."

She nodded but did not look at him as she continued. "I've seen several examples here—the Dudley men, Charles Gardner, indeed, your own example, sir. These godly examples have shown me that some men are kind and trustworthy."

Samuel felt a surge of satisfaction rush over him, followed by a knowledge of his own unworthiness. They reached the doorstone of the parsonage. He glanced about, saw no one watching, and reached for her hand, giving it a quick squeeze and releasing it. "Thank you for sharing that with me. I take it as a deep compliment that you would trust me with your thoughts and that you consider me an example to follow."

She swallowed hard and looked up at him, then away. "Feelings. . .they are so difficult to manage and to share. But they come from above, I am sure."

"Aye." He smiled, knowing he would pray that God would continue to bridge the gap between them. "I shall leave you here now and go back to my studies, though not for long." He looked up at the sun and saw that their trip had taken longer than he'd estimated.

"When do you want supper, sir?"

"I shall return in an hour."

He turned away, but he felt her watching him.

Thank You, Father, for this time together and this new understanding between us. Move us onward, if it be in Your plan, to a sweeter bond.

When he was halfway up the short path to the meetinghouse, he turned and looked back. She still stood outside the door. He raised one hand, and she waved back.

Chapter 14

On Saturday morning, Christine and Goody Deane both went to the parsonage. The elder woman was remaking one of the late Mrs. Jewett's dresses for Abby, and she offered to watch Ruth and sew while Christine and the older children joined the pastor in harvesting the rest of their corn.

As they husked the two bushels of ears they'd picked, dropping the shucks on a pile at the edge of the garden plot, Roger Ackley hobbled into the yard and hailed the pastor.

Samuel walked toward him, meeting him just a few feet from where they worked, and Christine could hear their conversation, whether she wished to or not.

"Brother Ackley," Samuel said. "What brings you out, sir?"

Christine hoped he wasn't here to insist that McDowell should be hung or to blame Samuel for the magistrate's delay. She nodded at Ackley but kept her head down after that, not looking his way but concentrating on her ear of corn.

"I've come to ask you to read banns for me on the Sabbath, sir. And to perform a ceremony three weeks hence."

Startled, Christine looked up. John, Ben, and Abby openly gaped at the man, though Constance appeared not to have noticed what he said and tugged tenaciously at the husks on her ear.

Samuel cleared his throat. "Am I to understand, sir, that you wish to marry again so soon?"

"That I do. You know the Lord says it ain't fittin' that a man should be alone. Now that's scripture." Ackley nodded emphatically.

Christine felt the color rise in her cheeks. She took Constance's ear of corn, quickly finished husking it, and laid it in the basket. "Are you finished?" she asked the other children. "I think we should go inside."

But they did not leave soon enough for her to miss the revelation of the intended bride's name.

"Alice's father won't let her come work for me anymore without I marry her," Ackley explained to the pastor. "And so I says to him, why not? Three weeks from Sunday is the day they chose for the weddin'."

By this time, Christine's ears pulsed with the infusion of blood, and she hustled the girls up the steps, embarrassed on Samuel's account as well as her own.

"Who's out there?" Tabitha Deane asked, laying aside her sewing.

"It's Goodman Ackley." Christine set the basket of corn on the table. "There, we shall have a good feed of roasting ears tonight."

"He wants to marry that hired girl," Ben said, shaking his head.

"Who? Alice Stevens?" Tabitha asked.

"Aye," Christine said.

"Ha!" Tabitha puffed out her breath. "Marry in haste, repent at leisure."

"Is that in the Bible?" Abby asked.

"Nay, but it should be."

"Come, Abby," Christine said. "Fill this kettle with water. John, you and Ben may bring in some more wood, if you please."

A few minutes later, the pastor entered the room. "Well, I seem to be performing another wedding."

"The children told me," Goody Deane said. "That pair seems rather mismatched to me, sir."

Samuel leaned against the mantel. "I told Ackley I will visit the girl at her parents' home and speak to all three. I've seen stranger things."

"She's not yet twenty, is she?"

"I'm not sure."

"Well, Roger Ackley be well past fifty." Tabitha shook her head.

"He should marry you, Goody Deane," said Constance.

"Ha! That's clever. You think I would wed that man?"

"Well now, perhaps we'd best turn the topic here," Samuel said gently. "All I know is that Goodman Ackley says he needs Alice to cook for the men he'll hire at harvest, and she can't stay at the farm to work unless they are wed."

"But that's—" Christine stopped and swallowed her words. It was not her place to object.

By evening, the pastor had made his trip to the Stevens house and returned. He said nothing while the children were about, but when Christine had hung up her apron and prepared to leave, he bade her wait and he would accompany her.

Her pulse beat quicker as she waited for him to don his hat and jacket.

"Children, I shall return in a trice," he called.

Christine felt a foolish smile tugging at the corners of her mouth as they stepped onto the path together.

"I would say you needn't escort me home, but I know it wouldn't change your mind."

"You are correct in that. I find it gives me a chance to speak privately with you. Do you mind?"

"Not at all."

"Christine, this precipitous marriage of Ackley's does concern me, but I find no grounds to refuse to perform the ceremony. The girl told me to my face she is agreeable, though she knows it to be a marriage of convenience for Ackley. Of course, it will elevate her status in the community. Ackley is better off than her own father, who is a mere laborer in the brickworks. But her parents seem to have no objection. Her mother even offered to go with her to the farm next week to help her cook for his harvesting crew."

"That was good of her," Christine said.

He frowned and shook his head slightly. "I asked her mother if she'd talked to Alice and explained what marriage would mean, and she said she was sure the girl would be fine." He glanced at her and halted, a few yards from Tabitha's door. "I'm sorry, Christine. I shouldn't burden you with this."

"Think nothing of it. You need someone to express your reservations to."

"Nay, I should take them to the Lord. But. . .I do enjoy talking to you. I've had no one to discuss such things with since. . ." He pressed his lips together.

Christine's heart wrenched. He missed Elizabeth, of course. And she was a poor substitute. "Well, sir, I do not mind if you speak to me about your concerns, and you can be sure that what you say will go no further."

"Thank you." He took her hand once again and held it. Her heart pounded. "Christine, your friendship means a great deal to me."

"And yours to me." She looked down at their clasped hands and took a careful breath. Could this really be happening?

"I expect that when I read the banns tomorrow, all the girls will gather around Alice and congratulate her, and yet. . .something about it bothers me." He seemed to realize suddenly that he still held her hand in his. He squeezed it gently and released it. "Forgive me. I presume too much."

"Do you, sir?" she whispered.

His eyes flashed with something—what? He drew in a breath and looked away. "I do understand a man. . .a widower. . .wishing to remarry."

She found it impossible to inhale. After a long pause, she squeaked out, "Do you?"

"Aye." They looked at each other. "Christine. . ." Samuel raised his hand and halted with it in midair, as though debating which to touch—her hair or her face. She thought her heart might burst if he did neither.

Behind her, Goody Deane's door creaked open. Samuel quickly stepped back a pace.

Tabitha chuckled. "I may be old, but I'm not blind. Don't you think it's time you began calling on this young woman?"

◆

The reaction to Sunday's public reading of the banns set Christine's sympathy for Samuel soaring, but she could not show it. The congregants gasped as one when the pastor read the names on the marriage intentions. Samuel spent the noon hour closeted in the meetinghouse with his deacons. When he emerged, there was no time for him to eat dinner, and Christine was able only to slip him a cup of cider and a slice of journey cake.

"Is all well, Samuel?" she whispered.

"Aye, and thank you, my dear." He pressed the empty cup back into her hand. His afternoon sermon, if anything, was more lucid and elegant than the morning's. Christine drank in every word. It was the one time she could stare her fill at him without arousing suspicion, and she took full advantage of it that day.

Once, when he called them all to join him in prayer, she noticed Samuel's gaze resting on her before he shut his eyes. Just for that instant, she felt his warmth and affection. She was glad all eyes were closed then and that she had the high wall of the pew at her back.

That night, he again walked her home from the parsonage after supper was over, but this time Goody Deane was with them.

"Some of the elders wondered if there shouldn't be a waiting period for remarriage after the death of a spouse," he told them.

"I never heard anything like it," Tabitha said.

"Nor I. And I've seen a woman who was with child married a week after her husband was killed by a bull. I suppose I could refuse to solemnize the vows, but to what end?"

◆

Nearly the entire village turned out Monday morning for the hearing at the meetinghouse. Catherine Dudley and Tabitha kept the children of several families at the parsonage with the young Jewetts.

Christine put on her Sunday best and went with the pastor, in expectation of being called upon to testify. She slid into the customary pew and felt people staring as Samuel joined her. The pastor had never sat in the pew before, to her knowledge. Certainly never beside her. The scrutiny of the villagers set her nerves on edge. Her hands trembled as she arranged her skirts.

McDowell was brought in and made to sit in the elders' pew between Baldwin and Paine, his wrists and ankles still chained. He stared down at the floor. A stranger in a cutaway coat and breeches sat near him, and Christine looked to Samuel and arched her brows.

"The lawyer," Samuel whispered. "I fear the crown must pay for his services, which means we shall be taxed for them."

The men had placed a table at the front, on the platform with the pulpit. The bewigged magistrate entered with great pomp and took his seat behind it.

When Christine was called to face the magistrate, she took her place knowing every eye was upon her. Her voice shook as she recounted how McDowell

"Probably not next week. He's holding court in Portsmouth and has several cases scheduled. He told William Heard to hold the prisoner until he comes. A lawyer will come, too, to represent the accused."

He wished this business was over with and McDowell gone.

"That is well," she said. "Are you hungry?"

"Aye, but the supper hour is past, and I must get to my studies."

"You shall eat something first. I saved portions for you and Ben." She went inside.

Lord, truly, she seems just what I need. Give me patience.

Samuel followed her and let the comfort of home refresh his tired soul.

had accosted her again and again, demanding food and other comforts.

"And did the accused ever harm you physically?" the magistrate asked.

"Nay, he never laid hands on me."

"Did he threaten you bodily harm?"

"Not I, sir, but others. He told me that if I did not do as he wished, he would hurt others who were close to me."

"And who would that be?"

She inhaled and glanced toward Samuel. His compassionate blue eyes looked back at her, and he nodded almost imperceptibly.

"The parson's children, sir." A sympathetic murmur went up from the congregation. "I be in charge of them most days, for the Reverend Jewett."

"And the accused said he would hurt them?"

"Aye. He showed me a knife the first time, and one other time. And more than once, he said he would hurt them. He said. . ." She shuddered, recalling his words. "Despicable things, sir. I do not wish to repeat them before the children' father."

Samuel's head drooped, and she thought she could see the sheen of tears in his eyes. A whisper rippled through the ranks of the people. The magistrate hit his gavel on the table and bade her step down.

Others went forward and told about the thefts they had experienced, and one farmer told how his dog had chased a man off one night, but he hadn' gotten a good look at the intruder. Captain Baldwin described the search for Mahalia Ackley, and at last the pastor gave his tale of the finding of McDowel in the thicket.

The magistrate recessed the hearing and went to the ordinary for his dinner Meanwhile, the people either went to their homes or milled about the common eating the refreshments they had brought and discussing the testimony.

Samuel and Christine walked back to the parsonage together.

"I'm sorry you had to go through this," he said on the way.

"It is needful."

The house was full of children. Samuel cast a woebegone look at Christine retreated into his bedchamber, and closed the door. She waited while Tabith fixed a plate and a cup of strong tea for him, then she took it to the door. Wher she knocked on the panel, he opened it a crack.

"You must eat, sir," Christine said.

"Thank you. I don't feel hungry, but I suppose I must." He took the plat and cup then looked earnestly into her eyes. "This will be over soon."

"Yes. Pray for justice."

Chapter 15

That afternoon, the hearing was reconvened. The magistrate asked McDowell if he wished to speak on his own behalf.

McDowell shuffled to the witness chair and took the oath to speak the truth.

"Tell us, then," the magistrate said, looking him over with narrowed eyes. "Did you commit the heinous acts described here this morning?"

"Aye, sir, all but one."

The people burst out in exclamations of surprise, and the magistrate banged on the table. "Silence." He fixed his gaze on McDowell, still scowling. "Make yourself clear, sir."

McDowell's attorney rose. "Your honor, the prisoner admits his guilt to the petty thefts previously alluded to and to intimidating Miss Hardin and threatening the children. However, he maintains he did not kill the aforementioned Mahalia Ackley." He sat down with a self-satisfied expression.

The magistrate tapped his gavel on the table once more. "The court finds there is enough evidence to hold the prisoner, Abijah McDowell, for trial. He is to be held locked up where he was housed heretofore until the trial. The Lord willing, I shall return here in a fortnight to carry out that business. Meanwhile, the prisoner's attorney will prepare his case."

The lawyer nodded, and the judge dismissed the hearing.

Christine stood, feeling a bit let down. "Seems nothing has changed," she said to Samuel.

"Aye. Another two weeks." The creases at the corners of his eyes looked deeper, and his eyes duller.

"You need rest, sir," Christine said softly.

"As do you. Come. Let us go home."

As they made their way out, they passed the attorney, who was speaking to the owner of the ordinary. "It sounds as though I shall have to lie over tonight at your establishment, sir. I regret I must remain here even another day."

" 'Tis not so unpleasant a place, sir," said the innkeeper.

"Nay, but I'll lose business I could be doing in Portsmouth for better pay than I shall receive for this, I'll tell you."

As Christine and Samuel walked toward the parsonage, they met several couples who had been to retrieve their children from Tabitha and Catherine's care. When they arrived, all of the children had left except the Jewett brood and Charles and Jane Gardner's little boy.

"I'll carry little Johnny over to the common," Catherine offered. "I expect Jane and Charles tarried there to talk to people."

She bade them good-bye and left with the baby and a bundle of his things.

John Jewett went to stand before his father. "Be they going to hang that man?"

"I don't know, son. Today was not the trial but merely a hearing to see if the case warrants a trial. The judge will return a fortnight hence, and the matter will be settled then."

"May we go next time?" Ben asked.

Samuel sighed. "I hardly think I want my children to attend such a proceeding."

Tabitha said sharply, "You young'uns clear out now. You can see your father's tired. Let him rest while Miss Christine and I get supper on."

"No, really." Samuel held up both hands and looked around at his offspring. "I believe I'd rather sit out under the oak tree with the children for a while. It does my heart good to see them around me, all strong and healthy."

Christine touched his arm. "Then you do that, sir. We'll bring you some refreshment out yonder."

She watched the children, quieted by their father's unaccustomed manner, surround him and head for the door. Ruth and Constance took his hands and pulled him along.

"That man is exhausted," said Tabitha.

"Aye." Christine reached for her apron. "Let me take him some cider, and then I'll get on a large supper for them all. You must be tired, too. Why don't you go home and lie down?"

"I'll help you. Then we shall both go home and leave them in peace for the evening."

Christine eyed her for a moment then put her hands on Goody Deane's shoulders and stooped to kiss the old woman's wrinkled cheek. "Thank you, dear lady. You are a blessing."

Tabitha waved her comment aside. "This will cheer you. This morning, Mrs. Gardner brought a haunch of venison, or rather, her husband did. And Mrs. Leeds, when she brought her three children, left a blackberry pudding. I made sure to put it up where the young'uns wouldn't get into it."

Christine gave her a weary smile. "Then let's get at it. The Jewett children and their father will feast tonight."

◆

The next morning, Christine took the three Jewett girls with her to the trading post. Samuel had taken the boys with him to the meetinghouse for lessons, and Tabitha had stayed at home to do her own washing and light cleaning.

Christine disliked going to the trader's, but sometimes it was necessary, and she found that they needed some hooks and eyes for Abby's new Sunday dress and a few stores for the parsonage larder. Samuel had entrusted her with two shillings that morning, and she feared it might be the last of his silver.

She and the girls entered and went to the counter where sewing notions were displayed. She was surprised to see Alice Stevens there as well, fingering rolls of braid. "Good day, Alice," she said.

"Hello." Alice seemed distracted as she compared the selection of fripperies.

"Good day, Miss Stevens." Abby dropped a pretty curtsy, and Christine felt a stab of pride. The eight year old's manners were better than many adults'.

Alice shot her a smile that was almost a smirk. "Soon-to-be Goody Ackley." She held out a roll of fancy black braid so Christine could see it. "The master—that is, my soon-to-be husband—has given me his late wife's clothing. I intend to cut down her somber old dresses and fix them up with pretty trimmings. Think you this would look well on her plum-colored wool?"

Christine gulped for air. "I'm sure I don't know. I'm. . .not one who knows much about fashion."

Alice looked her over for a second. "Aye, so you don't." She turned back to her shopping.

Christine inhaled slowly, feeling the flush creep up her neck. Abby's look of distress prodded her to control herself.

"Come, girls, let us find the hooks we need."

A few minutes later, they were outside the trading post and headed for home. Christine picked Ruth up to carry her and let Abby tote their small purchases in her basket.

"Miss Christine," Constance said, looking up at her soberly and clutching her free hand, "did she rude us?"

———◆———

Elder Heard blew the conch shell Sunday morning, and all the villagers hastened toward the meetinghouse. The temperatures had moderated, with a promise of autumn on the breeze, and all of the women donned shawls that morning.

As they reached the common before the meetinghouse, Christine spotted Alice Stevens approaching in the company of her parents. It did not surprise her that Alice wore her late mistress's plum-colored wool skirt and bodice or that the skirt was edged in swoops of black braid. She tried to forget the impolite words the young woman had spoken at the trader's. Alice's coming marriage seemed to have altered her attitude toward her neighbors. Christine hoped it was not a permanent change.

Jane Gardner hurried toward her with little Johnny on her hip. "Christine! Good day."

Christine smiled. "Ah, well met, Jane."

"What were you staring at?" Jane threw a quick look over her shoulder at the people entering the meetinghouse.

Christine ducked her head. "I'm embarrassed to say it, but I was surveying the future Goody Ackley's fashions."

Jane squinted toward the church steps. "Ah, a new gown?"

"New to the wearer. I met her at the trader's Tuesday, and she was buying trimmings for the late Goody Ackley's old clothing."

Jane nodded with comprehension. "Ah. It seems she has also acquired the mistress's fine scarf from England. Remember how Mahalia used to wear it to meeting?"

"Every Sunday," Christine agreed.

"Well, ladies."

Christine jumped at the pastor's voice. She'd thought him inside long ago.

"Good day, Pastor," Jane said with a smile. "Oh, here comes my husband. Pardon me." She hastened toward Charles.

"Surely you ladies weren't lingering to gossip this fine Sabbath morning?" Samuel arched his eyebrows.

"Certainly not, sir." Christine clamped her lips together.

All through the worship service, the scene replayed in her mind. By the end of the final psalm, she wallowed in guilt so low that she doubted she would ever leave the morass.

She took the children home and set out their dinner. She left them setting the table and ran out to see if the pastor was headed home. He came from the church, and she met him a short distance from the house. "Forgive me, sir, but I had to speak to you in private. You hit the mark this morning. My behavior was unconscionable."

Samuel eyed her keenly. "If you've aught to regret, Christine, I'm not your confessor. Take it to the Lord."

"Aye, and I have, to be sure. But I wish your pardon as well. For I not only gossiped with Jane, but I lied to you about it." Her voice quivered. "I wouldn't have thought I could do that, but it slipped out so easily!"

"This. . .gossip. Will it hurt the person in question?"

"I don't know, sir. I doubt it. But it has hurt me. It's made me see myself as mean-spirited, a character trait I do not wish to possess. Why should I care if Alice's affianced husband gives her his dead wife's skirts and English scarf? But I don't wish to be an example to your children of a petty, shrewish woman."

"Did the children overhear?"

She hung her head. "I don't think so. And when we saw Alice at the trader's, I believe I accepted her scorn without giving a poor example to the girls."

"Alice scorned you?"

She felt flames in her cheeks. "It is nothing, sir. What she spoke was true, but perhaps said unkindly."

"The same as what you did this morning, then, only to your face?"

"Aye."

He nodded. "My dear, I admire your tender conscience. Would that all my parishioners had such."

"Oh, Samuel, I promise you that with God's help I shall endeavor not to speak ill of others or to be uncharitable."

Samuel sighed. "Perhaps the Almighty had a purpose in your exchange with Goody Gardner."

"Oh?" She blinked and waited for him to speak further.

"Your talk this morning drew my attention to the scarf Alice Stevens wore." Christine was baffled. "And?"

"And I recalled that Goody Ackley nearly always wore it when going out in public, as you say. That is all."

Christine squinted at him against the sun, feeling certain that, on the contrary, that was not all.

Chapter 16

In the week before the trial, the nights turned chilly. Samuel spent much time in the fields, getting in his crops and helping the men of his parish harvest their grain and flax.

At last the magistrate and lawyer returned, along with a second attorney to represent the crown. The people gathered once more at the meetinghouse. Christine wished she could sit at the back of the room, but as witnesses, she and Samuel were bade to sit in the usual pew occupied by the pastor's family, along with Charles Gardner, who brought his wife this time. Samuel also allowed Ben and John to join them, and so the pew was nearly filled.

Christine felt quite warm in the close quarters and extremely conscious of Samuel's nearness. From time to time, one of them shifted, bringing their two shoulders into contact. Christine tried to ease away slightly, without drawing attention to the movement, all the while wishing she could relax and rest against Samuel's strong arm.

Goodman Ackley occupied his usual pew, though it was farther back than he would like. Alice, his soon-to-be wife, sat primly beside him, darting glances at the people around them. Her new attire reflected her future elevated status as the wife of a fairly prosperous farmer rather than that of a hired girl.

Christine was glad that when she had sat down, Alice could not see her. Not many in the congregation could. However, the magistrate, the attorneys, and the prisoner, as well as whoever sat on the stool used as a witness stand, had a first-rate view of her and the minister. She determined to stay alert and not give one tiny crumb of behavior that could be used to criticize Samuel.

She looked past Ben at Jane Gardner, and Jane gave her a feeble smile. The solemnity of the occasion was overpowering. Christine wondered if it would be better for her to sit on the other side of Jane, not beside Samuel. His proximity continually drew her thoughts to him, which might cause her to look at him often, which in turn might lead others to think malicious thoughts.

Joseph Paine, the trader who doubled as constable, stood and called the session to order. Much of the testimony seemed repetitious to Christine. She recounted the same facts she'd given at the hearing, and she couldn't see that the other witnesses added much to their previous information, until the crown's attorney brought forth the market basket Stephen Dudley had found in the woods.

Seventeen-year-old Stephen was called to tell how he discovered the item and where and when. "No more questions," said the lawyer.

"But it wasn't there a day earlier," Stephen said.

"No more questions," repeated the lawyer.

The magistrate looked at McDowell's attorney. "Your witness, sir."

The defense attorney rose, his eyes gleaming. "Now, Master Dudley, you said you found this basket near the camp in the thicket. That would be the same camp you and your brother found the day after the accused was arrested."

"Aye, sir."

"So you were there on the Friday with your brother."

"I was, sir."

"And you found no basket then."

"We did not. Richard can tell you, sir."

"Oh, we shall get to your brother, have no fear. Yet you say that on the Saturday morning, the basket lay there, on the ground, in plain sight."

"Exactly so, sir."

Christine was proud of the boy's calmness.

"How do you explain that, Master Dudley?"

"I don't, sir."

"So when you found this basket, on the Saturday morning, what did you do with it?"

"I took it along to the parsonage. I thought to ask the constable or the pastor about it."

"And what did they say?"

"They weren't t'home, sir. Both had gone to Portsmouth to ask for you and his honor to come."

"Ah." The attorney nodded in encouragement. "What did you then?"

"Miss Hardin said she would go with me to Goodman Ackley's to ask if it were his wife's basket, and I said mayhap we should get the captain to go, too. So I fetched Captain Baldwin and we went."

"And what happened at the Ackleys' farm?"

"The master and Alice Stevens, what were the hired girl, both said it were Goody Ackley's basket."

Richard Dudley and Captain Baldwin were summoned to the stand in turn, and both confirmed Stephen's testimony.

Goodman Ackley was next. In mournful tones, he told how his wife had gone off that morning and how he regretted not accompanying her on her errand. The crown's attorney asked if she had carried the basket previously introduced as evidence, and he declared that she had.

Alice Stevens was called next. She swayed down the aisle in her finery, took the oath, and sat down on the stool. Like her affianced former master, she bewailed the goodwife's disappearance and death, and she stated that Mahalia Ackley had indeed carried her customary basket that day.

The magistrate declared a recess at that point, and Christine and the Jewetts walked home for lunch, taking the Gardners with them. Samuel seemed preoccupied, but he joined in conversation with the guests and Tabitha while they sat at dinner.

As they left the parsonage to return to the trial, he murmured to Christine, "Forgive me if I hasten on ahead. I must have a word with the defense attorney before court reconvenes."

She watched him hurry off, surprised at his agitation.

"The parson's a bit on edge," Charles observed as they followed at a slower pace.

Jane said, "I thought so, too. Both during the testimony this morning and at dinner. Has this business made him restless, Christine?"

"Nay, but we would both like to see it finished well."

"Of course," Charles said. "But is there much doubt of the outcome?"

Christine watched Samuel as he hurried into the meetinghouse. Something wasn't right, she thought. Something other than the basket. Samuel must feel it, too.

They filed into the Jewett pew again, and Samuel joined them. His face was sober, but he tossed a faint smile at Christine as he settled beside her.

The boys traipsed in just before Paine stood to call the crowd to order.

Samuel leaned toward her. "Pray, my dear."

Startled, she nodded, unable to look into his face for fear she would betray the mixed apprehension and sweet pleasure his words brought her.

Mrs. Paine, the wife of the trader, was called forward. She acknowledged that she had waited on Goody Ackley the morning the woman disappeared and recounted the items the customer had purchased and placed in her large basket.

"And that was the basket you saw here this morning?"

"I believe it was, sir."

The crown's attorney then relinquished the floor to the defense council.

"Can you recall what the deceased wore that day?" McDowell's attorney asked.

Mrs. Paine eyed him thoughtfully.

Samuel's hands clenched into fists.

Christine listened carefully as the trader's wife spoke.

"Yes, sir, she wore her gray linsey skirt and a blue bodice over her shift, and of course her bonnet and scarf."

"A shawl, do you mean?" asked the attorney.

"Why, no, sir." Mrs. Paine sat up straighter and looked out over the meetinghouse. "I mean a particular scarf that she always wore into town or to meeting. Her husband had bought it for her at an emporium in Boston a year or two back, and she was very vain of it."

The magistrate tapped his gavel. "Keep your responses to the facts, madam."

"Aye, sir. But she wore it that day, and she often boasted that her husband had paid a great sum for it. Raw silk, she called it. Hmpf. I'm sure it's largely woolen, with perhaps a bit of silk woven in. If you'd like to see it, you've only to cast your eyes o'er the far pew, where the husband of the deceased sits now, with his betrothed and her family. In fact, your honor"—Mrs. Paine turned and gazed up at the magistrate—"Alice Stevens wore it when she sat in this very spot to give testimony this morning, and she wears it still."

A noise of whispering swelled amidst the people.

Again the magistrate clapped his gavel to the desk. "Silence."

The immediate stillness was broken by only the lowing of a cow on the common.

The magistrate studied Mrs. Paine. To the lawyer, he said, "Have you any more questions for this witness, sir?"

"No, your honor."

Mrs. Paine returned to her pew, and the crown rested its case. The defense attorney stood and turned toward the onlookers.

"The defense calls Doctor Elias Cooke, resident of Dover Point."

Samuel inhaled deeply as a man walked quietly up the aisle. The physician wore a powdered wig and a long, black coat and breeches. Christine felt Samuel's tension as Paine administered the oath to the physician, and when she glanced at him, she saw that Samuel's face was pale.

"Doctor Cooke," said the attorney, "you were called to examine Mahalia Ackley's body soon after it was discovered." The attorney stood sideways so that he could look at the witness and also at the onlookers if he wished.

"That is correct, sir."

"Why were you summoned here?"

"They have no physician in Cochecho, and Captain Baldwin asked if I would come and examine a dead woman to tell him what I could."

"And how long after her death did you see her?"

"I believe it was a few hours after death occurred. No greater than eight hours, from what I've heard of her activity that morning."

"And were you able to determine how Mahalia Ackley died?"

The physician looked up at him and said calmly, "Aye, sir. She had a wound on her temple, and her face was bruised, but I believe she was killed by strangling."

"Strangling, you say?"

"Aye. Her throat was marked where something had been pulled tight about it, and the blood vessels in her eyes had ruptured."

"And could you say what instrument was used to kill her?"

The doctor shook his head slightly. "I believe it to have been an article of clothing, sir."

The swell of low voices began again, but when the magistrate lifted his gavel, it subsided.

"A specific article of clothing, sir? For instance, would you say a belt?"

"Nay, not that." The doctor unbuttoned a few silver buttons and reached inside his coat. "The minister assisted me in my examination, and since he is one who often stands in as a healer in this community, I welcomed his aid. I pointed out to him an oddity pertaining to the wounds."

"And what was that, sir?"

"Fibers clinging to the creased skin of the victim's neck." He held out a folded piece of paper. "It may interest you and the magistrate to look at them. The Reverend Jewett"—Cooke nodded in Samuel's direction—"can tell you. He saw me remove several white fibers from the body. I believe the woman was strangled with an article woven of fine white wool and silk."

A shriek came from the rear of the hall. Christine looked at Samuel, but he had already jumped to his feet and turned to look over the back of their pew. Christine leaped up and looked toward the rear of the room.

Alice Stevens clawed the white scarf from about her neck, threw it on the floor, and crumpled into her father's arms.

Chapter 17

The uproar could not be silenced by the pounding gavel. Paine and Captain Baldwin leaped into the aisles in an attempt to calm the surging crowd.

Christine sat down hard on her wooden seat and shrank back against the pew, thankful she couldn't see what went on behind them but wondering what Alice Stevens and Roger Ackley were doing at that moment. She had an excellent view of McDowell, who craned his neck to see what was happening, grinning as he pulled against the leg irons and fetters that held him to the deacons' pew.

Samuel plopped down beside her and stared straight ahead.

After a good ten minutes, order was restored. The magistrate declared a quarter hour's recess, after which all witnesses were expected to appear ready to testify again if called.

John Jewett was standing on his seat, looking over the high back of the pew. As the crowd began to surge toward the door, he cried, "Father! Alice Stevens swooned. How can she testify again?"

Samuel shook his head. "We shall see, son."

"Her mother and father are trying to rouse her," Jane noted.

Samuel stroked his beard. Christine saw that his hand shook. "Perhaps I should see if they need assistance," he said.

"That doctor's looking at her," Ben reported, also peering over the top of the pew.

Samuel drew a deep breath. "We wished for justice, Christine. Do not cease your praying now." He patted her arm briefly and then clasped his hands in his lap.

"Do you wish to go outside?" Charles asked Jane.

"Mayhap we are better off to stay right here and see what befalls," his wife replied.

Christine was glad. She did not feel like facing the inquisitive stares and questions of the villagers. She sat stiffly beside Samuel, pondering all that she had heard. The two attorneys huddled with the magistrate at the front table. As Samuel had suggested, she leaned back, closed her eyes, and prayed silently.

After ten minutes, Charles left them for a short time and returned with a dipper of cold water, which he offered first to Jane then to Christine.

She took a sip, thankful for the cool liquid.

"Pastor, would you like a drink?" Charles asked.

Samuel took the dipper and drained it. "Thank you, Charles." He slumped back against the wall.

Charles took the dipper away. When he returned, he bent close to Samuel. "Goodman Ackley tried to bolt. Baldwin's got him in custody. They're going to bring him in last, when everyone's seated again."

"What about the scarf?"

"The attorney asked Alice's parents to give it to them as evidence. She's come round, but she still looks like death. They've moved out of Ackley's pew to another at the side."

Soon afterward, court reconvened. The defense attorney called Alice Stevens to the front of the room. Everyone stared at the hired girl as she rose, her face white. Her father escorted her to the witness stand, holding firmly to her elbow.

After she was reminded of her oath to tell the truth, McDowell's attorney directed his questions to her. "Miss Stevens, you were in Goody Ackley's employ at the time of her death?"

"Yes, sir."

"And where did you get the scarf you wore to court today?"

"My. . . Her husband gave it to me, sir."

"Why did he do that?"

Alice hung her head. Her answer was so quiet, Christine could barely hear it. "A week and more after she died, he asked me to be his wife."

"And you accepted?"

"Aye." She looked up quickly. "I thought—" She let out her breath in a puff and blinked as tears flooded her eyes and raced down her cheeks. "He gave me some of her clothing, sir. That were among 'em."

"And can you remember exactly when he gave you that scarf, Miss Stevens?" She shook her head. "A few days ago, I think."

"Did you see it the day your mistress died?"

"I. . .don't know, sir."

"Did she wear it when she left for the trading post?"

"I'm not sure."

The attorney took a few steps across the front of the meetinghouse as though deep in thought and turned to face her again. "Was she wearing it when they brought the body home?"

"Nay. Of that I'm certain, sir."

The men who had discovered the body in the woods off the road to Ackley's farm were called back and asked if the dead woman's scarf was on or near the body when they found it. All said no.

Next, Paine himself testified that Mahalia wore the article in question when she came in to trade on the fateful day. A woman who was in the shop at the time also swore that the deceased had worn the scarf.

Finally, Roger Ackley was called. The congregation hushed as he walked slowly up the aisle beside Captain Baldwin, dragging his feet with each step. He snuffled and took the stand. Again, the magistrate reminded the witness of his oath.

The magistrate fixed his stern gaze on Ackley's face. "Goodman Ackley, what say you? I have examined the fibers Dr. Cooke gathered from your wife's body and found them similar to ones I gleaned from the scarf you presented to Alice Stevens last week. So similar that I would not be loathe to say they came from that scarf. Have you an explanation?"

Ackley opened his mouth then closed it. He looked around, his eyes wild. He started to rise, but Paine and Baldwin, on either side of the stool, pushed him back down. He pulled in a shuddering breath. "My wife wore that scarf often. I gave a pretty price for it, and she doted on it. It is not unnatural that some of the threads should cling to her. . .skin."

The magistrate frowned. "The physician tells me they would not stick as they did from a casual wearing. Sir, your wife was strangled with this garment." He held up the white scarf. "I ask you, sir, where has it been since the day your wife wore it to her death?"

"I do not think she wore it that day, sir. Nay, she can't have. I found it later, among her things."

"As you found her basket?" the attorney asked.

"What. . .I do not understand you, sir."

"Where did you find it?"

"Why. . .in the chest at our home."

"You wife's basket was on her arm when she left the trading post. The scarf was about her neck. Her body was found a few hours later. No basket was present. No scarf. The basket turned up the next day at the outlaw's camp. Yet it was not there when he was captured. The scarf turned up in your wife's clothes chest."

McDowell's attorney swung around and addressed the magistrate. "Your honor, I submit that my client did not kill Mrs. Ackley. Rather, I ask you to believe the evidence. The poor woman was strangled by her own husband, who placed the basket at McDowell's camp to make him look guilty. But he couldn't bear to discard the scarf he'd paid so much for. Nay, sir. He had his eye already on a younger, fairer woman, and he gave it to her when he wooed her."

The magistrate held up both hands. "Sir, Goodman Roger Ackley is not on trial today. However, I instruct the captain to remand him into custody until a hearing can be held to ascertain whether there be sufficient evidence to pursue this line of inquiry. Meanwhile, the accused, Mr. McDowell, has confessed to several petty crimes." He picked up a piece of parchment and read them off. "I shall recess for one hour, and when we return, I shall pronounce sentence on McDowell for these lesser crimes. I find there is not sufficient evidence to convict said McDowell of murder."

◆

The next morning, Samuel walked to William Heard's garrison in a chilly downpour. Few people were about the roads.

The magistrate and lawyers had spent the night at the ordinary but planned to leave together after they broke their fast. Baldwin had commissioned two men to go with him to deliver McDowell to the jail at Portsmouth.

Samuel felt he needed to see the man once more before he left to fulfill his year's sentence in jail.

William Heard admitted him to the smokehouse. Baldwin was already there, checking the leg irons in preparation to removing the prisoner.

"Thank you for coming, Parson," McDowell said when he saw Samuel.

"I came to see if you needed anything and to tell you that I shall continue to pray for you."

"Thankee, sir. I know I deserve what I'm gettin'. I guess I can stand a year, so long as they don't throw me in a dank, cold hole for the winter."

"I trust they will see to your bodily needs. Do not lose hope, McDowell. Do not lose faith in God Almighty."

"I shan't, sir. He knows I'm sorry I done what I did. And He made it so I shan't be hanged for killing that woman, such as I didn't do."

Samuel nodded and turned to Baldwin. "Captain, this man is a brother in Christ. Please allow us to pray once more before you take him away."

An hour later, Samuel entered his house and removed his dripping hat. Christine was near the hearth, coughing as she stirred a simmering kettle. As much smoke seemed to billow from the fireplace as went up the chimney. The fire sputtered as rain pattered down on it. He looked about, mentally counting the children in the haze, and relaxed when he was sure all were safe within the walls of home.

"Ah, there you be, sir. Your coat at least is soaked, and probably your other clothing as well. You'd best change and hang your things here to dry."

He ducked into his bedchamber and closed the door. On his pallet lay a new suit of charcoal gray wool. He bent and ran his hand over it. So. She had finished her weaving and sewing, despite all that went on in the village.

Well, this suit was too good for him to loll about home in or to wear over to the meetinghouse for school time and preparing sermons. He put on the workaday trousers she had made him that summer and a different shirt. She was right; he'd gotten soaked to the skin.

He carried his wet garments out to hang near the fire. Christine had left the door open, and the smoke had cleared a little.

"Where are the children?" he asked.

"I sent them all to the loft under Ben's direction to crack nuts for me. I am baking a cake."

"I see."

"Do you, sir? Today is your birthday, you know."

That tickled Samuel, and he laughed. "I had forgotten it."

"Well, I had not." She wiped her hands on her apron and opened the crock where she kept pearl ash for her soapmaking.

He heard Abby's clear, ringing laugh and looked up. He could just see her back and Ben's. They were sitting on the floor chattering together while they worked. Despite the rain, despite the bleak events of the last month, he felt happier than he had in a long, long time.

"Christine."

"Aye?"

He stepped toward her and seized her hand. "My dear, you are lovely in your cap, with flour smudged on your nose."

She froze and stared at him.

"It is my hope that in the past two and a half years you've come to think of this cottage as your home."

"Oh, I have, sir," she whispered. She tore her gaze from his and looked down at their clasped hands.

Samuel smiled gently and tipped her chin up until she looked at him again. "It is also my hope that you will consider an offer to make this your permanent home. Christine, if you feel you can find peace here in this house. . ."

"I believe I can."

His smile grew without his trying to restrain it. "And if you can love my children as your own. . ."

"I do so already, sir. You know that."

"Yes, I do. And if you think perchance you might one day love me. . ."

She lowered her lashes. He waited, and after a long moment, she looked up into his eyes once more. "I do not believe in chance, sir."

He laughed and pulled her to him. "Marry me, then, dear Christine. Soon. I'll ask the minister from Dover Point to read the banns. May I?"

Her glowing smile answered him, although she got no words out before John called down from the loft, "Father! What are you doing?"

347

Epilogue

Whe the harvest was in and the golden days of October belied the coming bitter winds of winter, the Reverend Samuel Jewett took Christine Hardin as his lawfully wedded wife.

Her friends and the Jewett girls clustered about her. Jane and Sarah helped her dress in a fine new skirt and bodice. Ruth presented a bouquet of dried blossoms she and her sisters had made. The visiting preacher awaited them at the meetinghouse with Samuel and his sons. When they stepped outside for the short walk from the parsonage, Goody Deane hobbled out from her cottage and joined them.

James Dudley's wagon was tied up near the meetinghouse, and Captain and Mrs. Baldwin walked quickly toward the building. From down the street came the Heard family and the Otises. From the river path came the Paines and the fishermen and their families. Nearly all the people of the village gathered to witness the pastor's wedding.

Christine could think of only a few who were missing. Among those was Roger Ackley, who had confessed after a week's confinement and had been convicted a fortnight since of his wife's murder. He now awaited his hanging, but she refused to dwell on that. Thoughts of the grisly crime vanished as Christine waited.

Jane peeked in the church doorway, keeping watch for the right moment. At last everyone else was inside and seated. She and Sarah drew Christine to the doorway. Her two friends took the little girls and hurried to their families' pews.

James Dudley was waiting just inside the door. He offered his arm to Christine, and she slipped her hand through it.

She looked past the pews to the area below the pulpit, where Samuel stood with the officiating minister. Samuel looked at her with such love that she could only return his smile and walk toward him.

A rash of doubts tried one last time to assail her. Could she be a good wife? Samuel said she could. A good mother? He insisted she was already. A proper parson's wife? He would teach her.

He reached out and took her hands in his, and she gazed into his eyes. Peace filled her heart.

A Letter to Our Readers

Dear Readers:

In order that we might better contribute to your reading enjoyment, we would appreciate your taking a few minutes to respond to the following questions. When completed, please return to the following: Fiction Editor, Barbour Publishing, Inc., P.O. Box 719, Uhrichsville, OH 44683.

1. Did you enjoy reading *White Mountain Brides* by Susan Page Davis?
   ❏ Very much—I would like to see more books like this.
   ❏ Moderately—I would have enjoyed it more if _____
   _____

2. What influenced your decision to purchase this book?
   (Check those that apply.)
   ❏ Cover   ❏ Back cover copy   ❏ Title   ❏ Price
   ❏ Friends   ❏ Publicity   ❏ Other

3. Which story was your favorite?
   ❏ *Return to Love*   ❏ *Abiding Peace*
   ❏ *A New Joy*

4. Please check your age range:
   ❏ Under 18   ❏ 18–24   ❏ 25–34
   ❏ 35–45   ❏ 46–55   ❏ Over 55

5. How many hours per week do you read? _____

Name _____

Occupation _____

Address _____

City_____ State _____ Zip _____

E-mail _____

ALLEGHENY HOPES

Among the rolling Pennsylvania hills, three couples face the future together by letting love reveal the past. Meeting her college boyfriend after eight years means Adrianne is forced to bring a long-held secret to light. Living in a football city makes football-hating Brianna disgusted. . .until she meets one amazing quarterback. Leaving home to avoid an expected marriage, Katie returns to Amish country to face her family and be surprised by the man who will always love her. Watch as God takes the mistakes from yesterday and uses them to bridge a path to love.

Contemporary, paperback, 352 pages, 5⅜" x 8"

Please send me ____ copies of *Allegheny Hopes.* I am enclosing $7.97 for each.
(Please add $4.00 to cover postage and handling per order. OH add 7% tax.
If outside the U.S. please call 740-922-7280 for shipping charges.)

Name _____

Address _____

City, State, Zip_____

To place a credit card order, call 1-740-922-7280.
Send to: Heartsong Presents Readers' Service, PO Box 721, Uhrichsville, OH 44683

HEARTSONG
PRESENTS

If you love Christian romance...

$10.99

You'll love Heartsong Presents' inspiring and faith-filled romances by today's very best Christian authors. . .Wanda E. Brunstetter, Mary Connealy, Susan Page Davis, Cathy Marie Hake, and Joyce Livingston, to mention a few!

When you join Heartsong Presents, you'll enjoy four brand-new, mass-market, 176-page books—two contemporary and two historical—that will build you up in your faith when you discover God's role in every relationship you read about!

Mass Market, 176 Pages

Imagine. . .four new romances every four weeks—with men and women like you who long to meet the one God has chosen as the love of their lives—all for the low price of $10.99 postpaid.

To join, simply visit www.heartsongpresents.com or complete the coupon below and mail it to the address provided.

✂- -

YES! Sign me up for Heartsong!

NEW MEMBERSHIPS WILL BE SHIPPED IMMEDIATELY!
Send no money now. We'll bill you only $10.99 postpaid with your first shipment of four books. Or for faster action, call 1-740-922-7280.

NAME _____

ADDRESS_____

CITY_____ STATE _____ ZIP _____

MAIL TO: HEARTSONG PRESENTS, P.O. Box 721, Uhrichsville, Ohio 44683
or sign up at WWW.HEARTSONGPRESENTS.COM